Blood Pudding

Confessions of an Immigrant Boy
Pittsburgh 1920

A Novel

I V A N   C O X

Fulton Books
Meadville, PA

Published by Fulton Books 2021

ISBN 978-1-64952-435-5 (paperback)
ISBN 978-1-63985-561-2 (hardcover)
ISBN 978-1-64952-436-2 (digital)

Printed in the United States of America

To Martha, Anna, Alice
and to the memory of
Mary Ann

Note to the Reader

When my father died thirty years ago, we found this typewritten document under some stock certificates in his safe deposit box. Clipped to it was a note asking that nobody read it until 2020, one hundred years after his mother's death.

I offer this personal time capsule now, so that my father's suffering and triumphs as an immigrant boy in Pittsburgh should be known. I suspect there are many children of immigrants to America who share a similarly gritty but ennobling legacy.

Tadeusz Malinowski Jr.
Hunterton, Ohio
November 3, 2020

The Seven Children of Ignaz and Eva Malinowski

Their Ages at Eva's Death in 1920

Maksymilian (Max)—sixteen
Vera—fifteen
Urszula (Lucy)—twelve
Zygmunt (Ziggy)—eleven
Tadeusz (Tad)—nine
Kazimir (Kazzy)—four
Kasper (Blizzard)—two

Lightning Bugs

Mother died in November. Her sudden death left the seven of us to deal with Jumbo.

Vera, the older of my two sisters, had it worst. Mother wasn't cold in the grave six months when Jumbo started going after her.

One warm evening, the next June, while I was out chasing lightning bugs, I looked back and saw Jumbo cuddling Vera on the porch swing. He was coaxing her to tug on his mustache and urging her to sip on his homemade red wine. All the while he was feeling her up.

I had just turned ten. What did I know? But what I saw that night in the shadows on the porch seemed bad—his big rough miner's hand on her blouse, squeezing her nipple. Sure, Vera was blonde and built strong and had radiant green eyes like Mother, and Jumbo must have been lonely for a woman. But Vera was fifteen, and she was his daughter.

He did other stuff, too, and not just on the porch swing. Sometimes we heard Vera crying out from Jumbo's room, like Mother had done. More than once I heard him threaten Vera that if she went up to the church and told the priest anything, he'd take his razor strop to her. I tried to pump up my courage and go to the priest myself, but I didn't want to feel the scalding lashes of his strop either. None of us did.

I was ashamed for the family. If I told the priest and word spread around, what then? Would the mine company fire Jumbo and kick us out of the company house? Would we all be sent back to Poland?

None of us talked about it. We knew what Jumbo was doing was wrong, but we were afraid to mention it. Even my big brother Max, who was sixteen and tall and brawny and quick to throw a punch, feared Jumbo.

So, after Mother died, we plodded along from day to day in that crowded brick box on Robert Street in Rehoboth, Pennsylvania. We all shared grief and shame, and we wished Jumbo would stop hurting Vera. We prayed each night that he would sober up by morning and make his way to the mine. If Jumbo didn't go to the mine, he wouldn't get paid, and we wouldn't eat. We each might end up in an orphanage in Pittsburgh or maybe Poland.

Back on that terrible November day at the graveyard when we buried Mother, Vera announced she would quit school. "Somebody has to take her place and look after the family," she said, her pale chin poked out and her arms cuddling little Kazzy and baby Blizzard.

On the way home from the burial, Jumbo sighed. "I'm beat. I don't feel like cooking tonight."

"I'll do it," Vera said. "Spaghetti."

"Can you make it like she made it?"

"Taste it and see, Pop."

On that gloomy November day, Vera didn't know what she was in for. None of us did.

Poplars

Mother's cemetery was brand-new, almost empty. Her grave was the third they dug, set high up on a grassy hill. Half a mile down the long slope stood a straight line of young yellow-leafed poplars, separating the graveyard's acreage from a small stone chapel with an iron fence around it. On top of the chapel steeple was a tiny iron cross.

I knew Mother would enjoy that view. Often, she had told us that the rows of poplars here and there on the outskirts of Pittsburgh reminded her of Poland. Over in the old country, she said, the farm fields were separated by rows of tall poplars to shield the crops and animals from the strong winds.

There wasn't much wind that dark day by the new grave, but there was a steady cold rain. Everybody seemed in a rush to bury Mother fast and get out of it. The two cemetery workers holding the ropes dropped her so suddenly, her coffin cracked when it hit bottom. I knew that couldn't hurt her though, because she was dead. Two nights before, I had watched her die.

I was convinced that, broken coffin or not, her wonderful spirit would abide there on that hill forever, seeing the sun rise to the east and admiring the distant poplars and the stone chapel with the little cross and watching the cemetery fill up with more dead people. In church, I always heard the priests talk about heaven and purgatory and how we should pray to all the holy saints to help a person's soul after death. But those warnings confused me.

No, I knew Mother would remain right there, overlooking the chapel and the poplars, which meant I could come back and visit her, provided I was never sent back to Poland.

The older children, Max, Vera, and Lucy, had attended funerals before. They told us what to do. Ziggy and I watched them and tried to follow their cues. Once the men dropped Mother in the hole and yanked out the ropes, we each tossed a white rosebud on her and picked up handfuls of black dirt from the muddy pile and sprinkled small clods down on her. But when the workers started shoveling in big heaps of soil that banged hard on the coffin lid, Ziggy let out a loud grunt. He turned with a wild look in his eyes and took off like a shot, running down the hill.

I ran after him. Mother would have wanted me to.

Ziggy was two years older than me, but he was feebleminded and clumsy and had terrible eyesight and was easily upset by anything strange or different. Two years in a row, Mother had tried to start him in first grade at Rehoboth Elementary School, but each time, the teachers sent him home. The second time, bratty boys chased him all the way back to our house, shouting, "Ziggy piggy, Ziggy piggy!" They whipped his back with thorny switches and made him bleed and bawl.

The teachers told Mother that sending Ziggy to school was torture for him and a waste of everyone's time. Zig could barely tie his own shoes, let alone learn to add or subtract or read a clock or spell. School, they insisted, was futile. A state mental hospital or even the county work farm over near Beaver Run might be the proper place for him. In time, Ziggy might learn to do useful labor, they said. He would be in the company of other low IQ unfortunates, where he would feel equal and happy and possibly turn out to be productive.

Mother and Jumbo had decided that sending Ziggy to a mental institution or a work farm would cast a shameful light on our family. So instead, they kept him home and with me as his keeper.

Once I had mastered double knotting my own shoes and other basic grooming matters, Mother charged me with making sure Ziggy's laces were tied right. I was also to be sure he brushed his teeth and didn't pick his nose in public and flushed the toilet. I was to check that he buttoned his shirt straight and didn't let his underpants creep up over his belt and didn't leave his fly open to the breeze. I had to make sure he did not step on his eyeglasses or say odd things to the children on our street. Most of the girls were afraid of Ziggy and avoided him like a skunk or a patch of poison ivy. I also was to tell Mother whenever he wet the sheets, which was easy for me to detect, since Zig and I usually shared the same bed.

These duties with Ziggy kept me from starting school in Rehoboth with the other children my age. But Lucy, or sometimes Vera, tutored me at home in reading and writing and math. Meanwhile, if any mean boys came around to taunt Ziggy, I was to tell Max immediately, who would settle scores.

Mother's death did not change my commitment to Zig. I would be there for him, and he knew it. Now that Mother had been dropped fresh in the ground, my promise seemed all the more important.

When Jumbo saw us running away from the grave site, he hollered down the hill at us. By that time, we had almost reached the row of poplars and were out of breath.

We stopped, and I looked at Ziggy. He was panting and sobbing heavily. His face was messy with tears dripping down both sides of his blunt nose. Thin gray snot leaked over his trembling lips. Behind his horn-rimmed glasses, his eyes were swollen and red. He had rubbed his eye sockets with his muddy fingers. Particles of the grave dirt had lodged under the lids on both sides. Dense black finger swirls covered his wide cheeks and brow, right up to his curly blond hairline.

"Wait, Zig," I said.

I stooped and swiped my handkerchief on the wet grass to moisten it. Then I cleaned off his glasses and his face, as best I could. Zig let me dab the corner tip of the handkerchief under his eyelids. I had done that to him before many times, so he knew to hold still and not blink. He didn't want to risk another bad eye infection. He knew eye infections were trouble and could blind him.

When I was done, I hugged him hard. I knew he felt terrified and disoriented. I had seen Mother die, but Ziggy hadn't. He hugged me back and let out one of his long, heavy groans into my ear.

Jumbo saw us hugging on the hill and shouted down again for us to stop acting like idiots and to come back up to the grave. Jumbo also was terrified, now that Mother was dead. Of course, he would never admit it, not to us and especially not to any priest. My father had contempt for priests, and I'm sure they could tell and probably felt the same way toward him. In any case, Jumbo had been devastated by Mother's sudden death, and his reaction, instead of seeking consolation from somebody, was to boss us and raise his hand to cuff us, if we didn't obey.

I had witnessed the moments of devastation close up. I was there with him at St. Agatha's Hospital in downtown Pittsburgh two nights before, when they had rolled Mother back from the operating room. Max was there too. When the three of us walked onto the ward, the nuns opened the curtains around Mother's bed to let us be with her. When Jumbo looked down at all the blood on Mother's sheets, his face went gray. He started to shiver, something I had never seen him do.

During surgery, the doctors had transfused eight pints of blood into Mother. That included two from Max and two from Jumbo, as a last-ditch attempt to keep her alive. I wanted to give her blood, but I was too young. They said I didn't have enough to spare.

But it did not matter. The extra blood had not helped her.

I asked the main nun, who was only six inches taller than me and said her name was Sister Joseph, where all the blood was coming from. She whispered to me that it was coming from the place where Mother had had all her babies. The surgeons had given up. They had done everything and couldn't stop the hemorrhage. No matter how many pads and towels they stuffed into her, she bled through them all.

When they opened up her belly, they found she had abscesses all over her womb and her liver and her intestines, Sister Joseph said. So, they sewed her up and sent her back to the ward as a hopeless case, which is what we found lying in front of us.

On the sheets over her thighs we saw yellow and green pus mixed in with some of the thicker blood clots. The stink made me sick, and I almost puked right on her. Sister Joseph threw another white linen blanket over her to cover up the blood and the pus and the odor, but soon all of it had soaked through worse than before.

As I stared, mute and numb during Mother's final breathing moments, Sister Joseph whispered that she was bleeding to death, because of what had happened. Unfortunately, there was nothing more to be done, except to pray for a miracle.

When I asked her what she meant by "what had happened," Sister Joseph gave me an impatient frown and pursed her lips. She had tiny gray eyes and a crooked white scar running down from her left nostril to her mouth, apparently from a childhood harelip operation. The scar puffed out when she pursed her lips. I quickly moved my glance off her mouth to her eyes. But when I asked her again about what had happened, she looked away.

"He will tell you," she said, nodding toward Jumbo.

I peered over at my father. He seemed too pale and jittery about what was happening in front of his eyes to tell me anything about what had happened before to make Mother this way.

The nuns had tied a tight linen bonnet over Mother's wavy golden hair, and her beautiful rosy cheeks now were cement gray and getting darker by the moment. Mother's eyes were closed, Sister Joseph said, because she was unconscious and we shouldn't worry. Her eyes needed to rest before she opened them soon to see God and to beg forgiveness.

Sister Joseph said she hoped that the Holy Father would forgive her, but the way the little nun fluttered her eyes and shook her head when she said it made me think that Mother's chances of forgiveness from God were poor.

"I am not the one to judge," Sister Joseph said, tightening her lips again so that I could not avoid staring at the scar.

"Forgive her for what?"

"Ask your father, young man," she repeated. Then she pulled the curtains back around us and stepped out.

For half an hour, Jumbo and Max and I stood and watched Mother breathe fast and shallow. We saw her skin gradually turn a faint purple with wiggly white streaks in front of her ears, near her temples. It did no good to call to her. When I put my fingers on her arm, her skin was cold as clay.

The young hospital chaplain on night duty popped in through the curtains. He pinched his nose and closed his eyes for a moment. Then he looked down and reached into a black leather pouch and took out a small round silver jar. With his fingertips, he scooted back the edge of Mother's bonnet and dabbed a cross on her forehead with some sweet-smelling grease. Then he sang a few syllables in Latin and whispered a few more. Finally, he frowned dismissively at Jumbo and Max and me and wiped his hands on a clean white towel hanging on the bedrail. He disappeared through the curtains, leaving Mother with an oily gray cross above her motionless blonde eyebrows.

After the chaplain left, her body shuddered from her heels to her head, as if a bolt of electricity had jolted through her. Sister Joseph came back and put a wet white rag on her forehead, covering the cross the young priest had made. Then Mother's chest rattled feebly like there were dozens of tiny twigs rubbing together in her lungs. Then she stopped breathing for good.

Sister Joseph nodded to Jumbo and Max, closed her eyes, and bowed her head. They each gave the sign of the cross and leaned over and kissed Mother on her cold, darkened cheek.

When I put my cheek on the back of her hand, her knuckles felt like cold wet pebbles. Mother's hands had always been warm and strong and tender, especially at night when she tucked me in and caressed my face and my neck. As I pulled my nose away, the strong stink from under her sheets rose up my nostrils. That's when I knew this cold, smelly body wasn't my mother anymore.

Sister Joseph said she and the other nuns would clean Mother up, but it would take several hours. Jumbo could pick up her body the next morning, after the coroner came in to examine her. If Jumbo had any trouble finding a cemetery, he was to let Sister Joseph know.

Then we left Mother with the nuns and went home to our house in Rehoboth. While Jumbo and Max broke the news to everybody, I got into the bathtub and scrubbed as hard as I could.

I had been waiting for Jumbo to tell us what had happened to Mother to make her spew pus and blood from the place where her babies came out. But I was too confused to ask him. Explaining things to the children had always been Mother's job, and now I feared Jumbo was likely to leave all of us in the dark, even though there could never be a more important question in our lives.

At the cemetery in the rain, when I stood hugging Ziggy and looking up the hill at the other people by the grave, Zig's chubby shoulders jerked. Then he whispered in my ear, "It's our fault."

"What?"

"It's our fault, Taddy. You and me."

"Did Jumbo tell you that?"

"No."

"Who told you that?"

Zig started to blubber again.

"You don't know what you're talking about," I said.

Ziggy shook his head and pushed me away. "It's our fault. I'm going back up."

I grabbed his arm. "Zig, we did what Mother told us to do."

"It's our fault, Taddy." He jerked his arm away and started up the hill.

Climbing up behind him, even though it was chilly, I began to sweat. Then I trembled. My head spun, and I had to hold my butt muscles tight for a second to keep from crapping my pants. I puked very fast, twice on the grass, yellow green and thin. The liquid blended into the grass, almost as if it hadn't happened.

I looked up and saw Ziggy running toward the grave and waving his fists out spastically on either side of him, which was his odd way of running.

Dazed, I stood there in the rain. With a second quick vomit, my head stopped spinning. I took in some deep breaths of the cool, wet air. The rain felt soothing on my face, though my clothes were soaked and heavy all over me. I was able to put my feet in motion up the hill, though my tongue still tasted the bile.

They were all looking down at me from the grave site, and I felt embarrassed. Humiliation always hit me when people watched me from a distance. My limp looked more pronounced from afar. For as long as I remember, my right leg has been slightly shriveled and weaker than my left. Mother had told me not to worry. I wasn't born that way, and my legs would surely even up by the time I reached twelve or so. But now she would not be around to see if her prediction came true.

Apart from puking and putting my limp on display, what pained me most as I climbed the hill was what Ziggy had whispered to me. Despite his mental limits, Ziggy's instincts sometimes hit a bull's-eye.

Or it might be just another of Ziggy's misinterpretations of reality. His heart was so meek and generous that sometimes out of the blue he would up and apologize without any clear cause, as if he wished to take on guilt for misfortunes he had nothing to do with. It was a habit, like picking his nose, and I often discouraged him from doing it.

But this time, perhaps there was a just cause for his feeling guilty. And if Zig's instincts were right, I shared his guilt, though we did what Mother had said to do.

She had even drawn a map for us for where the slippery elm tree was, so we wouldn't goof up and bring her back the wrong tree bark. And we had burned the map as soon as we were done, exactly as she had told us to do. And she checked out the long slivers of elm bark we had carved out of the tree, and she said they were exactly what she had wanted. And later I even took what she called her blood pudding in the bucket out into the woods and dumped it out and buried it. Zig and I had done everything the way Mother had told us to do it.

Jumbo would get the official coroner's report, and that might explain the truth about Mother's death. That would have to wait. Right now, I knew we had to live one day at a time, take our steps one at a time without her.

At the top of the hill, except for Jumbo and the old priest and the men with the shovels, everybody was still kneeling in the cold rain, holding umbrellas and crossing themselves. Now their eyes were closed as they shivered and prayed, and I hoped they were asking the Holy Father to forgive Mother.

The men with the shovels had filled the hole all the way up, and now they were stamping down the mound of dirt, sealing her in there for good. Right over her head they pounded in a small pine cross that looked to be built from the same flimsy lumber they had used for the coffin. Somebody had typed out her name and dates on a three-by-five-inch file card that was pinned to the cross with a thumbtack:

Eva Marianna Malinowski
March 11, 1885—November 3, 1920

When he saw me standing there, Jumbo scowled. I kneeled beside Ziggy and asked the Holy Father for forgiveness for Mother and for Ziggy and me.

But then the priest, whose skinny red face was partially hidden by the brim of his black fedora, lit up a cigarette and started walking quickly back to his car, a long black Packard. He had seemed annoyed, even angry from the start of the ceremony.

Jumbo followed him. I watched the priest's uniformed driver hold up an umbrella and open the car door. The priest blew out cigarette smoke and put his prayer book into his vest pocket and jumped in while Jumbo approached. For a minute, Jumbo stood by the car, demanding something in Polish. I could not hear what.

Then the priest said loudly in Polish, "If you want a dog to bark, you must throw him a bone."

When Jumbo muttered something else, the priest threw up his hands and shouted in English. "You're lucky they allowed you to bury her here! I wouldn't have allowed it!"

Then the driver slammed the car door. Mother's burial was done.

Max told me later that Jumbo had asked the priest to say more than just the Lord's Prayer at the graveside, but since we couldn't pay the priest, he refused. As Jumbo's employer, Rehoboth Coal and Metals, had agreed to cover the burial charges, even the white rosebuds. But from the priest we got only the bare-bones burial, as Max said with one of his wry sneers. Max also said later that the new cemetery was the only Catholic graveyard around Pittsburgh who would accept Mother, because of what had happened. They let her in, because they needed the business and obviously had plenty of empty plots. And it wasn't actually a charity burial, since the mine covered the costs.

Again, the mystery of what had happened seemed to dangle in the air around everyone. After my whispers with Ziggy on the hillside, I began to hope the coroner would never give us his official report. It might be better if nobody ever found out what happened to Mother. In any case, we had promised Mother we would never tell a soul. And that's what counted.

It took four years till Mother's grave had a stone. Max paid for it. He rode me out there one day on the back of his Harley to show me. By then there were several hundred plots filled in, most with modest stones like Mother's but others with arches and columns and statues of saints and angels.

Mother's stone had just her name and dates, but Max was proud of it. I was too. That day we planted pansies in front of it, and it looked fine.

By then, Max was nineteen. He was newly married and had a baby on the way. He had opened his own cycle shop, Malinowski Motors. He lived with his wife, Benny, in an apartment over the shop's garage. Benny had urged him to buy the latest Kodak camera, so they could take pictures when the baby came.

At the cemetery that day, after we planted the pansies, he had me take a picture of him by the grave.

I still have a copy of it in my old scrapbook: Max squatting and grinning behind the tombstone, his muscular forearms resting on the flat top of the stone. His full black hair was greased back, and the afternoon sun lit up his high square cheeks and his fierce squinting Slavic eyes. In that snapshot, his forehead looked broad and slick, but only a month later a bad motorcycle spill cleaved out a deep four-inch gash across his brow. After that accident on the slag heap at the Rehoboth zinc plant, the scar on his face made him look like one of Genghis Khan's warriors.

In the picture, Mother's poplars had already grown tall and bushy. Behind Max, you can make out the trees down in the distance and the chapel with the little cross.

When we climbed back on the Harley that day, I asked Max if we could cruise down and take a closer look at the chapel, maybe go inside and light a candle for Mother.

"Bullshit." He laughed. He seized the handlebars, spread his wide shoulders, and rammed his foot down on the kick-starter. I climbed on behind him.

As we roared out through the cemetery gate, I looked back at her new headstone and whispered in Polish, "How I miss you, Mother. I'm sorry."

Ripple Brook Gardens

When we came from Poland in 1911, I was a baby in diapers. We first settled nine miles north of Pittsburgh in an area called Ripple Brook Gardens. By my first memories and by family accounts, everything started out happy.

My father had sailed over before us. Through a Polish friend's cousin, he had landed a job at Etna Metals, a sheet steel factory in Etna on the north bank of the Allegheny River. At first, he lodged in a barracks building owned by the plant.

Tall, broad shouldered, and quick-witted, Ignaz Malinowski mastered English promptly and worked tirelessly, grabbing every double shift the plant foreman offered him. His coworkers admired him. He was as strong and sturdy as an elephant, and they soon gave him the nickname Jumbo, which stuck.

In half a year, he had saved enough to book passage for Mother and the five of us born in Poland to join him. When I was eight weeks old, we sailed on the *Prince Oscar* from Gdansk to Philadelphia. From there, we took the train to Pittsburgh to join him and start our new lives.

Jumbo had managed to rent us a dilapidated but ample brick farmhouse in Ripple Brook Gardens, up on a hill with eight acres of overgrown meadows. There was also a neglected apple orchard with a dozen trees. In some old photographs of the property before we moved there, it is possible to make out the remains of a tiny vineyard near the orchard with rickety trellises and a few dozen scraggly vines with grapes.

The owner of the abandoned farm was Nicholas Wells Jr., a kindly old man in his eighties, whose father had first bought the land and cleared it for sheep grazing. Nicholas Wells Sr. built the house and operated the farm profitably for thirty-five years before bequeathing it to his son. Nicholas Wells Jr. and his wife had kept the farm going at a modest profit for over two decades.

When their son, Nicholas III, fell off a horse, broke his neck, and died outside the kitchen window, the couple were shattered. They sold their sheep, left the farm, and moved into Etna to live with their daughter, whose husband worked in management at Etna Metals.

For years, the old Wells farm had been up for rent, but no worthy tenants came forward. The fields and the orchard became overgrown, and the house and the outbuildings deteriorated. As the seasons passed and the property remained neglected, it seemed unlikely that anybody would ever be interested in renting or buying it.

Enter Ignaz "Jumbo" Malinowski, who heard about the farm from Mr. Wells's son-in-law. Jumbo went to see old Nicholas Wells and asked for a tour of the property.

The Wells farm was a half-hour bicycle ride west of the Etna Metals plant, and Jumbo estimated that this would be a reasonable commute. He told Mr. Wells that in Poland he and his wife both had plenty of farming experience, and that he needed space for her and their five children. He agreed to fix up the farm buildings on his days off from the plant. He vowed to put it back into a workable state, though he had no experience with, or interest in, raising sheep.

Nicholas Wells was surprised and delighted. He agreed to keep the rent reasonable and said not to worry about raising sheep, because he knew sheep were a full-time job, clearly impossible for a factory worker.

Nicholas Wells inquired about Jumbo at Etna Metals. The foreman told him Jumbo was popular, bright, diligent, and sober, one of the most reliable workers on their staff. The son-in-law concurred.

Greatly pleased and hopeful that his farm might be restored, Nicholas Wells prepared a lease, and the document was signed. Then the six of us arrived from Poland, and our new life in America started on the farm. Jumbo and Mother worked furiously to make the place habitable and productive, and they quickly succeeded. They cleaned out the house, fixed the broken windows and doors, restored the coal burner in the cellar, and rehabilitated the outbuildings. Jumbo reroofed the barn and purchased a few animals. Within a year, it was a fully operational farm.

Apart from the redbrick house, we had a wooden chicken coop with a corrugated steel roof, an outhouse behind it, a small barn with a horse and a couple of cows, a pigsty, a sturdy old buckboard, later a truck, and two large gardens with many different vegetables: lettuce, onions, potatoes, carrots, cucumbers, tomatoes, three kinds of beans, and half a dozen other vegetables, including corn, peppers, zucchini, garlic, and squash. I list all of these, because Ziggy and I spent many days helping Mother weed them. We also helped her harvest them. She forbade us from picking anything from her herb garden, which she relied on to make all her delicious stews and sauces and soups.

Our water supply came from a deep brick-lined well up the hill and near the edge of the forest. When we first moved in, Jumbo climbed down and cleaned out the well shaft. He scraped the moss off the bricks, pulled out the thick vines and a few spider nests. He also had to shoo out a colony of bats, messy work but well worth it.

The water, down eighty feet, always came up cool and clear in the bucket. Later he installed an iron hand pump, which made drawing from the well easier. Of all the many springs in the area, Mother boasted that our farm's water was the purest.

Around us were dense woods teeming with all the animals native to Western Pennsylvania: deer, woodchucks, raccoons, chipmunks, squirrels, rabbits, fox, skunks, porcupines, black snakes, plus all kinds of birds including owls, hawks, jays, and noisy packs of crows. We never saw dangerous animals like bears or wolves or cougars, but there were occasional sightings of those species as close as fifty miles north of us. Despite settling near Pittsburgh, the smoky industrial powerhouse of America, Jumbo had found us a farm ensconced deep in the forest and, in some ways, reminiscent of his rustic Polish roots.

We all did chores, and these were endless. But it was otherwise a wonderful place to be a child. In the little apple orchard, Max's responsibility, we found half a dozen pieces of flint, which Max said were Iroquois arrowheads, an excitement to Max's school friends and to Ziggy and me.

On summer mornings, Mother often took Ziggy and me into the woods to forage for mushrooms and wild berries. From Poland, she brought a lot of old country savvy and superstition. She said she was sure the abundance of raspberry bushes near our farm was providential. The name Malinowski comes from *malina*, Polish for raspberry, and Mother concluded in her mystical way that God's own hand had guided Jumbo to Ripple Brook Gardens. Weren't we lucky to be blessed so generously here in our adopted country!

She truly loved our farm and the forest around it. I remember her huge green eyes narrowing in a squint as she plucked the berries from the thorny bushes and dropped them gently into her cloth-lined wooden basket. She hummed while she picked. Occasionally she shook her head and grinned if a jay squawked or a squirrel barked from a branch. When Kazzy was born four years after me, she would strap him on her back like a little Polish papoose. Now and then, she would put her hand over her shoulder to offer the baby sweet berries to suck. I don't ever remember being in a papoose on Mother's back, but Lucy and Vera said she used to carry me around that way too.

When Blizzard was born (in a blizzard, which is how he got his nickname) two years after Kazzy, then Ziggy and Kazzy and I helped her with the same foraging ritual. By that time, though, we had moved clear across Pittsburgh to Rehoboth, where there were coal mines and the huge zinc smelting plant. The woods around Rehoboth were thinner and less populated by animals than in Ripple Brook Gardens. Rehoboth had only a few chipmunks and squirrels and mice and moles. For birds, there were mostly crows. Mushrooms and berries were harder to find there, and the water that came out of the spigots in the company house we lived in on Robert Street was orange tinted and smelled of sulfur.

To sum up, compared to Ripple Brook Gardens, just about everything in Rehoboth was worse, a lot worse.

In those first years, Jumbo worked hard to secure a foothold for our family. He bicycled to and from the factory in Etna and tilled our gardens whenever he could find time during the week and on Saturdays and Sundays. Max helped him tend the vegetables and the orchard, though Jumbo always grumbled that Max was lazy and never bothered to learn how to use a hoe. Still, the old Wells farm gave us sustaining nourishment, and the woods provided mushrooms and our family's birthright, raspberries. We had milk and eggs every day, sometimes grape juice from the vines, seasoning herbs (as they grew older, Vera and Lucy tended the herbs), and more apples and cider than we could consume or give away.

Sundays were the only times when I would leave the farm. Early in the morning, after putting on our church clothes, we walked down the hill and caught the bus on the main road that took us to Mass at St. Stanislaus's Cathedral in Etna. After church, Jumbo sometimes treated us to cherry phosphates or ice cream at the soda fountain in Kooperman's, the drugstore, where he also bought his cigars.

To supplement the family budget, Mother began to take in laundry from rich people in Etna. Word soon spread that her work was speedy and flawless. She became successful and busy and was always in motion. When she wasn't cooking or baking or mending our garments, she gardened or washed and wrung clothes in the hand-cranked wringer and tub on the back porch. She ironed the clothes at a long table behind the house. After school, Vera and Lucy helped her do the laundry.

When Mother's business increased, Jumbo erected a sturdy wooden tower, fifteen feet high. The structure supported a huge galvanized water tank. He and Max spliced a long series of pipes down from the well, so that water could be pumped down to the tower. An ingenious siphon effect filled the tank's five-hundred-gallon capacity. This was plenty to handle all of Mother's laundering tasks as well as our daily cooking and household needs. Jumbo also dug and poured two concrete coal-burning pits to heat up the large vats of water, which Mother and my sisters used for their laundering.

Several times a week, the servants of Mother's wealthy customers would arrive in carriages or fancy cars to drop off and pick up laundry. Sometimes well-dressed ladies would step out to meet Mother and tour "the laundry." She would always blush and bow her head to them respectfully, and they would leave her generous tips. Mother was beautiful and graceful, even in her workaday dresses, and probably to them she was exotic.

My task, if I saw a big expensive car heading up to the house, was to find Ziggy and keep him out of sight. Mother said she was not ashamed of Zig, but she knew that some snobby people simply might not be sympathetic to him. They might fail to understand that deep down he was a nice boy, especially if they saw him making monkey faces, which he did unpredictably and for minutes at a time. He shook his arms and banged his wrists together, because he was often nervous around strangers. Such shenanigans might cost her customers, she said, so I did what she asked me to do and kept Zig from their view.

I was fascinated watching Mother and the girls boiling the water and mixing the starch, which had a sweet odor. After the clean linen went through the wringer, they hung all of it with clothespins on thick steel wires stretched on half a dozen vertical I beams, also erected by Jumbo. I loved to play hide-and-seek with my sisters in the fluttering maze of sheets.

When Ziggy tried it, he often ran into trouble. Sometimes he couldn't find his way out, and then he panicked. Frustrated, he would tear down the sheets just to escape. Mother and the girls would scream at him, especially those times when they had to put all the sheets through the wash again. It wasn't long before the laundry area was off-limits to Zig, and it was my job to keep him occupied and far away from the laundry area, and not just when Cadillacs roared up to the house.

I sometimes resented being Ziggy's keeper, but most of the time, I enjoyed it. I loved him, and I tried never to laugh at him. Occasionally that was difficult. For example, Zig loved to shout and clap at our chickens for sport. He put his thumbs in the corners of his mouth and stretched out his lips. He thought this made him look scary to the chickens. Then he would stamp his feet and chase them back into the coop. He never tired of doing it, hearing them squawk and flap their wings, feathers flying in a noisy cluster of panic. And he was disappointed when the flock, once inside the coop, would stay there, because that ended the game. A few times I told him to go into the coop and chase them back out, but that always provoked such a ruckus that Mother scolded me for goading him on. The coop, she explained, had to be calm so the hens could concentrate on laying.

When Max brought older boys home from school, he liked to entertain them by shouting, "Hey, Zig! Go scare the chickens!"

Ziggy thought it was great fun, showing off in front of Max's buddies, and they laughed themselves silly at him. I thought this was cruel, and when I asked Max to stop it, he told me to mind my own business. They were his friends, not mine.

Once I overheard him say to them that he had two useless brothers, one an idiot and the other a cripple. Max had a mean streak, but my Mother couldn't do much about it, and Jumbo didn't seem to care. As long as the cows were milked on time and the orchard was tended, Jumbo never disciplined him. Max was strong and willful, like Jumbo, and he liked to boast that he could lick anybody in a fistfight and throw a baseball farther than anyone his age, which was true. But I got tired of hearing him say such things.

One particular afternoon when he was sitting on our front porch with his friends, Max reached into his pocket and said, "Hey, Taddy! I got something nice for you."

"What is it?"

He pulled a shiny silver dollar from his pocket and handed it to me. "Here. It's yours."

Astonished, I took it from the palm of his hand.

"Wow! Thanks, Max!" I sighed, feeling the huge coin with my fingers and rubbing Lady Liberty on one side and the American eagle on the other. I had seen very few silver dollars, and to have one for myself seemed impossible. My mind spun, as I thought at once about places where I could hide it. Maybe bury it out behind the barn? Or even better, give it to Mother for safekeeping. She had a special place for money and her jewelry.

"Now give it back."

"Why?" I squeezed the coin tight in my hand.

"Did you really think I would give you a whole silver dollar?" He cocked his head with a sneer, watching my confusion. Then he slapped me hard across the cheek and peeled my fingers back to grab the coin.

I broke into tears. Max and his friends laughed.

He held the dollar out again in the palm of his hand and said, "I was only kidding. Go ahead, take it."

I swiveled around and ducked inside the house. He yelled after me as I ran up the stairs, "Lost your chance, Taddy. You could have been rich!"

That cruel streak was pure Max. When Jumbo was not around, he enjoyed playing the boss.

It was hard to be his brother seven years younger. But Ziggy and I had no choice. I never understood what joy he found in humiliating us in front of his friends. Perhaps it made him feel powerful. Of course, Max being Jumbo's firstborn, what would anyone expect?

Max's cruelty may have toughened me for troubles I would face later, though I do not feel grateful for his bullying. Mother called him on it repeatedly, but it seemed, like Jumbo, he could not help himself.

In winter, the snow at Ripple Brook Gardens could fall thick and heavy. It bent the pines and birches in the forest and drifted high on the fences around our meadows. Jumbo had difficulty getting to and from the factory on his bicycle, and sometimes, when the roads hadn't been plowed and the buses weren't running, he had to wake up very early and walk to work. Later he finagled a deal on a beat-up Ford model T vegetable truck with a re-welded chassis. That clunker served us for years and carried him to and from work much faster, depending on whether the main road was plowed.

I loved the snow, and so did Ziggy. After Jumbo left for work and Max and the girls went off to school, we had all the snow on the farm, eight acres of it, completely for ourselves. We never missed a chance to build snowmen, one of Ziggy's favorite activities. We also made snow forts and snow bears and snow cats and bunnies and once a pig. When it came to molding images with snow, Ziggy surprised everyone. He seemed to have an odd artistic sense of how to sculpt forms to make them look realistic and how to pack snow that kept his creations solid for days on end.

"Step aside, Tad," he would order me, as we put the finishing touches on the snout of a bear. "Let me finish him."

I would stand back and marvel. He took his mittens off for the finer effects, wedging both his thick thumbs in a line to chisel the snow delicately and make the bear's snout smile. That skill impressed everybody, and yet, if you gave Zig a pencil and paper and asked him to draw a face, it came out as crude scribbles. Snow seemed to be his only artistic medium.

I vividly remember evenings when after dinner, Mother left the dish washing to the girls and took me outside with her to go sledding. We bundled up in our boots and heavy coats and set off, hand in hand. At the top of the hill, just beyond the chicken wire near the grape trellises, she would lie down flat on our steel runner Flexible Flyer, and I would climb onto her back.

"Hold me tight, Taddy," she would say. "Tighter! Don't fall off!" Then she would push off with her toes.

Off we went on a long and thrilling downhill scoot, zooming so fast, it scared me, and far off the edge of the property. We shot clear down to a cement gully where the sled blades scuffed on the bare concrete and sent out bright orange sparks that lit the snow around us. Whenever we went over bumps, I clutched her with all my strength, and she would let out her musical giggle from deep down in her belly, as though there was really nothing anybody should ever worry about, not when high-speed fun like this was happening. At the end of the ride, we would both roll over and look up at the sky, silent with joy at our thrilling descent through the snow and its spark-showering climax. I loved to listen to Mother breathe beside me. I watched the steam from her sighs rise gently above our faces and vanish.

If I was tired or if my gimp leg hurt, she carried me back up the hill to the house, the Flexible Flyer dragging behind us. I felt so safe and excited to be alone with her, having Mother all to myself as I looked out at the white ground and listened to the sled blades slip smoothly through the snow behind us. Above, the winter clouds pulsed with the vermillion blazes of the giant open-hearth steel ovens near the river. The searchlights from the coal barge tugs sometimes darted up in lines at the sky and sprayed all around on the glowing red clouds.

Even out where we lived on the Wells farm, the snow did not stay fresh for long. The next morning there was often a black granular film on the surface from the mill smokestacks. Ziggy and I would whisk it off if we wanted to eat the snow, one of Ziggy's favorite treats. Ziggy argued that snow was more than frozen water. He said it was white magic. He said eating snow was like eating magic. Did I think so too?

When I told Mother what Ziggy had said, she smiled in agreement. Ziggy knew what he was talking about, she said. Didn't he craft snow in ways that seemed magical to the whole family?

I said snow always melted and the magic often disappeared as soon as it happened.

"That is why it is so beautiful and mysterious. But you can find magic almost anywhere, if you look hard enough. God leaves it here and there. Ziggy finds it in snow."

I did not repeat to Ziggy what Mother said. With Zig, it was often best not to complicate stuff by making it abstract. No, better keep it simple. Snow and magic were the same thing. Agreed.

And that elusive moment of magic was exactly what I felt on those night sled rides with her. How often I have whizzed down that long white hill in my imagination, wishing Mother's musical laughter would never stop, hoping never to see those orange sparks fly up from the sled blades to announce the end of our ride!

I have often wondered why Mother favored me above all her other children. I know she did, but was it because of my shortened leg? Even after Kazzy and Bliz were born, and they were both cute babies with normal arms and legs and fingers and toes, she still seemed to favor me. She watched me carefully at all times and cuddled me more than any of the others. Maybe it was because my face resembled her brother Tadeusz, who was killed in the World War in Poland. I never had the courage to up and ask her if I was her favorite. Perhaps later that courage would have come to me, but by then she was not around to ask.

As a general policy, Mother and Jumbo claimed they loved us all equally. That was the family law, Jumbo said.

But when Mother died, Jumbo changed that law.

Glistenings

Jumbo liked to tell us that in Poland he had been chef and part owner of a small restaurant in a town near Vilnius. He had sold his share of the business to help pay for our coming to America. He also said he planned someday to quit his Etna factory job and open a bistro in Pittsburgh. With the many Slavic immigrants in the city, he had plenty of potential customers, he reminded us. We never saw any photographs of that restaurant in Poland, but Mother said the story was true.

Mother and Jumbo never showed us any pictures of their families in Poland. Mother said Jumbo had been in a rush when he first came over, and she had decided her photograph albums could be sent by mail to us later, since she had her hands full on the trip over with the five children, including me in diapers, and all our baggage. The photograph albums never arrived, so we all were totally in the dark about what our relatives looked like back in Poland.

"Not to worry," Mother used to say. "That was our old life. This is our new life, our real life. Here in America, where we are!"

We spoke mostly Polish at home. As I mentioned, I rarely left the farm property except to go to the church in Etna on Sundays, so I was delayed in picking up English. Back then there was no radio, and I relied on Vera and Lucy as my contacts with the outside world to help me learn to speak the American language. My sisters coached Mother too. I remember afternoons when they would take a break from their laundry work, and the three ladies of the family would sip tea at the kitchen table, while my sisters drilled Mother and me on vocabulary and basic grammar.

When we butchered the pronunciations, the girls looked at each other and giggled. Sometimes they took out the Pittsburgh road map and challenged Mother to read names of towns. A village in the next county had the rather musical name of Zelienople, and I recall Mother turning her mouth inside out trying to pronounce it. She also had trouble with tongue twisters like Aliquippa, Monongahela, and even Blawnox, a town not far up the river from us.

Sometimes these kitchen lessons would end quickly with Mother's exasperation. "Back to work, girls!" she would say, draining her teacup and heading back out to the washtubs.

Ziggy eavesdropped on our English lessons, and some expressions he picked up faster than Mother and me, an enduring family puzzlement. He was proud about this, and sometimes he ran around the yard, shouting "Zelienople" like a battle cry at the top of his lungs. He liked to say the word so much, he begged Jumbo to name a pig we raised Zelienople. The pig, originally Abner, had much worse than a name change happen to him, much to Ziggy's distress. But more about that pig named Zelienople later.

Re the restaurant. Jumbo scouted the small ethnic eateries across the river in Pittsburgh's Strip District, where the huge iron, cork, and glass factories employed thousands of immigrants, many of them Slavs. He said none of those restaurants met his culinary standards.

Max and Vera had memories of Poland, and they could recall the little restaurant. But they remembered Jumbo tending bar or waiting tables, sometimes playing the piano, rather than working as a chef in the kitchen. When we pestered Mother about the restaurant, she told us what was important now was working and living in America. Here in wonderful Ripple Brook Gardens, our new life was going well, and we should be happy and grateful for it and not think back about where we came from.

Jumbo also enjoyed telling us how we were descended from a prominent Polish nobleman and patriot, Count Tadeusz Malinowski, who supposedly had marched to Moscow with his brother Kasper when Napoleon invaded Russia. When we asked Mother to verify this, she was vague again and emphasized that Americans did not believe in nobility, and it would do no good to mention what Jumbo said about any aristocratic forebears. Yes, I was named Tadeusz, but after her brother and not the count who had served in battle under Napoleon.

Max, however, seized on this gilded pedigree claim and boasted to his buddies that "royal blood" flowed in our veins. Ziggy was proof, Max argued, since he had learned from an encyclopedia in the school library that many European aristocratic families often turned out idiots every other generation or so. How Max had gleaned this information about inbreeding in European families on one of his rare trips to the school library, none of us could figure out. But the theory seemed quite convincing to Jumbo, and he never disputed it.

As I learned later, there was actually no way of verifying our pre-America bloodline. Official birth records from the previous century, when Poland was not even an official country, but rather a colony of Russia, were unobtainable. Furthermore, soon after we left Poland, the World War broke out across Europe. More than half a million Poles and Lithuanians—young and old, soldiers and civilians—perished in the protracted chaos and carnage.

Poles were conscripted into the armies of both sides, so that Poles fought Poles, and the self-slaughtering was ubiquitous. From what Jumbo told us from the Polish newspapers, it seemed unlikely that any of our Malinowski relatives had survived.

Mother's parents, Vera and Marek Lisovski, were documented fatalities of the Great War. Their letters had stopped coming to her as soon as the first bloody battles broke out in 1914. She learned that they had been killed, as were her two younger brothers, by a Russian cannon shell that exploded in their house. She did not know where, or if, her family members were buried, since their remains had disintegrated in the explosion.

I knew it pained Mother to speak about her parents and her brothers. She told my sisters that our grandmother Vera greatly resented Jumbo, mostly because of his heavy drinking. And they felt betrayed when she left to go to live in America. Jumbo had missed my birth and baptism in Vilnius, since he was already working at the time for Etna Metals, and my grandfather Marek had held me up while the priest splashed my head with the holy water. Mother said my grandmother Vera was the last person to kiss me at the railroad station when we all piled on the train for Gdansk to leave Poland forever. Again, those photographs of such moments would have been precious for us all. Probably the pictures were blown up, along with the people whose images they had preserved.

I asked Max why he bragged so much about our so-called royal bloodline, especially if all our royal relatives were dead. He dismissed my question as stupid. Maybe it was. Max knew the best way to curry favor with Jumbo was to parrot his pronouncements. And to Jumbo, hearing his own tales come out of Max's mouth may have made them seem more likely to be true, especially when Max tacked on flourishes of his own, such as Ziggy's idiocy being proof of our family's elite status in Poland.

Several times I heard Jumbo relating this lore to his factory cronies when they visited our farm. They viewed Ziggy with fascination. I was pleased for Ziggy that he received some measure of respect, though the cause was dubious. Max liked to call Ziggy the royal idiot. His friends always got a charge out of that phrase. Ziggy, of course, had no idea what royalty was and why it might make him special. This, Max maintained, was even further proof, since most of the royal idiots in history had no idea whatsoever that they were royal idiots. When Vera and Lucy challenged Max to give one or two historical examples, he promised to bring the school encyclopedia and show them. But he never did.

Time proved, unfortunately, that in both Jumbo and Max any trace of noble descent and character was eventually crushed by rank alcoholism. But during those early years in Ripple Brook Gardens, Jumbo was always sober. That was one of the promises he had made to Mother and to her parents when he left for America.

A new life and a new country. A new Jumbo. No alcohol.

And she was proud of him. All of us were proud of him, and his bosses and coworkers respected him, hoped he would never leave the factory to start a restaurant. But Jumbo made it clear to the folks at Etna Metals that he did not see himself doing manual labor for the rest of his life. He told people he had not given up a successful restaurant near Vilnius to come to America and work like a slave, even though in those early years he was, in fact, a slave to Etna Metals and to our farm and probably, in his mind, to us.

Whatever was going on deep in Jumbo's soul in those early years at Ripple Brook Gardens, he always found profound delight in what he saw in the mirror: the strong jaw with a deep dimple in the middle, broad Slavic cheekbones, and those dark and penetrating widely spaced eyes hooded by arching black brows. He had no hair on the top of his scalp, and the scant gray bristles on the sides and in the back he shaved daily, buffing it all to a gleam.

Sometimes Mother or Vera would assist, but usually he did it solo, holding his straight razor in one hand and a small round mirror in the other. On summer mornings, I sometimes watched him from my bedroom window in the farmhouse. It was intriguing to see him use the front and back double reflections to guide the blade in quick strokes behind his ears and down slowly over the muscular nape of his neck. His shaving basin was set up on a shelf attached to the foot of the water tower, where in the summer he hung his mirrors and straight razor and shaving mug and his long rawhide strop.

He would hone the blade carefully then lather up with his shaving brush and execute these gestures with remarkable speed and efficiency. First the face, including the tricky area around the chin dimple, then the scalp and the neck. And as far back as I can remember Jumbo always sported a dashing handlebar mustache, which he waxed and sculpted, taking care that both ends arched up symmetrically at the points. Sharp-tipped scissors snipped the nose hairs and any overgrowth on his brows.

After shaving the whiskers, buffing the dome, and preening the mustache, nose, and brows, he added the final touch, slapping on a few drops of *Eau de Cologne 1411*. Then he inspected his work carefully, in profile on both sides and head-on. By habit, he would raise his hands to his nose and inhale the cologne fragrance on his fingertips, his pruned nostrils flaring with satisfaction as he sniffed and gazed at the mirror.

Always curious, I watched him dwell in his own image, some-times grimacing very close to the mirror at odd angles and testing the pliancy of the mustache. He gave himself that daily moment of private inspection and adulation before suiting up and setting off on his bicycle or in his truck to his shifts at Etna Metals or later at the Rehoboth coal mine and zinc smelter.

Why prepare for work in a sheet metal factory or coal mine or zinc plant with such a studied grooming ritual? That was Jumbo. Perhaps some vestige of the royal Malinowski blood had to affirm itself, if only for a proud minute or two early each morning in the mirror.

People were impressed, sometimes startled, when they first met him. He had an immense presence, those dark flashing eyes and the lyrical mustache. He was 6 foot 2 and over 220 pounds of rippling sinew and muscle. From his circus nickname, acquaintances often guessed he might once have been a professional big top strongman. He looked the part, everybody said.

No, he had never appeared in any circus, Polish or American, but yes, he liked people to call him Jumbo. He said it was his American name. Mother was the only person I ever heard call him Ignaz. To everyone else, even to his children, he was Jumbo, the imposing bar-rel-chested beast of a man whose roaring belts of laughter, when det-onated on our farmhouse porch, could send shivers down my spine, even half a mile off in the woods.

Up close, nobody missed the engaging, boyish sparkle in his eyes, especially when he grinned and showed off the glimmering gold cap on his left upper incisor, where he liked to park his cigar. Through the years, as Jumbo aged and drank homemade alcohol to excess, the gold tooth and the cigar remained, but the bright gaze, especially in the years after Mother died, faded gradually to a lusterless leer, and those once booming salvos of laughter petered out to hollow rasps.

But the deterioration came later. When Mother was alive and Jumbo was in his Herculean prime, he was truly an amazing spec-imen. When he moved his big body, no matter where he was, he seemed the man in charge, the boss, maybe even royalty. In church, as he strutted down the aisle to kneel and take Communion, he swung his arms as if leading a parade.

Sometimes Max strutted that same way right behind him. I thought Max looked foolish trying to copy Jumbo on the way to the altar, but I suppose I was jealous. When I practiced strutting in front of Mother's mirror, I could see my limp was more pronounced. No, strutting like Jumbo was out for me, royal blood notwithstanding.

I am often amazed at how clearly I recall the details of my early life on the Wells farm. I attribute this rich lode of memories to my sensitivity, which Mother cautioned me about in her wise way. But I know it is also the result of my ceaseless ransacking of my memory. As a prospector might pan for gold nuggets, I would search for traces of brightness and hope in my life before Mother died.

And these are not visions from dreams. In my sleep, I am often haunted by manifestations of my Mother. I always feel privileged when she comes to me in that generous and abiding presence. Such fantasies leave me refreshed and cheerful. I feel her love freshly. She is young, smiling, approving.

My dreams are different from my memories, which are gleaned through this unquenchable urge to dig into the past. This compulsion began abruptly with her death and continued relentlessly for many years. Regrettably, this process exposed me again and again to the pain, but it always seemed worth it. I could not stop it.

I refuse to believe it was denial, an inner disavowal of my complicity in Mother's death. As I have matured, my complicity now seems obvious, if innocent. Keeping Eva Malinowski alive by foraging for those memories, feeling her arms around me, her lips on my cheek, smelling her perfume, hearing her soft voice humming in my ear and telling me Polish folk tales, all those resurrections of Mother stay mystically alive and real in my soul.

Who are we but what we love? Not until many years later did I find the power in my heart to shed many of those memories and let them reside in the past.

Skills Galore

My love for Jumbo is a bitter task of loyalty. There were reasons to love him. Many people felt the urge. His physical bearing and charisma made him appealing. He attracted friends, and his many talents amazed them. I already described how he designed and constructed the water supply for Mother's laundry, an impressive engineering feat. But that was only the beginning.

Despite no training, he mastered many practical pursuits: carpentry, plumbing, sewing, cooking, wine making, and later automobile mechanics.

In addition, though he never finished high school in Poland and never had an appetite for books, he read a Pittsburgh newspaper several times a week, including the sports pages, and he subscribed to a Polish weekly that came from Chicago. When he talked with his friends about local or national politics or world events or boxing or even baseball, he appeared opinionated and up-to-date.

On the topic of books, we had several shelves of them near the fireplace in the living room, though Mother and the girls were the only ones who paid attention to the volumes. Jumbo did not. Among other titles I recall, there were Polish prayer books, a Polish Bible and an English Bible, a biography of Chopin in Polish, a collection of Mark Twain stories in Polish, a history of the partitions of Poland, and a beautiful red leather copy of *Quo Vadis* by Henryk Sienkiewicz, which my grandparents had given to Mother when she left Poland.

I once asked Mother about *Quo Vadis*. The title didn't sound like Polish or English. She explained the title was Latin, a language spoken in ancient Rome, where the story in the book took place. Latin, she added, was the secret language Roman Catholic priests used in the Mass.

"Is it hard to learn Latin?" I asked.

"I think the best high schools in America teach it. But nobody uses it except the priests."

"Does God speak in Latin?"

"God speaks every language, but let me tell you about *Quo Vadis*."

Mother went on to say that when Saint Peter was fleeing Rome to escape crucifixion, the risen Jesus appeared to Peter right there on the road.

"Quo vadis?" "Where are you going?" Peter asked the Lord. Jesus said he was going back to Rome to be crucified again, since Peter did not seem up to the task. When Peter realized it was Jesus, he was stricken with shame. He turned right around and went back to Rome, where he was crucified upside down.

"Why upside down?" I asked her.

"He asked for it that way."

"Why?"

"Someday you will read the book," she said. "The Roman emperor Nero was a monster. He tortured Christians and fed them to the lions in the Roman Coliseum. I know you will read it. Everybody in Poland has read *Quo Vadis*. Even your father."

The *Quo Vadis* story troubled me, especially the part about being crucified upside down. The book had no pictures in it, and it was over seven hundred pages long. To me it was beautiful on the outside, but the inside looked like a huge ocean of Polish words with dark meanings. This suspicion was confirmed when I asked Jumbo if he had actually read it.

He frowned. "I started to read it, but I stopped when the Romans wrapped the Christians in straw sacks and hoisted them up on poles. They drenched them with alcohol and lit them up for party torches. Too disgusting for me."

"Emperor Nero? The monster? Did he do that?"

"I forget. Wait. Yes. Nero was his name. Maybe someday you'll read it for yourself."

Though Mother said *Quo Vadis* was the best book she ever read, and it did look beautiful on our living room shelf, I understood why Jumbo didn't finish it.

On the other side of the living room from *Quo Vadis* and the other books stood an upright Wurlitzer piano, another manifestation of Jumbo's multiple talents. He had never taken a lesson and could not read the notes on sheet music. But if someone requested, he could sit at our piano and bang out the chords for almost any popular song he heard. His favorite American songs were "Over the Waves," "Beautiful Dreamer," and later "Hinky Dinky Parlez-Vous" and "Darktown Strutter's Ball."

He played Polish polkas, Strauss waltzes, and half a dozen marches by John Philip Souza. He sang in a booming basso and often went flat. Mother would roll her eyes and then smile when he found the right key again.

Our rattletrap Wurlitzer came second or thirdhand from the St. Stanislaus Church in Etna. When a wealthy dowager in the parish died and bequeathed the church her fine new Baldwin grand, Jumbo asked for and took the church's old Wurlitzer. That was before we got the Ford panel truck, so he had to haul the Wurlitzer out the road to Ripple Brook Gardens on our buckboard.

I can remember his spade-size hands hovering over those yellow keys and then jumping back and forth, up and down, always pumping his heel on the floor in time with the rhythm. He lacked delicacy but not enthusiasm. Because of his energetic pounding of the keys, the old Wurlitzer constantly went out of tune.

Not a problem. Jumbo ordered a piano manual and a tuning fork in the mail, and when the wires went flat, he knew how to screw all eighty-eight of them to the correct pitch.

Mother herself had taken some piano lessons back in Poland. She had a more refined touch at the keyboard, and she also had a beautiful contralto voice with a natural vibrato. She could sight-read music well, though she was always timid at performing. She taught

Vera and Lucy lessons in the fundamentals, and sometimes they would practice, but only if Jumbo was not around.

When Jumbo was in the house, hands off the Wurlitzer! The piano was his. Mother liked to play Chopin waltzes and Bach preludes and fugues, but again, only when Jumbo was off the property.

There is one of Jumbo's multiple talents, which I wish he had never developed: wine making. Not long after our arrival in Ripple Brook Gardens, he had gone out and separated and cultivated the old vines in the derelict vineyard on the property. After several test seasons, he enlarged the root cellar by the barn and brought in half a dozen large oak vats. Soon he had gallons of golden and red wine aging in that cool, sunken shed. Wine making and later vodka fermentation and distillation from our own potatoes were part of his master plan that evolved in stages to realize his dream to establish a restaurant.

6

Jumbo's Tavern

By the time I turned five, Jumbo and Mother had toiled to turn the little Wells farm into a sort of roadhouse, where on Sunday afternoons immigrant families, mostly Polish, would come and sit at long tables in the yard to drink Jumbo's wine and vodka and cider and play cards and feast on his and my mother's cooking. And they danced.

Our first customers were coworkers from the sheet metal plant, but in time word spread that Jumbo's Tavern in Ripple Brook Gardens was the place for authentically crafted dishes like *kapusta* and *bigos* and *kaszanka* served by Jumbo and his stunning blonde wife, and assisted by their sons and two charming daughters.

At sunset on summer evenings, we lit up torches and lanterns all around the tables, and Mother and Vera and Lucy served the customers. Max bussed tables and helped wash the dishes. I was too young to be involved, but I remember Mother smiling when I ran around with children who spoke Polish. Always keeping an eye open for Ziggy and me, she hustled through her tasks and supervised the older siblings.

The rolling meadows where the Wells family's sheep had grazed teemed with lightning bugs, and our fields, glowing and sparkling with magical yellow-green flashes, enchanted the visiting children. We ran out and caught the blinking insects in Mason jars and marched around proudly, showing them off to the children's parents at the tables.

BLOOD PUDDING

To Ziggy and me, the lightning bugs, *świetliki* in Polish, seemed another kind of magic. Like the winter snow that quickly melted, the light from the *świetliki* gradually blinked off in the Mason jars on the picnic tables and eventually became nothing but a pile of dead bugs. But weren't they wonderful for a while! Ziggy tried to make them flash again by shaking the jars, but it didn't work. I once tried to convince him that getting angry when he shook the jars wouldn't help bring the magic back. But he said he wasn't angry. He was sad.

Later, when Kazzy was born, what made Ziggy happy on those summer evenings was to push Kazzy's perambulator around to all the tables, showing off his new baby brother to the guests. Kazzy wasn't magic, but it did seem mysterious to Ziggy and me, even miraculous, that Mother's belly got very big over several months and then a new baby brother showed up.

"Kazzy, short for Kazimierz," Ziggy would announce, grinning with twitches in his eyes and jerking his head back and forth. The guests would nod, their attention often fixed on Ziggy's odd facial tics, rather than on the baby. The conversation usually died right there, and the guests looked relieved when Ziggy moved on to the next table.

After dinner, Jumbo rolled the Wurlitzer out onto the side of the back porch and clunked out polkas and waltzes and some popular American tunes. I have sweet memories of those gracious afternoons and evenings, often an accordion and violin playing along. Jumbo's massive hands rose and fell on the keys, and his mustache bobbed and quivered. His bass voice veered off pitch regularly, but nobody seemed to mind, since he was leading the show.

One favorite was a Polish patriotic song *"Hej, Sokoly!"* ("Hey, Falcons!") All the Polish families liked to stand at their tables and clap and sing with Jumbo.

Ziggy loved it when we walked up to the piano, and Jumbo took in a big drag from his cigar and blew smoke rings at us. Like frightening the chickens, getting blasted by Jumbo's smoke rings was another sport for Zig. But once or twice was all Jumbo would bother with before he told us to scram, gesturing with the cigar at the guests and shooing us away.

Jumbo danced well. Sometimes, to crank the party up a notch, he would command the accordion player and the fiddler to take over, as he twirled with my mother on the circular wooden dance platform he had constructed in the yard. Mother would take off her full-length apron to show off her white flowing party dress.

Jumbo looked grand in his starched white shirt with open collar, a red silk scarf round his neck, and a black swallow tail jacket with long tails. The polka was their favorite leadoff, and with Jumbo's infectious gold-toothed grin working the crowd, others soon joined in.

My visions of my parents waltzing to Strauss melodies in the torchlight of Jumbo's Tavern, surrounded by their happy friends and customers, are perhaps the dearest I have from those years. Mother's glowing green eyes and her broad excited smile as she twirled in his arms reassured me of their love. This helped me forgive much of my father's meanness and impatience, which were so often on display in our family and often to Mother.

The music and singing and dancing on those evenings, the flickering glow of the *świetliki* and the garden torches, and the gorgeous smile on my mother's face fixed in my early imagination a powerful longing for Poland. Though they had come to America, they had brought their music and traditions with them and were recreating them here on a little farm outside Pittsburgh. No matter how terrible they said Poland was as a place to live, with explosions and battles depopulating the country, I could not help but cherish that mystical place of my birth. Yes, people would say, Jumbo's Tavern is like a little piece of the good old Poland.

When couples started to schedule wedding receptions at our house, Jumbo imagined quitting his job at Etna Metals to devote all his time to a restaurant. Though there was no sign on our house, no menus on the tables, no advertisements in the papers, everybody at the plant and around Ripple Brook Gardens called the place Jumbo's Tavern.

Eventually Mother hired some young Polish women to help with the preps and cleanups, especially for the larger weddings. There was simply too much work for one family to do in catering to these large affairs. And the laundry business was thriving, too, which added to the pressures on Mother. But she never complained, always kept calm and steady, and seemed genuinely thrilled by our successes.

With our various sources of income, which included Jumbo's pay from the plant and Mother's laundry income and profits from the tavern, we had enough money coming in to buy clothes in the downtown Pittsburgh stores. I can remember one early September day when Mother took Max and me into town on the bus. We went to the boys' department of Joseph Horne's and bought Max two pairs of corduroy knickers and several shirts for school. I could see how proud Mother was, as Max tried on several pairs and the tailor measured Max's waist and inseam for the alterations. I imagined myself growing into Max's fancy knickers someday. I hoped Ziggy wouldn't get them first, because he might ruin them.

While Max's knickers were being tailored, we ate lunch downstairs in the elegant restaurant on the first floor, where the hostess and the waitresses were gracious and attractive, but not as beautiful as our mother.

The thrill of the day for me was when we rode the elevator clear up to the seventh floor, and in the children's toy department, she purchased a giant set of Lincoln Logs. The Lincoln Logs were a prize, no question, and I knew Zig would love them. But the store's elegant wood-paneled elevators amazed me the most. The uniformed operator was young, not much older than Max, and he seemed very sure of himself.

"Floor, please?" he said, smiling to each customer coming into the elevator. On the seventh floor he announced, "Welcome to seven. Toys. Sporting goods. Fishing equipment. Watch your step."

Little did I know how much time I would eventually spend operating elevators one day, after I had a chance to leave Rehoboth. But my first two trips up and down in Horne's were memorable. The young operator seemed so polite and polished, and I was sure he lived in the city, probably with sophisticated parents.

Another thrill that afternoon was a trip on the trolley car that took us up to the new Grand Theater, where we watched my very first movie, *Tarzan of the Apes*. The action scenes of all the African

45

animals amazed us, and for several weeks after that afternoon, Max walked around the farm pounding his chest and giving out what he thought Tarzan shouts would sound like. He had read the paperback of Tarzan, and sometimes he and his friends competed in bellowing contests.

These outbursts startled Ziggy. He did not know who Tarzan was, but he soon tried to imitate Max and his friends by screaming and pounding his chest. When Max saw Ziggy mimicking him, he stopped playing Tarzan. He did find vines on some tall elm trees deep in the forest and tried to swing on them like Tarzan, but the vines weren't strong enough. Then he discovered he could cut off a few inches of the vine, set a match to it and smoke it like a cigar. After that, he and his buddies went into the woods to smoke, not to swing. Mother scolded him about this, but he kept on smoking the vine sticks till he got bored with it. He went on to cigarettes shortly after his Tarzan phase.

This period of our lives was a golden time, when I would wander around the fields with Ziggy, and we would hear Mother playing Chopin on the Wurlitzer, and our lives were exciting. I asked Mother to give me some piano lessons, so that I could dream of someday playing for guests, just as my multitalented father did. And perhaps, when my legs eventually evened out, I could waltz or polka with her.

When I brought this subject up to Mother, she would smile and assure me that all I had to do was be patient and wait, and all the magic would happen, including the growing of the bad leg. She encouraged me to hope and believe, and I took comfort from her, though she never made much progress with me on the piano. I was too young then, probably.

Some Sunday mornings, when we walked down the church aisle in a line, I could feel people's eyes following my parents with admiration. We were the family that lived on the little farm out in Ripple Brook Gardens, where glorious wedding receptions were held, the family with the husky first son, the two eager young daughters, the boy with mental problems due to his family's precious pedigree, the boy with the bad leg, and the new baby, recently baptized. We were the Malinowski family, and didn't we look grand!

BLOOD PUDDING

Years later, that image of my family in church comforted me too. Despite the terrible events that happened subsequently, I could at least recall moments when it seemed my parents loved each other and cared for us, despite our quirks, and that we were all fully entitled to walk tall and relatively shameless through our lives.

The Black Madonna

At Jumbo's Tavern, I never saw for sure how the money was collected from the customers, but I recall that at the end of the evenings after everything was cleaned up, Mother pulled thick rolls of dollar bills out from under her apron. Sometimes, when I needed a little break from Ziggy, I slept on a cot in the corner of the kitchen, and when everybody had gone home, I saw her tug away the woven rag rug in the far kitchen corner where the pots and pans hung on the wall pegs.

Directly under a replica icon of the Black Madonna of Częstochowa, which Mother had brought with us from Poland, she squatted down and pulled up several bricks in the floor. Under the bricks and under the Black Madonna's watch were some large round coffee tins, stowed away where nobody could find them. After counting the take from the night, she hid the cash in the tins. She kept her few pieces of jewelry in a separate tin too. When the bricks were fitted back carefully into their places and the rug restored to its spot, she kneeled before the icon, crossed herself and prayed, and then kissed the Madonna. It was the last thing she did before she went to bed.

If Jumbo and his friends from the factory stayed up late playing poker out under the yard lanterns, he sometimes slipped into the kitchen and unearthed the coffee tins to hide his winnings or to withdraw cash to cover his losses. He never crossed himself or paid any regard at all to the Black Madonna. Jumbo never had religion on his mind the way Mother did.

And Mother made it clear to all of us that the family "bank" was off-limits, and that none of us should ever touch it, under severe penalty by the Black Madonna. As a saint and watchdog with her foreboding eyes and grim lips surrounded by a thick gold halo that melded with baby Jesus's own halo, the Black Madonna looked like one tough customer. Even Max knew to keep his hands off that rug and off those bricks.

My sister Lucy paid even more attention to the Madonna than Mother did. Sometimes when she thought I was sleeping on my special cot, she would come into the kitchen quite late at night and light a candle. She would pull up a stool and stare at the Madonna for almost an hour, often running her fingers over her rosary beads and squeezing them as she whispered prayers in Polish.

Pretending to sleep through her meditations, I would open my eyes just a crack and watch the smooth skin on her cheeks quiver slightly as she prayed in the candle's glow. When she was finished, she would put her rosary into the pocket of her nightdress. Then before she went back upstairs to the bed she shared with Vera, she would stand very quietly, kiss the icon, and then tiptoe over to me and kiss my forehead. I could barely feel her lips, but I could feel her warm breath and smell the shampoo fragrance in her hair.

She was as quiet as an angel through all her night vigils, and she probably thought I was always asleep and that I never was aware of her. In time, I began to look forward to watching her pray to the Madonna across the kitchen, so much so that I would stay awake, waiting for her. And I imagined that after her being in such close reflective contact with a powerful saint, receiving a kiss from Lucy was almost like receiving a kiss from Jesus's mother herself. Such a kiss might help my bad leg to grow, I imagined.

I was grateful to Lucy. She taught me to read and write English at an early age. Everyone said she was not as beautiful as Vera, but she certainly had beautiful qualities. She was wonderfully kind to Ziggy also, which was important to me.

Thinking back about my two sisters, I could say that Vera, who was tall and athletic and gorgeous to look at, shared the outer qualities of my mother, including her sparkling green eyes, whereas Lucy, who was not tall nor athletic and had brown eyes like the rest of us, bore Mother's inner spirituality, and I loved that about her.

I once asked Lucy if she thought I should pray directly to the Black Madonna about making my short leg longer. Lucy suggested I give it a try, but the Black Madonna looked too grumpy to me. Though she certainly could be trusted to guard my parents' money, I did not feel personally comfortable asking her about improvements to my own body. I told Lucy I would rather go to God for that one, which I did without fail every night.

A few years after Mother died and we were living in Rehoboth, Jumbo sold the Madonna icon to a traveling tinker without mentioning it to any of us. One day she just disappeared from the wall. Not a word to Lucy either. That was bad, but that was Jumbo, especially later, when we all wanted to escape from him.

I can trace his logic: with no money in the house to guard, the Black Madonna was useless. Of course, whatever money he received for the icon he would have spent immediately on a bootleg whiskey bender. That would have lasted him a week or less, leaving him again with no money in the house. And again, proof to him that the icon was no longer needed or relevant.

It occurred to me later that perhaps the Black Madonna herself wanted to escape, just like the rest of us. She surely was disgusted by what she saw happening around her in that house in Rehoboth. In her eyes, Jumbo's selling her might have been a big favor, though Jumbo would have been unaware of it. I hope she and her baby found a more wholesome and appreciative, hopefully Polish, home. I don't think Lucy could ever forgive him.

Zelienople

I have described how my father was gifted at any number of skills at the factory, on the farm, in the kitchen, and with the piano. The ugly death of our pig showed me, however, that there were limits to what Jumbo could do well.

Jumbo bought a pig to reduce the tavern's butcher bills. Pork was a major component of many of the tavern's signature dishes, to name three: *bigos*, a bacon-and-mushroom-stuffed sauerkraut; *galaretka*, or jellied pig's feet; and *kaszanka*, or blood pudding, a rich spicy sausage requiring large amounts of back fat and freshly bled pig's blood.

Pork loins and short ribs were also popular menu items, cheeks, tongues, kidney, and liver too. Some customers asked for brain, but we never offered that. It was said that an expert butcher could put to use every ounce of a pig, "all but the squeal," as the trade saying went. Jumbo's thinking was if we could raise and butcher our own hogs, the tavern overhead would lower and profits would rise. Mother agreed it was worth a try.

As an experiment, Jumbo bought Abner, a two-month-old and freshly weaned thirty-five-pounder, from Mr. Grant Murdoch, a hog breeder several miles out our road. Piglets purchased at that age are called weaners, a term at first confusing to Jumbo, who knew the word conventionally meant sausage.

Mr. Murdoch, who was not Polish, took time to explain the difference in meaning to Jumbo. He spelled out the two words on the sales receipt. Happy from the purchase and amused by the verbal irony, Jumbo showed off his new piglet with a punch line. "From weaner to wieners! See?" he would ask his friends, as he leaned on the pigsty fence post, puffed his cigar, and waited for the joke to register. By the time Abner had quickly enlarged to well over 250 pounds, Jumbo continued to crack the joke to visitors, his deep barrel-chested chortles blasting all over the property, though by that stage of the pig's development the joke was as stale as the pig was enormous.

Pink, fuzzy, and frisky, the weaner stole our hearts. We children had never seen a creature so animated and cute and with such an endearing personality. In the first month, all of us, including Max, would linger by the pigpen and adore the charming young Abner, who seemed to share our affection. He squealed when he was hungry, but also when he saw us coming over to visit him. It seemed as if that summer Abner became our favorite pet and the center of our family.

Abner had unlimited energy and for the first week or so enjoyed being picked up and cuddled. We loved to let him out of his gate, so we could chase him around the barnyard or up into the meadows. Jumbo crafted a leather collar for him, and sometimes we would take him on a rope over into the woods, where he would grunt with delight and root around busily, sniffing for mushrooms, acorns, berries, toads, chipmunks, almost anything.

He ate whatever we threw near him. One summer afternoon when Abner had been with us for a month and had tripled in weight, Max spotted and immediately sledgehammered a five-foot black snake, which had been lurking around the barn for mice.

When Max tossed the long limp carcass into the sty, Abner scuttled right for it. Then Max, Ziggy, and I watched Abner greedily crunch up the snake in three-inch sections and swallow it, beginning with the head and right down to the tip of the tail. It was rare for Max to shut up for so long, but the three of us were dumbfounded to watch the pig eat the snake.

When Abner had consumed all five feet and licked the final skin scales from his snout, he lay on his side to nap in the sun.

Max whispered, "Damn, that Abner can eat!"

Ziggy jumped down into the sty and kneeled beside Abner and petted him for a while. Then Abner suddenly woke up and puked up some snake bones along with what appeared to be the remains of a barn mouse the snake had swallowed whole. This startled Ziggy, and he climbed back out of the sty. Abner quickly gobbled up his snake and mouse again and went back to sleep. This made Ziggy laugh, and he talked about Abner and the snake and the mouse for a week.

Mother told us to put a limit on how much we loved Abner. Jumbo was raising the pig to be slaughtered. That was no secret. We should not forget that in six or seven months when Abner would grow to a massive three hundred pounds, we would kill him and drain his blood for the blood pudding and butcher him and serve him to the guests of the tavern. So, we were to be careful about our love.

This warning made only theoretical sense to Ziggy and me. The pig wasn't due to be executed till the late fall or winter, and that seemed a long time from summer.

Through the years, we all had watched Mother kill many scores of chickens quickly and humanely, sliding the squawking bird into a steel funnel with the head sticking out the bottom, slitting the neck vein with a sharp paring knife to release the blood, and then ramming the knife up through the chicken's open beak to pith the brain.

But chickens were stupid, and we had reared and slaughtered hundreds of them. Abner, however, was smart and unique to us, part of our family. He was the only pig we had ever known. He was the closest thing we ever had to a pet. True, we had nameless feral cats, who lived in the barn, kept aloof from us, and nourished themselves rather independently on mice, chipmunks, and toads. But we never had a dog, apparently because in Poland a fierce German shepherd had mauled Jumbo when he was only seven. Jumbo had hated dogs ever since. As mentioned, he felt the same about priests, though he never told us the reason behind that.

I once heard a boy ask Max why our family never had a real pet. Max snickered and said, "Ziggy serves that purpose fine around our house. He can even do some tricks for you, if you treat him nice."

Such hurtful comments from Max were never surprising, but I knew it was pointless and risky to call him on them. He would always shoot back some nasty quip about my having one and a half legs, and the laugh would end up on me. I usually would embarrass myself further by breaking out into tears. Max enforced the sibling pecking order regularly, and there was little I could do but to abide it and keep my mouth shut.

That summer if I lost track of Ziggy, I would usually find him with Abner, either grinning at him through the sty planks or sometimes flat down on the dirt in the sty, taking a nap, with his arm around Abner. The first time I woke Ziggy up and told him to get out of the sty, he broke into tears and stayed angry with me the rest of the day. After that, I let him sleep in the dry part of the sty, till Mother or Vera came out and shouted at both of us.

One day Ziggy said he wanted to change Abner's name to Zelienople, the name of the town Mother had trouble pronouncing. Zig said cryptically that the pig looked more like a Zelienople than an Abner. Since we all knew the pig would not live but a few months longer, nobody saw any reason not to make the change. He never really answered to his name anyway, so if it pleased Ziggy, why not? And once he had renamed the pig, Ziggy seemed to think that change made the pig more his own.

"Zelienople! Zelienople! Zelienople!" Ziggy would laugh as he ran to the sty. It seemed he felt empowered, thrilled by having us all go along with his suggestion.

Often that fall, Ziggy crawled up on top of Zelienople and rode him, bareback cowboy style, around the sty. I put the collar on the pig and led him around the yard with Ziggy on top of him, thrilled and giggling with pride. Mother and Eva looked over from the laundry area and laughed too.

"Zelienople!" Ziggy shouted.

"Zelienople!" Mother and Vera and Lucy shouted back at him.

It was great sport, and we all enjoyed sharing Zig's joy.

We all agreed that Ziggy's attachment to Zelienople was dangerous, but Ziggy was having so much fun, none of us wanted to ruin it.

Ziggy did not have many friends or joys in his life, and in this sense, the pig renamed Zelienople was a blessing.

Ziggy, of course, did not understand Mother's advice about limiting love. His mind and his heart could not grasp any of it, and thinking two or even one month into the future was impossible for him.

Jumbo took Ziggy aside and said that after we slaughtered Zelienople, we would quickly buy another weaner. Ziggy would find a new playmate to chase around the farm and take naps with. When he repeated this to Ziggy at the dinner table, I watched the tears well up in Ziggy's eyes. He ran outside to be alone with Zelienople and would not let me come near them.

One Saturday morning in late November, we woke up to find half a foot of wet snow on the ground. Jumbo came back an hour late from the night shift, because he had walked his bicycle most of the way home along unplowed roads. He was in one of his dangerous foul moods.

Mother told us that Grant Murdoch was coming over that morning, but none of us, except Max, knew what that meant. Vera and Lucy had gone out to bring in the eggs from the henhouse and then came back and started making breakfast with Mother. I had helped Max milk the two cows and muck the horse's stall. When I filled a bucket with soybeans for the pig, Max said I shouldn't waste them. When I ignored him and stepped out toward the sty, Max grabbed my arm and yanked the bucket out of my hand.

I ran back to the kitchen, and Jumbo asked me if Ziggy and I would like to build a snowman. I was surprised, because he rarely took an interest in what we did for fun. He said the best snow on the property was up at the other end of the barn beyond the vineyard and near the orchard. I said, if we built a snowman up there we wouldn't be able to see it from the house, but Jumbo said, "Your mother and I will come up in a couple hours to see how big you made him. Go out and get started. The snow might melt, and then you will miss your chance."

At the word "snowman," Ziggy's face lit up, and he ran to the closet to pull out his heavy coat. Mother bundled us up and poured a thermos of hot chocolate and gave us mugs to take along to keep our tummies warm. Lucy said she would like to join us, so the three of us set out to do our task. By this time, the sun was up above the trees, and our whole property was blanketed in beautifully glowing white.

It was still cold, and we were shivering when we climbed to the end of the meadow near the orchard. We immediately opened the thermos and stood a few minutes in the fresh snow, sipping cocoa. I put my mittens back on and kneeled and packed a firm ball to start rolling it around for the base of the snowman. Ziggy and Lucy, still shivering, kept sipping from their mugs.

I rolled my snowball up and down the orchard hill twice, and it quickly grew, accumulating more heavy snow with each revolution. I had a hard time pushing it, and I asked Lucy and Ziggy to help me. By then they both had finished their hot chocolate, but they were looking over toward the barn, where a strange truck had pulled up and parked. Jumbo was talking with the man, who drove the truck. There was no wind, and their voices echoed loudly across the snow right toward us.

"Oh, I recognize that man," said Lucy, who had been at the breeding farm the day Jumbo first went to buy a piglet. "That's Mr. Murdoch, the man who sold us Zelienople."

"Jumbo said he wants a snowman. We should keep building it," I said.

"Yes, that's definitely Mr. Murdoch."

Ziggy dropped his mug in the snow and bolted back toward the barn. Lucy set the thermos down and followed him. I kneeled and was starting a second ball for the middle of the snowman, when I heard Zelienople's loud squeals pierce the air. Then I saw Mr. Murdoch pull a rifle out of the cab of his truck before he disappeared on the other side of the barn.

I ran toward the truck, which had been backed up toward the sty. On the back of the truck bed there was a high scaffold with heavy hooks and a couple of long chains.

Zelienople's terrified bleats shattered the air. We had never heard him make such noises.

BLOOD PUDDING

I turned the corner and saw the pig lying on his side just outside the sty gate with his front and back feet tied up. Max held his back legs down, and Jumbo stood over him with the sledgehammer. Mr. Murdoch and Jumbo were arguing.

"No need shoot!" Jumbo shouted. "In Poland, we use hammer."

"You're gonna rile the pig and ruin the meat!" Mr. Murdoch shouted back.

Mother had her arm around Ziggy, who was shouting, "No! No! No!"

"I kill him!" Jumbo said. He raised the hammer with both fists gripping the handle and took aim at the top of Zelienople's skull. When he brought down the head of the hammer, Zelienople threw his neck back toward the sty. The hammer's head landed in the snow.

Squealing wildly, the pig kept jerking his head back and forth.

Frustrated and now enraged, Jumbo raised his weapon again, but Ziggy had broken free from Mother and threw himself across Zelienople's body. He held on to the pig and yelled, "No, Jumbo! No, Jumbo! I love him!"

"Get out!" Jumbo shouted.

"Let me shoot the poor animal," Mr. Murdoch demanded. "I don't have all day for this nonsense."

"Ignaz! Let him shoot it!" Mother screamed.

But Jumbo wedged the heel of his work boot into Zelienople's neck and cocked the sledgehammer high in the air. Again, the pig's head wrenched out of the direct path of the hammer as it came down. The hammer's head blasted through the snout and jaw, ripping a gash across his cheek and pounding his jawbone and his teeth off his snout and into the slush-covered ground. A red spray from the torn face showered over the snow. Zelienople's mutilated tongue sent a separate stream of blood flowing down his neck and flooding over Jumbo's boot.

Agonized bleats burst out of his smashed maw, and he lunged on the snow with Ziggy on top of him. Max held tight to the rope on the back legs till an explosion of pig turds sprayed onto him. He jumped back, disgusted and horrified by what he was seeing.

"Put down the hammer!" Mother shouted, walking over to Jumbo. "Mr. Murdoch, please shoot pig," she said. "Ziggy, step back!"

She grabbed Ziggy's shoulder and pulled him away from the pig. With blood all over his hands and his face, Ziggy grabbed on to Mother and hid his face in her arms. As soon as Ziggy had stepped aside, Mr. Murdoch charged in front of Jumbo, who had dropped his hammer and now started cursing at Ziggy.

Mr. Murdoch pressed the rifle barrel into Zelienople's skull and fired two quick shots then jumped back.

The shots provoked a convulsive writhing all through the pig that lasted a long minute. I stood beside Lucy, shocked and speechless. Lucy was in tears, as was Mother. Max stood by the pig's trembling body, just shaking his head. We had all seen chickens do quick death dances after their heads were pitted, but this massive seizure was sickening and terrifying and prolonged.

Ashamed of his failure, Jumbo let his rage loose on Ziggy. He grabbed the sleeve of Ziggy's coat, jerked him away from Mother then slapped Ziggy three times across his cheeks and kicked his back, till Ziggy was facedown in the snow.

Mr. Murdoch looked on silently. Then he said, "You people seem to have some problems up here today. Why don't you let me butcher the animal? I won't charge you much."

"First, I want blood," Jumbo said.

Mr. Murdoch pointed toward his truck. "Drag him over there, and we'll hoist him up."

Max and Jumbo pulled Zelienople's carcass, no longer seizing, over to the back of the truck. Mr. Murdoch slipped a hook into the rope around the back legs and cranked him up with a heavy iron winch, so his mutilated face was just at the level of the truck bed.

Mother brought two large empty milk buckets over. Mr. Murdoch slashed a quick gash in the neck artery near the breastplate. The blood gushed down into the buckets, one then the other, till they both were nearly full. After all the commotion, the only audible sounds now were the diminishing squirts of the blood into the steel pails and Ziggy's muffled whimpers.

Jumbo said nothing. He stood breathing heavily, steam coming out of his nostrils. He watched as the last drops of our dear pig's blood flowed out of him. Mr. Murdoch explained to me that you have to drain a pig as soon as you slaughter him. Otherwise the meat will taste bad.

"Sonny boy, did you ever have some blood pudding?" he asked. I nodded to him and started to cry.

"Good, ain't it?"

I nodded again.

"I'll have this critter all butchered up nice for you folks in about two hours. I'll keep the back fat in a special bucket for your pudding, Mrs. Malinowski."

"Thank you, Mr. Murdoch," she answered. She picked up the two buckets of blood and started walking around toward the kitchen door. Mr. Murdoch climbed into his truck and drove down toward the main road with Zelienople swinging back and forth, leaving a dripping path of red splotches in the snow all the way down the hill.

I did not want to be near Jumbo or Ziggy, so I marched back up the hill beyond the vineyard and worked on the snowman again. My heart was not in the project, but I knew I should do what Jumbo had told me to do.

Every moment of the pig's slaughter stuck in my memory. The images continued to haunt me for many years, especially Jumbo's cruelty to Ziggy. Much later I thought that perhaps that cold, snowy morning was the first moment I witnessed my father cracking from the strain, which this new life and identity in America had forced upon him.

There was no reason for Jumbo to lay into Ziggy the way he did that morning. And I never understood why he refused to let Mr. Murdoch shoot Zelienople's brain right from the start. We never served brain at the tavern. The result was a cruel, mutilating death witnessed by our whole family. We all felt injured.

My parents were intelligent but not richly educated in Poland. They took what they found in America at face value, often clumsily. Jumbo never really told us why he left Poland, except to say that if he had stayed, he would have been drafted into the czar's army and would most likely have been quickly killed. So, he said, we all should feel lucky about what was happening to us in America.

And as I mentioned, for most of that time in Ripple Brook Gardens, I was happy. But not the morning we killed Zelienople, and not for a while after that.

Later that day, when Mr. Murdoch returned with the butchered parts, Jumbo spent a few hours preparing the blood pudding, heating up the ingredients and squeezing them into Zelienople's own intestines. The next morning Mother fried up some slices of the blood pudding for breakfast before we went to Mass. Everybody ate it but Ziggy and me. Jumbo and Max took our shares.

After that, Mother never allowed Jumbo to buy another pig, though Ziggy sometimes asked her if we could.

"There was only one Zelienople, Ziggy," she would say, hugging him.

"Yes, only one Zelienople. Only one. Can we get another one?"

Ownership

A year after Kazzy was born, Jumbo began to talk about purchasing our farm. The idea came to him in a dream, he said. At first, he had dismissed it as nothing more than an impractical vision. But the vision would not leave him alone, and he decided to speak casually to our farm's owner, old Mr. Wells, and ask if there were any chance at all of our owning the place.

Mr. Wells said he had not recently considered selling the farm, but now that he was well into his late eighties and his son-in-law had no interest in working the place, the idea struck him as attractive. He promised to put in a positive word with the bank in Etna about giving us a mortgage, especially since Jumbo had done such an outstanding job at rehabilitating the property.

The bank would, of course, require a substantial down payment, but that would be between the bank and Jumbo. If Jumbo could work it out with them, then Mr. Wells was all for it and maybe could help with a loan for the down payment.

By this time, Jumbo had cut back on his hours at the sheet metal plant and had declined recent offers to move up to foreman. He wanted to devote more time to the farm and the tavern. He still received a steady paycheck from Etna Metals, though an amount less than he earned previously. And the prospect of paying a monthly mortgage charge, rather than rent to Mr. Wells, seemed possible and appealing.

Mother was cautious on the matter. We were doing well finan-
cially. Perhaps it would not be wise to press our luck and go out on
a dangerous limb of debt to a bank. Jumbo complained that such
backward thinking was one of the reasons why he had left Poland. He
had come to find opportunity, and what else did the farm and tavern
represent, if not that?

America had been built on dreams and risks, and Jumbo was
anxious to dive into the process and become successful. Much of the
food supply for Jumbo's Tavern was produced on our farm, including the wine and vodka and cider, and Mother's laundry business
brought in a growing year-round sum. The time to move ahead with
the purchase was exactly now. Jumbo could see no reason to wait.
And Mr. Wells was old. If he died, there was no guarantee his daughter and son-in-law would want to continue renting to us.

Other imaginary scenarios crept into Jumbo's thinking. What
would happen if a stranger suddenly came by and made old Mr.
Wells a cash offer for the place? What if Mr. Wells sold it right out
from under Jumbo and after all the work we had done? What if,
for example, one of the wedding reception guests fell in love with
the farm, approached Mr. Wells behind Jumbo's back, and made a
generous offer outright? Maybe the vision that came to Jumbo in the
dream was, in fact, not a fantasy, but rather a practical and prudent
venture for the family's future. Look at all the thriving industry in
the city of Pittsburgh, and surely all those successes represented a true
manifestation of the American way of being confident in one's own
abilities and convictions.

A stranger could step in at any moment. If our family waited to
buy, the house, the farm, the laundry business, and Jumbo's Tavern,
all could slip right through our fingers with the stroke of that rich
stranger's pen.

Jumbo's fears grew and may have swayed Mother's opinion. Her
husband had a point. If Mr. Wells were to sell the farm, it would
be hard to find another place that offered what we already had. Eva
Malinowski did not want to search for another neglected property
and repeat what she and Jumbo had done over the past six years.
God's hand had guided Jumbo to this farm on the hill amid the forest

with the abundant wild raspberries and the apple orchard and the delicious fresh water, and maybe it was time to trust in what God had provided us. She said she would think about it.

The idea of owning the land at Ripple Brook Gardens became a compulsion. Jumbo was tormented by nightmares of old Mr. Wells arriving at our front door with a constable and forcing Mother and the rest of us out of the house at gunpoint. These dream visions, he said, resembled the grim scenes he had witnessed as a boy in Poland when the czar's Cossacks evicted families in the middle of the night.

He had to do something fast, he said, before Mr. Wells died or had a stroke or made a move with a third party. Mother understood that there was no turning back. So, Jumbo made an appointment at the bank, and one morning he put on his Sunday suit and walked into the bank in Etna with Mother and Mr. Wells. He came out with a plan that was possible, though it meant that Jumbo would need to come up with a down payment. The Black Madonna's treasury was good for only half of that large sum. But Mr. Wells generously agreed to lend us the remainder.

"We can lock it in!" Jumbo said that night at the dinner table. "We can lock our farm in for good! Monday, I will go to the bank with Mr. Wells and close the deal."

His eyes prowled around the room at Mother and at his six children, as if we should all understand what this big step meant. None of us except Mother and maybe Max could foresee any real change in our lives. All our chores on the farm would be the same, and business at the tavern would continue just as it had for the past several successful years. All the cooking and linen cleaning and vegetable harvesting and wine making and cider pressing would remain the same, possibly increase in intensity. So, none of us could grasp why, in Jumbo's eyes, our buying of the farm was such a big event. Why would buying the farm bring about changes?

But things did change, almost imperceptibly at first, and then in a spiral that permanently corrupted our futures.

Change of Luck

Shortly after Jumbo signed the mortgage papers with the Etna bank, he threw a lavish party at the tavern. He invited Nicholas Wells and his family along with all his friends and coworkers at the plant. Even some of the Etna Metals management showed up, which tickled Jumbo and Mother. The attendance of the executives gave Jumbo confidence that his purchase of the property was a solid bet.

The party lasted all night with dancing and singing and poker games till the sun came up. Our new life and Jumbo's ownership of the farm were joyously launched. We finally owned our piece of Ripple Brook Gardens. Jumbo had officially purchased a slice of the grand American pie, and it tasted splendid.

About a week later, Etna Metals again called him into the management office and offered him another promotion and a large pay raise. They were enlarging the plant, and they wanted him to help train new workers, more than a dozen fresh lads in from Poland. Two of the management team had been at Jumbo's party at the tavern, where they had seen that he was a leader among the Polish community and the ideal man for the job.

Jumbo could not resist. Once he had signed the mortgage papers with the bank, his nightmares about being run off the farm by the constable had transformed into a new terror, being strapped by enormous debt. He had vowed to pay off Mr. Wells for his help with the down payment, and he reckoned the increased income from Etna

Metals would help eliminate that obligation quickly. This meant he would have less time to devote to running the farm and the tavern, but he hoped his regular customers would be patient and understand.

Jumbo intended to pay off Mr. Wells within a year, a reasonable goal, but the onerous twenty-year mortgage preyed on his soul. At the plant, he took to playing numbers on payday in the hope that a lucky windfall might help him chip a chunk out of the down payment and the principal. He also started to place bets on horse races and baseball games and boxing matches. Eventually Mother began to wonder why Jumbo's take-home pay had not increased, despite his promotion and the added hours he was putting in at the plant. We could feel the tension in the house, and sometimes Jumbo's seething ire escaped his control.

Now and then, Mother and he squared off in front of the Black Madonna and exchanged increasingly bitter words. Rather than admit to where the money was going, he stared at her silently. Several times I saw him, red-faced and quivering with rage, glare at her and shout that buying the farm had been her idea to begin with, and why couldn't she find more laundry customers?

Once, I saw him slap her. She shrieked and slammed the bedroom door on him.

Things did not improve. Sometimes we saw bruises on Mother's arms and on her face, but she gave us excuses. It was hard for all of us to hear my Mother, who always told us to tell the truth at any cost, fib about her wounds and try to convince us that she had slipped on soapsuds and banged her head on the laundry wringer.

The stress became habitual in our house, and though we continued to cater wedding receptions and serve meals on weekends, some of the steady customers at Jumbo's Tavern seemed to have found other weekend rendezvous spots. The quality of the food and drink had not changed, but the atmosphere was somehow less relaxing, less spontaneous, less welcoming.

As months went by, there were fewer family outings, less music and dancing and singing. Jumbo rarely played the piano, and the musicians with the violins and accordions stopped showing up. In their place came gamblers, men who liked to linger late and play poker. Games of chance had always been amusements at the tavern, but soon they dominated the attention of the clientele and eventually the tavern's host.

Max said one night he watched Jumbo slam his losing poker hand down on the table. One of the men across the table said, "Why don't you take a drink? It might change your luck."

Jumbo looked around and saw that Mother and the girls had long since cleaned up the kitchen and were up in the house asleep. A large flask, uncorked and full of his own homemade vodka, stood on the table near him.

"Fetch me a glass, Max!" he commanded.

Max brought a tumbler out from the kitchen. Jumbo ordered him to fill it up halfway.

The other men refilled their glasses and raised them in a toast. Jumbo insisted they wait till Max ran in, brought another glass, and poured himself a drink too.

Max said they all chanted in a chorus, "To a change of luck!"

And then they laughed and slapped Jumbo on his shoulders.

"Now double your luck!" One of the men laughed, pouring another full glass for Jumbo.

Darkness

A thick veil shrouds my memories of what happened in our family after Jumbo took those first sips of vodka. Everything changed for all of us. There was no transition period.

Though always narcissistic and imperious through our years at Ripple Brook Gardens, overnight my father became much more impatient, unpredictable, and cruel. All of us were immediately aware of the terrible change.

Most of my recollections from those early days of my childhood are vivid, as though the events had happened recently. They are all indelible: my adventures with Ziggy, my moments of affection with Mother, my humiliating bullying sessions with Max, my cordial hours spent with Lucy and Vera tutoring me, and, of course, the glorious family celebrations at Jumbo's Tavern.

But my recollections of the year after Jumbo started drinking are repressed or obscured, because of how painful they were to me and to all of us.

Deep in Jumbo's personality, a tightly coiled spring had snapped. It seemed that the acknowledged master of so many skills, the gregarious and charismatic champion, the brilliant strong man at the plant and on the farm, who had royal blood running in his veins, the pianist, the dancer, the master of the house—all of those fabulous traits—rebelled from being a slave to the responsibilities he had taken on in America. That he became a slave to his old liquid master did not apparently occur to him in any meaningful way.

At first, Mother tried to shield his habit from us. She laughed at his jokes that were not funny, and she teased him about how, perhaps, he should realize he had drunk too much vodka and he should be careful not to drink more for fear of not being effective at the plant the next day. But nothing could make him see what he was doing to us.

Hoping to find some advice or support, Mother went to see the priest at the church in Etna. After a few frustrating discussions, she gave up. Her husband had jumped the tracks and gone back to the old habits he had followed in Poland of nightly drinking and daily recovering from hangovers. The priest said he could do nothing for Jumbo, unless Jumbo presented himself for confession.

She tried to convince Jumbo to go to the priest, but he said the church had nothing to offer him, and come to think of it, he might forgo Mass, now that Mother had embarrassed him by blabbing to the priest.

Did she want him to walk in there and be embarrassed? Whose side was she on?

We noticed bigger, darker bruises on her arms and on her face. When her laundry customers dropped by, she covered her arms with long-sleeved blouses and smeared the facial bruises over with makeup. Her customers might not have noticed, but we did.

Even heavily hungover, Jumbo still spent his early morning moments meticulously preening himself in front of the mirror. That was one of the few things in the house that seemed the same. Then that changed too.

"Quo vadis?"

The following spring, the Etna bank foreclosed on our farm.

Mother sold our animals and the Wurlitzer and what she could of the furniture and some of her laundry equipment, and early on a sunny Saturday morning in May, we packed all our clothes and kitchenware and farm tools and everything else we owned, including the Black Madonna, up onto the truck. The packing had taken two full days and most of Saturday morning. All our energy was used up, and we barely were able at the last minute to upload Mother's two washing machines and her old Singer sewing machine and a steam mangle. She would need these, she said, where we were going.

The bank wanted us off the property by noon. The auction was at two.

Prospective buyers had been snooping around the property for weeks. Mother had spoken to the bank and asked them to tell everyone to stay away and leave us alone. Still, we saw people in strange cars driving up to the barn and turning around slowly at all hours.

Max said he heard a rumor circulating that oil had been discovered on the property, and that the bank was planning to set a high starting bid when the auction finally got going. The oil gimmick was surely a put-on, because the bank would have come and done tests on the property before putting it up for auction. In any case, we were leaving. The Wells farm and any make-believe oil under it were up for grabs.

We had not seen nor heard from Jumbo for over three months. Not long after taking up the bottle again, he had also taken up romantically with a young secretary at Etna Metals. The company had fired both of them when they failed to show up at work for two weeks straight. Mother received Jumbo's last paycheck a couple of days after Lincoln's birthday, and with it, she paid off some debts to a few of her laundry customers who had taken pity on us.

I was far too young to fathom what had happened, and I don't think Mother could come to grips with how quickly our fragile little paradise had fallen apart. Jumbo, for the good and the bad, filled a large space. When he was gone, he left a huge hole for all of us to fall into.

We survived that winter mostly from the root cellar and eggs from the chicken coop, though by March, Mother had started to slaughter the last of the hens. We ate our goat. Max, who had an accurate throwing arm, nailed a few wild rabbits with rocks, and Mother boiled them in a stew that was mostly potatoes, mushrooms, carrots, and various herbs. After a week of it, we began to resent the taste. Max asked if she wanted him to bag some squirrels or raccoons, but she told him to hold off, because we still had a few more chickens in the coop.

Max, Vera, and Lucy stayed in school that winter, and Max took an after-school job as a gasoline jockey at a Texaco station. He also helped the mechanics with grunt work on weekends. At the Texaco, he heard rumors that Jumbo and his girlfriend had fled to Florida to look for work. Nobody knew for sure, but one thing was clear: Mother was destroyed.

Jumbo had never said a word to warn us that he was leaving. He had been gone from the house since Christmas, had not worked since January, and the Etna bank said they had no choice but to take the farm. We had hoped that Nicholas Wells might take pity on us and buy the farm back, but we learned he had passed away of a heart attack on New Year's Day, and his family felt no obligation to help us. They were disturbed that we were now losing a property, which they felt should have been theirs to inherit, especially now that someone had said there was oil on the acreage.

One of the bank's lawyers confided to Mother that Mr. Wells had admired Jumbo so much and was so impressed by what we had done with the farm over the years that the old man once considered writing us into his will to bequeath Jumbo the property outright. Mother said the bank lawyer was cruel to mention all this now, because the year had already brought her so much else to regret.

It may seem jarring for me to report this terrible turn of events as a cruel surprise, but that is what it was for all of us. Even in his violent outbursts, he had never threatened to leave. One day Jumbo was there, and the next he wasn't. The only personal items he had taken with him, apart from underwear and stockings and his black Sunday suit, were his mirror and shaving tools and cologne.

At first, we were relieved that he was gone. Since he had started drinking, his dominating presence, always a burden, had become unbearable. And once he left, there was peace for Mother, at least, and that seemed a chance for her to heal. But she could not feed and dress all of us from her laundry business income.

Through the St. Stanislaus Church in Etna, Mother established contact with a priest over in Rehoboth, a tiny company-built coal mining and zinc smelting town twelve miles west of the city, not far from the West Virginia line. The priest in Rehoboth, a certain Father Fernando, had urgent need of a laundress and cook to work full-time in the rectory, where he and five other priests lived. There was a house owned by the diocese behind the rectory that would accommodate her and the six children. The job and house were available immediately.

We all resented this move away from Ripple Brook Gardens, but Mother convinced us that the Rehoboth job and the house opening up for us were a near miracle. Mother also regretfully reminded us that back in Poland, Jumbo had been a heavy drinker. He had vowed to quit alcohol forever, if she would follow him with us to Pittsburgh.

As we all had seen, forever had not lasted as long as we would have hoped. With that original gulp of vodka at the late-night poker table, Jumbo's fierce drinking habit took control again, even worse than his years in Poland. Mother saw his personality deteriorate and his commitment to the family vanish. All the achievements and responsibilities at his job and on the farm and tavern seemed suddenly onerous and expendable. She watched the wine vats, previously reserved for tavern guests, being steadily depleted. He had drunk through the vodka supply in two weeks.

He smelled of wine and vodka early in the morning. In the evenings, he staggered and ordered us around and threatened to cuff us if we were slow to obey. As mentioned, my memories of this period are dark and scant, repressed perhaps because they involved witnessing Mother's increasing desperation.

We saw her peppy spirit change to a resigned glumness. Her beautiful face, normally rosy, animated, and gleeful, now drooped most of the time with fatigue and melancholy. Her glorious green eyes no longer danced and sparkled. At Christmas, Jumbo played no carols at the piano, and Mother seemed in no mood to sing or to play herself. We each received one toy on Christmas Eve, after which we piled into the back of the truck in our church clothes and attended High Mass, which seemed more like a funeral to us than a joyful Christmas celebration. Jumbo did not attend, which was probably best, because he was wobbly on his feet.

When Jumbo disappeared after the New Year, Mother had tried to keep up a resolute attitude. We went to church on Sunday mornings. At Mother's orders, the older children stayed in school and took care to finish their homework assignments. Max picked the coal bin clean for our basement furnace and managed to refill the bin partly from a railroad coal hopper he discovered parked and unguarded on a side ramp along a stretch of track that led up toward the town of Butler.

We all became lean, but we had survived the winter without Jumbo. And now that it was May, the leaves in the forest were sprouting, the birds were singing, and we were on the way to a new life.

Mother dreaded abandoning the home and farm, which she had once thought God had provided for us, but she held in her tears as she climbed up into the truck. Vera handed Kazzy up to her. Then Max, who was barely twelve but could already drive the truck expertly, jumped up into the driver's seat in the cab. He took out the Greater Pittsburgh road map we had used in our English lessons.

Max had drawn a red line all along our route, following the river-banks of the Allegheny, then across the bridge at the foot of Mount Washington, and then on Route 22, about a dozen miles west to Rehoboth. Vera and Lucy sat on some kitchen chairs on the right side of the truck bed, both of them in tears, and Ziggy and I lay down on our sides, butt to butt and silent on the side of the truck bed opposite our sisters.

Max pulled the choke and started the engine. Sad but excited, we quivered with the truck's vibrations.

We heard the hand brake release, and then we started rolling down the hill. Max snapped in the clutch, and the engine propelled us along the driveway and almost to our mailbox on the main road.

Before pulling out onto the pavement, the truck idled for several minutes. Had Mother or Max forgotten something? Ziggy and I wondered what was the delay, so we both stood up to look.

Pedaling toward us up the main road and wearing his Sunday suit and a black derby hat came Jumbo.

Max turned off the engine. Jumbo drew near the truck and looked in past Max to Mother.

"*Quo vadis?*" he asked.

She did not answer.

Ziggy and I stood wide-eyed and silent for a while.

Then Ziggy yelled, "Jumbo! It's Jumbo! He's back!"

Max jumped out, took Jumbo's bicycle, and lifted it up to us. We cleared space for it and squeezed our bodies together, the three of us sitting in a tight slot between a couch and an old leather suitcase Mother had brought with her from Poland.

Jumbo vaulted up into the driver's seat. He took a quick glance at the route sketched by the red line on the map, turned the key in the ignition slot, and started the truck engine. Then he pulled a cigar from his coat pocket, lit up, and puffed.

"To Rehoboth!" he shouted.

He let out the truck clutch, and we pulled up the road.

Cuddling Kazzy, Mother stared straight ahead.

We were on our way to Rehoboth, the coal-mining and zinc-smelting town beyond the western suburbs of Pittsburgh. Our new life was about to start, but not as Mother had planned.

Father Fernando

Father Fernando, young for a holy man, could not keep his eyes off Mother. And both Vera and Lucy could not keep their eyes off Father Fernando.

He was probably in his midthirties, about Mother's age, not tall but with full black slicked-down hair, dark eyes, swarthy skin, and teeth as white as his crisply starched priest's collar. Later, Lucy said she was afraid to look into his eyes for long, because he reminded her of pictures she had seen of the famous movie star and national heart-throb Rudolf Valentino. Vera agreed. The resemblance was remarkable. I remember staring at his hands, which were large, delicate, and finely manicured, so different from Jumbo's.

Father Fernando was new to the diocese, transferred recently to Rehoboth from Philadelphia. He told us his parents came from Madrid when he was an infant. The kind and generous people in Philadelphia, where his father worked at the Continental Hotel as a bellhop and later as the senior concierge, had helped his family when they first came to America. He felt obliged, through his calling, to help immigrant families in any way he could. He was perplexed that Jumbo had shown up in the truck with us and our furniture and pots and pans and clothes. He said he had understood clearly from the St. Stanislaus priests over in Etna that Mother had been abandoned.

There followed a difficult silence. We all stood by the truck parked beside the rectory, and Jumbo, shifting his derby hat from one hand to the other, stared at the ground and said nothing. Mother, holding baby Kazzy in her arms, looked imploringly at the priest. We all feared we might have to crawl back onto the truck and drive off again. But to where? Ziggy stood beside me, rocking back and forth in his usual fitful rhythm, clenching his fists and pounding his wrists together.

When I sneaked a glance over at Jumbo, I saw actual tears of humiliation welling in his eyes. "I made a mistake, Father," he said, still staring at the ground.

"Will you come to confession tomorrow?" Father Fernando asked.

"Yes, Father."

Father Fernando's glance drifted up to the towering hodgepodge of household items and laundry tubs and garment trunks piled on the back of the truck. Then his eyes dropped down again, lingered a moment on Ziggy's curious fist banging, and then locked on Mother. He squinted slowly, his pupils enlarging, as though, despite Mother's beauty and grace, there was perhaps too much confusion and misery in front of him to absorb all at once, even for a priest.

Father Fernando looked at Jumbo. "Come and talk to me. Your sins will be forgiven." Then he smiled first at Jumbo then at Mother.

Jumbo nodded. "Thank you, Father," he said and then slid his black derby back onto his head. With a slow sigh, he adjusted the brim and fingered his mustache on both sides to even up the points.

Mother said, "We are very grateful, Father. I am sure the children will love it here."

"Think nothing of it, Mrs. Malinowski. They look like wonderful children. Now let me show you the rectory and your new house. Does anybody need to use the bathroom? It's just inside the door on the right."

Ziggy grabbed my hand and shot for the rectory door. Vera and Lucy were right behind us. They started giggling about Father Fernando's good looks and how wonderful it would be to go to confession with him.

"Just like Valentino," Vera whispered.

"He could be a movie star, for sure," Lucy agreed.

"Those deep dark eyes! And a priest!"

I know for a fact that Jumbo never followed through with that confession to the good-looking priest. Jumbo had not gone to confession at the church in Etna for years. And why would he go now and confess to a strange new priest?

Besides, Father Fernando had already promised him forgiveness.

Our New House

So, it seemed we did have a new home. Our move across the city of Pittsburgh from Ripple Brook Gardens to Rehoboth was successful. Despite his initial hesitancy, Father Fernando gradually appeared delighted with our arrival. He spoke to Mother with a broad and charming grin, and he said he truly needed her services. I liked him very much. His gentle baritone voice had an engaging lilt that seemed unlike any priests we had met before. There didn't seem to be an ounce of crankiness in him.

He took us inside the large brick house behind the rectory and showed us around. When Mother asked him questions, he answered eagerly and took care that she understood him clearly. He apologized that he did not know more about the history of the house, but he had just arrived himself a few weeks before and had not found out the details of any prior occupants. He also said he was sorry that he had not shopped for groceries for us, but Mother would be allowed to help herself in the rectory kitchen and bring over whatever we needed. Jumbo remained silent during the tour.

Upstairs were four big bedrooms and a bathroom with a huge and sparkling porcelain tub. All the sheets on the beds were freshly laundered and ironed.

"I wanted you to feel welcome," Father Fernando said.

Vera and Lucy rolled their eyes at each other, because, like Father Fernando, the house felt too wonderful to be believed. It seemed that we were moving into a fancy hotel. In fact, we could have left much of the furniture on the truck back at Ripple Brook Gardens, because the house was already tastefully appointed.

Downstairs was a large sitting room, a spacious kitchen, a dining room, and one tiny bedroom with its own bathroom sink and flush toilet. Other features included an oil furnace and water heater in the basement, and a front and back porch. The house had no fireplace, but Mother told Father Fernando that it was otherwise more than ideal.

"I'm so happy you like it." He grinned.

"We will take good care," Mother answered, smiling right back at him.

I had not seen her beam like that for close to a year, and sometimes she even blushed, which made me know she was really happy. I had difficulty grasping how lucky we were to find this house. We weren't looking for perfect, but this house seemed as close to perfect for our needs as one could ever find.

Out the back windows on the second floor we gazed across the little valley to the town of Rehoboth. Further west and on the other side of town was an imposing stark facade, the coal mine's pithead, or entrance, braced by two orange brick administration buildings.

Further beyond the mine loomed four tall smokestacks rising from the four slanting zigzag roofs of the zinc smelting plant. Each stack sent out a plume of cloudy orange discharge. Two miles beyond these widemouthed cylinders rose a separate and immense brick smokestack. With red and white rings painted all the way to the top, it gracefully pointed high into the sky above the trees like a giant, brightly striped soda straw. This smokestack was the tallest in Pennsylvania, according to Father Fernando, and it was the emissions release for another plant beyond the zinc works. This other factory smelted molybdenum. Its stack towered 270 feet above the ground in the next hollow, dwarfing the zinc factory smokestacks, and shooting out a thick white plume that fanned out high in the wind above the four orange plumes from the zinc plant.

In the truck on our way up to the rectory, we had bumped over the railroad tracks at the crossing near the town center, where we had asked a policeman for instructions on finding St. Anthony's Church. From the windows of the new house, we could see how those tracks led further on to the mine and the zinc plant and beyond to the molybdenum operation.

When Max asked the priest about molybdenum, Father Fernando explained that moly, as it was called by people in the town, was a metal used to increase the strength of steel in bridges, military equipment, trucks, tractors, and automobiles.

Father Fernando told us the town's six hundred workers, predominantly immigrants, were employed about equally among the mining and zinc and moly operations, and that each facility furnished housing for the employees. All the houses and the buildings, including the coal-burning powerhouse and the company store for the employees, had been designed and built and were now operated by Rehoboth Coal and Metals Inc., with offices in Rehoboth and in downtown Pittsburgh.

Father Fernando added that the company provided a medical clinic for the workers and their families right inside one of the administration buildings by the pithead. Father Fernando also mentioned with a sincere smile that the company donated liberally to the four churches in town: the Roman Catholic, the Methodist, the Presbyterian, and the Greek Orthodox.

He said the coal for the zinc plant came up out of the bituminous shafts in the ground under the town. The zinc ore that was smelted into industrial-quality metal was actually mined in Missouri and shipped east by rail in mammoth hopper cars over six hundred miles to Rehoboth. Beyond the smaller factory smokestacks we glimpsed rows and rows of tall orange mounds of slag, the abundant but useless byproduct of the zinc smelting process.

Another byproduct of the zinc plant, this one valuable, was sulfuric acid. Father Fernando said it was used in large quantities in manufacturing fertilizers. The acid was poured into huge railroad tank cars and shipped out to Cleveland, Toledo, and other fertilizer-producing centers.

In conclusion, Father Fernando said that every day the Rehoboth operation produced over fifty tons of zinc and one hundred tons of sulfuric acid. He was not sure exactly how much molybdenum was produced, but he understood that the moly ore was shipped in by rail from Idaho, smelted, and then sold to the big steel plants in Pittsburgh.

Thus far on the tour, Ziggy had been silent and withdrawn, but for some reason, he perked up when Father Fernando said the word "molybdenum."

As Zig gazed out the window at the giant smokestack, he started to repeat the word in a whisper, "Molybdenum, molybdenum, molybdenum." It seemed he had latched on to a word, like Zelienople, that caught his fancy and gave him a kick to pronounce.

As Zig's annoying whispers of "molybdenum" grew louder, Father Fernando offered a smile, but he was clearly indisposed. Mother squeezed Zig's shoulder firmly and raised a finger in front of her lips to signal silence. Ziggy complied, but then I saw his lips continuing to move for at least a minute. He grinned at me, as if he were having a private joke that he wanted me to share.

I nodded to reassure him, but I felt embarrassed. We were trying to have Father Fernando like us. Ziggy was not helping our cause. Ziggy was a handful to understand, even for people who knew him well. Mother would have to do some explaining later about Zig to Father Fernando, but our first hour in the new house seemed an awkward time to make her do it.

As we were turning away from the upstairs windows, Mother said, "One question, Father."

The kindly priest smiled again at her. "Yes?"

"What stinks?"

I had wondered about the odor myself, and I watched Father Fernando's forehead redden as his lips pursed. He nodded toward the four zinc plant smokestacks and said, "Mrs. Malinowski, I have lived here for over a month now, and I almost don't smell it."

Max pointed to the giant smokestack and said, "I think the stink comes from way over there. Smells like sulfur."

"Well," the priest said and shrugged his shoulders. "You simply have to get used to it, but you will. After a week, you barely notice it."

"Farts," Ziggy said and laughed. "Smells like farts. Molybdenum farts. Molybdenum. Molybdenum."

"Zygmunt, stop it! You are acting rude!" Mother scolded.

Ziggy shut up, made two fists, and started tapping his wrists together, a gesture which attracted Father Fernando's attention only briefly.

"Thank you, Father. We'll get used to it quickly," Mother said. "It's a beautiful house. We are grateful. Can we move our things in now?"

The priest seemed pleased that the tour and the conversation were finished. "Yes, and I am happy to help. I must say that is all I know about Rehoboth, but the people here are very friendly and warm. Your children will find many friends, and the schools in the town are excellent."

"Yes, that makes a big difference! Here in America, education is important."

The priest smiled at all of us. "You will be happy, I know."

As soon as Mother decided which rooms each of us would sleep in, we started unpacking the truck. Max was to sleep in the small bedroom off the kitchen. The rest of us were to be upstairs. Vera and Lucy were to share one room near the front, and Ziggy and I would sleep in a big bed in our own room near the back. Kazzy's crib would occupy the room opposite the bathroom, and Mother and Jumbo would take the big master bedroom at the top of the stairs.

Father Fernando helped us unpack. When he saw the Black Madonna, he seemed thrilled. Mother let him pick out the best spot for her. We hung her by the landing on the front stairway. As soon as you walked in the door, she glared down at you.

Father Fernando seemed to know a lot, and not only about the zinc and moly plants. He told us that of all the saints, Saint Luke was his favorite. He asked if Mother had heard the Catholic legend that Saint Luke himself had rendered the original Black Madonna of Częstochowa with his own hand. Luke, of course, had known the real Mary and consequently had a clear image of her face when he painted her likeness. Another interesting detail: Saint Luke had painted the portrait of Mother Mary and baby Jesus on the actual tabletop from the Holy Family's home in the Holy Land.

Lucy asked Father Fernando if he knew what the little book in baby Jesus's hand could be. "Is that the Bible?" she wondered.

"Good guess," Father Fernando replied with a wink. "Of course, the New Testament had not even been written at the time Saint Luke painted the icon, so that book would have to be probably the Old Testament."

When Father Fernando mentioned all this important information, Mother looked deeply and slowly at him. She had never heard that legend in Poland. When she was a little girl, her family had once made a pilgrimage to the church in Częstochowa, at a monastery in the heart of Poland, where the real Black Madonna hung. She said she knew from her Bible school in Poland that Saint Luke had been a physician as well as an evangelist, but she never knew he also was the painter who had rendered the icon, the symbol of the identity of the Polish nation. And Saint Luke had painted it on wood from the Holy Family's kitchen table!

Grateful for this amazing new background on the origins of her icon, Mother immediately crossed herself. We children did, too, and Father Fernando closed his eyes in front of the Madonna and crossed himself with all of us.

The moment instantly glowed in my mind. I had never met a kinder or more knowledgeable priest. Again, Mother exchanged glances with Father Fernando, and then they both looked up at the Black Madonna in silent reverence. Just then I thought leaving Ripple Brook Gardens might not be so terrible, after all. Mother would work for this wonderful man, and we would live in this spacious house under the watchful eyes of the Black Madonna with her baby, apparently painted by an actual saint and disciple of Jesus. Could we have prayed for and received anything better?

And Father Fernando also explained that the two dark and oblique lines on the cheek of the Black Madonna were not falling tears, as I had always thought, but rather knife slashes inflicted by Protestant heretics, who hideously defaced holy icons back during the religious wars in Europe.

"Yes, they do look like sorrowful tears," Father Fernando said, "almost as though she is weeping for the souls of the heretics who cut her cheek. Thank goodness, their cruel knives never got to the baby Jesus in her arms! Even Protestant heretics knew not to do that!"

Mother smiled that whole afternoon. We all were smiling, all except Jumbo.

When Jumbo asked why Mother had not packed any clothes for him to wear, Father Fernando reassured him that there were abundant high-quality secondhand garments over in the basement of the rectory. The priests kept a large inventory of clothes for immigrant families arriving in Rehoboth. Most of these strangers, of course, wouldn't have money until their jobs were arranged, either at the mine or at the zinc or moly plant. The clothes were donated by wealthy families around Pittsburgh and channeled here by the diocese for distribution in the growing town of Rehoboth.

When Mother looked over at Vera and Lucy, Father Fernando quickly added that, of course, the children could avail themselves of the trove of donated garments too. As soon as we were settled in, he would take us over to pick out clothes for Sunday Mass, if we needed them.

"Can we do it now?" Vera asked.

"Be patient, please," Mother insisted. "Don't be greedy. The father has already been so kind to us!"

The offer proved to be a bonanza. In less than an hour, all Mother's children found clean and durable attire, even shoes and belts and gloves and hats. The garments fit fairly well, and all were for free. Jumbo stocked up, too, including a black and burgundy smoking jacket, tailored from fine Chinese silk, that must have been donated to the diocese by the widow of a big banker or one of Pittsburgh's powerful steel executives. Who, besides Jumbo, would feel comfortable wearing such a glamorous item?

That evening, Father Fernando brought us over beef stew and two cherry pies from the rectory kitchen, all of it prepared by volunteers from the parish, who had been helping out the priests temporarily, until Mother arrived to take over these duties. After our months of relative starvation on the farm, which was no longer ours, we feasted hungrily and joyfully.

What an amazing day it had been for all of us! How had all this actually happened? At one point, I went over to the Black Madonna and explored her face for an answer. Father Fernando had explained to us that if a copy of a holy icon is touched to the original, the powers of the true icon are passed on to the copy. I felt certain that our Black Madonna had surely been touched to the original back in Częstochowa, who knows how long ago! And now look! We were living proof of her power, weren't we?

After dinner, Jumbo lit up a cigar in his new silk jacket, and one by one, Mother directed us to take baths in the huge tub. Vera and Lucy helped to bathe Kazzy.

Later that evening, Mother came into our new bedroom to tuck us in and listen to our prayers. She told Ziggy and me that Jumbo had promised her he would never gamble or drink any vodka or wine anymore. Not even beer. Our father was back with us again, and he would find a job either in the mine or at the zinc or moly plant or somewhere nearby. Before long, our family would be back up on our feet here in Rehoboth, our new home.

Yes, we loved Ripple Brook Gardens, but Rehoboth seemed like a nice enough place, too, if we could get used to the smell. We said an extra prayer to God to thank him for Father Fernando. The priest had already taken a special place in my heart, and from the look in Mother's eyes, I could see the same was true for her.

That night as Ziggy and I lay restless and wide-eyed beside each other in our new bed, I asked him, "What do you think it would be like to be a priest?"

"A priest? You want to grow up to be a priest?"

"I'm just wondering what it would be like. Father Fernando seems like he probably knows God better than anybody else I ever met."

"You have to die to know God."

"I hope not. Who told you that?"

"Nobody. But I think you have to die."

"I'll ask Father Fernando tomorrow."

"I would hate to be a priest."

"Why?"

"You could never get married. You could never fall in love with someone like Mother. You wouldn't be allowed to. Priests aren't allowed to fall in love, Taddy. Don't you know?"

"You're right, Zig. Good night."

That was one of those times when I knew Ziggy thought a lot deeper about things than people gave him credit for.

Rehoboth

The next day, Jumbo skipped morning Mass and drove over to the coal mine to ask about a job. The weekend foreman told him the hiring office was closed on Sundays, but they were desperate for workers, especially strong and eager English-speaking fellows like Jumbo. They were likely to put him right to work, so he should get there before seven. Jumbo then drove on to the zinc plant, heard the same story, and returned to our new house.

He was sipping coffee in the kitchen, when we arrived back from Mass. He told us the good news with a grin, which did not last long.

"Eva, where's the piano? You didn't forget to pack it?"

We were surprised and frightened when Jumbo said this. In the dying days of Jumbo's Tavern, in the months before he left the farm, he had never touched the piano. Now suddenly he wanted to play?

"Mother sold it," Max said.

"Sold it?"

Mother glared at Jumbo. "Twelve dollars. We needed the money. And we couldn't have lifted that piano up onto the truck. There wasn't space for it."

"No clothes? No piano? Makes me wonder why the hell I came back to you people."

"A month ago, it was sell the piano or let the children starve," Mother said. "You weren't around. Remember?"

"Not that again today, please. I'm beginning a new job in the mine tomorrow. Don't spoil this day with your complaints."

"You never worked in a coal mine in your life. You're sure they'll hire you?"

"Always skeptical! Things are coming back to me now, things I tried to forget about."

"Ignaz! Not in front of the children."

"You are always looking on the worst side of everything."

"Go! Go back to Florida or wherever you went. Put on your smoking jacket and your derby hat and be gone!"

"Don't make jokes. I have to be at the mine tomorrow morning."

"Yesterday you begged me to take you back. Now you want to change the story? I'm going upstairs to put the baby down for his nap."

Vera and Lucy followed Mother up the stairs.

Jumbo peered around at his sons, all of us silent. Then he drained his coffee and said, "Let's all go for a ride. Max, you want to drive?"

"Sure."

"Let me show you boys the mine and the zinc plant. And this town of Rehoboth isn't bad. They even have a little movie theater and an ice cream parlor."

We hurried out to the truck. Jumbo and Max climbed up into the cab. Ziggy and I jumped up in the back. As Max started the engine, I looked up and saw Mother sitting by the upstairs window. Kazzy was sucking on her. She was crying.

We drove up past the rectory, and Father Fernando waved at us. Max didn't slow down. Through the back window, I saw Jumbo looking straight up the road.

It was obvious Jumbo resented the handsome priest. I had not heard him thank Father Fernando the day before for all he had done for us. As I have mentioned, Jumbo's contempt for priests was a given in our family, but I wished he would make an exception for Father Fernando, who seemed like a nice, regular person, rather than a priest. He had been our savior. We were total strangers to him, but he gave us a job for Mother, a house for all eight of us to live in, clothes for us to wear, and food for our table.

But even Max would have been afraid to tell Jumbo a thank-you was in order. We all feared our father might cuff us, or Mother, at any time or abandon all of us again. On the other hand, if he left again, our current living circumstances did not seem dire. Apart from its ubiquitous sulfurous odor, Rehoboth appeared quite livable.

The town had been designed and built by the Coal and Metals company twenty-five years before. It had mostly brick and stucco buildings on a dozen streets, all paved. It took about thirty minutes for Max to drive around and scout it all out, which meant six times we crossed the two pairs of railroad tracks which ran through the center of town. We passed the school, and then a Presbyterian church under construction, a little town hall, the Greek Orthodox church, a grocery store, a movie theater named the Bijoux, Hanlon's Pharmacy, Rosey's Ice Cream Parlor, a bicycle shop, a five-and-dime, a bank, a blacksmith's stable, a coffee shop with a bus stop in front of it, and a Texaco station almost exactly like the one where Max had worked in Etna.

Most of the houses in Rehoboth were smaller than the one Father Fernando had provided for us, and this made me feel lucky and strangely proud. Again, I wished Jumbo would give the priest a chance.

The streets of Rehoboth were fairly deserted on a Sunday, but as we cruised through our new town, Ziggy looked interested yet fearful. Ripple Brook Gardens had been a protected place for him, but now we were living close to the center of a town, and he may have felt threatened. He, too, had seen Mother crying at the window of the new house, and this clearly upset him.

Zig was sensitive to tension, especially between our parents, so I put my arm around his shoulders and told him Jumbo would always love Mother, and things would improve. Jumbo just had to get used to us again and vice versa.

"I'm afraid, Taddy," he said. Then I saw tears dripping around the soiled lenses of his glasses. I helped him wipe his tears and clean his glasses with my handkerchief.

I was surprised to feel tears in my own eyes, since I really wasn't sad or afraid, certainly not of Father Fernando or of our big new house. I suspected my tears were from the slightly acrid air blowing into our faces as we stood on the top of the truck bed.

We drove up to the mine buildings and the pithead. Jumbo jumped out, waved at the entrance guard as if they were old buddies, and then talked to us about the mine, explaining that the zinc plant on the other side of the hill needed to burn tons of coal every day to fire up the smelting process. The same went for the moly plant. As Father Fernando had already informed us, the zinc ore came all the way from Missouri to be processed there at the Rehoboth plant. Most of the mine's coal was sent into Pittsburgh steel plants, but a quarter of it was needed here for the zinc and moly plants. Again, we had heard all this from Father Fernando the day before, but it was just like Jumbo to assume we had ignored what an inexperienced young priest might have to say about important industrial processes.

"It stinks bad here," Ziggy said.

"Shut up, fat boy," Max snarled from the cab. "We're learning about the mine."

"It stinks."

"You stink."

"You stink worse. You stink like poop. And you're a bad truck driver."

"Really, Zig? Like you're ever going to drive a truck in your life!"

Quickly Ziggy was on the verge of bawling. "Can we go home now, Jumbo?"

"Shut up," Jumbo shouted and hopped back into the cab.

We drove further and passed a line of railroad tank cars and the zinc plant entrance. We didn't go through the gate and onto the grounds, but we surveyed it all through the wire mesh fence: the factory itself with smokestacks, the railroad flatcars that carried away the finished zinc, and far beyond the rows of slag heaps, the immense moly smokestack. The moly stack was the tallest structure I had ever seen.

We craned our necks to look up.

"That's where the stink comes out," Ziggy said. "See that smoke?" His nostrils twitched. "That's the stink. Stinky zinc."

"Stinky zinc!" I echoed, and I laughed extra long at his rhyme to put him in a better mood, even though he was referring mistakenly to the moly smokestack.

"That there is stinky moly!" Max shouted from the cab.

"Stinky moly! Molybdenum. Molybdenum!" Zig shouted back.

The stinging fumes emitted from the high orifice of the smoke-stack surely must have been deadly poisonous to inhale up close. The combined odors from the zinc and moly plants were far less pungent up by the rectory and our house, but nowhere in Rehoboth could anybody fully escape them. The forests immediately surround-ing the two plants were blighted, most of them consisting only of tough-looking scrub pines and oaks and hardy birches and weeds.

Max drove on.

Laid out less than a mile from both plants were houses built in neat rows for the workers. Twenty-five years back, the company had cleared the woodlands and built the houses. Not far from the houses were several clearings that widened into meadows. Max cruised us around the back roads, and we came upon a weird treeless region of abandoned strip mines not two miles from the workers' houses.

Again, Jumbo made Max stop the truck, so that he could jump out and explain about the two kinds of mining. This was information that we had not heard from Father Fernando, so we paid attention.

Jumbo explained that shaft mines consisted of a hole in the ground and deep horizontal shafts dug into the earth hundreds of feet below. The coal was picked and shoveled or blasted out of the shafts and delivered up in small hopper cars by a deep-plunging ele-vator that came out at the pithead, the same elevator the miners went down in. Strip mines, on the other hand, used bulldozers and steam shovels to gouge shallower coal out of the layers near the surface. The strip mine operators hauled off the coal in big trucks to the rail yard, where it would be unloaded and used locally or shipped. The shallow coal had all been picked clean from the strip mines, and they had been abandoned some years before.

As Ziggy and I listened, we stared at the severely scarred land-scape left after the mining was done: no trees and no grass anywhere near the old mines. We could count the many colored mineral seams of earth in the high mounds and deep gullies. The coal taken from these mines had been no more than a hundred feet from the surface, much of the abandoned terrain still terraced in irregular curlicue layers.

We drove past several large pits filled with stagnant rainwater, some orange, some yellow or brown, depending on the color of the mineral in the soil around the edges. Ziggy laughed when we spotted three naked boys swimming in an orange pool. We could see their clothes lying on the dry weedy mounds above the water.

"What if we snitch their clothes?" Ziggy laughed.

"How would they get home?" I asked.

Ziggy looked out at the boys and rocked back and forth, grip-ping the truck's top rail as we scooted along on the lumpy ground. "Yeah. How would they get home? We better not do it."

"Not on our first day here. We want to make friends, not enemies."

"We shouldn't be naughty."

I shook my head and hugged him.

"But it looks like fun. Let's do it someday."

"We won't let anybody steal our clothes."

"Yeah, how would we get home? Run naked like crazy people?"

Ziggy started to laugh and was still grinning when we got back home to Mother.

"So, do you like your new town?" she asked, polishing the counter of her shiny new kitchen with a moist towel. Her mood seemed to have improved.

"Yes. Everything but the smell," I said.

She shook her head. "Nothing to be done about that."

Mother would say that same phrase often in Rehoboth. In time, we all adopted it as a comforting, if ironic, mantra.

"Nothing to be done about the smell. Nothing to be done about Jumbo."

Whatever Rehoboth was, we simply had to give the place a chance.

Adjustments

The Rehoboth mine worked two ten-hour shifts, 6:00 a.m. to 4:00 p.m. and 4:00 p.m. to 2:00 a.m. As the new man, Jumbo had to take the late shift. He went into the cage and down into the tunnels late in the afternoon, and he came up in the middle of the night. To save gasoline, he wore his miner's helmet with the light on so he could see his way to pedal home on his bicycle. He left his dirty mining clothes outside on the back porch or in the hall outside our kitchen. Then he tiptoed up the stairs and scrubbed off in the bathtub before climbing into bed with Mother. He worked six shifts a week. The mine was closed on Sundays. As far as Mother and we could tell, he did not drink alcohol.

Jumbo had two sets of heavy denim mining clothes, supplied by the mine. Mother laundered one of them daily in the rectory laundry, separately from all the towels and tablecloths and linen and clerical shirts from the six priests who lived there.

Mother was glad we had hauled her two washing tubs from the farm. There was only a pair of large tubs in the rectory laundry when we got there, and she needed all four to complete her daily loads. As before, Vera and Lucy pitched in after school to help her. They were by now expert at ironing and mangling, because Mother had already trained them on our farm. I found out the circular white of the priests' collars slipped out of the full black shirt, so the two components were laundered and ironed separately. Each priest had

93

his name stitched into the inside collar of his shirts, and the stockings and underwear had tiny nametags sewn on them too. The first week, Mother and the girls organized the laundry room with six separate sets of hooks and cubbyholes, so we could always keep track of each priest's garments. They liked that.

Father Fernando said he was amazed at how smoothly Mother had taken over the job and delegated work to her energetic assistants. Once again on sunny days, there were rows of sheets hanging out on lines to dry. When Kazzy was up walking and running, Ziggy and I sometimes chased him around in the maze they formed, but there was less excitement to it than back on the farm. Also, there was less time for it, because once the linen was dry, Mother and the girls took it in to avoid soiling it with tiny orange or brown particles from the zinc and moly plants' effluents.

We did not see much of the priests who lived in the rectory. A car came for them at dawn every morning and took them around to their various churches in the diocese to perform early services. Then the group would come home in the evening and have dinner prepared by Mother in the rectory mess. They were all a lot older than Father Fernando, and rarely we would see them out strolling through the town, usually with their hands clasped behind them as they paced, as though they were thinking about something holy or important. Father Fernando never walked like that, and he was by far our favorite. Jumbo ignored them all, including Father Fernando.

I could not help noticing that when I saw Mother talking with Father Fernando, the two of them seemed to be in their own private world. His eyes would sometimes flash with delight, and Mother always looked animated and content. The thought struck me more than once how wonderfully different our lives would be if Father Fernando were our father, not Jumbo.

But that was a selfish and impossible wish, for as Ziggy had pointed out on our first night in Rehoboth, they were not allowed to love each other. He was a priest who could not marry, and she was already married to Jumbo, a man ten years older than her and with six children by him.

On the other hand, it wasn't totally selfish to wish for it. I wanted Mother to be happy, and I could see how perky she was when she talked to the priest. I suspected Father Fernando was happy, too, and I wanted that to be true. Sometimes I wondered what he said when she went into the booth every week and confessed her sins to him.

Was it awkward? Would she ever hint that she loved him? If she did, would he make her recite a hundred Hail Mary prayers as penance?

I thought the world of Father Fernando. I hated the idea of him growing old and someday walking around Rehoboth or any other town with other old men, holding his hands behind his back and with his mind in the clouds. He was caring and humble, and he had taken a special interest in our adjustments to our new town.

Within a week, Max had landed a job at the Texaco station. The owner, Joe Curtiss, had a son, Roscoe, who was exactly Max's age. Joe was surprised that Max already knew much more about cars and engines than he had taught Roscoe.

Max and Roscoe soon developed a rivalry at the station, showing off what they could do as budding mechanics. Max had been working at the station not more than two weeks when an axle jack slipped and crushed Roscoe's right ring finger.

"What a laugh!" Max chortled. "I hollered at him to get his hand out of the jack, but he left it there, like he was daring me to smash it. I told him he would have trouble pitching a baseball for the rest of his life. Of course, he'll never be as crippled as you, Tad. You're the real item when it comes to cripples."

Joe Curtiss didn't seem too concerned about his son's accident. Joe himself was missing two thirds of his left pinky. Roscoe knew not to try and even the score with Max. Their rivalry simmered along, and I think Joe Curtiss was pleased to see his son challenged by the spunky new kid in Rehoboth.

Because Max worked for him, Joe Curtiss let Jumbo buy gasoline at the Texaco for half price. I remember a couple of times when Jumbo stopped to fill up and Max pumped in a full tank and then winked and shooed us away without Jumbo paying a cent. You see,

Jumbo and Max thought alike, especially when it came time to take advantage of another person or situation.

I judged myself more like Mother and maybe even more like Father Fernando. I told Max there was a difference between being kind and gentle versus being a sissy. Max didn't see the difference. I am not sure Jumbo did either. Max liked to call me a sissy in front of Roscoe Curtiss and the other boys who hung around the Coca-Cola cooler at the Texaco. But there was nothing I could do about it, so I avoided the place as much as possible.

He would also tease my sisters, telling them they were stupid and ugly and that neither one of them had a chance to grow up and be as smart and beautiful as Mother. But Vera and Lucy weren't afraid to slap him. I was. I knew Max's temper could ignite and explode, just like Jumbo's, and the older we grew, the less I liked being around Max. I decided to stay away from the Texaco, even when Max wasn't there, because Roscoe began to mock me the same way Max did, and Joe Curtiss didn't seem to care at all.

It did not take long for Max to make enemies in Rehoboth. He flirted with girls who already had steady boyfriends. This caused some fistfights that he always won, whether or not he ended up with the girl. Not surprisingly, Jumbo never scolded Max about it. If anything, he seemed to admire Max's brawler side. Probably it reminded him of his own youth in Poland. When the scuffles happened, Jumbo always wanted a full rundown of every blow, as though he were a boxing coach, not a father.

In those first spring and summer months, I suppose we all were simply adjusting to our new lives in Rehoboth. Again, thanks to Father Fernando, we were clothed and eating well, and we had a strong roof over our heads. Jumbo was not drinking, and we weren't being evicted. I grudgingly realized that Rehoboth was the town where I would grow up.

Everything had changed for our family, but we were together and healthy. The years on the farm at Ripple Brook Gardens and the parties and wedding receptions, where we fetched fireflies for the guests at Jumbo's Tavern and the snowman building with Ziggy and the thrilling sled rides on my Mother's back down the snowy track through the woods on the Wells farm, all of these were a different and finished part of my life. Growing up meant accepting these changes, and I did.

After all, if we had moved all the way from Poland to Pittsburgh, we could surely make the most of our move from Ripple Brook Gardens to Rehoboth, stinky zinc and moly and all.

The Beckwith

Because Jumbo worked full-time for the mine, we could buy dry goods and shoes and groceries on credit from the company store. Their emporium, a cavernous brick building situated halfway between the town and the mine entrance, also offered an impressive array of carpenter and mechanical tools, automotive equipment, and household items. The prices were said to be much lower than in regular stores. Mother compared them with what she found in the Sears Roebuck catalog, and she agreed that "our store" gave the workers a break on nearly everything, plus credit, if needed. Any special orders were arranged through the manager, an affable, chubby, red-cheeked butcher and retired US Navy man named William "Daddy" MacAdoo.

One Saturday morning, a delivery truck from the company store drove up to our house. Jumbo, lounging in his smoking jacket and puffing his cigar, stood up from his kitchen chair.

"It's here!" he said excitedly and snuffed his cigar. Then he ran outside.

Daddy MacAdoo and his Negro assistant, the short muscular Ernie Dobbs, rolled a large upright piano on a four-wheel dolly down out of the truck. Then they set up a plank ramp on the front steps and rolled the piano up through the front door, past the Black Madonna, and into the living room.

"Where did you want it?" Mr. MacAdoo asked.

"Over there." Jumbo grinned. "Against that wall. Yes, between the windows, please."

"What is this?" Mother asked, nodding to Mr. MacAdoo and Ernie Dobbs.

"What's it look like? It's a brand-new Beckwith stand-up piano. Daddy Mac was kind enough to order it special for us. It's only three dollars a week."

"For how long?"

"Three years, Mrs. Malinowski," said Daddy Mac. "Jumbo tells me you want the girls and maybe Taddy to learn to play, don't you?"

"Yes. That would be good."

Ernie Dobbs grunted intermittently as he centered the new Beckwith between the living room windows. Mother gazed silently at its massive height and breadth.

The Beckwith was of solid dark oak, carved with fluted pillars on either side supporting the keyboard. There were clusters of leaves at the top of each pillar, resembling decorations outside a courthouse or church. Under the music stand was a pair of brass candleholders that swung out on hinges to illuminate sheets of music.

The Beckwith was a beast, almost as tall as Jumbo himself. The elaborate wood carving on it was similar to the decorative forms on the front of the pulpit in our church back in Etna.

"Is this for us, Ignaz?"

"Yes, of course. We live here, don't we?"

"But it's such a luxury."

"You sold the other one."

"We had no money, and now we still have no money!"

"But we have credit and plenty of it. I've worked my ass off in that mine for two and a half months, and we're going to keep this, whether you like it or not! And in your spare time, you'll teach Vera and Lucy and Taddy to play!"

"She should be in good tune." Daddy MacAdoo grinned, dusting off the piano with a cloth and then running his fingers up and down the keyboard." You folks will have thousands of hours of joy from this gorgeous instrument. Mr. Malinowski made a smart choice."

Vera stepped over to the keyboard and played a C scale. We all stood and listened as the notes echoed all through the living room and right up the stairway.

"Sounds like you've got talent in the house, Mrs. Malinowski. Now you can develop it."

Daddy Mac winked at Vera, which made her blush. Quickly she retreated to the kitchen, while Mother stared at Jumbo. Suddenly, Mr. MacAdoo looked uncomfortable. He told Mr. Dobbs to roll the dolly out to the truck and bring in the piano stool.

I was stunned. Our Wurlitzer back in Ripple Brook Gardens was nothing like this beauty.

The Beckwith's swivel stool had details to match the piano. It was a four-legged claw-foot with a round seat with a shiny surface and oak leaves around the edges. The seat could be screwed up and down to fit the player's height. Daddy MacAdoo and Ernie Dobbs were barely out the door when Jumbo plunked himself down, adjusted the seat to his comfort, and then began banging out "Over the Waves." After that came a medley of Sousa marches.

"Yes, she's in perfect tune! Just listen to her!"

The piano had a huge resonating voice, almost like a pipe organ, and Jumbo's face broadened into a wide smile when he pounded the chords. Ziggy and I stared on, confounded by the overwhelming sound and bulk of this booming monster, newly arrived and now hunkered solidly into our house, and with the master of the house regaled in black and burgundy Chinese silk.

As Jumbo played on, fleeting visions of our wonderful after-noons and evenings at Ripple Brook Gardens flooded into my mind. I caught myself wondering briefly whether Jumbo might want to set up another tavern right here in Rehoboth. But that was silly. A tav-ern situated in a house owned by the diocese and located smack-dab beside a rectory and a church? I quickly discarded those thoughts. No, this was our new life.

Kazzy began wailing in his crib upstairs. He could not be con-soled, even when Mother went up and offered her breast. Jumbo ignored the baby's wailing. Nothing was going to stop his music making. The Beckwith was here to stay, we all realized, and it did feel reassuring to have Jumbo's huge personality finding an emotional outlet at the keyboard.

Later, Mother asked if Jumbo had thought to ask Father Fernando about the piano before bringing it into the house. Even with the front door locked and all the windows shut, the rectory and the church were within easy earshot of the big Beckwith.

"Those priests could use a little music to cheer them up. They walk around like cadavers," he said, swiveling back to the keyboard and to a march by Sousa.

Mother flipped through her Sears Roebuck catalog and saw a picture of a piano exactly like ours. She took out a pencil and made some quick calculations. Jumbo's three-dollars-per-week payments over three years to the company store would end up equaling nearly double what the piano would cost if we saved up and then purchased it.

"Buy it outright? Come on, Eva! Where am I going to get money like that?"

"But we will pay twice what it's worth."

"Look, Daddy Mac is the nicest guy in the world. I get on with him great. I've been talking to him about it for a couple months. He ordered it through Sears and put it on my account. He should get a little something for helping us make this deal."

"But almost double?"

"Just listen to that deep bass! Vera, come sit down and try it out!"

After that, Mother held her tongue. I presumed she concluded the giant Beckwith, again like many things in Rehoboth, was something for which nothing much could be done.

In those first few months, the town itself seemed friendly enough. Father Fernando introduced us to some of the families from the church. Most of the fathers worked in the mine or the smelting plants, and many of their children spoke poor English. We felt quite lucky to be living in such a large house and with plenty of grassy ground around it to play tag or kickball. Sometimes after Mass, we invited other children to come over for sandwiches and to play. Vera and Lucy became popular and often had girlfriends over for tea parties in the afternoons.

Sometimes on hot days, we walked into the town center for soda pop or ice cream at Rosey's. I always enjoyed hearing the loud clangs of the warning bells at the Rehoboth railroad crossing. Ziggy and I liked to stand licking our ice cream cones and watching the giant coal hopper cars roll through the middle of town and out the track toward the Pittsburgh steel mills. The roar of the steam engines as they picked up momentum was fearsome. The concrete sidewalk trembled under our feet from the vibrations of the huge iron wheels as they rolled by. Even if we yelled at each other, Ziggy and I could hear and feel only the deafening roar and powerful reverberations of the iron giant gaining speed just a couple yards from where we stood. All that enormous power in motion was a sharp contrast to the sweet smooth ice cream melting on our tongues. That was part of the fun. Sometimes Ziggy would reach for my hand for reassurance, and I was happy to offer it. Standing so near those huge rotating wheels was scary, and I sometimes needed the reassuring touch of his hand too.

Curiously, I never thought of the tons of coal in the hopper cars as being a product which our father helped to produce. Though we noticed that his shoulders and his biceps were becoming even more massive from wielding his pick and shovel down in the dark mine, what he did down there seemed unrelated to what we saw up here in the daylight in the middle of town and contained in these massive hoppers rolling out of town in front of us.

Like eating ice cream by the rail tracks, we gradually found ways to adjust to our new town. My sisters pestered Mother to start piano lessons, but she was so consumed by her cooking and laundering duties at the rectory that those training sessions were rare. All I ever heard from the girls were scales or "Chopsticks." Vera worked hard on Beethoven's "Für Elise," but she never really mastered it.

Sometimes Mother would take a break from the laundry or the kitchen and play her favorite Chopin preludes and waltzes. She had a delicate touch on the powerful Beckwith, and the sad but soothing Chopin melodies drifted gently around the house, almost as though her soul were singing to us. And even today when I hear those haunting Chopin passages, I feel Mother's own soul wafting straight to my heart.

Still More Changes

In July, Mother started vomiting in the morning. She asked Vera and Eva to take over more chores in the laundry. She also asked the girls to cook breakfast. Jumbo complained that after his late shifts he couldn't sleep in the morning with her making such miserable noises.

By August, Mother was feeling better and took over her laundry work full-time. We were relieved to see the usual pink return to her cheeks, and with Vera and Lucy starting school in September, the timing worked out well. Then Mother told us that she had gone to the company general practitioner, Dr. McAllister, and he said she would have a baby in February. This news made everybody happy.

Everybody but Jumbo.

"Do you think it will be a boy or a girl?" I asked. He was at the mirror in the bathroom, shaving before work.

"Boy or girl?" I repeated.

"Get out and shut the door!" he barked.

The new baby idea cheered the rest of us for a couple of weeks. We enjoyed debating girls' and boys' names with Mother. We wondered which room the new baby should sleep in.

The last question became irrelevant in late August when Father Fernando knocked at our front door one Sunday afternoon after Mass and went into the kitchen with Jumbo and Mother. He said he had some unfortunate news, which would affect us soon. The girls and I stepped out of the kitchen, and when Mother closed the door, we put our ears to it and listened.

Father Fernando said the bishop of Pittsburgh had suddenly decided to transfer him to a parish in Detroit. This same bishop, who had first approved our staying in the house by the rectory, had changed his mind about us too. He had been told last winter that Mother had been abandoned and needed housing for her and her six children. Now someone had come to him personally and explained that Mother's husband had moved back in with her and was working full-time, earning solid wages at the coal mine. Mother was no longer an abandoned woman, and we were no longer a deserted family. Therefore, despite her excellent work for the rectory residents, we no longer were eligible to live in the house owned by the diocese and would have to move out by the middle of September.

The bishop was quite sure we could find housing in one of the coal and metal company's houses, which would be closer to the mine and an easier commute for Jumbo. The bishop had already secured two women to take over Mother's laundry duties, and they would report to work in Rehoboth by the middle of September. They each had children and would be living in what had briefly been our dream house. They were abandoned women, which Mother no longer was.

The news crushed Mother. She asked Father Fernando if there was any way to appeal this decision by the bishop. Perhaps we could pay rent to the diocese?

"It's final," he said.

The conversation continued with Father Fernando apologizing at length. He said he so enjoyed having Mother working for the church and also getting to know the Malinowski family as his neighbors. He was very attached to us, and he assured Mother that her work and her cooking had been top-notch. He said several of the priests at the rectory had complained about the loud piano music, but otherwise we had been a perfect family.

When Mother started to sob, we expected Jumbo to blow up at the priest. Oddly, he remained silent. When the door opened and the three of them stepped out into the living room, Jumbo's face looked oddly smug.

BLOOD PUDDING

"I hear wonderful things about Detroit," he said, nodding as they stood at the front door. Then he put his arm around Mother and added, "I'm sure you will be popular out there. Good luck, Father, and God bless."

Robert Street

In September, we moved into a small orange brick house at 7 Robert Street, a mile from the mine and only a five-minute stroll through a small forest to Curry's Meadow, a large fallow field suitable for cattle grazing. On the far side of Curry's Meadow were the abandoned strip mines, which we had seen on our first day in Rehoboth.

We were told the streets in the row house development were named after the company owner's children: Robert, Phyllis, Paul, Mary Ann, Blanche, Rupert, and Roger. As the entire town had been designed and built two and a half decades before we moved in, we assumed that by now these seven rich children, on whose streets we now lived, had probably grown up to be rich adults.

The humble houses on the streets named after them, however, were far from opulent, all being kit houses shipped in from a warehouse in Oklahoma. The bricks were supplied locally, but everything else had been prefabricated in Oklahoma, including the woodwork, kitchen cabinets and appliances, toilets, sinks, basement boilers, front and back doors, and our number 7 mailbox.

The structure had very low ceilings. The only items we could jam into the tiny parlor were a small couch, an easy chair, the majestic Beckwith with its twirling stool, and the Black Madonna on the parlor's back wall. With three people sitting in the parlor, it was difficult for a fourth to turn around without having people move their legs to make space. In such a confining chamber, Jumbo looked odd, puffing his cigar and reading the newspaper in his silk smoking jacket. And when he pounded out Souza or Strauss, the Black Madonna trembled on her nail and vibrations penetrated through every corner of the house.

The music drilled out onto the street, and the neighbors on three sides complained immediately. The little houses on Robert Street were only about ten paces apart, and to contain the sound Mother had stuffed a thin layer of quilt batting near the wires on the inside of the piano. Jumbo did not like that, but Mother convinced him that she had to do it.

The kitchen in the back of the house had a table with low benches on either side. We could all barely squeeze in and sit for a meal with Jumbo on a low stool with his back to the icebox. Mother's washtubs were on the other side of the kitchen screen door that led out to a little back porch. From the kitchen table, you could see the shed at the end of the yard and a small neglected vegetable garden at the edge of the property.

All the houses on Robert Street had swinging benches on the front porches, and in the evenings, we saw neighbor children watching our house as they swung back and forth in the dim yellow porch lights above each door. Nobody came over to welcome us to the neighborhood, and I suspected the reason: when he sat alone on the front porch swing, Ziggy sometimes talked to himself and made faces and giggled. That might have scared off the neighbors.

Also, when Mother tried to enroll Zig at the Rehoboth Elementary, the school sent him home on the first day, and that failure may have given the neighbors further reason to steer clear. We could not keep Ziggy off the front porch, because he loved the swing, so I spent a lot of time out there, too, as usual keeping an eye on him.

Zig also liked to spin around on the piano stool with his eyes closed till he felt dizzy, but Jumbo put a stop to that with a loud unannounced slap across Ziggy's forehead that sent him crashing into the corner of the couch. He lay there dazed on the floor for several moments, while Jumbo ranted at him. Then he ran upstairs and never did any more spinning. But the front porch swing took plenty of action from him. He said he felt happy there and safe.

Off the kitchen hallway, Mother and Jumbo shared a bedroom with a half bath with a sink and a toilet. Upstairs there were three small bedrooms and a bathroom with a large copper tub. Our first week there, Jumbo constructed a triple bunk bed for Max, Ziggy, and me. Vera and Lucy had to sleep in their own bunk in the same room with Kazzy's crib. Once the new baby came along, he or she would take over the cradle Kazzy had outgrown.

Mother's tummy grew a bit bigger each week, so we were all aware another baby would show up before long. One Sunday evening after dinner, Ziggy blurted out, "Fernando! Let's call the new baby Fernando!"

Jumbo jumped up from the table. His eyes darted down to Mother's belly.

"That would be nice. I miss Father Fernando," I said.

"We all do," Mother added, smiling.

I was looking at her and smiling back when Jumbo's huge palm and fingers smashed across my scalp and ear. I felt a severe pain at the top of my head, and my forehead burned from the blow. In my left ear, I felt a throbbing ache, and a loud ringing sound had started. Then the pain disappeared, but I could not hear from that ear.

"Look at that," Jumbo sneered. "Crying like a baby. We have too many babies in this house already."

Ziggy started to weep beside me.

"You too?" Jumbo snarled. He went into the bedroom and grabbed a cigar. "I'm going out."

"Should I come along?" Max asked.

"No. Stay and help your mother clean up. And we don't need a baby named Fernando."

When the front door slammed, we all felt relieved.

"Tad, the skin on your forehead is all red," Mother said. "Come here."

I cupped my hand to my ear. Blood smeared onto my palm. I couldn't stop crying from the shock and from the headache. "This ear doesn't work, Mother. And I'm not a baby!"

Not till Halloween did my left ear begin to hear again, and Mother was quite relieved. After none of Jumbo's violent flare-ups did Mother ever apologize to us or try to explain them. We didn't expect her to. She lived under the same threat. She always consoled us, and we tried to comfort her when she seemed sad.

Now that we were all squeezed together in this tiny house and with neighbors peering our way suspiciously, tension seemed to mount. Mother began to complain of headaches, similar to those she had suffered in the months before Kazzy's birth. We could see that her health was an issue, now that her pregnancy was progressing and she clearly was having trouble keeping up with her usual activities. With her washers and wringers out on the porch behind the kitchen, she tried to start up her laundering business again. But after only three customers, she gave it up. Throbbing headaches and overwhelming fatigue halted her efforts. We all tried to help out, but nothing we did made her headaches go away.

Yule Tidings

Mother told us that our first Christmas in Rehoboth would be the bare minimum, not to get our hopes up. It would not be like the celebrations we had at Ripple Brook Gardens. She would prepare fried carp for Christmas Eve dinner, our customary dish, and we would all attend midnight Mass. But Mr. MacAdoo, the company store manager, had limited Jumbo's level of credit, so none of us should expect gifts.

We didn't even have room in the house for a tree, and there was no fireplace for Santa. We hung stockings on the stairway banister, and the most we were hoping for would be some oranges and candy bars.

We were not as poor as we were last Christmas, but we were still very deep in a financial hole. Jumbo had a job, and we should be grateful for that. Also, a new baby would be on the way, so we could look forward to that.

Mother tried to explain that Christmas was about love and hope and the baby Jesus, not about silly presents or gorging ourselves on a dozen different fish dishes, as we had done on the farm. We should thank God for the blessings we had and pray for other families less fortunate than we were.

A week before Christmas, my bad ear became fully functional. I could hear whispers from across the room and crows cawing outside. I made sure to thank God for that. Both ears were now back to normal. This little miracle encouraged me to hope my short leg might also grow enough to match my left leg, as Mother had predicted it eventually would.

"Mother, my hearing came back. I don't need another gift," I told her.

She smiled, kissed both of my ears, and then hugged me.

We received a Christmas card with fancy stamps from an old friend of Mother's over in Poland. A few of Mother's laundry customers sent her greetings, two with ten-dollar bills and one with a five. She said that would help pay for Christmas dinner. There was also a curious picture postcard from Father Fernando. It showed a couple driving a car with a Christmas wreath on the front and the printed inscription, "You auto be in Detroit! Merry Christmas!"

Mother laughed and explained the joke. She showed us the funny picture then hid it, so Jumbo wouldn't see it and start asking questions. A couple of years later, after Mother died and Vera was cleaning out her dresser drawers, she found the card with a few more letters from Detroit in Father Fernando's handwriting. Vera showed them to us but burned them up before any of us, including Jumbo, could read them. Later I thought that was probably the best thing to do, but I wish I could read them now.

We all had suspected that Jumbo was jealous of Father Fernando from the first day we moved to Rehoboth. This did not make sense to anybody, because the kindly priest had taken a vow never to get married or even fall in love with a woman.

Then, years after I had left home, Max told me that while we were still staying at the rectory house, he and Jumbo had driven the truck all the way into Pittsburgh one afternoon to the central office of the diocese. Max waited outside the building while Jumbo went inside and talked to the bishop. A few days later, Father Fernando was notified of his immediate transfer to Detroit.

So, I don't doubt Jumbo's jealousy was the reason why we were forced to leave the rectory house and squeeze into the little brick box at 7 Robert Street. All of us spoke about how different our lives might have been if Jumbo had never come back from Florida or if

Mother had not accepted him back that morning, when he rode up the hill to the farm on his bicycle and in his derby hat.

Once Jumbo was back, we all seemed to be shackled tightly into our fate. Even when he was not drinking alcohol, we all had it in the back of our minds that the most important part of growing up for us all would be escaping from him.

A quarter mile deep in the Rehoboth mine, the coal shafts ran right back under our house, and Jumbo was down there for ten hours a day with his pick and shovel digging constantly at the coal seam, just as he dug at our souls up on the surface, taking from each of us, but mostly from Mother, a daily painful gouge.

Dr. McAllister

Not long after Christmas, Mother's headaches increased and then became constant, pulsating, and much more terrible. Her vision deteriorated. Finally, she went to old Dr. Virgil McAllister, who worked for the company, in his office on the first floor of the administration building. He examined her and told her that her blood pressure was extremely high, directly related to her pregnancy. The sooner she had the baby, the better. Once the baby came out, the blood pressure should come down, he predicted. She should stay in bed and try to do as little as possible around the house, or she might have a stroke. He gave her aspirin for the headaches, which did not help much.

He also told her that she should never get pregnant again, or she might die.

By day, Vera and Lucy were in school, and Ziggy and I helped as much as we could with chores around the house and with changing Kazzy's diapers.

January brought several heavy snowstorms, and the school closed for a week. That meant Vera and Lucy could stay home and lend Mother a hand. Some children in the neighborhood invited us to go tobogganing with them, but we didn't, because we were worried about Mother. Her headaches and her vision were worse. Dr. McAllister had predicted the baby would be born around Valentine's Day, and when he made a house call to examine her in late January, he was even more concerned. Mother's pressure was dangerously high, and the baby's head was in the wrong place for a normal delivery.

I was sitting in the kitchen with Ziggy when Jumbo stepped out of the bedroom with the doctor. Both men looked worried.

Dr. McAllister was a short, stooped white-haired man with a pink wrinkled face and thick wire-rimmed eyeglasses. When he emerged from the bedroom with Jumbo towering over him, he was sweating heavily. He wiped his brow and then pulled off his glasses to clean them. I saw white flakes of dandruff sprinkling onto the black rubber tubes of his stethoscope. He dusted these off before coiling the instrument into his doctor's bag.

"Can you turn the baby around?" Jumbo asked, looking down at the little doctor in our cramped kitchen.

"Tricky," Dr. McAllister said, licking his lips. "We call it a breech presentation."

"Yes, I know about breech," Jumbo said.

"How do you know about breech?"

"This boy Ziggy here was a breech delivery back in Poland. He came out an idiot."

Ziggy sat rocking back and forth on the kitchen bench and rubbing his eyes under his glasses, which he often did whenever he was embarrassed about something.

Jumbo's voice began to boom. "Don't tell me we're going to get another half-wit! This other boy has a short leg."

The old doctor's high-pitched voice started to tremble. "It would be best to send her into Pittsburgh to St. Agatha's and deliver the baby surgically. We call it a Cesarean section."

"She won't let you cut her, Doc. And I won't let you cut her."

"It wouldn't be me. It would be a specialist at St. Agatha's. It's a very fine hospital, one of the best in Pennsylvania. As I said before, with her blood pressure so high, she could have a stroke."

"Paralysis?"

"Sometimes death."

Jumbo's nostrils twitched above his mustache. His head jerked back. I saw his eyes moisten. He stared at the doctor for a long time.

This was a situation he could not easily bully through, and I watched his broad shoulders start to slump.

"Think about it," Dr. McAllister warned. "Right now, your beautiful wife is in double trouble. She has very high blood pressure and a breech presentation. It would not be wise to wait too long. We could lose her and the baby too. Then where would we be?"

Jumbo stared around the kitchen, his head nodding in thought. Vera and Lucy were in the parlor with Kazzy, and Max was out shoveling the snow in front of the house. For several seconds, all we heard were Max's shovel scrapes.

"I'll be back tomorrow morning to check on her," Dr. McAllister said. "I must be on my way home now. They predict more snow for tonight, and I forgot to put the chains on my tires."

"Thank you, Doctor," Jumbo said. "Yes, I'm due back for my shift at the mine in an hour. I have to be on my way too."

The doctor nodded to all of us, put on his coat, hat, and gloves, and went out. Ten minutes later, Jumbo left for the four o'clock shift.

I went in to see Mother. Her eyes were closed, and she moaned slightly.

"Mother," I said, "Jumbo went to the mine. Can we get you anything?"

She looked up and smiled from the pillow. "No, Taddy. Thank you. The doctor said if I live through this, I must never get pregnant again. My head hurts so badly."

"I love you, Mother."

"I love you, too, darling. I will call the girls if I need anything."

I stood and watched her. Gradually her moans diminished, and when it seemed she had fallen asleep, I crept out of the bedroom.

I was scared. Mother had always been robust and energetic. To think she could die seemed impossible and terrifying, but I had heard it straight from Dr. McAllister. When I went out in the kitchen, I told Ziggy I was not worried. That was a lie, and he knew it.

Jumbo came back in the middle of the night, as usual, and none of us heard him, because we were all deeply exhausted.

Mother was calm through the night, but shortly after dawn, she began to scream with belly pain. She told us she was going into labor, and she knew something felt very wrong. She was also having trouble seeing around the edges of her eyes, and her headache was the worst it had ever been. The room was beginning to look black, except where she focused her eyes.

Another foot and a half of snow had fallen, and when we looked out the window, Robert Street was silent and white.

"Where's that doctor?" Jumbo said.

"Maybe we should take her into Pittsburgh in the truck," Max suggested.

"You want her to have the baby in the truck and in the snow?"

"No, but if we drive fast…"

"Shut up. She's staying right here till that damn little doctor comes back. She could die, you know that? Did you hear the doctor say that yesterday?"

"I was shoveling snow," Max said.

"Yeah, so what? She could die. Now you know. So, come on, let's get our shovels and clean off the street for the doctor."

For several hours, we heard no automobiles anywhere in the neighborhood and no snowplows. We began to doubt that Dr. McAllister would be able to get to us. Meanwhile, Mother's screams started to come about every five minutes.

Around ten that morning, the snow stopped, and the white sun poked through some breaks in the gray clouds. Ziggy and I looked up the road and saw a man on horseback slowly making his way down Robert Street. It was old Dr. McAllister, his medical kit stuffed in the saddlebags. We ran to him and greeted him anxiously.

"Good morning, boys. Couldn't get my car started. Had to borrow my neighbor's horse. How's Eva doing this morning?"

"I think she really needs you, Doctor," I said.

The doctor tied his horse to the front porch rail and came inside.

As soon as he stepped through the front door, Jumbo's fingers squeezed the little man's hand hard. "No way to get her into the Pittsburgh hospital today, is there?"

Dr. McAllister, still stamping his boots free of the snow, pulled off his scarf and glanced out the window. He shook his head and frowned. "I'm sorry. I'm your hospital today. But I'll need some helpers. And some clean sheets and lots of boiling water. Sounds like she's near time. I better check her pressure first."

"Max, take the horse back to the shed," Jumbo ordered.

I was glad Jumbo had not put on his wine-colored smoking jacket that morning. I don't think the doctor would have been impressed by it.

We took the doctor's coat and hat and scarf. He carried his bag into Mother's room. On the way in, he waved for Vera and Lucy and asked them to prepare the sheets and water and to join him with Mother. At the doorway, he turned and frowned at Jumbo. "You stay out, hear me?"

"You're not going to cut her yourself?"

"Not if I can help it. Please stay out of this room."

Jumbo watched, as my two sisters disappeared in the bedroom. Then he sat in the easy chair in the parlor. He picked up his Polish newspaper and stared at it.

"Can Ziggy and I go out and make a snowman?" I asked him.

Jumbo looked up, annoyed. "Where's Kazzy?"

"Upstairs in the crib. Lucy gave him his bottle."

"Your mother is on the verge of death, and you want to make a snowman?"

"Yes."

"Go make a snowman. Get out of here."

Ziggy and I played outside, and Max helped us stack up three big balls of packed snow. We were grateful for Max's help with our project, which took our minds off what was happening with Mother and the new baby, if there would be a new baby. I let Ziggy sculpt the snowman's face, his specialty. All the while, we heard Mother groaning and screaming in intermittent blurts. We focused on our manual work.

Later, Vera said we were lucky that Dr. McAllister was a short man with little hands, because he had to wiggle his fingers way up inside Mother, almost to his elbow, and with his other hand press on her tummy and flip the baby's body upside down inside her. A big-handed doctor might not have been able to do that, Dr. McAllister had pointed out during the procedure.

First, the doctor had injected some medicine into Mother's arm to ease her pain and calm her down. Vera said he explained that the medicine helped to loosen the womb and belly muscles and let him get started on the maneuver, making the baby do a somersault inside the womb and come out the normal way, which was head first.

Outside, Max and Ziggy and I noticed that her screams had quieted, and just as we were finishing our work with the snow, putting on a hat and a scarf and some buttons down the chest, we heard the new baby start to scream. We dropped our mittens and ran inside.

Vera was holding a little pink boy, who was wiggling around in a white pillowcase. Vera and Lucy had washed off the birth fluids, so he looked clean and soft. His nose had a point to it just like Jumbo's. He also had a tiny dimple in the middle of his chin.

We looked in on Mother. She was fairly unconscious, and the doctor did not want us to go near her. He said it would take another hour for her to wake up but that she would probably be exhausted for a week or more. He had never had such a difficult delivery, except for two when the babies had died. This baby looked lively and alert and hungry and very much resembled his father.

Lucy warmed up a bottle of milk, and the little creature went for the rubber nipple.

"We will call him Kasper," Jumbo announced, puffing on his cigar and appearing very relieved. "My grandfather's brother's name was Kasper. As you know, they both had royal blood."

"Let's call him Blizzard!" Ziggy laughed. "He's a blizzard baby!"

My sisters laughed. "Shouldn't we ask Mother when she wakes up?"

"I already decided on the name," Jumbo said. "He's Kasper. Hear me?" At some point during the delivery, Jumbo had changed into his smoking jacket, which seemed to make him feel proud and important.

"I call him Blizzard!" Ziggy shouted. "No matter what his real name is!"

Jumbo opened up the top of the Beckwith and pulled out the batting and let loose on the keys with Strauss's "The Blue Danube."

Dr. McAllister looked completely spent. Vera, who was taller than him, put her arms around his shoulders. She nudged him, swaying in front of him. Then they waltzed a few steps in the little space in the parlor, but he was too tired to keep up with her. He smiled weakly. He looked totally relieved and perhaps amazed by what he had just done.

"If I had vodka, I would give you a shot, Doc. But we don't have any in the house."

"That's fine, but thank you."

"I wish we could celebrate big. I guess she didn't need the Pittsburgh hospital after all, did she?"

Dr. McAllister nodded weakly and collapsed in a chair. Vera brought him a cup of tea.

"Yes, that's my favorite celebration drink. Thank you."

Mother had lost little blood during the delivery, and Dr. McAllister said that was quite lucky. If she were to need a transfusion, it would be likely that she wouldn't have lived. In a Pittsburgh hospital with a blood bank, she would have survived, but not here on Robert Street, where the whole hospital rode in on horseback.

The doctor sipped his tea till Mother woke up. He went in and examined her again, carefully measuring her blood pressure. As he predicted, it had come down to a safe level. The darkness in her vision was improving, too, and the headache was almost gone.

When the exam was over, Vera brought little Blizzard in and put him in Mother's arms. We watched the baby with the dimple on his chin hook onto a real nipple. Soon Kasper, or Blizzard, was sucking full force, and Mother finally smiled. She looked at the little doctor. "You are my hero. You saved my life. And you saved my baby. I will always remember."

The doctor leaned across the bed and hugged Mother. "Thank you, Eva. I'll be back to check on you tomorrow. You have shown great courage. You and the whole family should feel proud."

Max went out back and saddled the horse again and brought him around to the front of the house. Dr. McAllister bundled up and tossed his scarf around his neck.

"Did you really save Mother's life?" I asked him near the door.

"Of course, he did," Jumbo said and slapped the doctor's shoulder.

The little white-haired man with the glasses looked exhausted and very old. "I'm not sure I could do it again. Next time she gets pregnant, you're going to need a younger man. But it would be better if she did not get pregnant again. We were lucky this time. Next time maybe not."

"We got seven kids already, Doctor." Jumbo smiled over his cigar. "That's a lucky number. Maybe we'll try to keep it at that."

"Good idea, Mr. Malinowski. And, Vera and Lucy, thanks so much for your help. I really needed you."

"Doctor, what's your fee?" Jumbo asked.

"The company pays me. Don't worry. Thanks for working in the mine. Your labor helps me get paid."

"Never thought of that," Jumbo said.

"Well, it does. That's how it all works out."

For such a hero, the doctor seemed humble. I figured he and Jumbo were about as opposite as two men could be. I watched him climb on the horse and ride away, leaving us with baby Blizzard and Mother, both of whom had almost died.

After the doctor left, Ziggy and I went out and finished the snowman's face and buttons. We gave him sticks for arms, and we tied an old, ragged scarf around his neck. We put a small bucket on his head for a hat, and I insisted that we name him Virgil, after Dr. McAllister. We even found an old cloth seed bag in the back shed and tied it over one of the sticks, so he looked like he was carrying a doctor's bag.

When the doctor came back again on horseback the next day, he looked better rested. I told him we named our snowman after him.

He grinned. "I'm very honored. Thank you, boys!"

Standing together with their scarves floating in the wind, the two Virgils were just about equal in height.

"I wish we could make a real statue for you, Dr. McAllister," I said. "You deserve one."

"I think a snowman is quite enough of an honor. You know, that face does looks a bit like me. How did you do it?"

"Ziggy's an artist," I said. "Aren't you, Zig?"

Ziggy's cheeks, already pink from the chill, reddened deeply.

The doctor nodded. "Why, that's the best snowman I've ever seen!"

Then Ziggy surprised me. He lunged at the doctor and hugged him hard. "Thank you, Doctor. You saved her! What would we do if she died?"

"Let's not let that happen, young man," said Dr. McAllister, smiling back at Zig.

Ziggy grinned. "We sure won't! We promise! Right, Taddy?"

"Yes, Dr. McAllister! We promise!"

Head Lock

Right from the start, baby Blizzard was colicky and loud about it. Even when Mother tried to nurse him out of his screaming fits, he refused to be consoled. His shrieking and bawling often set Kazzy to crying too.

If Jumbo was back from the mine and trying to sleep, Ziggy and I were assigned the tricky task during the day of keeping Blizzard and Kazzy under control. We did our best, but sometimes the noise and confusion in the house seemed intolerable. We wanted Mother to rest, and we feared our father's anger could flare at any time. The first week we tried to bundle up Kazzy and run outside to play in the snow as often as we could.

We made a baby snowman, called him Bliz, and laid him down beside Virgil, who was mostly melted. This amused Mother when she saw it from the window, but she barely had energy to smile at us. Along with her breast milk, the real baby Bliz was sucking out all her energy and spirit.

For the first month, Vera and Lucy did most of the shopping and cooking. Ziggy and I tried not to mess up the place too badly, though with Ziggy's clumsiness and his tendencies to slobber and drool, to eat sloppily, to miss the toilet when he tinkled and forget to flush the toilet, even when he pooped, made being his keeper a challenge. Since Ziggy often did not understand exactly why he was being punished, I took much of the scolding for his messes.

BLOOD PUDDING

After Blizzard's birth, Max avoided hanging around our house. Sometimes during the day, Jumbo would take over Max's bunk to escape the chaos. Max did not mind. He was either at school or at the Texaco. This started a continuing pattern of Max seeming more and more detached from the house and us. That did not bother me.

Max made enough money now to buy cigarettes, and one of the brands he preferred, True Champion, came with photographs of skimpily dressed women. Max sometimes flashed these pictures to Ziggy, whose eyes went large as he tried to grab them from Max's hand. One time on the back porch, as Ziggy's thumb clamped down on the picture, Max jerked it away. The picture ripped in half, and before Ziggy could apologize, Max cuffed him across the mouth.

"Stupid moron!" Max shouted. "Can't show you anything nice."

Ziggy started to cry.

"He didn't mean to tear it," I said.

Max grunted and slapped me hard on the back of the neck. "You're too young for pictures like this, anyway!"

"If Ziggy can see them, I can too!" I shouted.

"You want another smack?" Max warned.

"Mother says you shouldn't be smoking cigarettes."

I had raised my voice loud enough that Blizzard started wailing upstairs.

Max sneered and whispered, "Jumbo says I'm old enough to do what I want. I got a job. I get paid. I might just drop out of school and work full-time at the Texaco. How would you like that, Tadpole?"

"You shouldn't drop out. You should stay in school."

"What do you know about school? You've never been."

"People learn stuff at school. Important stuff. Stuff you should know for later."

"Taddy boy, I've been watching you for a while, and I think maybe some of Ziggy's stupidity is infecting you, too."

"Take that back!"

"Make me." Max laughed and tucked the torn picture of the woman back into the True Champion pack. He pulled out a cigarette, struck a match, and lit the tip.

Ziggy watched him puff.

"Want a drag, Zig?"

"Yeah."

"Don't, Zig!" I warned.

"This will be good," Max said. "Tell you a secret. Never suck on the hot end."

Max put the cigarette to Ziggy's lips.

"Suck hard, Zig. Maybe you can blow smoke rings like Jumbo."

Zig sucked, and his eyes bulged.

"No, breathe it in! Inhale! Breathe it in!"

Ziggy's tongue wiggled inside his mouth, and his cheeks turned gray. His drool was soaking the cigarette.

Max grabbed it, but when the cigarette came out of his lips, Ziggy puked out a huge wad of yellow vomit all over Max's arm.

I laughed. Max grabbed me and put me in a headlock and wiped Ziggy's smelly puke all over my face.

"I told you not to make him smoke."

"Shut up!"

Ziggy got scared and ran back into the house. Blizzard was still screaming inside. Then Kazzy started up too.

"And why don't you leave and go live at the Texaco?" I said, still with my neck clamped in Max's arm.

"I should. This little house is full up, and I'm tired of having a crippled little shit like you bothering me."

Then I started to cry, and Max let me go.

"I'm disgusted," he said. "Too many babies around this crap hole for me!" He tossed the wet cigarette out into the snow and walked out to the shed and closed the door behind him.

Free from his grip, I breathed deeply and rolled my neck around and tried to rub out some cramps. Then I went into the backyard and scooped up some snow and wiped my hands and face with it. I didn't want to walk into the house with Ziggy's puke all over me. It was dark yellow and disgusting.

I didn't regret telling Max to leave and go live at the Texaco. He could go out and bully plenty of other boys in school or at the gas station, if he wanted to. I never knew what kind of special thrill he took from bullying us, his brothers, but probably now that Mother was still recovering from childbirth, he figured we would not run and tell her when he was mean to us.

But on one point, I agreed with him. Our little house was full up. We weren't in Ripple Brook Gardens anymore or the rectory house. As Max said it, we were living in a crap hole.

Cowboys

When the warm spring nights finally came along, Blizzard calmed down, and Mother was able to sleep and find her strength. The pink glow came back to her cheeks. She smiled and giggled again, acting younger and more like the mother we had always known. She and Vera and Lucy sometimes walked around the neighborhood with Blizzard in his perambulator and Kazzy in a stroller. The three looked like sisters, not a mother with four of her children.

We loved to hear her sing in the kitchen. She started to take in laundry again, and she often would softly warble Polish songs, while she was ironing men's shirts and ladies' blouses. She had only a few customers, mostly wives of company employees in the administration building. Later, she attracted some rich customers, who drove up to our little house in big cars, the way the customers had done at Ripple Brook Gardens.

From time to time in the evening after Jumbo had gone to the mine, she would sit at the piano and play Chopin. Ziggy and I liked to sit in the swing on the front porch and listen to Mother's music and pretend that Rehoboth was not such a terrible place. Mother reminded us often that, small as it was, 7 Robert Street was now our home and each of us was responsible for making it a happy house.

One thing was different. Back when we lived on the farm, we all had unlimited chores, so many that it seemed our work was never done. The little vegetable patch behind our house on Robert Street was a joke compared to our big farm gardens and orchard. I suppose we slowly realized that our identity as farm children was deep, and naturally we all missed the freedom of roaming through the meadows and into the woods.

I was pleased when Jumbo told us he had bought a pair of cows cheaply from one of his fellow miners. He planned to keep them in the shed behind our house.

"Tad, you and Ziggy will milk them in the mornings and then take them over to Ben Curry's meadow to graze. I talked to Ben about it. We give him a couple quarts of milk a week, and the cows can eat their fill in his field. We drink a couple gallons of milk every day, and these cows will pay for themselves in a few months on saved milk money alone."

Mother agreed.

The cows, Rose and Mary, arrived mid-May, around my birthday. They were Holsteins: black-and-white, big and loveable and kind of funny. Early in the morning, their milk bags drooped almost to the floor of the shed, and Zig and I had to hoist up their udders to fit the buckets under them. Ziggy and I had chores again, and I welcomed that change, especially if it helped us to save money.

Vera and Mother did most of the shopping, usually at the company store. When they came home, they would unpack the groceries and store everything in the kitchen cupboards. Zig and I enjoyed helping them.

We wondered why Mother was always so delighted to buy Heinz products, which were produced locally in the factory along the Allegheny, upriver from Pittsburgh and downriver from Etna. Though we thought nothing of the pickle jars and mustard and onions on our shelves, Mother told us that in Poland it was rare to find packaged food products like these in jars and cans in stores. America was where new things, like pickles in jars, made life better. We now enjoyed the option of not having to preserve and store our own vegetables. And she was particularly proud that Heinz said they sold fifty-seven varieties of pickles. Even as a little girl in Poland, fifty-seven had been Mother's lucky number, and now many of the jars on her shelves had "57" right there on the label.

She told us, also, that long ago in Poland when she was a little girl, a mystical woman in her village had told Mother that she had a special "57 angel" watching over her and guarding her. She said the Heinz factory here in Pittsburgh, with its special "57 varieties," was a manifestation of that angel's continuing influence in her life.

One might think that with the "57 angel" and the Black Madonna of Częstochowa closely looking out for her, Mother's fate in America would have been better. But we learned that angels and saints obviously have limits to their powers.

Mother surprised me that May with a real birthday gift: a Hohner Marine Band harmonica, made in Germany and with a squeeze button on the end for the half step passages called chromatics. One of Mother's laundry customers had bought it at a music store in Pittsburgh, but that woman's children showed no interest in learning to play it. After a few tips from Jumbo, who somehow knew his way instinctively around a mouth organ, I picked up a few songs. My first was "Little Red Wing" and after that, "Clementine" and "Oh, Susannah!"

The rule was I couldn't play it in the house, whether or not Jumbo was sleeping. The harmonica riled my little brothers, and I understood. I certainly did not want to start them wailing away, as they sometimes did the first few times I tried out my new instrument.

After a week, Mother said she was astounded by my progress and that I was obviously gifted musically. Ziggy was jealous that he did not have a harmonica, so I tried to teach him. But he was quickly frustrated and once threw it down on the floor and bent the corner of it. I revoked his harmonica privileges, but he didn't seem to mind. I was glad about that, because he always handed it back to me filled with his slobber. That meant I had to shake it out hard and run water through it and blow it out to dry it and make it sound good again.

The Hohner came in handy. Most mornings, Ziggy and I milked Rose and Mary and carried the heavy buckets into the kitchen. Then after breakfast we headed off to Curry's meadow. Mother packed us sandwiches, and off we clip-clopped down the street, over the little stream, through a small forest with a few oaks and birches in it, and then through Ben Curry's gate and out into the meadow. Rose and Mary followed us, each on a rope.

My harmonica ditties could entertain Ziggy for only so long, and one day I brought along *Tom Swift and His Motorcycle*, a book Max had borrowed from the Etna Public Library but never read and never took back. Somehow, Tom Swift had stowed away on our move from the farm. Thanks to Lucy's tutoring, I could read out loud to Ziggy. Some of the longer words were tough to understand, but I would just skip over them and Ziggy would not notice.

I was never sure how much he understood. Often, he would lie on the meadow grass and gaze up at the sky, while I read to him. This was a fun way for me to express my love for Zig, and I know he was grateful for it. Also, it gave me a great opportunity to practice reading, which I loved to do.

We found out there were many more Tom Swift books in the Rehoboth town library, and Vera and Lucy would check them out for us. That first spring and summer, we went through three or four of them, all while tending Rose and Mary. Sometimes Zig would ask me to read a whole chapter again, especially those filled with action. I wondered if someday I might want to grow up to be an inventor, just like Tom Swift. Of course, if I wanted to become an inventor, I would have to go to school. For now, I had Lucy and a cow pasture as my school, so I decided to make the most of it.

I recalled Dr. McAllister's phrase when he delivered Blizzard: "I'm your hospital." So, for now, at least, I would have to be my own school.

Another book I read to Ziggy that summer was a paperback Max had picked up at the Texaco station. It was *The Curse of Capistrano*, and it featured a Spanish don named Zorro, a masked horseman who fought for the peasants of the early California colonies against the corrupt military government. By day, Zorro was actually a dapper gentleman named Don Diego, who pretended to be a coward and a dandy, so that nobody would realize he was Zorro. Then at night, he would put on his mask and his cloak and ride through the hills, solving crimes and sometimes punishing the wicked villain by carving a Z with his sword tip on their foreheads. Zorro means fox in Spanish.

When I read him that section, Ziggy reacted with a loud laugh. He grinned to think that a bad character would have to wear a Z on his forehead for the rest of his life, so that people would know he was an exposed criminal.

When I showed Ziggy how to make a Z with a stick in the dirt and told him it was the first letter in his own name, he seemed excited. I was hopeful that I could teach him more letters of the alphabet later, but he never showed any interest. All he wanted to know was Z.

I was tempted to carve a Z for Ziggy in the bark of one of the trees on Mr. Curry's property, but Mother refused to allow us to take knives out of the kitchen drawer to bring along with us to the meadow. So, the Z in the tree did not happen until much later.

Mr. Curry's property was huge, Max said at least eight acres, and at the far end, on the other side of the wood rail fence and over a hill, was an abandoned strip mine, the same mine we had spotted from the truck on our first day's tour in Rehoboth.

One hot, sunny day when Ziggy was tired of listening to my harmonica and hearing about Zorro's adventures, we walked Rose and Mary down to the far end of the meadow, tied them to the fence poles, and hiked up one of the high mounds to look down at the mine pits.

The peak of the mound offered a commanding view of the entire mine's extent, several square miles of excavations as deep as hundreds of feet cut in giant gouges into the terrain. All displayed the stacked layers of minerals in weirdly striped geological array.

Lucy had once shown me photographs in her science textbook of the Dakota Badlands in the American West, where scientists had unearthed dinosaur skeletons. The thought occurred to me that similar giant bones might be sticking out from the ground in the Rehoboth area. Why not? On later trips, we kept looking for bones and for dinosaur eggs, but Ziggy and I never found any. The deep gullies were filled with settled rainwater, various orange and yellow and even green-shaded pools, some stretching thirty feet across.

On that first day, which was hot and humid, Ziggy yelled, "Swimming!"

Off he went, rambling down the mound toward the closest pool, a large orange-shaded pit at the base of a mound shaped like a half moon. I ran back to the top of the hill and looked back to check on Rose and Mary. Both were grazing contentedly by the fence. Then I followed Ziggy down to the water.

Ziggy's impulse to jump into the pool frightened me. He didn't know how to swim, and neither did I. And we didn't know how deep the pit was or whether the water was toxic. But we recalled seeing the boys swimming in the same pool on our very first day in Rehoboth, so we probably weren't in danger of being poisoned or burned by harmful minerals. We also were not at risk for mosquito bites or any water snakes; the chemicals in all these pools famously prevented any animals or plants from living there.

Ziggy pulled off his glasses. We removed our shoes and stripped off our clothes and left them in a pile between some rocks on the side of the mound. Naked in the sun, we gingerly stepped down the squishy bank into the water, which was warm as a bath in our copper tub and smelled like sulfur. To be safe, we held hands on our way in and were up to our belly buttons when we let go of each other.

I showed Zig dog paddle strokes, which I improvised. We looked at each other and grinned, feeling the soothing water slip into every crack in our bodies. I had never been in a river or even a pond, so my heart was beating hard as I moved my arms and legs as fast as I could. I was worried that if anything bad happened, I would be blamed and punished. But then if we both drowned, Jumbo couldn't punish us and Max might be sorry that he had bullied us so much. Fat chance of that, I thought, thrashing about in the water as best I could.

After about a minute of panic and desperate splashing by both of us, Ziggy's grunting laughter started, and I couldn't help myself, either. It was an odd and wonderful feeling. We didn't need to thrash our arms or legs. We floated without moving a muscle. The water's heavy mineral content buoyed us up, so that even if we remained stock still on our backs, we didn't sink. Ziggy rolled over and floated, motionless, staring up at the sky and chuckling, his pale freckled belly, a white mound on the orange water.

We were thrilled and amazed, because we didn't have to worry about going under. Though you could barely see your hand in it, this water was probably the safest water in the world. We both laughed and spread out, our heads back, staring up at the sky. We were speechless for a long while. The pool was like a huge quivering wet magic carpet.

"Nobody can see us," I said.

"Yeah, but if somebody was up on the moly smokestack, he could see us."

I looked up over my shoulder. He was right. There was nothing visible in the sky beyond the pit mounds, except the top of the moly smokestack, which was several miles away.

"Nobody ever climbs up that stack, Zig."

"But what if they did? What if they did today? There's a ladder that goes all the way to the top."

"Up there, they wouldn't pay attention to us, not from so far away. They would be too busy holding on so they wouldn't fall down."

"Well, okay," Ziggy said with a soft laugh.

"And they could not steal our clothes, not if they were on the top of the moly stack."

"Yeah!" Ziggy seemed to lose himself in laughter. We both felt joyous and free.

I decided to lie back and enjoy myself in the sun, stretched out limp in the heavy orange liquid. Not that I would have fallen asleep there, of course, but it was so cozy and sensuous, feeling wet and defying gravity. Soon I fell into a trance, closing my eyes, feeling the sun on my skin and listening to the crows calling to each other on the other side of the mound.

After several minutes of silence, I looked over and saw that Ziggy was lying flat with his fingers around his dinky, moving his hand up and down.

"Stop it."

"Max showed me."

"Well, what?"

"I'm doing what Max told me to do. Try it."

"It looks bad."

"Max says it can make you feel real good."

"Do you feel good?"

"Well, sort of. My dinky feels good."

"Stop."

"No, he says if you do it long enough, it really makes you feel good. I watched him do it, and white stuff came out."

"White stuff? Do you believe everything Max says? He's always baiting us."

"I saw the white stuff. Max says girls really know how to do it best, but if you're all alone, you can do it yourself."

"What kind of girl would do that?"

"Max said a pretty girl named Louise did it to him in a car back behind the Texaco. In fact, she did it twice, he said."

"Your dinky looks big."

"Yeah. Max says the longer and harder it gets, the better you feel."

"That's stupid."

"Try it."

"We should check on the cows."

"Can't we stay longer?"

"Go ahead. Stay."

I got out of the water and went to put on my clothes. Ziggy finally followed me.

"So, did you feel real good?" I asked him, when we were hiking back up the mound.

"Yeah. You don't know what you're missing. It's fun. We should come back here again tomorrow."

"Did white stuff come out?"

"A little bit at first. Then I couldn't stop it!"

"Zig? Are you telling the truth?"

"I did it just like Max showed me."

"You really shouldn't do everything Max tries to trick you into. Max can be mean, you know. Something bad might happen."

"Like what?"

"I don't know. Just bad."

"Like the white stuff?"

"Yeah."

"It's not bad, Taddy. It's sticky, but it's not bad. It's good."

"I say it's bad."

"Do you think Mother would ever do that to Jumbo?"

"Stop, Zig. Don't talk crazy."

"Max says she does."

"You mean like what he says that girl Louise did to him in the car?"

"Yeah. With Jumbo's dinky. And Max says that's how babies are made."

"Wait a minute! You can't believe what he says a lot of the time. Max lies."

"Not about that."

"Hey, look at those cows. Rose and Mary haven't moved an inch."

"See. Nothing bad happened. You worry a lot, Tad."

"But I don't do everything Max tells me to do."

"Neither do I."

"Well, you were doing it in the water back there."

"I want to come back here tomorrow. Can we?"

The Bunkhouse

Once Ziggy had a notion in his head, he wouldn't let it go, especially if it made him feel good. This applied to what Max had told him about stroking his dinky. And Max kept asking him about it.

Max also started calling Ziggy and me the cowboys, since we spent a lot of time with Rose and Mary. And he called our bedroom the bunkhouse. Some nights when the three of us were stacked up in our bunk, Max on top, me on the bottom, and Zig in the middle, the dinky stroking above me was noisy and annoying and often accompanied by loud whispers, grunts, and groans.

"Are you doing it, Zig?"

"Yeah. Are you?"

"Yeah. Oh yeah. Oh yeah."

"Mine doesn't work."

"Keep at it. Mine always works."

"I'm doing it just like you said. Maybe I'm too young."

"Shut up. Shut up."

"What?"

"Shut up!"

"What's happening?"

The bunk would rock back and forth and slam against the wall as if wolves were jumping above me.

"Hey! You'll wake up the baby. And Mother needs her sleep!"

"Shut up!"

"Yeah, we're doing it," Ziggy would add. "Try it yourself."

"You're not going to like it when Jumbo pops in here and slaps us silly for waking up the whole house."

"Jumbo's at the mine. Nobody will bother us."

Max was right. No matter how much noise they made, Mother or the girls never came into our room, even when I was sure they could not help but hear us.

One night when Max was out late and Ziggy was snoring above me, I decided to try for myself. It felt good, but there was no payoff like they talked about. No white stuff.

I decided to stop. Maybe it was something I had to grow into. And I certainly wasn't going to complain to Jumbo or Mother or the girls about Max and Zig doing it, especially since now, once in a while, I was experimenting with it on my own.

One time when Ziggy and I stopped at the Texaco to share a soda pop, a car pulled up to the pump with a pretty girl and her father in it.

"Hey, Ziggy!" Max shouted, pointing his thumb behind him at the girl as he filled the tank. She was looking over at Max's arm, running her eyes along the muscles in his back.

When she saw us looking at her, the girl dropped her eyes. When the car drove off, I asked, "Is her name Louise?"

Max nodded again, "Yeah."

Ziggy said, "She's…"

Max grinned. He looked very proud. "Don't tell anybody, okay? Not to anybody, hear me? Or I'll slug you guys."

Ziggy and I sighed. Louise looked to be about Vera's age. I simply couldn't imagine Vera doing something like that. Or Lucy, for that matter.

When we got back to the house, I asked Vera if she knew a girl named Louise. She said she did and why did I want to know about her.

"I think she likes Max."

"She likes a lot of the boys in the school."

"I never see her at Mass."

"Her parents are Presbyterians. They don't go to confession, I hear."

I looked at Vera and asked, "Do you think she should go to confession?"

Vera blushed. "What are you asking?"

"Just asking, that's all."

"Her business is her business. And it certainly isn't yours. And it shouldn't be Max's either. But don't tell him I said that."

The Addition

Later that summer, Jumbo told us he had decided to build an addition to the shed. He said he bought Rose and Mary not thinking how much space their stalls and the hay bin would take up, and now he wanted a workshop.

It took him a month and a half to complete the project. Ziggy and I helped. We stood around holding tools, sanding boards, bringing him coffee from the kitchen, and generally pretending that we were useful. I enjoyed watching his huge deft hands at work. When crafting, he was competent and exacting. He whistled and smiled and seemed almost kind, different from the way he usually acted around us. And I liked the smells of the sawdust and turpentine and the various wood stains he used on the boards to preserve them and make the grains stand out. Besides, he was doing something to give us more living space, which we all craved, and it meant he would be spending more time outside of our house, a relief to everyone.

When it was done and the tar paper roof had been sealed around the edges, Jumbo had clearly doubled the size of the shed. It looked and smelled beautiful. Now he had a large worktable with several vises on it that Ziggy and I liked to twirl. Jumbo fashioned a large utility wall with pegs and shelves and slots and cubbyholes for tools and nails and hinges and other hardware gadgets that he said were essential. The shop had a plank floor reaching better than halfway across the space, but then the floor stopped.

Jumbo surprised us by starting to dig out the dirt at the far end of the shed. He carved a large square pit, deep enough for him to stand up with his head coming to just below floor level. He hauled all the dirt and stones from the hole in a wheelbarrow down to the little forest on the edge of Ben Curry's meadow and spread it out along the fence. Once the hole was dug, he sealed the sides of the pit with cinderblocks and mortar and poured in a concrete floor. Atop the pit he stretched more floorboards and a trapdoor, so that with a burlap rug over it, the rough flooring appeared continuous. Glancing casually, nobody would guess there was a secret concrete vault under the workshop.

Maybe a week after the work on the pit was completed, he brought in some equipment, which looked familiar to me from the old Ripple Brook Gardens root cellar. Max said he and Jumbo had driven out one Sunday to our old farm, which was still unoccupied, and without finding anybody to ask permission, loaded the old wine vats and the vodka still up onto the truck. There were several dozen empty bottles, too, in big cardboard boxes, and these they had hauled back and loaded down into the pit.

"Don't tell anybody what I'm doing," Jumbo said one evening after dinner in the kitchen. Everyone else had gone outside for a walk, and I remained at the table with Mother and him. "It's against the law, and I could go to jail. And you could too. If anybody says anything to anybody, I could lose my job and go to prison and where would we be then? Think about it! Do you want us all maybe to get sent back to Poland?"

I was confused. After all the excitement I had enjoyed from watching Jumbo construct the workshop and the big underground vault, now how was I responsible for some kind of crime?

He stretched back from the table, stood up, and walked out the back door to the shed. I looked at Mother, and she put her hand on my arm.

"He's only going to make vodka and sell it, not drink it," Mother explained. "And he might make wine, too, if he can find the right grapes."

"Why would he go to jail? Why would they send us back to Poland?"

"A license is required to make alcohol, if you're going to sell it. He could get away with it when we were living on the farm because we were out of the way from everything. And we only sold it to our tavern customers."

"He will make and sell vodka?"

"We need money. I spoke again yesterday with Mr. MacAdoo, and he has stretched our credit limit again as far as he can. He's very kind, but he runs the store, and he is limited to what he can do in terms of credit. I begged him, but he said we are far behind in our debt. The bill is so high I don't know how we will ever pay it back. The tools and materials for the addition to the shed put us even further into the red ink."

"Is he going to drink the vodka?"

"He promised me he would not."

I watched Mother's brow furrow and her eyes squint, as if she were trying to make me think she believed what she had just said.

"Very well, Mother. But what if somebody finds out?"

"That's why we are talking to you. The others all know. We all have to be very careful. Can you be careful?"

"Yes. But what if Ziggy says something? You know Ziggy."

"Nobody believes Ziggy. Besides, Jumbo won't start doing it for a few months. It takes a while to produce the vodka and the wine."

"But what if they find out? Will they really throw us out of America?"

"Your father knows what he's doing. Just keep quiet, and everything will be fine. I had a very long talk with him before he built the addition."

"But when he started to drink vodka, Mother, that's when things went bad on the farm. And he left us."

"That's not going to happen again. I'm sure of it."

"Mother, why do you love Jumbo?"

She stared at me, smiling tenderly at first, her elbows on the table, her chin resting in the palms of her open hands. I felt privileged being alone with her, having her confide in me.

"I have no choice. None of us has a choice. We must love him. He is a man who needs our love. And he is doing his best to improve our lives."

I nodded to show her I understood, but she probably could see I was pretending to go along with it.

And then, in front of my eyes, I watched her facial features strangely dissolve. As her eyes moistened and twisted close, her high strong cheekbones seemed to give way and sink into themselves like bread dough. Her large smoothly curved lips tightened and trembled, and then pulses of red flashed up into her cheeks and forehead. She started to sob convulsively, and a stream of tears swept down her cheeks into little skin wrinkles beneath her nose and her lips, wrinkles I had never before seen and now filled by her tears.

Mother's pain was in front of me. It was as if, maybe only this one time, she could no longer conceal all the weight and strain of caring for her seven children under increasingly abject circumstances. Or was it rather all the injury inflicted on her by Jumbo, who was now pushing her further with a project that would supply our family with money but probably greater chaos.

I jumped up at the table to put my arms around her. As I embraced her strong shoulders and rested my cheeks against her thick blonde hair and her quivering face muscles, I could feel through the bones in my chest her pounding heart.

Many times, I have recalled that moment when I tried to comfort her in the kitchen, held her as tight as I could to calm her. Jumbo was off in the shed, and I was alone with her. This was my moment to be her loyal son.

I kissed her and said, "Mother, I know things will turn out all right."

Later I have realized that moment in the kitchen was my first glimpse of her despair for being complicit in Jumbo's folly. Making alcohol in the shed might give us a foot up out of our hole of debt to the company store, but ultimately it would be destructive. I did not see why we had to cheat to survive.

But what were any of us to do? Though I was feeling for the first time the horrible depth of my mother's regret, still I kept up the pretense.

I whispered feebly as I cuddled her, "I will be as careful as possible. I won't tell anybody, and I won't let Ziggy spoil the secret. I promise."

26

A Family Business

At Jumbo's request, Max sneaked home empty soda pop bottles from the Texaco, and these were to serve as vodka containers for the new business. Ziggy and I washed them out and lined them all upside down, six in a row, on some portable wooden racks Jumbo had crafted. Mother gave us old pillowcases to cover them, because she felt it best that the neighbors would not see them. For all they knew, we were making jelly.

The corks came from *Piccolo Palermo*, an Italian restaurant in Rulandville, the next town over, where gallons of Chianti were served every night. Jumbo drove over in the truck and picked up a couple hundred of them in a large box. The owner, Mr. Pasquale Papallardo, asked if Jumbo wanted old bottles, too, because he had plenty of them. Jumbo declined the offer, figuring that hauling wine bottles and corks from the same source would look too suspicious. And the soft drink bottles were smaller and more portable. Mr. Papallardo told him to come back when he needed more corks. No questions asked.

Ben Curry began to deliver several bushels of potatoes to our house once a week. He brought barley, too, in heavy burlap sacks.

"Growing family!" Mother said with a smile, each time he drove up and stepped out of his truck to unload the baskets. The laundry vats that were busy during the week served well to boil and mash the potatoes on weekends. The distillation happened in the secret new pit in the shed.

After only a few weeks, Jumbo had product to sell. Of course, he had to taste it to be sure it was of good quality, but he didn't swallow it, he said. He was true to his oath to Mother, at the beginning.

By now Jumbo was working mostly day shifts, and every afternoon when he came back from the mine, he would take the clean bottles back into the shed, fill them up, cork them, and then bring them back into the kitchen.

He started selling the vodka in mid-September, and word spread fast. Soon he could not keep up with the demand. By the end of the first month, half a dozen customers might come by every afternoon. Mother had to turn down some folks. Business doubled by November.

When customers knocked at the door, Mother interrupted whatever she was doing to take the money and hand them a bottle. One to a customer was the rule. By Thanksgiving, we had paid off enough of the debt to buy new clothes and shoes on credit, and just before Christmas we went to the company store and picked out warm winter coats.

We all pitched in to make the vodka, hauling water, cleaning and slicing the potatoes, helping Mother boil them, adding in the barley and sugar, watching the mash cool, and cleaning the still with strong vinegar. Oddly, we felt again like a farm family working together, and Mother seemed happy that the extra money was helping us to live more like the way she wanted us to live.

We knew that we could be in trouble quickly if word leaked out. Why, after all, were people suddenly coming to our house and walking away with a bottle in a brown paper bag?

I was frightened one day when a pair of policemen showed up at the door, but Mother did not seem worried. She handed them six bottles for free, as this was the deal Jumbo had cut with the police chief.

Apparently, Jumbo had a special gift for distilling vodka, and he began to tell people that it came from an old family recipe handed down by a grand uncle, Kasper Malinowski, who was said to be of Polish noble blood and who had invaded Russia with Napoleon.

Jumbo never went so far as to put a label on the product, but he liked it when people asked for a bottle of Kasper's Tonic or, more simply, KT. Then he could march out his pedigree story to people who would bother to hear about it.

Royal recipe or not, when Jumbo raised the price, nobody minded. In fact, some customers drove clear out from downtown Pittsburgh and from as far west as Hunterton, Ohio, and as far south as Wheeling, West Virginia, to buy Kasper's Tonic. When they came that far for it, Mother changed the rule to six bottles per customer.

Jumbo read articles in the paper that soon all across the United States alcohol sales would become illegal. It was a movement called Prohibition, and most states had agreed to ratify it as the law of the land through a constitutional amendment. By this time, he was making almost as much money from his vodka business as he was from mining coal. If it were not for the threat of Prohibition, he told Mother, he had half a mind to quit his job at the mine and start an official distillery.

Apparently, the Rehoboth police chief had told him some good news: even if Prohibition was passed, Jumbo could continue his business. The police would not interfere. He had to keep everything discreet, but people would always want to drink alcohol, no matter what the politicians and the crazy temperance movement ladies tried to make everyone believe.

A highly unfortunate coincidence occurred in those first months of Jumbo's vodka business, which helped to boost sales. The Spanish flu epidemic swept through the country. Western Pennsylvania had many thousands of cases. American soldiers returned from Europe infected with the terrible disease, and doctors had no treatment for it. Seventeen workers at the mine and smelting plants succumbed to it, along with some of their children.

It was common that fall and winter to see whole families wearing black armbands. Then Mother heard the news that dear Dr. McAllister had caught it from one of his patients, had passed it on to his wife, and they both died within a day of each other. So, Mother cut and sewed black armbands for herself and for Jumbo and Max.

When Max ran a high fever, she feared we all could catch it, too, but that didn't happen. Following an old Polish folk tradition, Jumbo treated Max with a shot of vodka every six hours. Miraculously Max snapped out of it in two days. Soon word spread that Kasper's Tonic, with its mysterious Polish noble recipe, could save lives, certainly better than anything the doctors around Pittsburgh had to offer.

Vodka production in Jumbo's shed tripled. Again, the police gave him no trouble about it, seeing how, if rumors were true, the vodka could actually be saving lives in the community. The price per bottle stayed the same, because Mother felt it would be unfair to charge more to customers who were buying the product for medicinal purposes. She refused to gouge the clientele for blood money. If only Dr. McAllister and his wife had tried it! If she had known they were sick, she certainly would have brought some by his house.

Eventually the Spanish flu plague subsided, but sales of the vodka continued. Mother even had an idea that if, in a year or two, Jumbo could pay off his account at the company store and hoist us out of debt, we might be able to move back to Ripple Brook Gardens and buy back the old farm.

Then we heard that the Etna bank had sold the farm to Etna Metals, and row houses like the one we lived in on Robert Street were now being constructed on the old Wells property. The new houses were for new workers at Etna Metals. Mother's dream of going back to the old farm and our former life stopped. She no longer talked about it. It would have to remain a memory.

Our chances of going back to Ripple Brook Gardens were as likely as our going back to Poland and starting life all over again there. Neither place now existed as it once had.

Some changes are permanent, like it or not. As Mother often said, "Nothing to be done."

27

The Strop

On a chilly February morning, Max showed up at high school drunk. He was expelled for the rest of the year. When Jumbo heard the news, he grabbed Max by the arm and hauled him out to the shed. "Tad, bring me my strop," he ordered, as he slammed the back door.

Reluctantly, I took Jumbo's razor strop down from its hook by the upstairs bathroom mirror and went out to the shed.

"Now get out!" Jumbo ordered. "Take your shirt off, Max. Take it off!"

I stood outside. The blows simply would not stop. Jumbo whipped Max over and over, each loud lash prompting a grunt of agony.

"Look me in the eye!" he shouted each time, as he would bring his arm back and lash Max's shoulders and spine. "Look me in the eye, I said! Big man! Think you can show up to school drunk!"

I heard Rose and Mary making urgent lowing noises and shifting their hoofs on the shed floor.

"You want to get us all arrested?" Jumbo bellowed.

More lashes and screams. Rose and Mary started to stamp around.

"Drunk at school? Drunk at school?"

"I only sneaked a little last night!"

"Nobody drinks in this house! You hear?"

"I won't ever..."

"No, you won't! I'll go to jail, and the rest of you will go back to Poland. Do you want that?"

"Even Blizzard and Kazzy? They were born here!"

"Shut up, you stupid drunken pig!"

I heard Jumbo slap Max hard on the face three times.

On the last blow, Max started wailing in pain. "Stop!"

"You're talking to the wrong person if you think I will stop. I haven't even begun on you."

"Please, stop!" Max whined. "Please, please…"

Then I heard a horrible crash and a loud splintering collision of Max being thrown against a shelf of bottles. I heard liquid spilling out in many streams on glass shards. I imagined dozens of bottles of our product wasted on the floor of the shed, some of them drenching Max.

Apart from those noises, only silence came from the shed. Neither Jumbo nor Max said a word. The crash had startled Rose and Mary into stillness.

Then the shed door opened, and Jumbo strode out, his razor strop in his hand, fire in his eyes. As soon as he saw me, apparently as punishment for my standing there, he swung the strop back above his head and then down over my left shoulder. The steel ring on the end of the strop whipped up around my other shoulder and banged me square on the nose and lip. Jumbo wrenched it back without even looking at the damage he had done and marched back toward the house.

My upper lip felt numb. I put my hand to my nose. Blood pooled in my palm.

At the back porch, Jumbo turned and pointed at me, his hand raising the strop as if there were more blows coming. "Clean up the shed! Clean it up now! Your brother's out cold. I don't want a thing out of place when I go back in there!"

The ring on Jumbo's strop had bashed my nose and split my upper lip below the left nostril. Blood spilled over my mouth and down my chin. I couldn't tell where it was coming from. I pressed my other palm to my face and saw two red streaks close together at the base of my thumb, but I was too concerned about Max to worry about my small wounds. I knew I should get in there in a hurry and clean up the mess, because Jumbo could easily come back to give me more strop lashes.

Rose and Mary continued their silence. I could hear nothing else coming from that side of the shed, but I knew Zig and I were due to milk them soon too.

I took a long breath in and out and opened the door. Vodka fumes were everywhere. Max lay faceup on the floor, his brow and cheeks flushed and covered with welts and broken glass. He was moving his head slowly and his eyes were blinking around. I saw no blood on his face, but he was at risk of cutting himself, if he tried to pick off the shards.

"Wait, Max. Let me clean you up. Don't move! Don't even talk."

"Goddamn Jumbo! Motherfucker!" he whispered.

"Shut up, Max. Don't talk about Mother that way!"

Tears and vodka were puddled on his face. His left front tooth had broken off halfway down. He poked his tongue out and spit the square tooth fragment out onto his chin. Blood sprayed out with his saliva.

"Fucking motherfucker!"

"Stop that."

"I don't care. He's a fucking motherfucker!"

Jumbo had to report to the mine that afternoon, so he never returned to check the shed. Max and I spent three hours cleaning it up.

Just before we were finished, Mother came out to look in on us. She put my face up to the electric light bulb and switched it on to examine me closely. Her eyes ran slowly over my nose and lip, and she murmured, "I'm sorry. I'm sorry for this." She touched the tip of her index finger to my lip, which had stopped bleeding.

"I'm sorry, too, Mother."

"It will leave a scar on your lip! My best-looking boy! I'm so sorry."

"Not your fault. Nothing to do."

Then she pulled Max over to the light, ran her fingers through his hair, her head moving back and forth. "You are like your father,

Max. Just like your father. Someday you will probably make some woman hate you."

I saw tears gathering in her big green eyes. She looked into the buckets, where we had deposited the remains of the broken bottles. Her head moved dolefully. "We lost money. Look how much! I will talk to your father."

Max tried to put his arm around Mother, but she shoved him aside. "Pfuew!" she shouted. "You stink! Both of you! Upstairs and take a bath right now! You smell like vodka factory!"

We turned off the light and walked back into the house. Max looked at me skeptically. He and I both doubted Mother would mention anything to Jumbo about this event. Not tomorrow or anytime.

The fact was Jumbo had clobbered Max not for being expelled for drinking, but for putting the family vodka business at risk. We all knew Jumbo was indifferent as to whether Max should continue with his education. None of the miners Jumbo worked with had any schooling at all, and Max was almost big enough now to go down into the shaft. So, the message Jumbo delivered to Max in the shed that afternoon could also have included a challenge to leave the house and go out on his own or think about going down into the mine to earn a living. I could never imagine Max doing work that hard, but I kept my mouth shut.

All through that winter, Max was out of school, and he worked double shifts at the Texaco. I hardly saw him, except late at night when he crept into our room and climbed up into his bunk. When he left in the morning, Ziggy and I were usually out milking Rose and Mary. Max never touched Jumbo's vodka again, as far as I could tell, and eventually he and Jumbo started joking again, as if nothing bitter had ever happened between them. Jumbo would even tease him, "Hey, how'd you get that hole in your teeth?"

Now and then Max would take a chaw of Mail Pouch and spit the juice out through the new gap in his grin. He did this with remarkable accuracy. He could hit a dime with a hawker from six or seven paces. He also showed off by sucking in on a cigarette and then sneering widely with the butt stuck in his front teeth, but this did not go over well with Joe Curtiss at the Texaco, who told him not to look like a jackass Polack in front of customers

Ziggy overheard Roscoe Curtiss calling him this and took a liking to the phrase "jackass Polack." I heard him call Kazzy and Blizzard that a few times, till Mother put a stop to it. Ziggy had no idea what a jackass Polack was, though in my mind that phrase sometimes fit Max perfectly.

And as for the razor strop cut on my lip and nose, it healed up with only a tiny scar. Mother was relieved, though I am sure she never talked to Jumbo about how it was inflicted.

Mother was a very strong woman, but on some things, she was weak.

The Harley

At dusk one Saturday in March of that year, we were finishing dinner at the kitchen table when we heard a loud motorcycle rumbling down Robert Street. The noise diminished suddenly, and then the motor idled in front of the house. When Max shouted to us from the street, we jumped up and ran outside.

Max stood with his big gap-toothed grin, lifting a pair of motorcycle goggles up over his forehead and straddling his first Harley Davidson. That day, he announced over the continuous growl of the engine, he had shelled out his first cash down payment for it at an army surplus store on Liberty Avenue in Pittsburgh.

The motorcycle was painted military green and had a sidecar, which was shaped something like a sturdy baby carriage and with thick steel panels and a spoked wheel the same size as the two on the motorcycle. Stenciled on the gas tank were a white star and the words "U.S. Army."

The salesman at the store had told Max the Harley was a veteran of the Great War, and that it had proved itself practically indestructible in numerous battles in France and possibly also in Italy. The removable sidecar was equipped with a machine gun mounting cylinder, also detachable.

The war department was unloading these motorcycles to the American public in bulk, which accounted for the low price, payable over twenty-four months. Max proudly pointed out two deep circular dents in the front fender and another three on the door of the sidecar, which the salesman had said were probably impacts from ricocheted bullets, courtesy of the kaiser's rifles.

With Max's permission, I ran my fingertips reverently over the dents, while Ziggy stood back, his eyes huge and blinking with excitement. We had never seen anything so strong, beautiful, and exotic. The idling engine sounded like a purring cougar.

Max told us more and pointed proudly to each feature. The Harley had a fifteen-horsepower dual cycle engine, and it came with a new headlamp, a brand-new pair of Goodyear tires as well as a third for the sidecar, four spare spark plugs, a tire repair kit and pump, a five-gallon portable spare gas canister, and an army-issue wooden toolbox, also with stars on it, that contained wrenches and screwdrivers and gauges, and snapped tightly on the back fender with four heavy steel latches.

All of us, including Jumbo, stood speechless. Max said that when he told the salesman where he lived, the guy said it was quite possible the strong steel on the Harley's fender and sidecar had been forged with molybdenum smelted in Rehoboth. Jumbo was especially pleased to learn about this.

"Christ, you should feel this baby fly!" Max gloated loudly, sensing our awe. "Who wants to take the first spin? Mother?"

Mother ran inside quickly and came out, putting on her coat and wrapping her scarf over her head. We watched her open the little sidecar door. She stepped gingerly inside and then took her seat beside Max, hunching as low down as she could in the seat. Ziggy jumped over and put his arm around her, but she shook her head and said, "I will be safe, Ziggy. Don't worry."

Lucy and Vera exchanged concerned glances. We were afraid, especially when Max, who we all knew had driven a motorcycle only once or twice before in his life, slipped his goggles back on, revved up the engine, snapped on the headlight, and popped the clutch.

Mother's neck jerked back. She gave a loud frightened shriek over the roaring engine. Seconds later, they were off down the corner and out of sight into the darkening evening.

We all stayed silent for a long moment. We listened as the Harley's drone dimmed in the distance.

"He is a fool," Jumbo murmured, shaking his head and walking back into the house to light a cigar.

We went back inside to clean up the dinner dishes, but we said nothing. We worried about Mother riding with Max, declared a fool by our father at the moment, when he was probably showing off by speeding around the country road curves and getting an odd thrill by terrifying our Mother.

"Maybe he took her clear into Pittsburgh," Ziggy said.

"Don't say that," Vera said.

"No, he wouldn't take her that far. It's dark already," Lucy added.

"He has a headlight," Ziggy replied. "He can take her anywhere. You can ride anywhere at night with a headlight. Right, Taddy?"

Twenty minutes later, to our great relief, we heard the Harley roar back down Robert Street. Mother's perilous absence had seemed much longer than that. When she stepped back into the house, she was shivering and her teeth chattered. She immediately went into the parlor and began a whispered conversation with the Black Madonna.

Max stood by the Beckwith, apologizing for all he was worth. Mother would have nothing of him.

"You frightened me close to death!"

"I didn't mean to, Mother."

"To death you frightened me. Why do you like to do this to me?"

Jumbo peered up from his Polish newspaper and puffed on his cigar, regarding them both. Mother nodded and pointed at Max. "Like you, Ignaz. Like you!"

"I never drove a motorcycle!"

"Don't get any ideas from your daredevil son!"

Max stood with his motorcycle goggles on his forehead, working his broken tooth with his tongue. "I thought you were enjoying yourself."

Nothing more was said that evening about the motorcycle, and Mother seemed too upset to tell us about her ride. But the following day, which was a sunny Sunday, Max took first the girls then me and then Ziggy for rides in the sidecar. Jumbo refused. He was probably too big to fit into it, anyway.

My ride lasted almost an hour, and I was grateful for the thrill. We went west and crossed the state line into West Virginia and then drove up and down some forested hills that had unpaved narrow roads that bounced me almost out of the sidecar. We passed some huge farms and a state park with a big pond with clear water that looked perfect for swimming in the summer.

We stopped for gas and Coca-Cola at a Gulf station in a small West Virginia village. Max lit a cigarette and strode around. I stayed in the sidecar and felt the sun shining warmly on me. A boy only slightly older than me pumped gas into the Harley's fuel tank. I loved sitting there and imagining that American soldiers in the Great War had ridden in that same seat during battles, protected by metal that was partly produced at the foot of the moly stack. I put my fingers on the bullet holes and imagined myself manning a machine gun against the German soldiers. I shivered at the adventure Max was giving me.

That was one of the only days I could recall in my entire boy-hood when I remember Max acting in an affectionate way toward me. Of course, I was only along for the ride, and he didn't have to say anything to me, and he was clearly just exploring the world on his new machine and showing off. But he was almost kind to me, as if I was a valued brother to him and not an embarrassing cripple. I had no real inkling that some years down the line, Max's motorcycle would do me a life-changing favor. Now remembering that feeling I had in the sidecar, I want to say it was similar to what I felt in the elevator with Mother in the Joseph Horne's department store. But I could be making that up in my own mind, since both the Harley and the elevator moments were to be repeated importantly in my future.

In any case, I recall the boy pumping the gas. He was blond like me and skinny, but he had dark eyebrows that curved up at the ends. They lined up exactly with the upturned curve of the sides of his mouth, as though he had been born with a permanent smirk and could not control it. As he pumped the gas, which took less than two minutes, his eyes flashed back and forth between Max and me, both of us drinking our Cokes.

"What are you looking at?" Max asked him.

"Nothing," the boy said.

"The Harley?"

"Yeah. Looks old."

"That Harley went through the war," Max said. "It was my uncle's. He got hit in the arm by German fire, but he shot the Kraut and then rode away. He gave me his motorcycle when he came back." Max drained his Coke.

"Is that so?"

"See the bullet holes?"

"Them ain't holes. Them's dents."

"How do you know? You ever go to war? Wipe that smirk off your lips."

"I'm not smirking."

"So, what's with the look?"

The boy pulled the nozzle out of the tank and hung it on the pump. Then he screwed the lid on the tank. "Forty-three cents, please."

Max approached the boy, glaring at him in a standoff. "What's with the look?"

The station owner stepped out of the office. "You got a problem out there, Lyle?"

"No, Dad."

"Let's go," I urged Max.

Max handed the boy two quarters and said, "Keep the change, squirt."

The boy's hands trembled when he took the coins from Max. I had seen it before. Max's glare could make a total stranger's hands shake, just like mine did.

Max handed me his empty bottle and jumped on the Harley. He rammed the kick-starter, and we zoomed away without further conflict. I was relieved, and I felt sorry for the boy at the station. There was no need for an argument, but Max seemed to want to start one up.

Incidents like that at the fuel pump over in West Virginia were not unusual for Max. My feelings for Max had changed though, ever since I saw him in such a defeated state that afternoon in the shed, when he was covered with vodka and glass.

Yes, Max was a bully and headstrong and very much like Jumbo. But Max was my brother.

And on another afternoon some years later, his Harley-Davidson changed my life much for the better.

29

Miss Bainbridge

Ziggy and I were bringing Rose and Mary back from Ben Curry's pasture on a sunny afternoon later that spring when we saw a strange car parked in front of 7 Robert Street. We assumed it was a vodka customer, but as we led the cows around the house, Mother opened the front door and called to us to hurry. Mother was frowning, though she was trying to look calm. She said there was a woman inside who wanted to meet us.

We quickly led the cows back into the shed and filled their feed pails with alfalfa. We washed up in the kitchen, where Kazzy and Blizzard were both snoozing in their shared playpen.

Mother sat there with a young bony-cheeked woman, whom Mother introduced to us as Miss Bainbridge. They were drinking tea. Jumbo had volunteered to work an extra night shift, and he was trying to catch up on his sleep. Mother's face looked tense.

I remember Miss Bainbridge as being pale. She wore a plain black suit and a blue felt hat with a black silk bow above the brim. She was blue-eyed and blonde but younger and much thinner than Mother. She smelled like the lemon-scented talcum powder Mother sometimes used after a bath.

Ziggy and I stood silent and felt her glance beam up and down at us. Beside her on the couch lay a brown leather briefcase with two manila folders on top of it. I saw my name typewritten on the label of one of them.

Suddenly jittery, Ziggy stared at the floor and rocked back and forth. In moments like these, Ziggy could not do eye contact. "What does this lady want? I'm scared, Taddy. What does she want?"

"I don't know, Zig. Let's listen."

Miss Bainbridge smiled and nodded to both of us. "I'm the new social worker for the mine company. I dropped in to meet your mother and to see how your family is doing."

Ziggy rocked harder and pounded his wrists. I feared an outburst was likely. I looked up at the Black Madonna and shot her a quick open-eyed prayer to help Zig and me through this, whatever it meant. I did not know what a social worker did, but this sounded serious.

"We're wondering why you two boys are not in school."

Both of us stared at Mother, who now looked alarmed. She nodded to me, as if I should not be afraid to speak.

"All the other company children go to school."

"I have a bad leg," I said.

"That's no reason not to go to school."

"I think my leg will be normal when I turn twelve. I look after my brother Ziggy most days. My big sisters already taught me how to read, and I'm pretty good at arithmetic. I know some geography and history too. I can recite the names of all twenty-eight presidents. Washington, Adams, Jefferson—"

Miss Bainbridge raised her hand to silence me. She squinted skeptically. "That's wonderful, but you can't wait till you turn twelve to go to school."

"I tried school!" Ziggy shouted. "The teachers kicked me out!"

"Your mother explained that you had difficulty at the Rehoboth Elementary School."

Ziggy started to slobber. I handed him my handkerchief.

"We might be able to find the right school for you," Miss Bainbridge said, "a place where the children are more like you."

"The teacher was mean to me."

"Really? Why would a teacher—"

Ziggy would hear no more. He bolted upstairs to our bedroom and slammed the door. This startled Blizzard and Kazzy. Both started to wail.

We heard the door to Jumbo's bedroom jerk open. "Jesus Christ! Shut up, everybody!" he roared. Then the door slammed loudly.

We heard Kazzy trying to climb out of the playpen, so I stepped over to keep an eye on him and Blizzard.

Miss Bainbridge stood up. "Oh, dear! I'm so sorry, Mrs. Malinowski! I seem to have disturbed the whole house. Maybe I should drop by another afternoon."

Mother stood and walked the social worker toward the front door. "Could I stop by your office sometime?"

Miss Bainbridge fumbled with our files and hurriedly jammed them back into her briefcase. "Yes, please come by next week. We won't want the boys starting school till the fall, of course, but I do want to make some plans. Perhaps a day when your husband can come into my office too? I'm in the main building, right beside where Dr. McAllister's office used to be."

As Mother was about to open the front door for Miss Bainbridge, we heard a loud knock.

Mother opened the door, and old Mr. Cronyn, our neighbor's father from up the street, appeared with a paper bag in which he had three clinking empty soda pop bottles. "You open for business today?" he asked.

Miss Bainbridge stared curiously at Mother.

"Come back tomorrow, Mr. Cronyn," she said. "Fresh out of lemonade."

The old man eyed up Miss Bainbridge and took the hint. "Yes, you sure make real fine lemonade, Mrs. Malinowski. My grand-daughters just love it. Kasper's is the best lemonade, we all agree!"

"Tomorrow I make more special for you, Mr. Cronyn."

As Mr. Cronyn walked back out to the street, Miss Bainbridge handed my mother her business card. "I'm so sorry," she said. "I caused a fuss, didn't I?'

"I will come visit you at your office next week. I bring you some lemonade too."

"Thank you so much. But you really don't have to. I'm so sorry that I upset Zygmunt."

"He is a sensitive boy."

"I will try to find a fine school for him."

From the window, I watched Miss Bainbridge drive away. Then I went into the kitchen. Mother was trying to console Blizzard with a bottle of juice. It might have been lemonade.

"So, Tad. Maybe we will send you to school in September. Would you like that?"

"How about Ziggy?"

"Miss Bainbridge says she will find a school for him. She seems nice. I hope she can help him."

We could hear Ziggy pacing back and forth in the upstairs hall, listening to what we were saying about his future. Ziggy always had trouble when it came to thinking about what might happen in the future. And none of us, especially Mother, could help him on that score. Perhaps it was fortunate that at least Miss Bainbridge was trying to call our attention to it.

The thought of going to school with other children my age excited me. It was hard for me to find friends if I spent all my time with Ziggy and Rose and Mary. Miss Bainbridge had planted the seed in my mind about finding a real education. I obviously needed to learn many things in school, including what exactly a social worker was.

Kennywood Park

That Fourth of July, Rehoboth Coal and Metals closed operations for the day and treated all the employees to a giant all-day family picnic at Kennywood, the famous amusement park on the Monongahela, a few miles upriver from downtown. Nine large buses picked up everybody at the mine entrance at eight o'clock in the morning. We traveled into Pittsburgh and then east along the riverbank to Kennywood, whose tall twin Ferris wheels and towering roller coaster we saw from a mile up the river road. The company was generously covering everything that day, including transportation, picnic lunch and drinks, all the rides and game booths, swimming in the park's giant pool, a barbecue picnic supper, a band concert, and then a huge fireworks show after sunset.

We had been looking forward to this event since it was first announced in May, and Mother had sewn us all new swimsuits for the outing. She and Lucy packed up towels and diapers and other clothing and some snacks and drinks in two large baskets. Mr. Cronyn's son had promised to look in and milk the cows late in the afternoon, and so all nine of us piled up into the truck, and Max drove us over to the mine entrance to meet the bus. Max had asked if he could bring a girlfriend, but when Jumbo said Max would have to pay her way, his date's invitation was cancelled.

As a special commemorative bonus, the mine hired a photographer to shoot family group portraits outside the mine entrance prior to our departure for Kennywood. Not only were these pictures free of charge, but the photographer offered a choice of six different scenic screens as backdrops.

Not asking any of us which we preferred, Jumbo picked the Swiss Alps. The photographer told us that we were the only family to choose that background, and Jumbo said that was exactly why he had chosen it. This picture of the five older children clustered around Jumbo and Mother and with Blizzard and Kazzy cuddled in their arms was the only one anybody ever took of all of us.

Jumbo and Max sported new straw boaters, cocked rakishly for the camera. Vera and Lucy and Mother wore flowered bonnets. Ziggy, Kazzy, and I were in sailor suits and caps, and Mother had sewn a cute red, white, and blue golfing outfit for little Blizzard, with plaid knickers, white stockings, an argyle vest, a red bow tie, and a blue golfer's cap with red and white tassels on the top. It was an unusual outfit for a little boy, and Blizzy got plenty of attention from the other employees. We all did. Our costumes were a sensation, and Mother was clearly proud of us. Of the many mining and metal working families, we were the largest and by far the most carefully and outlandishly clad. The picture of us posing proudly at the base of the snow-crested Matterhorn was unique and preposterous, yet it was a fitting souvenir of that magnificent daylong outing.

The July sun shone bright and hot, but there was a mild wind that cooled everyone off. Miss Bainbridge said hello to us, and she could see we appeared to be, if anything, a model, harmonious family. Ziggy again avoided eye contact with her.

Kennywood was jammed that day with revelers from all over the Pittsburgh area, and we never had had so much pure fun. Mother was worried all day that one of us would get lost, but we didn't.

Ziggy and I rode right behind the girls and Max on the roller coaster called the Jackrabbit. Jumbo sat alone behind us to make sure we held on. We did, and we were thrilled. As the cars cranked up to the highest peak, we looked out before us and saw the whole stretch of the Monongahela and the bridges over it and the green hills that sloped down on either side. Then suddenly the Jackrabbit whipped down fast and swung wide, so that it felt like you might get tossed right out into the river. Ziggy puked into his mouth a couple of times, but he swallowed it fast. He also almost lost his glasses on the first ride, and we solved that by stowing them in the pocket of his sailor suit. He looked terrified at first, but then he adjusted and started to squeal with delight on the sharp curves and on the plunging downgrades.

The twin giant Ferris wheels went up even higher than the roller coaster, and when the carriage stopped and rocked back and forth at the peak, we looked around downstream and saw clear back to the city of Pittsburgh with all the heavy smoke rising from the steel factory on the other side of the river operating that day, even though it was Independence Day, the national holiday.

When Ziggy and I were perched at the top, I wondered whether we were actually as high as the moly stack back in Rehoboth.

"Higher!" Ziggy giggled. "Higher!"

"You sure?"

"Yeah! Higher than that little smokestack!" He grinned and nodded his head with certainty. "That smokestack is puny next to us now, way up here."

I'd never seen Ziggy so thrilled. When he smiled hard, his wide cheeks puffed with pleasure, and his eyes narrowed tightly. He sometimes banged his wrists together, too, though this was not possible on the roller coaster or several other rides, since I kept reminding him that he had to hold on tight.

Several times we vowed to come back soon to Kennywood, but Ziggy and I never would.

There were at least two dozen other rides. We did not have time to try them all, but we loved the Tumblebug, the Tilt-A-Whirl, the Roundup, and the Mad Mouse. But the Jackrabbit and the giant twin Ferris wheels were far and away Ziggy's and my favorites. I knew he would be talking about them for weeks.

After lunch, Jumbo took Mother out in a rowboat in what they called the Lagoon. It was a huge fake lake with an island in the middle that had a small windmill whose arms twirled around, even though by that time there was not enough wind to move them. I looked out at Mother in her bonnet and Jumbo in his straw hat, pulling the oars gently in the sun, and it seemed that day that we all were in a lovely and exciting dream.

The day was a pleasure from beginning to end. We ate cotton candy and drank lemonade, and there was a special moment for me when Zig and I were on the merry-go-round. I looked over from my horse and noticed that a girl in a pink dress was looking hard at me. She was smiling from her pony. She was about my age, and it seemed like maybe under her blonde bangs she was blinking her eyes and trying to flirt with me. Her mother was riding beside her, and when I looked at her, she smiled, too, while her pony rose up and sank down on its pole. Then the little girl saluted me and giggled, showing off the dimples in her cheeks, and I wondered why. Later I realized it was because I was wearing a sailor suit. She was giving me a nautical salute, which I should have answered with a salute of my own instead of freezing in her glance.

At the end of the ride, we all went our separate ways. I had to be sure Zig got off his horse, and that distracted me from watching the girl leave with her mother. Later that afternoon, I looked for her as we walked along the different game stalls that offered Kewpie dolls and fuzzy animals for prizes. Max would have asked for her name, of course, right there on the carousel, if she had looked at him that way. But of course, she was much too young for Max, but just right for me, probably about nine or ten, I thought. Her mother was gorgeous too.

When I was up on that pony, bouncing along with the calliope music, it was likely that she did not notice my shortened leg. Had she seen me limp when we got off the merry-go-round? I hoped she didn't, though what would it matter? I did not know who she was or where she lived or anything about her, except that she had bangs and dimples and a beautiful mother, and she smiled at me in a way that made me think she admired me. And she was pretty. She was very pretty.

Those blinks meant something about her and me, but I supposed I would never find out. There was nobody in my family I could mention it to either.

But it happened, and it felt wonderful, even though she remained almost a mirage to me. I caught myself imitating her gesture, blinking my eyes and wondering if perhaps I should have blinked back at her, the way you are supposed to with cats. Surely, I should have saluted her, but I didn't, and I regretted that. If I ever saw her again, I would not miss my chance.

This incident on the Kennywood carousel may seem a poor excuse for a romantic encounter, but I never forgot it: her smile, her salute, her blinks, our ponies bobbing up and down as we went round and round. A sliver of my soul still rides that carousel, still longs to know what happened to her.

Before sunset, they gave a rousing band concert. Jumbo grinned when they performed some of his favorite Souza marches. At the end, they played the national anthem, and everybody stood up from their benches, the men took their hats off, and most of us sang. Meanwhile, I looked everywhere for the girl in the pink dress but didn't see her.

Then we all sat down and waited for the fireworks show.

Next to the blinks and the salute from the girl in the pink dress, the fireworks were the biggest thrill of all. The pounding concussions rocked our bones, and the brilliant flashes shocked us—red and yellow and green and purple—erupting into giant blazing arabesques that faded with stabbing reports as they dropped over the river. The brilliant explosions lit up the entire park and illuminated all the amusement rides in delirious, silhouetted splendor. I looked up at Mother's excited face, splashed by the crazy colors. I loved to see her so thrilled by the flashing and crackling feast in the sky.

When the fireworks finally ended, the smell of gunpowder rife in the air for a minute after the climax, all the mining and metal families found the buses to head back to Rehoboth. As it turned out, we never did go swimming, but we didn't care. We were too busy to go swimming. Delighted and exhausted, the Malinowski family piled into the last bus and arrived home not long before midnight. It had been a spectacular excursion. For us, nothing like that day ever happened again.

On July 5, Jumbo went back into the mine. Mother started doing her laundry duties with Kazzy and Blizzard under watch. Max went early to the Texaco. The girls helped Mother with the laundry. Ziggy and I milked Rose and Mary and took them out to pasture, where we read from a Tom Swift book and went swimming in the nude. We all did again what we routinely did.

And afterward, what we had done on that particular Fourth of July in 1920 was about as unreal and unlikely for us as maybe all of us moving to Switzerland and living at the foot of the Matterhorn, which that odd family portrait pretended to show.

Mrs. Lewis

One of my mother's favorite laundry customers was Mrs. Lewis, a chatty gray-haired woman probably in her late fifties. Usually on Tuesday afternoons, she came by our house to exchange bundles of laundry, and she often stayed for tea and gave Mother advice on all kinds of topics. Mrs. Lewis wore an expensive French jasmine-scented perfume, and it was easy to guess who had been in the house after she left.

She was much older than Mother, but she was tall and about the same size as Mother. She sometimes brought over blouses and sweaters and skirts she no longer wanted to wear. Mother was pleased to accept whatever was offered, because she said Mrs. Lewis had classic taste, and her hand-me-down garments were always of top quality, some of them imported from France or England. Mother's clothes closet began to smell like Mrs. Lewis, and we teased her about that, but she did not mind.

Mrs. Lewis once brought over a litter of baby kittens, hoping Mother would adopt one or two. But Mother explained that our family could not afford to feed a cat, which shocked Mrs. Lewis. After that, she took an increased interest in Mother and in what might happen to her seven children as we grew up. She was wealthy, kind, and a Presbyterian, and she seemed determined to make our lives better.

BLOOD PUDDING

Mrs. Lewis's husband owned a hardware store over in Rulandville. Years before, due to his uncontrolled drinking of whiskey, Mr. Lewis had almost lost his store. When Mrs. Lewis threatened to divorce him and move out with their three children, her husband stopped drinking. He turned his life around and saved his hardware business. Now he had three separate stores in Pittsburgh suburbs. He and Mrs. Lewis had become active in the local temperance society, which often met at the new Rulandville Presbyterian Church.

Mrs. Lewis was thrilled about the coming Prohibition law. She loved to celebrate the merits of teetotalism. She felt the new amendment to the Constitution would surely foster sobriety and improve lives for everyone across the nation. Her husband was a walking example of what strict abstention could achieve. They had sent their children to private boarding schools, and now the two boys were attending Princeton and planning their professional careers in law and medicine. Their daughter boarded at the Baldwin School in Philadelphia and had plans to spend a semester at the American Academy in Florence, Italy.

Mother confided to Mrs. Lewis that a few years before, Jumbo had lapsed horribly, lost his job at the Etna sheet metal plant, and then ran off to Florida for several months with one of the company's secretaries.

She told Mrs. Lewis how we had to forfeit the Ripple Brook Gardens farm, but that, thanks to the wonderful Father Fernando, we had landed in Rehoboth. Providence or the influence of the Black Madonna, or some kind of divine intervention had allowed us to start anew. We were struggling, but with her laundry business and Max's earnings at the Texaco and Vera's new part-time job helping out afternoons and weekends at the company store with Mr. MacAdoo, we were getting by.

Several times Mrs. Lewis had mentioned to Mother that she had heard rumors about a house on Robert Street that sold home-made liquor, specifically vodka. At first, Mother was too ashamed to admit the truth, but eventually she came around to confessing to Mrs. Lewis that, yes, Jumbo had sold vodka to help boost us out of debt, but that now that we had paid off the bulk of our burden, he would stop selling alcohol.

During that particular visit, I was sitting in the kitchen, minding my two little brothers, so I could eavesdrop on the conversation out in the parlor. This was the first I had heard that we were opting out of the vodka business, and I was surprised and relieved to hear the news.

"Just in time." Mrs. Lewis smiled. "He could go to jail, or worse if the authorities found out. They might even want to throw him and your whole family out of the country."

"Ignaz has paid close attention to the newspaper stories about Prohibition. He said it was time to stop. So that is what we are doing."

There was a pause in the conversation, during which the two women sipped tea. I waited silently.

"And he never drank any of it?" Mrs. Lewis wondered.

"Never."

"Are you sure?"

"He pledged not, and he never did. Never."

"Just like my husband, Charles. Not easy for our men to stop, but they are so proud of themselves when they do, don't you think?"

"Yes, very proud. Me also."

"So do you have any of the vodka still left in the house?"

"No."

"That's good news, Eva. Just so you know, scientific studies have shown that most serious drinkers find it impossible to resist indulging when alcohol is on the premises."

"There's no alcohol here."

"How about the equipment? I believe they call it a still? The new law says you can go to jail if you possess a still."

"Yes."

"What about it? I presume he destroyed it."

"Yes."

"Whew! You certainly avoided a disastrous tragedy, didn't you, Eva?"

Again, Mother's response surprised me. I knew that two separate cars from Pittsburgh had stopped at our house that same morning, and Mother had sold each six bottles of Jumbo's latest batch of Kasper's Tonic. Of course, the key fact Mother was reporting was true, that as far as any of us knew, Jumbo had not started drinking again. But I knew for sure we had plenty of inventory on hand.

About an hour after Mrs. Lewis had left, Jumbo came home from the mine. As usual, he dropped his boots and his filthy work clothes on the back porch and walked through the house in his underwear to go upstairs and wash. As he passed through the parlor, Mother said she wanted to talk to him after he had taken a bath.

Jumbo stopped and sniffed. "That Lewis lady?"

"Yes. That's what I want to talk to you about."

"What? Another lecture?"

"It was mostly about the new law, the amendment to the Constitution. Mrs. Lewis said if somebody finds your equipment, you could go to jail or be thrown out of the country back to Poland."

"Maybe Poland would be a better place to live. They don't have anybody named Mrs. Lewis there."

"Don't talk foolishness, Ignaz."

"Foolishness is what I call Prohibition."

"Go up and clean yourself off. We can talk about this later."

The next week, when customers arrived to buy vodka, Mother informed them that we would soon stop selling it. This would be their last order. After a month had passed, the cars stopped pulling up to our house, and Jumbo wondered why business had declined so abruptly.

"It's that damn Mrs. Lewis, isn't it? She's a bad influence, Eva."

"I don't want you going to jail or being sent back to Poland."

"So, the business is closed?"

"I think you should destroy your equipment and get rid of all that extra vodka. You won't be selling it, and I don't want you feeling the temptation to drink it yourself."

"You want me to pour it all out?"

"The sooner, the better. It's poison to you and us!"

"I've been sober. You know that. And I will stay sober. It has not been easy, but I've done it. And think of the money we have made!"

"Mrs. Lewis's husband gave up whiskey completely, and he saved his hardware store and his family, and he put his money in the bank and bought stocks, and now they are all very happy. And they are rich."

"But I already did that. I stopped drinking."

"So, it should not be hard for you to pour out all those bottles. Mrs. Lewis says that there are scientific studies which say having alcohol around is too great a temptation for anybody with a drinking problem."

"We're going to miss the added income. And I no longer have a drinking problem."

"Ignaz?"

"Have I been drinking?"

"Not lately."

"That's all you can say?"

"Ignaz! If Henrietta Lewis heard about a house on Robert Street where alcohol is sold, then it's likely that many other people know about it, not just our customers. Before the authorities come and pour out the vodka, wreck your equipment, and haul you off to jail or deport you, you must pour it all out. The risk is too great. You should start by telling Mr. Curry that you don't want any more of his potatoes or barley."

"Mrs. Lewis should mind her own business."

"She is concerned about us. She's a kind person."

"I don't want her in this house again. Tell her you won't do her laundry anymore."

"I will not do that."

"Tell her to find somebody else to wash her clothes and listen to her sermons."

"I have no choice, Ignaz. No choice at all. Neither do you!"

As far as I could tell, the topic of vodka sales was not brought up again for several weeks. No customers came to the house, and no vodka was sold. And Mr. Curry stopped delivering the ingredients.

Nor did Jumbo pour out his large inventory or destroy his still. Mother had not given him a deadline for doing it, so he apparently felt no need to take action that would mean capitulating to her nosy customer, a Presbyterian busybody with stinky perfume. Still, the matter was palpably present, and none of us wanted to disturb the silence about it for fear of provoking another confrontation between Mother and Jumbo.

At the dinner table, we steered clear of the vodka topic. When Max showed up for a meal, he bragged about how free he felt working at the gas station and zooming around on his Harley, and how girls he met at the Texaco loved to go for rides with him, sometimes in the sidecar, sometimes not.

Vera brought us up-to-date on her new job at the company store and about how kind and caring Mr. MacAdoo was to all the customers and to her. She really liked working there, and it felt good to earn money and help the family. Lucy talked about who she hoped would be her teacher when school started again at Rehoboth Elementary. I talked about Tom Swift and Zorro and Rose and Mary, but nobody except Ziggy showed any interest. We all tried to find some excuse to keep conversations going without ever allowing our homemade vodka family business to come up for discussion. We kept our mouths shut about it, because we knew Jumbo would bring up the subject when he was ready.

One afternoon in late August, Ziggy and I walked the cows home. We were slow getting back, because after our swim, while I read to Ziggy under a large oak tree at the edge of the pasture, we both fell asleep. In the hour or more we were dozing, Rose and Mary had wandered down to the far end of the pasture, and we had to find them and lead them back home.

When we brought the cows in, we saw Jumbo's bicycle lying outside the shed. There was no noise coming from the workshop side of the shed, so we peeked in and saw the rug pulled back and the trapdoor flung open. The open padlock dangled on the latch hook. We entered the shed and looked down into the pit. On the concrete floor, Jumbo lay motionless beside the still.

Ziggy shouted, "He's dead!" and ran into the kitchen to find Mother.

I climbed down into the pit and saw four empty vodka bottles, set neatly in a row near Jumbo's right hand. He was snoring deeply, and his nose was puffed up and bruised and bleeding from both nostrils.

Mother rushed into the shed with Ziggy. She climbed down beside me and surveyed Jumbo's bruised face and his limp body.

Then she nodded and whispered, "Leave him here, but let's take all the vodka up and pour it out before he wakes up."

"Is he going to die?" Ziggy asked.

"Not today," she said, a wince in her brow. "Not today."

"Mrs. Lewis was right, wasn't she, Mother?" I whispered.

"Yes. Let's get to work!"

32

Blood Blisters

I had hoped that in September I would be allowed to start school at Rehoboth Elementary, but Mother told me she still needed me at home. She had not followed through with Miss Bainbridge, the well-intentioned social worker, who said she would find a school for Ziggy. Then Mother heard that Miss Bainbridge had married and moved away to Cleveland. No replacement had yet been named. That meant no special school for Ziggy, and he was greatly relieved not to have to go somewhere strange.

On the first day of classes, Mother took Ziggy up to Rehoboth Elementary again. Later that day, four nasty boys chased him home, taunting him and shouting, "Ziggy piggy! Ziggy piggy!" His back had bloody ripples welling up through his shirt around his shoulder blades, where the boys had lashed him mercilessly with thornbush switches. The next day, Mother received a note from the principal, explaining that Ziggy had misbehaved and that he was never to enter the school again.

With Ziggy still home, I would have to stay home too. Now that Vera was helping out at the company store after school, Mother needed me more than ever. Lucy was thirteen now, entering eighth grade, and I was worried she would stop tutoring me after school. But she was committed to helping me with my studies, and she gave me assignments every day, some in American history, geography, as well as grammar and diagraming of sentences. I looked forward to our sessions at the kitchen table every day, and I know Mother was grateful for Lucy's efforts.

Mother had lost her interest in improving her English. Though she listened in to some of my tutorials with Lucy, she no longer participated actively. In fact, since Jumbo's vodka binge, when we found him bruised and unconscious down in the shed pit, Mother had seemed weary of many things, not just learning the details of English grammar.

Something had changed. That day, while Jumbo was still passed out for several hours in the shed pit, we had poured his inventory out in the kitchen sink and then loaded the dozens of empty bottles into the truck and thrown them away at the town dump. Jumbo had woken up later that night, still drunk. Somehow, he had made it to the mine the next morning on his bicycle and worked a full shift.

When he came home from work that afternoon, he and Mother fought. Ziggy and I arrived with the cows and found Mother weeping in her bed. She had bruises across her cheeks and purple blood blisters on her forearms where his hands had squeezed her. You could make out the outlines of his fingertips just above her wrists. I remember being afraid to touch her where Jumbo's thumbs had made the purple ovals.

Vera prepared dinner that night, and Mother retreated to her bed. Jumbo had taken the truck and didn't say where he was going. When I went into her room and asked her where he was, she sighed and said she didn't care where he was going. She wished he would go to Florida again and never come back. Somehow, we would all get along without Jumbo, so none of us should worry, she said.

Lucy looked after Kazzy and Blizzard that evening. Ziggy and I sat with Mother in her bedroom for several hours. Vera cooked spaghetti for us. We sat silent in the kitchen as we ate. We didn't know if Jumbo would come back, but he did. We heard the truck pull up in front of the house, and Jumbo strode in the front door. He was smoking a cigar and smelled of red wine. He put his fingers into the spaghetti bowl and pulled out the remainder of the noodles, lifting them high and sucking them into his mouth then licking his mustache.

"Sorry, I'm late," he said. "Had drinks with my buddies. I'm going to bed."

A week later, I heard Mother talking with Mrs. Lewis over tea about what options she might have. Mrs. Lewis said the next time Jumbo hit her, she must notify the police.

This set off in Mother's mind the bitter fear we all had that at any time, if we broke the law, we could be sent back to Poland. Not just Jumbo, but the lot of us. Mother said she would have to think about what she could do.

"Don't wait till he hits you again before you take action," Mrs. Lewis warned. "That man is so strong he could kill you with one hard punch. Then what will happen to all your children? Can you imagine what their lives would be if you weren't around?"

One night I heard Jumbo apologize to Mother. He was not drunk, and it was a lush Indian summer evening. They were sitting together in the moonlight on the porch swing, and I saw them kiss. The next day, the tension returned.

Mother seemed preoccupied, resigned, sometimes given to tears. On certain days, she seemed vague, almost in a daze, and in a way that none of us had ever seen. Previously, Ziggy and I had always found ways to cheer her up. And Kazzy was beginning to clown around a little, which was amusing. Even Blizzard seemed to be developing a bit of a devilish, but charming, personality.

I will never know what Mother really was thinking during those last weeks of her life. I doubt I would have understood if she had told me. All I could really have suspected at my age was that she was unhappy, and maybe she was giving up. And I don't think she would have wanted us to know that.

I would have done anything to help her. Whatever she asked, I was ready to do.

Slippery Elm

On that chilly November morning, Mother was too sick to get out of bed. Vera and Lucy made pancakes. After Jumbo had left for the mine, the girls considered staying home from school. But Mother heard them talking about it and wandered out into the kitchen in her bathrobe. She shouted at them both to clean up and go.

"You look sick," Vera protested. "We'll stay home and help you."

"You must go to school today. No staying home. I soon will be better. Just a mild flu. That's all."

"You look gray, Mother," Lucy said. "Do you have a fever?"

"Go! You are late already. I will be better in a few minutes. I need time in bed. Go!"

Vera and Lucy did not obey. They started to wash up the breakfast dishes.

Mother came up behind them and pinched their ears hard. She did this when she wanted us to follow orders without further discussion. She rarely resorted to this tactic, which meant she intended to be obeyed. The girls reluctantly gathered their schoolbooks and coats and went out the front door into the brisk and windy morning.

That left Ziggy and me in the kitchen and the two youngest boys in their room upstairs, Kazzy in his playpen and Blizzard in his crib.

The front door had barely shut when Mother opened it. She weakly shouted, "Did you feed the baby?"

Vera and Lucy couldn't hear her, because her voice was so weak. Through the window I saw them hurrying up Robert Street to the road.

It was a cool, dark day. A steady breeze blew down Robert Street, and rain seemed to be on the way. Ziggy and I had already milked the cows, and I did not feel eager to walk Rose and Mary out to the pasture. It would be cold out there in the wind, and Ziggy would not want to sit still outside. Lucy had brought back a new book for us to read from the school library, *King Arthur and His Knights*. But if it rained, the book might be damaged, and I did not want to take it out in Ben Curry's meadow. But we did not want to have Mother pinch our ears for staying in the house.

I saw Mother stumble back into the kitchen and lurch toward the sink. She leaned over it and puked hard, but nothing much came out, only some thin yellow bile. Ziggy went over and put his arm around her waist. Blizzard started bawling upstairs. This stirred up Kazzy.

Mother looked too weak even to climb the stairs, so I filled Blizzard's bottle with some warm milk and took it up to him. That was what he wanted, and when he calmed down, I gave Kaz a cookie to munch on. In a few moments, they both were back asleep.

I came downstairs again and found Mother sitting on the kitchen stool with a moist towel over her face. "Thank you, Taddy," she said.

I sat down beside her. "You've been sick three mornings now, Mother."

"I know what is wrong with me. It will pass."

"Should I run and get the doctor?"

She sighed and then frowned. She looked very worried. "No. I don't need the doctor."

She went back to the sink and washed out her mouth with water. That must have stimulated nausea, because she puked again and headed back toward the bedroom without rinsing the bile down the drain. As she hobbled past me, I saw her eyes roll around, and I thought for sure she would collapse on the floor, but she didn't.

She groped for a handhold on the table. She squinted hard at me, as though she could not see me.

I looked over at Ziggy. He was scared. He was banging his wrists together slowly under the table. We had hardly ever seen Mother sick, except when she was pregnant with Bliz and then almost died when he was born. That time, old Dr. McAllister saved her.

We wanted to help her. I couldn't figure out why she had insisted that the girls go off to school that morning, because they would have been more helpful than Ziggy and me.

I washed the remaining breakfast dishes. Ziggy dried and stacked them.

Ten minutes later, she came back out of the bedroom. "Boys, do you want to help me feel better? You can do me a big favor."

We nodded. We were desperate to make her feel better, and running an errand might help us forget about our fear.

"But you must keep it a secret, and only the three of us will know. Do you promise?"

We nodded again, and we both kissed her.

"People can die from the flu, Mother. I don't want you to die like Dr. McAllister," I said, cuddling her.

She smiled at me, but her eyes looked so very sad and tired. I could see she was really suffering.

"I know exactly what will make me better, and you two boys are the only ones who can help me with that."

I grinned proudly at Ziggy, and he looked pleased that she was asking us to help.

Then Mother startled us. She pulled a carving knife out of a drawer and took a big white dish towel from the shelves beside the sink. She wrapped the knife in the towel. The knives on the rack were strictly off-limits to anybody but the older kids. Now it seemed she was willing to trust us with one. Why?

She took a heavy paper grocery bag and smoothed it out on its side on the table in front of us. With a dark pencil she sketched a rough map of Robert Street and the half dozen other streets that led up toward town. She filled in landmarks like the Episcopal church, the cobbler's shop, the old blacksmith's stable, a couple of empty lots opposite the town park where the bandstand stood, and the Gulf station, whose owner had died of the Spanish flu.

Then she took a red crayon and drew a line from our house to one of the empty lots near the bandstand and the Gulf.

"You see where we are and where I want you to go?"

Ziggy was puzzled, but I knew all the places she had drawn on the map.

"We live here, Mom. Of course, I know all these places."

"There is a field across the road from the Gulf. You know that field?"

"Yes. We play hide-and-seek there sometimes."

Suddenly she stood up, lunged for the sink, and vomited more bile, a deeper green than before. She heaved hard at the sink, and her face was covered in sweat. Ziggy and I waited, very afraid, but she came back and took a couple deep breaths, wiped her mouth on her bathrobe sleeve and pointed at the map again. It was obvious she wanted to make our orders clear.

"Mother, we can't leave you alone."

"Nonsense. We must do this together, and we must do it this morning. I would do it myself, but you see I am too weak."

"Shouldn't I run and get the doctor?"

"No. I already told you I don't need a doctor. Listen to me and do what I tell you."

She looked cross and pointed her finger at us. Ziggy and I nodded. He straightened his shoulders and stood tall like a soldier. We were ready and willing.

"As you walk down the road past the Gulf, there are three big oak trees with leaves still on them." She drew the three oaks for us.

"Sure, Mother," I said.

"Behind those three oak trees, there's a small elm. It's a slippery elm. The leaves are now yellow and rough, like sandpaper. But the inside of the bark is slippery to the touch."

"I know that tree. We used it as the goal when we played hide-and-seek last summer. Remember, Ziggy?"

Ziggy's face twisted up in difficult thought, his mind lost somewhere on the map.

"As I said, I would do this myself, Tad, but I don't have the energy. You're a big boy now. I trust you and Ziggy to do it for me. I don't think I would get far before I would vomit and pass out. I don't want anybody to see me this way. They would rush me to the doctor. But I do not need a doctor, and we must do this today. We must do it this morning."

"Is it for the flu? Does slippery elm cure the flu? Have you taken it before?"

"Yes, I took it once back in Poland, and it worked like magic."

I remember feeling a thrill right there in the kitchen when Mother gave me a very weak smile. There was a rush of pride in my heart that Mother would rely on me to do what was obviously an important job, perhaps a job that she would trust nobody else to do, not even Vera or Lucy or Max. When she finished with our instructions, I kissed her. "We can do it, Mother. We can do it today."

"Take your time, boys, but don't be too long." She went back into her bedroom and closed the door.

Ziggy and I bundled up in our coats and gloves. As we hustled through the chilly wind on our mission, we felt like we were on an adventure. This was much better than walking Rose and Mary to the pasture. This mission involved a long knife.

"This is like we're Zorro, Zig. Are you afraid?"

"Yes."

"Zorro would not be afraid. We have to be brave like him."

The streets were quiet, but the wind was strong. We walked fast. We saw hardly any cars or people on our way.

We easily found the slippery elm tree and snapped off some low twigs and compared the leaf outlines to what Mother had drawn on the paper bag. They were an exact match, yellow and rough. They felt like the sandpaper in Jumbo's workshop, as Mother had predicted.

Then we took the long carving knife from the towel, and as Mother had ordered, we shaved off long slivers of the elm bark from the side of the tree.

I did the first cut. It took some firm pressure with both of my fists to wedge the blade deep enough, but I was careful. Under the bark the wood of the tree had a reddish shade, and it smelled sweet.

She had told us it would. So we knew we were right. She said she knew all about the slippery elm, because the same tree was abundant in the forests of Poland and was a popular medicine for certain types of illness, including the flu. And we both heard her say it had worked like magic for her.

She wanted each sliver of bark to be thinner than my pinky finger and a little less than a foot long, or from my chin to my belly button. I did the first two. Then Ziggy insisted on doing a couple of slices himself. His were longer than mine, but he did a neat job. I told him if we took off too much bark we might kill the tree, so I stopped his slices at two.

We were fairly sure nobody saw us, but we thought, who would care anyway?

When we were done, we wrapped the knife and the shoots of bark back in the towel and stowed them in the grocery bag. Then we headed home. The air seemed even colder and the wind stronger, so we trotted all the way back, taking care that our precious cargo would be as fresh as possible for Mother.

Blizzard and Kazzy were still asleep when we came home, and Mother had cleaned up the kitchen. She looked a little livelier, and she had taken a few sips of tea. She said her stomach felt much better.

"Maybe you don't need this bark medicine?" I said. "Are you going to put it in your tea?"

She waved her hand to dismiss my question and took our bag. She put it on the table and took out the four bark slivers and the twigs with the sandpaper leaves, comparing them to her sketches.

"Excellent," she said. "You boys did a perfect job. Thank you. You have been a wonderful help to me. I will feel better soon. And I will thank you for helping me."

Then I could tell she had another surge of nausea, and for a moment, she put her hands to her head and pressed firmly on her temples, as though she wanted to crush a headache away. I looked at Ziggy, and I could see he was again as scared as I was. She really needed the bark medicine, we thought.

When she was feeling a little better, she laid out the bark shavings on a wooden cutting board and splashed water on them. Then she ran her fingers over them. They were slick.

"Slippery," she said, nodding.

Ziggy and I put our fingers on the bark. It started out gray and rough, but the water made it darker and smooth.

Then Mother lined up the bark strips, picked up the knife, and cut them into thinner slices.

"What's this for, Mother?" I asked. "Are you going to boil them?"

She frowned and rolled the towel around the strips. "Please don't ask. You boys did wonderfully. Now that you brought my medicine, can you take the cows out to the pasture? Just for a couple hours or so? I would like to be alone. The babies and I will be fine."

I glanced out the window and saw that the sky had brightened. Ziggy poked his jaw out proudly and gave me a smile. We had performed our secret mission flawlessly. Zorro would have been pleased.

Then Mother's forehead turned green again. Tears glistened in her eyes.

"Maybe we should stay with you," I offered.

"No. I want to be alone. I packed you each a cheese sandwich for lunch."

"Are you sure you are feeling better, Mother?"

"I will be much better very soon once I take the medicine. Now, go on! Please leave the house. Take the cows away." She spanked our butts lightly to emphasize that it was our time to leave her alone. "You boys have been a big help."

I watched her pick up the towel with the bark slivers in it. She sighed deeply and cleaned the knife and put it back in its drawer. She passed me in the hall and went out into the parlor. She closed her eyes, standing in front of the Black Madonna, and whispered a prayer.

Then she turned and went into her bedroom and closed the door. I thought for a moment that it was too bad we had discarded all the Kasper's Tonic. If it worked for the Spanish flu, maybe it would have been good therapy on her condition this morning.

I have relived my activities on that November day thousands of times and always with painful regret. Ziggy and I had followed her orders in every detail. We figured the sooner she took the medicine we had brought her, the quicker she would feel better. So off we went to spend what otherwise would have seemed a rather typical day shared in the meadow with my brother Ziggy.

Ziggy and I could not have realized that, while we were tending the cows, our lives would change in the worst possible way through the effects of those slivers of slippery elm bark, which we had harvested and delivered so devotedly and efficiently.

I took my harmonica and the cheese sandwiches, and Ziggy brought the cows around front. We decided to forgo reading any King Arthur tales that day, so we left the book on the parlor table.

We followed our usual path down past the two blocks of company houses, into the little clearing at the end of the pavement, through the forest and on into Ben Curry's pasture. We untied the cows and spanked them gently. Slowly they wandered over to the little spring where they always drank, their long tongues lapping around the rocks in the shallow stream. Cows' tongues are pink and three feet long, and they need the whole length to wrap around grass clumps and pull them into their mouths. Ziggy and I were often entertained by watching Rose's and Mary's tongues work the grass in Ben Curry's meadow. When they dipped them into the stream on a chilly day like this to lap up the cold water, they turned purple, a fascinating sight. Ziggy said Rose had the longer tongue, but I thought both their tongues were about the same size. He dared me once to compare them with a ruler, but I told him that would be hard to do and a waste of time anyway. Who really cared which cow had the longer tongue? Still, it was an interesting topic to bring up with Ziggy if I wanted to kill some time by keeping his mind busy, which is what I wanted to do that morning.

I reminded Ziggy that Mother had told us to stay away from the house for a couple of hours. But the wind started blowing hard and cold, and I could see he was unhappy. He started walking back toward the house.

"Do you have to pee?" I asked.

He nodded.

"Pee here. Nobody can see you."

While he was peeing, I took out my harmonica and started to play his favorite song, "Little Red Wing." After he was done, he walked back toward me and started to smile. Then he said he was hungry and wanted to eat his cheese sandwich right away.

I told him to wash his hands in the stream, which he did. I joined him, and while we were kneeling by the water, Ziggy spotted a crawfish in a small isolated pool on the side of the stream. The crawfish entertained him as it scurried among the pebbles. He picked up a twig and poked at it for a while. That kept him distracted briefly, and then he remembered about the sandwiches, and we sat on our usual favorite rocks in the field and ate our lunch early. There was a golden delicious apple tree at the far end of the field, and it still had a few dozen ripe ones waiting for us. So, we picked off a couple for our dessert.

As we were walking back, munching on our apples, Ziggy said he wanted to bring down another apple or two to give Mother, just in case her appetite had improved. So, he went back to the tree, climbed up into the crotch of a low branch and shook one of the higher boughs to make the biggest apples fall. While he was crouching there in the tree with his arm tugging on the branch, half a dozen apples dropped down onto the grass. One of the apples must have landed on a yellow jacket nest, because before we knew it, a swarm of them shot out of the ground and charged toward us. We were doubly surprised, because we hardly ever saw yellow jackets this late in the season.

Ziggy jumped down, and we both dashed off across the field. The yellow jackets followed us with vengeance. Ziggy began to scream in terror, and we separated, so the yellow jackets would have to choose between Ziggy or me.

"Change directions, Zig!" I shouted, and we both started zigzagging over the field to fool the yellow jackets. When Rose and Mary saw us running like crazy, they started to look agitated and moved toward us.

"Turn around! Yellow jackets!" Ziggy shouted to the cows. As he ran, he waved his hands at the cows like a windmill, and they stopped, confused.

After several minutes, the buzzing ceased. Out of breath, we stood stock-still. Then we looked all around and checked our clothes to be sure there were no tiny yellow-striped monsters on us. We checked the cows too.

When the danger was over, Ziggy's eyes lost their panic, and then we started to laugh. Nothing worked up Ziggy as much as wasps or yellow jackets, and we chuckled with relief, part of it laughing at ourselves as we shooed the cows away. We decided to skip going back for more apples. Not today, we said. Maybe tomorrow, when Mother's appetite surely would be better.

I noticed that Ziggy's cheeks were moist with tears. His fear of being stung had caused them. When I wiped his face with my handkerchief, he said, "I'm not a baby, Tad. Am I a baby? Max calls me a baby."

"Not at all, Zig. Kazzy's still almost a baby. And Blizzard is a baby."

"Yeah, Bliz is a baby. But we're not. I'm not."

"No. But nobody, baby or not, likes the feel of a yellow jacket sting."

"Boy, are you right! Nobody! Especially me! Even though I am not a baby."

As we watched the cows wander ahead of us, Ziggy kept repeating the phrase "Nobody likes a yellow jacket sting!"

"And certainly not Blizzard," I added.

"Yeah. Blizzard's a baby. And Kazzy's almost a baby too. And babies don't like yellow jacket stings either."

"No, they don't!"

"Ha ha! No, they don't. Nobody does!"

"Zig, Mother would never send a baby on a mission like we did for her this morning. Hear me?"

"Yes, no baby could do what we did."

We both felt a certain release in our emotions, now that the yellow jacket threat was gone. But after another twenty minutes or so, rain clouds gathered, and we both shivered. The cows had meandered back toward us, as if they wanted to head home too. So, we roped them up and jogged them back through the fence and then up the street.

After we led the cows back into the shed, we went inside the house. Ziggy said he had to poop, and then he wanted to take a nap. The excursion and the excitement had tired him out, but the bathroom came first. I agreed.

I heard Mother moaning in her bed, and I went in to see her.

She held her rosary beads in her fingers and was praying in Polish. Her palms were red, and I saw some blood streaks on the sheets and some red splashes on the floor.

The slivers of slippery elm bark were lying in a line on the dish towel. Four of the slivers were bent crooked, and the one closest to Mother had lots of blood all over it. Mother's wrists were crusted with blood.

Outside, the storm had churned up, and a flood of rain was beating down. Suddenly I felt very alone with Mother.

She said something to me in Polish that I couldn't quite hear, so I went over to her and put my hands on her face. She was sweaty, and her skin felt hot.

"You're not better, Mother. Should I send for a doctor?"

"No doctor, no."

"What can I do, Mother?"

"Can you do me another secret favor?"

"Anything."

"First, take this map outside and set a match to it. Burn it all up. Then look out on the back porch. There's a bucket there under the bench."

I ran outside and burned the map. Then on the porch, I found the bucket. It had a bloody towel covering it. I brought the bucket inside.

"No," she said. "Take it out and bury it. Bury it deep, so the dogs and raccoons don't get at it. Take the slippery elm bark too."

I looked out the window. Most of the thunderclouds had moved onto the east, but the rain was still strong.

"Can it wait?" I asked. "I'm worried about you. I think I should run and get the doctor."

"No! No doctor. Take Jumbo's shovel and go down past where the road ends. Go into the forest. Bury it there."

"What's in the bucket?"

"It's blood pudding. It went bad before I could make it. We have to throw it out. Do what I tell you, please, Tadeusz. Do it now."

Zig was finished in the bathroom and had gone up to the bunkhouse to nap. Bliz and Kaz were slumbering quietly. So, I took the bucket and the elm bark and one of Jumbo's spades, put on my coat again, and went down in the rain and dug a hole in the place Mother had told me.

There was no wind in the woods, and nobody saw me work. I dug a hole almost two feet deep. I was glad Ziggy wasn't with me, because he would be asking a lot of questions I could not answer. I knew that Mother had made up the story about the blood pudding. Mr. MacAdoo at the company store didn't sell it in his butcher's department, and Jumbo would have said something about it if he had purchased some pig's blood somewhere.

What I dumped into the hole was not blood pudding. It was bloody, all right, but it looked like a little lifeless red and purple tadpole. At one end, it had some little purple fins coming out from it. It had a long vein wrapped around it that ended in a soft, lumpy pool of black clots. There was also a separate wad of red jelly that resembled a little sponge, but it was dark red and had fibers in it.

It made me sick to stare into the hole, and I was very worried about Mother. So, I quickly spaded the earth back into the hole and stamped down the mound of dirt till it was level with the ground. I spread pine needles and vines over it, so it looked mostly the same as the area around it.

I was fairly certain no animals would get into it. Jumbo always had said that wild creatures tried to shy away from human odors, so before I left, I pissed in a circle around the little mound to protect it. Then I went over to the spring and cleaned out the bucket and rinsed the blood from the towel, wringing it out half a dozen times.

Mother was unconscious when I returned to the house. Her face was gray and sweaty. I could hear her heart pounding fast. There was much more blood all over the sheets, and some of it was dripping off the bed and onto the floor.

I heard Blizzard and Kazzy screaming upstairs. Ziggy was standing halfway up the stairs with a milk bottle.

"Mother. She looks terrible," I said. "I have to run and fetch the doctor."

Ziggy started to cry in fear, the bottle in his hands. Suddenly I felt paralyzed, not wanting to leave Ziggy in charge of the house with Mother looking worse than she had looked just when Bliz was born.

Then Vera showed up with Lucy, both back early from school. They said the teachers had let them out to attend to Mother.

Vera was horrified. She stuck a thermometer in Mother's mouth, and she did not have to wait long till she pulled it out and read it. She said Mother had a high fever and asked did I know what had happened.

"I better get the doctor," I said. "Mother could die. She has the flu."

Vera and Lucy looked down and saw bloody footprints on the floor. When they raised the covers, we saw blood all over the sheets, soaked into the mattress.

"Run, Tad! Go get the new company doctor. I think his name is Dr. Zankowski! Mother does not have the flu."

"That's what she said she had."

"This is terrible, Taddy. Run fast!"

Mother's Secret

I told Dr. Zankowski and his nurse Sarah that Mother had felt very sick in the morning. She told us she had the flu, and she ordered Ziggy and me to leave her alone and go watch the cows, all of which was true.

I said that when we came back a few hours later with the cows, she looked all sweaty and pale and could hardly talk, except to mumble some prayers with her rosary beads. We saw blood on her sheets, some of it running onto the bedroom floor. Then she closed her eyes and stopped talking and was sleeping so hard, I could not wake her up. I told them nothing about the slippery elm bark or the "blood pudding" I buried with the bark slivers.

I had seen Dr. Zankowski in church a few times. He had moved to Rehoboth six months before and seemed young and nice and always wore a black suit, just like a city doctor. He had taken the place of Dr. McAllister and was from Poland and could speak Russian and German and a little Italian as well as English. We heard that he was doing a great job, and with his language skills, he was immediately popular with the mine and zinc and moly workers and their families. Nobody in our family had ever been to him till now.

Vera had told a neighbor to run to the mine and tell Jumbo about Mother's condition. By the time he arrived home, an ambulance had come to take Mother to St. Agatha's in downtown Pittsburgh. Just before the ambulance pulled away, Jumbo reached into the ambulance and squeezed Mother's ankle through the sheets.

Dr. Zankowski went in the ambulance with Mother. His nurse Sarah waited till Jumbo had showered off all the coal dust and grime and put on his Sunday suit to go to the hospital. Nobody knew where Max was, but we figured he could ride into the hospital on his motorcycle.

I cleaned up fast, put on my Sunday suit, and went in the car with the nurse and Jumbo. Vera and Lucy stayed home with Zig, Kazzy, and Bliz. As Nurse Sarah drove away from Robert Street on our way into Pittsburgh, I remember hoping that Ziggy would not forget to milk the cows. When we passed by the empty lot near the bandstand, where the slippery elm stood, I looked closely at the tree. Zig and I had stripped our slivers from the back side of the tree, not visible from the street. Nobody passing by would ever notice the bark gouges in the back.

And who would think to look, except me? Or Zig.

It seemed that neither Dr. Zankowski nor his nurse felt that I had told the whole truth. When he rushed back from the mine and saw Mother in the ambulance, Jumbo didn't appear to believe me either. But her ghastly appearance was so dreadful, nothing about what was happening seemed believable. Nobody could put the pieces together to explain it.

On that trip to the Pittsburgh hospital in Dr. Zankowski's car, I began to feel a dreadful sensation of falling, which would linger long after that day. It was as though whatever happened around me was a reality separate from the plunge my soul was taking into despair. As courteous and kind as Nurse Sarah was to me in the car, and as patient as Jumbo was trying to be toward me, all I could feel was my soul falling.

And as soon as that sensation possessed me, I knew I must keep it secret from everybody. Mother wanted it that way.

35

"What Do We Say?"

Vera found the black armbands Mother had sewn after Dr. McAllister's death and insisted we all wear them for at least three months, so everybody would know we were in mourning. She and Lucy sewed enough for all of us, plus a few extras in case anybody lost theirs.

She did not insist that Kaz and Bliz wear them, but all the rest of us were required to.

She had quit school to take on the task of trying to keep our household together, beginning with the armbands. She had just started the tenth grade, but now school was permanently over for her. Sophomore year was as far as she ever would go.

For a long time, she had shadowed Mother closely in all the cooking and laundering and house cleaning. She had shopped with Mother for groceries and household items each week. So, she had already acquired many of the practical skills required, even though she was only fifteen.

She had to give up her part-time job at the company store, but Mr. MacAdoo had taken a shine to her and told her he would love to have her continue to work, even for only an hour or two a week. She had made excellent grades in school, and Vera had a particularly quick instinct for figures, which Daddy Mac noticed immediately. He had encouraged her to step into his business office from time to time and familiarize herself with the basic accounting principles required to run the store. One afternoon when I was there, he said,

"Taddy, your brilliant sister takes to numbers like a duck takes to pond water. Never seen anything like it." He said she could whip through a list of hardware or grocery inventory on his new Victor adding machine faster than anyone. "That includes me," he said with a big chubby-cheeked grin.

These skills helped Vera take over Mother's household bookkeeping. Jumbo was impressed when he saw she could keep track of our giant debts and our measly assets on a formal ledger, just like in Mr. MacAdoo's office at the store. Mother had never done that, Jumbo pointed out.

For the first few months, Jumbo did not resort to alcohol for consolation. This surprised us all. But we figured Mother's death had sobered him in a way her scolding and prayers never could. But how long would it last? We were afraid to guess.

He took only one day off from the mine after Mother's burial, and he and Vera straightened out Mother's dresser drawers and her closet, which still smelled like Mrs. Lewis. At fifteen, Vera was almost Mother's size, and so many of Mother's garments fit Vera quite well. Jumbo told her she did not need to move all of Mother's clothes out of the closet. Whenever she wanted to wear a dress, she could step into their bedroom and help herself.

Vera washed and ironed his work clothes every day and cooked our meals. She also led us all down the aisle at Mass on Sunday mornings. People were amazed at how closely Vera resembled Mother in appearance, especially when she wore Mother's dresses. Everybody seemed to think we were doing remarkably well, despite the tragedy, and we followed all our routines as Mother would have wanted us to do.

Jumbo told everybody that Mother had died of hemorrhage from a miscarriage, which was true. Jumbo added that she had a problem with high blood pressure during pregnancy, and the high pressure had made the bleeding unstoppable. Also, there was a blood infection involved.

I remember him shrugging his shoulders and saying, "Three strikes and out," borrowing a baseball phrase that stopped the conversation from going further. The listener usually nodded in sympathy.

BLOOD PUDDING

I recall feeling strange whenever I heard Jumbo using that baseball analogy, which he did often. Every time I heard it, I half imagined Mother in a baseball uniform stepping up to the plate with a bat in her hands, and that impossible thought cheered me up for a moment. Mother had never shown any interest in baseball, and the idea of her playing the sport was laughable. But Jumbo had adopted it, and when they heard it, most people stopped asking questions.

It was hard to know how Blizzard and Kazzy felt after Mother's death. They both would cry out for her, and Vera or Lucy would jump to cuddle them. Max seemed the least affected by her loss, but he was home so little that it was hard to notice. Ziggy cried a lot for a couple months, and I had to give him hugs.

"Did she really die? You saw her die, didn't you?"

"Yes, Zig. I saw her die."

"We helped her die, didn't we?"

"We did what she told us to do. I don't think she wanted to die."

"No. She wouldn't leave us ever."

"We have to get along as if she were still with us. That's our job, Zig. You and me, that's our job."

After a few months, Zig seemed to get used to having Vera cook and launder and run the home, so he appeared to recover from his grief faster than one might expect.

The biggest family problem after Mother died was me. I wished to be with her. I so wanted to take a bus clear across Pittsburgh and see that new cemetery where we had buried her and maybe lie down on the grass or even in the snow by her grave. I asked Jumbo and Max if they would drive me in the truck or on Max's Harley, so we could perhaps put some flowers on her grave. They both asked what that would prove. It would take up half a day to make the trip, and neither of them had that much time to spare. Mother wasn't going anywhere, they both said, and we would have plenty of time to go visit her, maybe in the spring, when the weather warmed up.

Sometimes I would go into Mother's bedroom when nobody was downstairs and look through her closet, touching her garments and inhaling the French perfume still redolent from Mrs. Lewis's garments, several of which Mother never even had a chance to wear. I liked to open the doors in the kitchen cabinets and peek up, just to see the Heinz 57 labels on the jars of ketchup and mustard and think of her. Anything that made me feel close to Mother I would do, almost always when nobody else could see me do it.

Sometimes I would hear Vera singing in the kitchen or see her walking home from the company store with a bag of groceries in her arms, and for a fleeting instant, I would imagine that she was Mother. The feeling that my soul was falling, sinking down from the weight in my heart would lighten for a second. Then I would have a quick pang of anger against Vera for wearing one of Mother's dresses and because she wasn't Mother. And then the falling of my heart would start all over again.

Vera saw how despondent I was at moments like that, and she held me close to her body and bumped her cheek teasingly against my head. She would whisper in my ear that everything would be better, but it wasn't Mother's whisper. Vera did everything she could to comfort me, but it was impossible. I knew it was unfair for me to resent Vera, but there were moments when I couldn't help it. I never told her of my resentment, but I am sure she felt it. I was a challenge for a fifteen-year-old to try to console. But she kept trying.

The only thing I could do to feel truly close to Mother was to go down into the woods to the hidden place where I had emptied that bloody bucket into the earth. I would bend down on my knees and whisper prayers.

I had placed a round piece of shiny blue slate on the ground to mark where I had dug the hole. On another day, I crafted a small cross with birch twigs and twine to put on the spot beside the slate. Then I recalled that Mother had wanted me to bury her blood pudding where nobody would find it, and it didn't make sense to put a cross there and risk detection. People might wonder what the little cross was supposed to mark, even if it were made out of tiny birch sticks.

I thought probably a small round piece of blue slate wouldn't mean much to a stranger walking by; maybe they would figure somebody had buried their cat or dog. I took the little cross home in my pocket and put it under my pillow. Sometimes I would fall asleep holding the cross. Nobody would know about it except Mother and me. That comforted me for a while. Then the little cross disappeared from under my pillow. I suspected Max swiped it, but I never asked him. Why make an issue and stir up trouble? I figured maybe he gave it to one of his girlfriends to butter her up.

Not a week after I put the blue slate disk down, I went back to my secret spot, and the disk had disappeared. Then again, the slate was so smooth and flat and remarkably blue that I assumed somebody had decided to pick it up and use it, perhaps, as a handsome beverage coaster.

I didn't really need a marker to tell me where I had dug the hole, between a couple birch trees and a towering oak and an old maple stump. That became my favorite place to be when I wanted to be alone, or rather when I wanted to be with Mother.

My melancholy became problematic for the others.

"I guess you're the new baby in the family!" Max wisecracked.

"Be a man," Jumbo ordered. "We all lost her, not just you. And you know she would not want you to cry."

"She's not coming back," Vera would pitch in. "You have to face that, Tad. We all miss her, but we have to carry on. You too."

Ziggy knew more than the others. We had always been closely bonded, but now that we felt complicit in Mother's death, our attachment was strained, somehow less chummy. What I did not want to share with Ziggy was that I feared some punishment or retribution would surely come my way and maybe his way too. It went along with the falling feeling that I couldn't stop or control. But I did not want to infect Zig with such fears of something unknown and terrible. I have mentioned how Zig would take a thought and wring it in and out in his mind. So, I kept this guilt and fear of chastisement to myself.

Perhaps going to a priest and confessing would have helped, but I had not yet been confirmed in the church. Confirmation would not happen till I was twelve, and sins committed by children weren't supposed to require confession, Max said. Vera and Lucy said that too. I thought my sin was much bigger than most children's sins, but

I was afraid to go to the priest, because it could also mean blabbing on Mother too.

I had been looking forward to turning twelve, not because of confirmation, but because that was when my legs were supposed to even out. But now, I wasn't as eager to hit twelve, not if it meant coming clean to a priest about Mother's death.

In my worst flashbacks, I would see Mother's blood streaming everywhere. I was back at St. Agatha's Hospital, and I would smell the pus from her deep wounds creeping all over her bedclothes and the chaplain's weird greasy cross of a death blessing on her forehead that then quickly was covered.

In my best dreams, I would be holding on to her as we caromed down the sled track at the farm, hearing her laugh magically as we flew through the snowy night. And sometimes we would be standing by the well on the farm, and she would pump up enough to fill the stainless steel mug we kept chained to the well pipe. She would offer me a sip and then take one herself, and we both would smile with our mouths full of the cold clean spring water and then swallow it.

"Nobody has sweeter water, Taddy," she would say. "This water comes from God, don't you think?"

I never asked Ziggy if he had dreams like mine, or if he felt guilt. Ziggy was compromised mentally. Most of the dreams he told me about involved elephants and lions and frogs, creatures who put on parades or wore silly costumes, he said, innocent adventures like that. No real nightmares like some of mine. At least, he never confessed to nightmares. I usually slept right beside him or beneath him, and the only thing I would hear when he was asleep, besides his snoring, was frequent giggling and the time he said, "Don't tickle me, Taddy. Stop it!"

And as a general principle, there are some things that an idiot should not be told, because idiots do not have the intelligence to process certain issues, for example, the moral consequences of what we did to Mother. I wasn't handling that one at all well myself.

Mother had lied to me when she said slippery elm bark was a cure for the flu. I was blindly obedient. I should have been more suspicious. I remembered the wave of Spanish flu that had killed Dr.

McAllister. Never during that flu epidemic had Mother ever gone out to slice bark from a slippery elm. Never during that entire ugly contagion did I ever hear anyone mention slippery elm bark as a cure for the flu. Kasper's Tonic? Yes. Slippery elm bark? Never.

But recollecting that terrible gray November morning in 1920, as I did compulsively, all I could see was how miserable Mother looked. I had to do exactly what she said to help her.

As the months passed, I was resigned to the fact that something horrible would happen to me. I was falling toward something bad. I hoped it was not as bad as what happened to Mother.

A few times at night when everybody else was asleep in the house, I would light a candle in the parlor and stand before the Black Madonna and whisper prayers to her, the way Mother and Lucy sometimes did. But I found no consolation in the saint's dark face.

If anything, the Black Madonna seemed to confirm my fears. The look in her eyes, as she held the baby Jesus close to her, seemed to mean, "What do we say to a boy who did what you did?"

36

Miss Wilson

Ziggy and I squirmed in a pair of squeaky metal chairs by the window radiator. It was a snowy day outside, but the iron grid beside us was piping hot. From time to time, it released spurts of steam from the escape valve on the bottom pipe. We were in the office of the mine and metal company's new social worker, Miss Wilson. She was younger and skinnier than Miss Bainbridge and prettier, too, with a porcelain-smooth brow and cheeks. But she seemed stiff and possibly mean, until she smiled at me and announced, "Tadeusz must enroll in school immediately."

High on the wall behind her hung a large framed photograph of our dour, straight-faced president, Woodrow Wilson. As I sat there feeling the radiator's heat, I wondered if she might be the president's daughter or maybe a niece. Her lean hands were folded on the desk, and her black hair was pulled up in a tight bun that seemed to stretch her face muscles taut, like the president's flat cheeks up in the picture on the wall. Rimless spectacles on her sloping nose would have completed the family resemblance, but I was glad she didn't wear glasses, because her blue eyes were tender and soft.

Jumbo, wearing his Sunday suit, faced off with Miss Wilson across her desk. He was perched on the edge of a heavy wooden chair. His huge forearms rested on the front of her desk with his fists tucked behind his elbows. He had shaved and doused himself with his cologne before we came over. I was sure Miss Wilson could smell it as she looked curiously at this Polish giant with the meticulously arched mustache and widower's armband.

A pair of manila folders lay on the desk between Jumbo and the social worker. The labels on the covers read, "Malinowski, Z." and "Malinowski, T." I recognized them as the same folders Miss Bainbridge had brought to our house that afternoon when she spoke with Mother. But now they looked slightly thicker.

Jumbo shifted his weight on the chair. He offered her a pleading smile. "But what am I to do with Zygmunt? Tadeusz looks after Zygmunt every day. They watch our cows together."

"Tadeusz is very bright. You must not waste his formative years by making him tend cows."

It was odd to hear both of them pronounce our actual given names. I was sure Zig felt the same way. People rarely said our real names. We both were frightened when we first walked in, but now hearing our formal names called out in this strange overheated office with President Wilson on the wall and a woman who looked like his daughter sitting in front of us seemed to tighten the vise of fear.

It was as though our very identities were under scrutiny, which was the case. And the heat from the radiator was also warming up our chairs. Ziggy and I both were sweating heavily. Miss Wilson was not. We should have slid the chairs away from the heat, but we were too scared to move.

Jumbo darted a quick glance at me and then back at Miss Wilson. I could see he liked her, because she was young and delicate and pretty. He did not like that she had ordered us into her office for an interrogation, but his foreman had told him we all three had to go. So, we did, and here we were, armbands and all.

"My daughters have helped keep Tadeusz up with his studies at home. He reads and writes well and does figures faster than me. And he knows much more about American history than I do. Don't you, Taddy? And what's that book you've been reading to Ziggy?"

"*The Hound of the Baskervilles.*"

Miss Wilson's graceful eyebrows jumped. "Sir Arthur Conan Doyle?"

I wiped some sweat off my forehead with my handkerchief and nodded silently.

Jumbo looked above her. I watched his glance dwell briefly on the president, and I half expected him to ask her if she was related, but he didn't. The resemblance was strong. But that wasn't why we were in her office, I realized. And it would not matter either way.

She picked up my folder and leafed through it. "Tadeusz scored much higher than his age level on all our achievement tests. Your daughters have done a fine job as his coaches. But let us be serious, Mr. Malinowski. Tadeusz needs to have regular classes from trained teachers, not from his sisters."

She waited for Jumbo to respond, but he only squeezed his fists under his elbows and remained silent.

She blinked expectantly for a few seconds then continued, "Of course, as you say, the boy mopes around since his mother died. He's in pain. You can see it clearly on his face. Any boy would pine for months or more under these circumstances, especially a bright and sensitive child like your son. So, you must get him out of your house every day and let him meet and play with other children, not cows or his siblings. He needs to keep his mind active. He should not be obsessing over his mother's death. He may have a shortened leg, but he's hardly handicapped, and he should not be pampered."

Jumbo shrugged his shoulders. "But what am I to do with Zygmunt?"

While they were talking about me, Ziggy had begun to rock back and forth on his chair. His fingers had fidgeted with his armband and squeezed it to a thin black strip. Then his wrists started a repetitive batting together, faster and faster. He breathed with loud grunts as he rocked harder and harder. His jerky groans were louder than the jets of steam shooting from the radiator valve.

Miss Wilson and Jumbo stared mutely at Zig.

Suddenly Zig's wrists stopped beating. He glanced out the window at the snow drifting against the windowpane and stood up. "Me and Taddy we made Mother die. We helped her die. We did it. We helped her die." He started pacing in the room with his wide-based gait, panting very hard and grunting. Again, his wrists, drenched in sweat, slapped together hard.

Miss Wilson watched cautiously. Ziggy wasn't finished.

"We helped her die. Me and Taddy. Helped Mother die!" He chanted the words between grunts. "Zelienople died. Then Mother died. Zelienople then Mother. Died. Died. They died. I loved Zelienople and I loved Mother. And Mother loved Zelienople. And they both died. They both got killed. They got killed."

She whispered to Jumbo, "The boy has a wild imagination, it seems."

Ziggy's brows arched desperately. "Tell her, Taddy. Tell her."

Jumbo frowned. "Sit down, Zig, and shut your mouth right now!"

Ziggy turned to me. I wanted to support him, but I was afraid to agree with him. His eyebrows were cocked up, and his lips twisted tight between his grunts. With his face gnarled up and lathered with sweat as he pounded his wrists, he looked very crazy, even for Zig.

Miss Wilson sighed and smiled. "You see, Mr. Malinowski, it's not at all unusual for children to feel guilt when a parent dies. The textbooks clearly state that children sometimes conjure up things that are obvious fantasies. I wouldn't be surprised if Tadeusz had some of these feelings. Do you, Tadeusz?"

I shot a quick look at Jumbo. My face flushed. "Maybe a few," I said.

Ziggy's eyes started dripping tears. Rivulets of wet snot rolled out his nostrils. "Tell her about the tree bark that morning, Tad! Tell her how we cut the tree bark. Then we brought it back to her. The bark made her bleed, made her bleed. Zelienople lost a lot of blood, and Mother did too. Lot of blood. They got killed."

I went over to Zig and pulled his handkerchief from his pocket. I started to mop his brow and his nose, but he pushed my hands away.

"Don't, Tad. I'll hit you if you do. I'm not a baby. You know I'm not a baby! And I know the truth." His lips curled at me. I could see he felt I had betrayed him.

Jumbo jumped up, shoved me out of the way, and grabbed Ziggy's wrists. "Get back in your chair, Zig. Stop screaming like an idiot! You sit, too, Taddy. Sit!"

While Jumbo cleaned up Ziggy's face and his glasses with the handkerchief, Miss Wilson sat up very straight in her chair and breathed in deeply. It was hard to tell what she actually thought of the three of us. I looked in her expressive eyes for a clue, but I couldn't find one. Since our interview with Miss Bainbridge, I had found out more about social workers. They are given training in how to help people. But how would she possibly deal with us?

It took Zig a long minute to start breathing slowly in the chair beside me.

Jumbo went back to his perch in front of Miss Wilson's desk.

She stood and walked over to us. "Boys, listen to me, please."

Her face, which had been blank an instant before, softened. Her smooth brow wrinkled in a sympathetic frown. "Your father showed me the report from the doctor, who examined your mother's body in the hospital after she died."

I looked up into her eyes and begged silently for forgiveness.

"Boys, the report states it all very clearly. Your mother was pregnant, but she had a miscarriage. She had a tiny baby inside her, but she lost it. And nobody could find it. That's what the doctor reported. That's what happened. She was going to have a baby in several months, but then the baby inside her must have gotten very sick before it was big enough to live. Does that make any sense to you? I know you are very young to hear all this."

"Tad watched Eva die in the hospital," Jumbo said.

"That must have been impossible for you."

"Yes," I said. "It is."

"And you're still sad, aren't you?"

I felt my lips quiver. My shoulders shook hard. Tears filled my eyes and dripped down my cheeks, worse than Ziggy's.

Ziggy snorted. "How did they know the baby was sick? The poor little baby, little baby."

Jumbo glared at Ziggy. "I told you to shut your mouth."

Ziggy ignored him. "We did it, Tad. You know it. We made the tiny baby sick."

Miss Wilson took my hand, leaned down, and then put her arm around my shoulders. She nodded at Ziggy. "I'm sorry, Zygmunt, but the doctor's report said the baby was lost. So, nobody will ever know why the baby was sick. You should not feel guilty. Not at all."

Ziggy was afraid to look over at Jumbo. He clenched his jaw tight and did not speak. His face was again wet with sweat but no tears.

Miss Wilson was soft and smelled faintly of roses. Seated on the warm metal chair, I melted into her embrace and continued to cry. She did not feel at all like Mother. She was bony with almost no flesh on her ribs and back. But she was warm and held me very tenderly to her. I was embarrassed that I had been sweating so much and crying, and her blouse had become moist with my sweat and my tears.

For a while, we all were silent. She was patient. I stopped shuddering. I looked up at her. Her kind smile soothed me. I stood and put my arms around her and embraced her hard. I could tell she wanted to comfort me, not punish me.

"Tadeusz, we're going to send you to school tomorrow morning," she said.

I could feel her chin moving and her voice vibrating on the top of my skull as she spoke, and it tickled me. Her words tickled me too. This was the best news I had heard in a very long time.

"To Rehoboth Elementary?" I asked, not quite believing her.

"Yes. And don't worry about Ziggy. We will find a place for him."

"What place?" Ziggy yelled.

"A nice place."

"Jail? Will you send me to jail? We didn't mean it. Did we, Tad? We got her the bark. That's all we did. We took the knife and got her the bark."

"Don't talk about jail, Ziggy. Your father tells me your family used to live on a farm."

"Our farm. We had vegetables and we had Zelienople. Jumbo had a tavern."

"Really? Well, would you like to live on a farm again?"

"Not a jail?"

"It's not too far from here. Tadeusz can come and visit you. Your father and your sisters too. I have already telephoned to them, and they have a place for you."

"Can Taddy come and stay there with me?"

"No, I'm afraid he can't. Tad will be going to school here in Rehoboth."

Ziggy came over to her for a hug. The two of us latched on to Miss Wilson for a long while.

Jumbo broke the silence. "You boys go home now," he said. "Let me talk to the lady. We must make plans."

Miss Wilson smiled warmly. "Would you boys like to come back and see me another time?"

Ziggy and I nodded. She hugged us again, and then we headed for the door and took our coats off the wall pegs. We both were hot and sweaty, but we knew it would be cold outside.

"Things will be fine," she said. "And someday you will come back and tell me how you are doing, both of you."

"Are you related to President Wilson?" I asked.

Miss Wilson smiled and glanced back at the portrait on the wall. She shook her head. "No. But I admire him greatly."

"I thought I would check," I said. "He looks like he could be your father. And can I have another hug?"

"Yes. One hug for each of you."

We put on our coats and walked out the door of the administration building and down the steps. It had started to darken outside, and the snow was wet, good for packing. As we walked past the parking lot and onto the street, the cool air felt tingly on our wet faces. The street was quiet, and we walked in the silence, enjoying the crunch of the snow under our boots. I thought about my hugs from Miss Wilson.

We were turning the corner onto Robert Street when Ziggy stopped and said, "I'm scared, Taddy. I'm really scared."

"The baby was sick inside her, Zig. Miss Wilson says Mother's tiny little baby was sick inside her. You should stop worrying."

"But I'm still scared. She wants to send me away."

"Are you too scared to make a snowman?"

Zig grinned. "No, never that scared."

"I think we have just enough daylight left to make a good, solid one."

Ziggy picked up his pace. I hustled to keep up with him.

"Max says I will always be a baby. He's wrong, right?"

"You and I, we're both growing up."

"I want to grow up fast," Ziggy shouted. "When I'm grown up, I'm going to hit Max in the nose. Hard. Then he'll know I'm not a baby anymore. He won't call me a baby anymore."

37

Bunnies in the Moonlight

Though I went to bed early that night, I woke up around midnight and could not sleep. I was too excited. It seemed dawn would never break. Finally, before the sun came up and without disturbing Ziggy, I went out to the shed and milked Rose and Mary. I brought the pails with their usual four gallons into the kitchen. For some reason, they did not feel as heavy as they usually did, but I figured maybe I just felt much stronger that morning. Then I bathed and dressed before Jumbo came in to clean up and shave.

I woke up Vera, and she helped me pick out my outfit for my first day in school. She surprised me with an old pair of blue corduroy knickers which Max had outgrown. They were the knickers Mother had bought him at Joseph Horne's the day we saw the *Tarzan* movie. Vera had washed and mended them especially for me to wear on my first day. She gave me long socks that Max had grown out of, so I could tuck up the tops under the knickers cuffs. She told me not to wear the mourning armband, because that might keep other children from talking to me.

Then she let me help her make breakfast. I was disappointed when she reminded me it was Friday, which meant only one day of school that week.

"One day is a start," she said, sounding like Mother.

"It sure is! And I can't wait!"

Then she pinched my ear and said, "You're going to behave today, right? Not like Ziggy did last September."

"Stop!" I said. "That hurts. Mother never pinched us that hard!"

I was not sure of what she meant about Ziggy. I was too thrilled with anticipation to think much about what Ziggy had done last September.

After Jumbo shaved and dressed, he told us that on Saturday morning we would drive the truck clear down past Wheeling, West Virginia, to a town along the Ohio River called Murphy's Forge. Miss Wilson had found a place for Ziggy there. They had a special school and work farm for slow children and teenagers like him.

As Lucy and I left the house, I saw immediately that the snowman Ziggy and I had crafted the afternoon before had been shoved over into the snow. The round head had rolled off intact, and the eyes and mouth, fashioned from nut-size clumps of coal into a charming grin, were now directed upward. His carrot nose angled straight up at the morning sky. The body and base, with coal cubes for buttons, had holes kicked in them. The cutoff broomsticks with mittens had been thrown into the neighbor's yard.

This decapitated and dismembered figure, I presumed, was Ziggy's reaction to the news from Jumbo that Saturday morning we'd be driving him to a place in West Virginia, where he would stay for a long time.

It hurt me to think Zig had destroyed something we had built together. I recalled how he and Mother had once agreed that snow was magic. But my bruised feelings about the snowman were trivial compared to Ziggy's pain at leaving all of us at home. He was going somewhere he had never heard of. It was a giant change for him, and he took his emotions out on the snowman, the last one I would ever make with Zig. No more white magic. Today I was heading up to Rehoboth Elementary, and tomorrow we would ship him down to an institution, which sounded to him like a jail.

On my way to school, I stopped fretting over the mutilated snowman. I knew I would miss Ziggy, but the idea of not having to mind him anymore, coupled with the prospect of meeting my teachers and dozens of children my age at Rehoboth Elementary, put me into a buzz of anticipation. I thought of how proud Mother would have been to see me on my way, at last.

Halfway there, I started giggling out loud, and I told Lucy all about Miss Wilson and how at first she seemed stiff but then was nice. Miss Wilson was true to her word too. Here I was, on my way to school, and tomorrow Ziggy would be on his way to Murphy's Forge, West Virginia. I also told Lucy how Miss Wilson had praised my test scores and how she said Lucy and Vera had done a fine job tutoring me, particularly in geography, in which I had achieved a test score at a seventh-grade level.

Lucy seemed annoyed. She said I had told her all that information at dinner the night before, and asked if I wasn't feeling a little full of myself.

I asked her to forgive me, but I couldn't help it. I had been shackled to Ziggy all my life, and suddenly Miss Wilson had unlocked the door to my future and freed me from being Ziggy's keeper.

I was deeply indebted to Lucy for all she had done for me, but sometimes her selflessness and humility grated on my nerves, especially on a morning when I was feeling the opposite of humble.

I asked her how she felt about the plan to take Ziggy to Murphy's Forge.

She confessed that she, too, would feel relief to have Ziggy out of the house. Mother's death seemed to have unhinged his wilder tendencies, and now that he was bigger and stronger with facial hair that soon would need shaving, he sometimes frightened her. Almost every evening she heard a lot of disgusting noises coming out of our bunkhouse, and the special school in Murphy's Forge was just the place for him, she hoped.

She still heard wisecracks at Rehoboth Elementary about the day when Zig had caused such a fuss in the first-floor lavatory. She warned me I might encounter similar remarks. Among her friends, Ziggy was known as too weird and scary. I was afraid to ask what Ziggy had done to cause such a stir at the school, but I assumed I would learn soon enough.

Lucy said she felt sure Murphy's Forge would be the right step for the whole family, and maybe Mother should have thought about it long ago. Ziggy was a problem, that's all there was to it. She hoped at Murphy's Forge he would learn how to control his impulses.

I hoped that too. Nobody knew better than me about Ziggy's impulses, especially now that he had begun blurting everything about Mother's death out to Jumbo and to Miss Wilson.

That had to stop. We had found Murphy's Forge just in time. But Murphy's Forge was tomorrow, Saturday, for Ziggy.

Today was Friday and for me.

I had made some special preparations. I always noticed that when strangers in public places first saw me walking toward them, they often glanced down at the lower part of my body and then looked up again at my face. The adults would smile politely, but children's eyes would often widen and search me for further flaws. I imagined they were taking a quick inventory, as if maybe I should also be cross-eyed or have a nervous twitch or a rash on my face, or maybe I should also drool, the way Ziggy often did. When they realized there was nothing peculiar about my face or the rest of my body, no obvious defect apart from a tiny shallow scar under my left nostril from Jumbo's razor strop, the children often stared down again at my foot to confirm their first impression about my limp and leave it at that, inventory complete.

This inspection routine was invariable, believe me.

Knowing this pattern, I hoped to prevent it on my first day at school. I had cut half a dozen round patches from an old wool sock and stacked them in the heel of my right shoe to jack up the foot and make my stride less uneven. The knickers were a bit baggy and fell down about midcalf level, so it might be hard for people to observe the difference in the thickness of my calves.

"Notice anything different about me?" I asked Lucy as we approached the school.

"No," Lucy said, "except you are full of yourself today. That sort of attitude will make a very bad impression on your first day. Be careful, Taddy. Be humble and nice."

Rehoboth Elementary was a three-story structure, built with a standard institutional design for a public school and with the same orange bricks the company had used for its administration building near the mine entrance. In fact, the two buildings could have been twins.

They used the same bricks for the power plant, the company store, some of the workers' houses, and for the town fire station and police department. Choosing that color was wise, because over the years the fine orange soot that wafted from the zinc plant smokestacks, a constant nuisance to remove from other buildings and houses in town, had settled and blended perfectly with the company-built major structures, including the school. I doubt I was conscious of this coincidence when I was entering the fifth grade just as, within a month of our moving to Rehoboth, we all had stopped noticing the town's acrid air odor.

As Lucy and I climbed up the steps to the school, I took a deep happy breath of that air and felt my heart racing with excitement. We passed between the pair of tall marble columns that marked the main entrance. How often I had seen those columns and dreamed of walking through them! And now it was happening, thanks to the kind and beautiful Miss Wilson.

On our way through the main hall, we passed several children. None of them pointed or smirked at me, so I was hopeful that my heel booster pads were working.

First, we went to the principal's office and filled out forms. This took longer than we had expected, and I knew it would make Lucy late for her first class. But she helped me with everything very patiently, just as Mother would have done, and signed her name for Jumbo on the last line.

"Down the hall and around the corner. Miss Beck is expecting you," said the principal's secretary. Lucy took me to Miss Beck's room, opened the door, and pushed me in.

I walked slowly to Miss Beck's desk, feeling eighteen pairs of eyes sinking and rising at me in synchrony with the teacher's. Miss Beck was a stocky woman, a maiden lady with wide shoulders and hips and steel gray hair parted in the middle and woven peculiarly in thick braids like earmuffs on either side. I had never seen a woman's hairdo like hers, but I realized that at my new school I should see new things. That was school. I was here to see and learn.

Miss Beck's smile was gracious as she stepped down from the platform where her desk was perched. She took my hand. "Class, this is Tad Malinowski," she said. "Please stand and welcome Tad."

The eighteen children stood at once at their desks and chanted in loud unison, "Welcome, Tad!" as if rehearsed. Then they all stared at me. My hands trembled, and I felt the blood rush into my face. I was much relieved when Miss Beck told them all to sit down.

"Tad, please go to the back row on the right. You'll find a free desk with some books on it. That's your place, and those are your books. Welcome to fifth grade. The nurse will be in to check you for lice in a few minutes. Right now, we're discussing the geography of South America."

I walked carefully toward my desk, while Miss Beck pointed to a huge roll-down map of South America hanging in front of the blackboard.

"Lice?" I asked.

A few children giggled.

"Yes, there was an outbreak last week. We just want to make sure you're clean."

"I took a bath this morning."

"Excellent. You look very clean. And we've heard you're very bright."

I turned and nodded to her. "I have a bad leg, but it will get better before I'm twelve."

"Wonderful! I'm sure it will. Tad, I don't want to put you on the spot on your first day in class, but do you by chance know the capital of Venezuela?"

I took a hasty glance at the map.

"Caracas?"

"Well, yes, indeed. How did you know that?"

"There's a star up there on the map. That usually means the city is the capital."

My cheeks burned as I sat down. Lucy had drilled me on knowing the capitals of countries, and she knew Miss Beck was a geography fan and a stickler for knowing capitals. You might call that cheating, but I considered it simply being prepared. In any case, I had made a good impression with Miss Beck, and I hoped it didn't look like I was showing off by giving the correct answer. I did not want to seem too full of myself, as Lucy had warned.

The nurse arrived in a white uniform and shoes and hat. She wore white gloves and sat me down to inspect my hair. She had a flashlight, tweezers, a fine-tooth comb, and a magnifying glass. She tickled my scalp with her instruments for several minutes, while the class talked about the major natural resources of South America, most of which Vera had already taught me.

"Clean!" the nurse announced to the class. She patted me on my shoulder and nodded at Miss Beck. Before she departed, she whispered to me, "You have a very stubborn cowlick in front, don't you? Your mother should dab it with Vaseline. Keep it under control."

I did not mind her comment. I was excited. I had been in the classroom for less than ten minutes, and already I had scored two victories: Caracas and no lice.

Right off the bat, I loved school. This was exactly where I should be.

The rest of the morning and afternoon proved equally rewarding. I turned in all correct answers on the multiplication and spelling quizzes, and I hadn't even done the homework assignments.

In the playground at recess, I spoke with several of my classmates. They all seemed friendly and encouraging. One boy named Jasper Slattery with freckles and red hair was said to be smart and the best artist in the class. When Miss Beck gave us a thirty-minute art lesson, Jasper went up to the teacher's easel in front of the class and drew a fancy picture of rabbits dancing under the moon with large curly clouds in the sky that partially covered the face of the moon. Moonbeams shot down on the bunnies from the edges of the clouds, and Jasper filled in the spaces behind the bunnies with vague shadows. When he was done, everyone in the class applauded him. It was a memorable drawing, and I was jealous at once. Jasper seemed to be very advanced. I immediately decided that I wanted Jasper Slattery to be my friend and do art with him.

When Lucy met me after school to walk home together, I told her I couldn't wait for Monday to come so I could go back to school.

The sun was shining brightly and melting much of the snow, so the pavements were clean but moist. Wisps of mist rose from the evaporating snowmelt. I saw them as tiny fairies dancing happily for me in triumph.

Lucy hugged me and gave me a kiss and said, "Do you know how proud Mother would be of you today?"

"All I did was go to school like any other kid."

"But isn't that wonderful?"

"Oh, believe me, Lucy. I know I'm going to learn so much and so fast!"

Once we were home, I showed Ziggy how to draw rabbits dancing under the moonlight with clouds over the face of the moon and shadows behind the bunnies. I told him he might be able to make a good impression at the Murphy's Forge school on the first day if he showed the other boys that trick. But Zig couldn't get the knack of it. He kept trying to draw the whole moon first and then put clouds over it, which didn't work. And he made some of his shadows much bigger than the bunnies themselves.

"Zig, you have to draw the clouds first and then fill in the rim of the moon behind the clouds. And don't draw a little rabbit and then a giant shadow. The moon is almost right on top of them."

I showed him three times, but he just had to put the whole moon down first, and all of his shadows were out of control.

"Keep practicing," I said. "I wish you could meet Jasper Slattery. Maybe he could teach you."

I should not have pressed Ziggy. I could tell he was resentful of my day at school, and he probably did not want to concentrate on what I was demonstrating. He was scared of what tomorrow would bring. And maybe I was also acting a little too full of myself.

He said he had missed me all day. I told him I had missed him, too, but we both really knew it wasn't as true for me as it was for him.

In fact, I had not missed Ziggy even for a second.

I didn't mention the ravaged snowman in front of the house. Most all the remnants had melted in the sun, so it was easy to forget.

Nor did I tell Ziggy what Jasper Slattery had confided to me: that the previous September on Ziggy's first day at school, the janitor had caught Zig in the lavatory teaching a second grader how to play with his dinky. The janitor told Zig's teacher, and she sent him home. Some of the nasty boys in the school heard about it, and decided to punish him with thornbush lashes.

This incident further explained why Ziggy was banished from Rehoboth Elementary forever and why most of the girls in our neighborhood ran away from Zig as soon as they saw him. Such news spreads fast, and the girls' parents likely warned them to steer clear of my brother, the halfwit troublemaker. Who knew what he might do next, they probably whispered.

Thanks to Miss Wilson, the neighborhood girls would not have to fear Ziggy anymore. It was hard for me to imagine Zig as any kind of menace, but that's what Jasper told me. It was four months later, and still people in the school were talking and the older boys were laughing.

I wondered if the other children would view me with suspicion. I was Zig's brother. Telling everyone that he would now be living far away in West Virginia might reassure them and take the taint off me, I hoped. I would confer with Jasper about that. It felt so good to have a new friend.

Again, I felt very grateful to Miss Wilson for intervening with our family and insisting that I stop tending cows. I loved school immediately, and she had made it possible.

I questioned myself later that night why I should be having such negative and selfish thoughts about Ziggy. I knew him as a goofy but wonderful brother with a gold heart, someone I dearly loved despite his shortcomings. And the stuff about Zig playing with his dinky did not surprise me much. Ever since Max showed him how, it was something Zig did a lot. But I'm sure a second grader on his first day at school might not see it that way, and the janitor was probably right to call the teacher's attention to it before it started happening regularly.

I realized, too, that Mother's death had changed my feelings about Zig, and not in a good way. With my head on the pillow that night, I tried to keep my mind off the brother snoring above me in the bunk, who minutes before had rolled back and forth, playing intensely and turbulently with his dinky till at last he fell asleep.

I tried to force my thoughts away from Ziggy and on to something new and pleasant. Quickly I envisioned cute bunnies dancing in the moonlight and how I would try to draw them as beautifully as my new friend Jasper.

The bunny gimmick worked. For several minutes before I fell asleep, I didn't think about Ziggy or Mother at all.

Just bunnies in the moonlight, bunnies and their shadows and clouds and the moon. And before I knew it, I was asleep.

See that! My first day at school, and already I had learned something very important and useful.

Belvedere

We were to be at Belvedere, Ziggy's new school and work farm near Murphy's Forge, West Virginia, by ten on Saturday morning. Jumbo had been told they wanted to put Zig through some tests before they formally accepted him.

In our suits, Jumbo and Ziggy and I climbed into the cab of the truck and set off early. The roads were mostly all clear of snow, and there was little traffic. The drive down to Wheeling took an hour. Then we followed the road along the Ohio River further south for another twenty minutes. We arrived at the school at ten sharp.

Vera had baked some lemon cookies and put them in a tin. Jumbo had stowed the tin with a thermos of milk under his seat and told us we could each have a snack if we kept our mouths shut the whole way down to Wheeling. We did. Apart from gnawing on what was left of his fingernails, Ziggy stayed calm. I put my arm around him a few times, and he seemed grateful for that.

Jumbo drove straight through the streets of Wheeling without telling us where we were. Ziggy and I had never been down this way, so we did not know when to ask for the treat under the seat. We had already passed in and out of Wheeling when we saw Belvedere itself set up on a round hill two miles south of the little village of Murphy's Forge and overlooking the river. I suspect Jumbo simply forgot about the cookies, and when Ziggy and I looked out and saw Belvedere and its tall spiked iron fence surrounding the grounds, we forgot about them too.

A uniformed guard swung the front gate open and let us in. Suddenly Ziggy was sweating and drooling profusely. He wiped his hands on his face and mouth and then rubbed his fingers on his suit pant legs to dry them. When he saw the spear-like points on the iron fence, he started to bat his wrists together. I noticed two of his cuticles were slightly bloody, but not dripping, from his nibbles. I offered my handkerchief, but he pushed my hand away.

"West Virginia, Zig," I said. "It's wild down here. They have plenty of bears and bobcats in the woods. Good thing they put that tall fence around the school."

Ziggy's eyes blinked fast. "Bears and bobcats! Maybe lions too. Need a tall fence. Build a tall fence. Build it tall."

"No lions, Zig."

"How do you know, Taddy? You've never been here. You've never been to West Virginia. Max told me they have mountain lions all over the place in West Virginia."

"Even if they do, a mountain lion couldn't jump over that fence. It's very tall."

"And strong. Has to be strong, strong! Tall and strong."

"And pointy."

"Pointy!" Zig echoed.

Jumbo wanted this drop-off mission to go smoothly, so he didn't contradict us. "Bears and bobcats for sure, Zig! I hear the mountain lions around here are tiny. So, I think you're plenty safe."

We pulled up to a three-story Victorian granite mansion with bars on all the ground-floor windows and the word "Belvedere" chiseled in large letters on the overhang of the pillared portico.

Jumbo rolled down his window, jumped out, and pulled Ziggy's suitcase from the back of the truck. "Get out."

"Cookies!" Ziggy demanded. "We didn't eat the cookies. We want our cookies, don't we, Taddy?"

Irritated, Jumbo jerked open the truck door again and pulled out the cookie tin and the thermos from under the driver's seat. He slammed the tin down on Ziggy's lap. Then he leaned over and slapped Ziggy's cheek so hard, that Zig's forehead bumped against my chin. Jumbo glared at Ziggy. "Eat fast, stupid, and get out of the truck. We don't have all day to waste while you eat your damn cookies."

The slap had hit the edge of Zig's lower lip. Immediately a welt rose up at the front part of his cheek. I thought he would cry, but he didn't. His swollen lip quivered, but he did not cry. He opened the tin and pulled out two lemon cookies. When he stuffed them into his mouth, blood leaked off onto his fingers, and I realized he had bit his tongue when Jumbo popped him. Fortunately, Vera had left a dish towel in the tin, and I used it to clean up Zig's hands and face as best I could. The tongue bite wasn't bad. When he kept his mouth shut, you could not see if he was bleeding or not.

"You can eat my cookies, too, Zig," I said.

Jumbo turned his back, slammed the door, and stomped away from us.

After Ziggy had eaten all the cookies and washed them down with a few gulps of milk, I checked him again. His left cheek had two other pink welts. The finger marks wouldn't go away when I rubbed them with the dish towel, but I tried. He had a bruise on the right side of his forehead, where he had bumped my chin, but no more blood came out of his mouth. This was a relief. We wanted him to look as presentable as possible to the Belvedere people.

"Ready now?" I asked.

He nodded, and we jumped out of the truck.

A tall Negro man, also in a uniform, came out of the heavy front door and up to the truck. He took the suitcase. "Mr. Malinowski? Please follow me. Which one of the boys is Zygmunt?"

"He's the taller one. Call him Ziggy."

"Come, Ziggy. Dr. Horvath wants to meet you. He's the head of the school."

"That other one's my other boy, Tad."

"But we're only taking Ziggy, right? Only one boy is staying is what I was told."

"Yes. The taller one."

"Boys? Come along, please."

I pushed Ziggy forward and held his hand as we walked into a high-ceiling receiving room with rich leather chairs and couches. There was a giant stone hearth with a blazing fire and thick Persian rugs on the floor. Over the fireplace hung a large oil portrait of a stocky young man with a full red beard. His arms were folded, and he stood proudly in front of a factory billowing smoke by the river. The oak paneled walls had huge tapestries like the ones Lucy and I had read about that adorned walls of old castles in France. The receiving room also had a giant grandfather clock standing beside the staircase at the far end of the hall. In one corner stood a pair of high oak book-shelves filled with at least a hundred leather-covered volumes. I had never seen such an elegant room. I was glad that Jumbo had insisted we wear our Sunday suits.

The kindly attendant in uniform parked the suitcase beside the grandfather clock and went up the staircase to tell Dr. Horvath of our arrival.

"Gosh, you're lucky, Ziggy," I said. "What a beautiful school!"

"Yes. Beautiful."

"This place makes Rehoboth Elementary look like a pigsty."

Ziggy nodded. "Don't say that. I miss Zelienople."

"Me too."

"She bled like Mother bled. Lot of blood, Taddy."

"I remember. But that was a long time ago."

"I miss Mother. That wasn't long ago."

"I miss her, too, Zig. She would be so proud of you today."

"Do you think?"

"I'm sure of it."

The light in the receiving room was subdued, so Zig's latest facial injuries were not as obvious as they had seemed outside in the truck.

Dr. Horvath stepped down the stairway in a white laboratory coat. He was quite tall and skinny, older than Jumbo, but equally bald. He descended the stairs with stooped shoulders, his hands resting in the side pockets of his coat. His dark eyes were kind, but his face was long, and he had a large jaw with a wide mouth that at first seemed fixed in a scowl.

He stopped at the bottom of the stairs and smiled. "Malinowski. Polish?" he asked with a thick accent, as he shook Jumbo's hand.

"Polish," Jumbo said.

"Dr. Gabor Horvath. I'm Hungarian. Welcome to Belvedere."

The two men eyed each other cautiously. Neither smiled. Ziggy began to bang his wrists.

Finally, Dr. Horvath spoke. "I had a long conversation yesterday with Miss Wilson, the social worker in Rehoboth. Now I would like to take Zygmunt into my office and give him some tests. First, we need to find out what is the level of his intelligence. Will you come with me, please, Zygmunt?"

"Call him Ziggy," I said. "He likes that name."

"Very well, Ziggy, please come with me. By the way, Mr. Malinowski, don't be fooled. It is oddly quiet here today. Usually there is much more activity, but this morning the entire student body went off in buses to the movie theater in Wheeling. They're watching *The Sheik* with Rudolf Valentino. It's supposed to be quite wonderful. All the boys love going to the movies."

"Wow!" I said. "We happen to know a priest who looks just like Rudolf Valentino," I said, "but he moved to Detroit."

Dr. Horvath ignored me. He and Ziggy headed down the hall.

Jumbo and I went over and sat on a couch by the fire. After less than a minute, he went outside to smoke a cigar. I went over to the bookshelves in the corner and pulled out the thinnest book I could find, *The Autobiography of Benjamin Franklin*. Then I took a seat on the couch by the fire, put my feet up and started to read. At around page 7, my mind wandered onto bunnies in the moonlight.

I woke up when Ziggy's hand shook my shoulder.

"I like it here, Tad," he said.

I looked up. Dr. Horvath and Jumbo peered down at me.

"Looks like you might want to stay here at Belvedere, too, young man," said Dr. Horvath.

"Yes, it's very nice here," I said, yawning and sitting up.

"Nice." Ziggy nodded quickly. "And no mountain lions either! Dr. Horvath told me."

Dr. Horvath sat down on a chair and signaled for Ziggy and Jumbo to sit down too. He clasped his hands in front of his chest in prayer position and looked at the three of us with a slow smile. To me, he looked like some of the older priests living in the Rehoboth rectory building, but he was wearing white, whereas all of those priests wore black.

Ziggy was grinning at him. The pink welts on Zig's cheek had faded completely.

"Yes, we had a pleasant talk," Dr. Horvath said. "And I gave Ziggy a few tests, several of which I have invented and published in professional journals myself."

"So, what did you decide?" Jumbo asked. "Can he stay here?"

"I have some good news. Ziggy can stay with us. In fact, we've recently received a federal funding grant that will enable Belvedere to give him a full scholarship. Of course, he will participate in our farmwork program, which brings a significant income to the school. Our students agree the work program offers them a chance to interact cooperatively with their colleagues and exercise their bodies fully every day. Zygmunt assures me he will enjoy the work."

"Ziggy, he has problems finishing jobs," Jumbo said.

"You can be sure we won't let him get away with that! Will we, Ziggy?"

Ziggy laughed. "I'm not a baby, am I, Dr. Horvath? Not anymore."

Dr. Horvath winked at Ziggy and echoed, "No, not anymore. No babies here at Belvedere."

I watched with amazement and growing relief. Dr. Horvath's somber face had changed to a large smile. It seemed that Ziggy's awkward charm had registered with the school's director.

I shot a glance over at Jumbo, who was wiggling the tips of his fingers in his palms, a nervous habit Ziggy sometimes did. I caught myself starting to mimic the same gesture, but I stopped. It was a rare moment when I was in total sympathy with my father. We were both full of hope that Ziggy would be acceptable to Dr. Horvath, and it seemed he was.

"You see, Mr. Malinowski, after going over the tests with Ziggy very carefully, I have concluded that his scores correspond to an intelligence quotient of about 60. That fits him into the category of low moron or high imbecile, depending on whose articles you read. But he is certainly not an idiot!"

Jumbo's eyebrows leaped up his scalp. "Not an idiot? Are you serious?"

"Definitely not," Dr. Horvath affirmed. "Idiots are individuals with IQs below 25. Ziggy's is more than twice that figure."

Jumbo smiled. "Well, that is good news."

"Not an idiot!" Ziggy repeated. "Not an idiot! And not a baby!" He began to rock back and forth, beaming at all three of us.

I patted Zig on the back. "I'm very glad we took you down here."

"More good news. He's fully trainable!" Dr. Horvath insisted. "Now, would you gentlemen like to see our school? I'm happy to give you a tour. After all, Belvedere will be Ziggy's new home. You might want to know how all this came to be. And don't be deceived that it is so peaceful here today. If it were not for Rudolf Valentino, there would be a beehive of young men buzzing around everywhere."

Ziggy jumped up and cut a few awkward twirls in front of the fireplace, beating his wrists together and whispering "Not an idiot!" As we began the tour, he started to swing his arms and strut, similar to Jumbo and Max in church. I had never seen him do that, and yet, I felt he had a right to strut at the good news from Dr. Horvath, an obvious expert on intelligence and other such matters.

Dr. Horvath told us that Belvedere had originally been built as a private estate by the local iron baron, Archibald Murphy, whose portrait hung over the fireplace in the front lobby, but who had perished in his early thirties without an heir. A yachting enthusiast, Murphy was a victim of a terrible tragedy on Lake Erie when, on his honeymoon, a sudden squall capsized his boat *Nereid*. He, his beautiful young bride Rebecca, and four crew members drowned. Murphy's attorneys divided the shares in his three iron foundries along the Ohio, the biggest in Murphy's Forge, among board members. What to do with his personal estate remained problematic.

When the United States mobilized for the war in Europe, the government of West Virginia took Belvedere over by eminent domain and constructed barracks on the grounds. The mansion and its outbuildings then served as a temporary induction center and military academy during the war.

After President Wilson signed the armistice, the West Virginia Department of Public Health acquired the facility and eighty-seven acres of adjacent farmland and turned it into what it now was, "a school for idiotic and feebleminded persons." Two hundred boys came from all over the state, some also from Ohio and Pennsylvania, to be housed and fed in a humane arrangement and, according to the new positive scientific theories and recommendations, trained to serve in a capacity appropriate for their various mental handicaps.

Dr. Horvath walked us through the barracks, each of which accommodated thirty-two boys. The walls were wood shingled, the roofs corrugated sheet metal, similar to the product Jumbo had once helped fabricate at Etna Metals. For all we knew, Jumbo said later, he might have been the guy who put a roof over Ziggy's head.

The dormitories were clean but smelled of body odor and shoe polish. Ziggy was given a bed and a wall locker, and we quickly stowed all his personal clothing and items in a steamer trunk at the end of his new bed. Dr. Horvath said he would receive two sets of denim working clothes later that day. On Monday morning, he would receive a new pair of high-top work boots. He would have all day Sunday to adjust to his new surroundings and to meet his new friends.

Ziggy looked scared but pleased. He lay down on his bed and bounced a few times to test the bedsprings. "Wow!" he said. "Softer than home, Taddy!"

I was surprised not to find any bunk beds in the dormitories. Considering my own personal experience, I was glad nobody at Belvedere would have to be Ziggy's bunkmate.

We wondered when all the other boys would be coming back, and Dr. Horvath advised it would be best if we did not linger at the school. The boys were usually agitated after seeing a movie, he explained, and it was school policy to limit visitors on such occasions. We would have opportunities to meet Zygmunt's new companions the next time we drove down from Rehoboth, but we should definitely notify Dr. Horvath before we planned a future visit.

"The boys get agitated?" Jumbo asked.

"It happens every time," Dr. Horvath explained. "Once they step out of this safe environment, they go a little crazy for a while. If there are strangers around, their behavior becomes all the more unpredictable. And today, it's Rudolf Valentino. You won't want to be around after that film, believe me. Those boys all will be worked up." Dr. Horvath rolled his eyes around twice, a gesture which implied the impending chaos he wanted us to avoid.

Ziggy had rarely been to a movie. Mother and Jumbo had been afraid to take him. But now he was in a school where all the boys went together!

"See, Zig," I added. "Now, you'll be able to go to movies with all your new friends!"

Zig giggled, holding on to his tummy.

"Don't pop your belly button!" I said.

He liked my joke and started laughing louder.

We visited the classroom buildings, the laundry facilities, the horse and cow barns, the football and baseball fields. Finally, we skirted the edge of the rolling land devoted to crops and grazing. All work was done using horse-drawn or handheld implements, Dr. Horvath noted. It was risky to let these boys use any farm machinery. The major cash crops were potatoes, yams, cabbage, carrots, winter wheat, and hay, though they also had large vegetable gardens to feed the school in the warm months.

At the end of the tour, we thanked Dr. Horvath. Jumbo signed the papers to enroll Ziggy, and we found out he could stay there as long as he wanted.

"Even in the summer?" Jumbo asked.

"Oh, we will need Ziggy especially in the summer," Dr. Horvath said. "That's when our farm is busiest. And all the boys love it, especially on hot days after work, when they all run over to the large pond at the edge of the property to take a refreshing dip."

"Sounds wonderful!" Ziggy shouted.

Jumbo's brow relaxed. He surely felt the same profound relief I was feeling. It seemed that Ziggy now had a future in a safe and happy place with boys similar to himself.

"Here, young man," Dr. Horvath said, as we were heading out the front door. He handed me the volume of Benjamin Franklin, which I had left lying on the couch by the fireplace. "I saw you took an interest in this book. Please keep it and read it. Bring it back next time you come to visit your brother."

I gripped the volume tightly and shook the doctor's bony hand. Ziggy was beaming, and I was feeling happier than I had been since Mother died.

Jumbo hugged Ziggy hard and kissed him on the forehead.

Then it was my turn. We had a long embrace.

"You're safe here, Zig," I said. "We love you."

He put his lips to my ear and whispered, "Tell Max I'm not an idiot!"

On the way out through the front gate, the spears on the tips of the iron fence did not look as fierce as they did on the way in. Our truck rolled away from Belvedere, and I looked back and saw Ziggy and Dr. Horvath waving at us. I waved back out the truck rear window.

No, we weren't leaving him in a jail. And Ziggy wasn't, despite the fears he expressed to Miss Wilson, being punished for what we had done to help Mother die.

Those pointed iron bars were protecting him against the bobcats and bears. He didn't have to worry. Possibly for the first time in my life, I almost envied Zig.

Jumbo drove north silently. Just outside of Wheeling, he lit up a cigar. As he rolled down the window and tossed the match out, he glanced at me. "Hungarians," he grunted. "Never trust them."

"But Dr. Horvath is nice. I like him. He lent me this book about Benjamin Franklin."

"Sneaky people are nice. Let's not talk about it. Have you ever been to Ohio, Tad?"

"No. You know I haven't."

"How about I take you for a ride across the Ohio River? Would you like that? I want to say hello to a friend up in Hunterton. It's only half an hour up the road on the Ohio side."

Hunterton

We drove north up through Wheeling and then took a left turn at a bridge over the Ohio. We continued north along the riverbank for a dozen miles and then stopped for a late lunch at a roadside diner.

Jumbo and I were both in fabulous moods, as we munched on our ham sandwiches and potato chips in a booth by the window. We looked out across the dark flowing river toward the banks of white snow layered thick in the forests in West Virginia. I was thirsty, so I had a second mug of root beer. It was frosty and foamy and delicious, and I guzzled it eagerly. As I ran my tongue over my lips to taste the last sweet drops of the root beer, I decided at that moment that I really liked Ohio, even though I had been in the state for only half an hour. As Jumbo's eyes followed a coal barge down the river, I saw his normally tense cheeks soften and relax. Now that we had apparently, almost magically, solved a major problem for our family in depositing Ziggy at a place where he seemed secure and happy, we both felt giddy, miraculously relieved.

I wondered if this day might signal a change in our fortunes.

Yes, Mother was dead, but we had to move on to our new and different lives. We had not worn our armbands to Belvedere that morning, and I somehow felt better without it. Maybe we shouldn't wear them anymore. I hoped Vera would consent.

After all, just as we had crossed the Ohio River into a new state, perhaps we could move into a new realm of tranquility and positive thinking and action, which had already begun yesterday with my enrollment at Rehoboth Elementary. As I chewed on my last potato chip, I toyed with the idea that I could actually love the man staring out at the coal barge, the bald, mustached creature sitting across from me. Could I feel genuine affection for him, stop resenting him so much?

And not only here in Ohio, but also at home in Pennsylvania?

When I let out a loud burp, he looked over at me and grinned, baring that gleaming gold incisor for all it was worth. Then he put his palms together and started beating his wrists together, the way Ziggy always did. He looked comical, rolling his eyes and moving his head back and forth spastically.

I smiled back. "Yeah, poor Ziggy!"

When I started to beat my wrists together, Jumbo's smile vanished.

"Can that!" he ordered. He looked around the diner to see if anybody had noticed our bizarre gestures. I had not sat in many restaurants till then, but I realized that maybe imitating a brother, who was no longer considered by the authorities as an official idiot but whose odd mannerisms appeared idiotic, might make strangers uneasy. I looked around, too, but none of the other restaurant customers seemed to be paying any attention to us. I so enjoyed sharing that short moment of mirth with my father, even though it was at Zig's expense.

"How do you feel?" Jumbo asked, after we both leaned back in the booth.

I sat silent for a few seconds and peered at him carefully. I could not recall Jumbo asking me how I felt or almost anything else about me.

"I guess I feel pretty good," I said. "I will miss Ziggy, but he seems safe where he is."

"Feel like letting off a little steam?" he asked.

"Yes, I guess that's what I feel like."

"Ziggy is as okay as Ziggy ever will be. That's clear. I don't trust Dr. Horvath, but he might be good to his word. What do we have to lose? So, let's forget about Ziggy and Belvedere for a while, Taddy. I want to let off some steam!"

Jumbo waved a two-dollar bill at the waitress and told her to keep the change for a tip, almost half the charge for the meal. Such unusual generosity from my father shocked me.

After lunch, we piled back in the truck. As we drove further north toward Hunterton, I asked Jumbo to sing some of his Polish songs to me. "Sing the song about the Polish falcons!"

He needed no further prompting. With his fists clutching the steering wheel, Jumbo suddenly belted out *"Hej, Sokoly!"* He continued for numerous verses along a dozen miles up the river. I joined him on the choruses, and he seemed to like my harmonizing. I wished I had brought my harmonica along, but I had no idea when we left Rehoboth that I would have a need for it. That seemed like a long time ago, back in the Ziggy days.

Here we were now in Ohio, my new favorite state, and I was singing with my father! Ohio seemed great.

Near the outskirts of Hunterton we saw a large steel mill across the river. I counted eleven smokestacks towering up above the slanted factory roofs, and each was puffing out thick billows of variably colored smoke, from dark brown to snow white, and with several orange shades in between. This was clearly a bigger plant than what we had in Rehoboth with an entirely different product, but there was a similar-sized lumpy field of slag piles extending along the riverbank for nearly a mile.

I saw that Hunterton had its own mill, too, with even larger smokestacks and factory buildings, located between the road and the river and all separated off with high barbed wire paneled fences. As we passed, I mused to myself, why such tall fences with barbed wire? Were thieves really going to go in there and steal the steel?

The giddy relief I felt since arriving in Ohio made me whisper to myself, "Stealing steel. Stealing steel."

"What did you say?" Jumbo asked, cracking half a smile. "Something about stealing steel?"

"Guess I'm just letting off some steam," I said. "Ha ha!"

Jumbo pointed at the factory. "Like all those smokestacks?"

I laughed again and nodded, surprised that Jumbo was enjoying himself in my company.

"You know, I think I like Ohio," I said.

"I do, too, Taddy, old boy!"

I felt tempted just then to call him Dad, but I didn't.

We drove through the center of the town, which was five blocks up from the river. The Hunterton air had a slight stink to it, but not like Rehoboth. There were plenty of stores, almost every kind. The busy streets were paved with cobblestones intersected with streetcar rails. The horse-drawn streetcars looked like they would be fun to ride.

We passed three movie theaters, triple what we had in Rehoboth. I noticed there were several haberdasheries, hardware stores, two five-and-dimes, multiple restaurants, and what looked like taverns, a jewelry store, a couple of department stores, several bakeries, two pharmacies, a blacksmith, a Texaco, a Shell, a Sohio, a Chevrolet dealership, and a large elementary school named after President Ulysses S. Grant. A few blocks up the hill, but still very close to the center of town, stood a coal tipple, similar to the tipple by the mine in Rehoboth.

All in all, I counted eight churches that we passed near the outer parts of the town. Around them stood neighborhoods with stately houses back toward the river, each with a lovely garden and an expansive view across the river of the snow-covered West Virginia cliffs. Looking in the other direction, higher up on the Ohio hills west of the river, were more houses and more churches.

It seemed the city of Hunterton had spread up and west as it grew, and one of the main streets stretched straight westward, probably toward suburban churches and houses. Everybody on the busy sidewalks looked well-dressed, the ladies in hats and woolen coats, and the older men, especially, wore rich-looking suits of thickly woven wool and wide-brimmed fedoras.

To me, everything about the town seemed appealing. It was not huge like Pittsburgh or tiny like Rehoboth. It was just the right size for a town that was almost a city, and within ten minutes of driving around, I was no longer aware of the pollution in the air.

We stopped at a corner to let some cars pass, and Jumbo pulled his wallet out of his breast pocket and fingered through a sizable wad of bills inside it. He tugged out a small square of paper that had an address scrawled on it and then put his wallet back in his coat.

After asking directions from a friendly couple walking on the sidewalk, we pulled onto Water Street, which had houses on both sides that were not as nice as what we had seen further up in the richer neighborhoods. Jumbo parked the truck in front of a modest-looking house with a broad porch.

"Wait here," he said. "I shouldn't be long. If you get bored, read your book."

I had a strange wish. Perhaps Jumbo was thinking of moving all of us to this Ohio town, which was at least ten times bigger than Rehoboth. Maybe he was going into this house to inquire about employment. Or maybe he went in to ask about a house to rent.

I remembered our move from Ripple Brook Gardens to Rehoboth, and I saw no reason why we couldn't move now to Hunterton. Moving the Beckwith would be a burden, but I knew Jumbo could find a way to do it, once it was paid off.

While I looked up and down Water Street, I saw a long fancy car, possibly a Maxwell sedan, pull up and park on the other side of the street. An elegantly dressed man stepped out of the car and walked up the steps of the house directly across the street from the one Jumbo had entered.

A few minutes later, a man walked out of the house where Jumbo was. A woman inside waved to him from the window. Gradually I noticed this seemed to be happening in several houses on the block, and I soon realized I was getting bored watching men step in and out of doors, so I took Jumbo's suggestion and opened my book.

I discovered that I had several things in common with young Ben Franklin, beginning with the two of us having large families. Actually, there were even more children in his family than in mine. He wrote that he could remember thirteen kids sitting around the dinner table, all his brothers and sisters. He helped his father make candles and soap, whereas I helped out the family by tending cows. Ben Franklin lived in Boston, Massachusetts, near salt marshes, whereas I lived in Rehoboth, Pennsylvania, near abandoned strip mine runoff pits. Ben learned to swim fairly early in the ocean, and I had learned to swim, too, but not expertly, again in strip mine ponds. Like Jumbo, Ben Franklin's father had "an excellent Constitution of Body," was very handy in the use of tradesmen's tools, and was also musically gifted, being able to sing tunes to psalms and play the violin at the same time.

Well, my father could play the piano and sing, too, though he hardly ever sang hymns or psalms.

I couldn't wait to tell Jumbo all these fascinating discoveries, especially since he had been in such an ebullient mood since we had dropped off Ziggy. But as the afternoon wore on, I grew tired of reading. Eventually, I lay down on the truck seat, covered my shoulders with the dish towel Vera had wrapped the cookies in, conjured bunnies in the moonlight, and fell asleep.

I woke up when I realized I really had to pee badly. The double mugs of root beer I enjoyed with my ham sandwich had primed my system, and I didn't have to let off steam, but I certainly had to let out some urine.

The sun was falling in the sky, and the lengthening shadows on the west side of Water Street were making it very cold. When I realized I could not hold it any longer, I jumped out of the truck cab and ran up to the door Jumbo had entered.

I knocked hard. I heard jazzy gramophone music inside, so I knocked harder. I had to go so bad that I squeezed the tip of my dinky with my fingers to keep it from losing control right there on the porch.

Nobody answered the door. I started to shout, but then I realized that pee was rolling down my leg. So, I just let it happen. Now I knew I couldn't go inside that house, because they would probably see my pants were wet. I stopped shouting immediately, so that nobody would come out and discover what I had done. Also, I no longer needed to go in to use the bathroom.

I started to walk back down the porch steps toward the truck, when the door opened.

BLOOD PUDDING

A tall dark-haired woman opened the door. She had on glittering rhinestone earrings and a necklace to match with silver link bracelets on her wrists and several big gemmed rings on her fingers. She was smoking a cigarette. She looked down at me and chuckled.

"You're too young, sonny boy. Scram. What would your mother say if she knew you were down here on Water Street? Should I call her?" The woman didn't seem to notice the puddle of pee at my feet.

"I'm sorry. I don't live in this town," I said. "Have you seen my father? His name is Jumbo."

Then she laughed and said, "Jumbo? Let me see if I can find him upstairs. Is he a big man with a mustache?"

"That's him. Would you remind him I'm in the truck? My name is Tad."

"Sure, Tad. Tad and Jumbo. I'll remember. I would invite you in, but you are too young. And don't say anything to your mother, okay? I don't want Jumbo to get into trouble at home. Let it be a secret between you and me?"

When she shut the door, I walked back to the truck and jumped inside. My Sunday suit pants were soggy, and I took the dish towel and tried to rub them dry, but that didn't work.

I waited there in the truck at least another half an hour, and the streetlights popped on. I started shivering. Then I started to cry, because the woman at the door had said she might call my mother. Then I saw other men walking in and out of the houses, and I wished that one of them could be my father, so I could go home and take a bath and change clothes.

When Jumbo finally stepped out of the door, a different woman, also with bracelets and earrings and a necklace, walked him to the edge of the porch and kissed him. He wobbled on the steps and reached several times into his suit pocket for the key to the truck. Then he looked up and down the street, as though he was not sure which vehicle was his.

I rolled down the window. "Jumbo!" I shouted.

He held out his finger, pointed at me, and grinned, his gold tooth glowing in the shadows as he pointed the truck key in my direction. Then he went around in front of the truck and opened the door on the driver's side. He vaulted up awkwardly and landed in the seat. My nostrils were hit with a powerful wave of perfume mixed with what smelled like vodka and cigars. He had plenty of lipstick on his cheeks and neck.

"Are we moving to Hunterton?" I asked.

He fired up the ignition and started to laugh. "Great idea, Taddy! All of us move to Hunterton! Great idea!"

He did not notice that I had wet my pants, and I was relieved about that. If I smelled of my own urine, he didn't say anything about it. I did not speak all the way home. I knew he was drunk, and I did not want to distract him in any way. The truck swerved several times going over the Hunterton Bridge and then a few times up the hills through the thin panhandle part of West Virginia. Now and then, he sang a few verses of *"Hej, Sokoly!"* But I was too tired and too scared to sing with him.

Finally, we made it back to Robert Street. I felt lucky that he did not smell my stinky pants, because usually that would mean he would hit me. Vera quickly realized that he had been drinking, and she became cross. But what could she say to him as he stumbled toward his bedroom and slammed the door? He was our father.

Besides, I had wet my best Sunday pants, and I hoped she wouldn't come down on me too hard for that. I couldn't wear them to Mass the next morning, that was certain, but Vera didn't seem to notice, either.

After I stepped out of the bathtub and put on my clean pajamas, Vera asked, "And how was Ziggy's new school? Does he like it?"

"He loves it," I said. "We accomplished a lot today. We really did! And they gave me a book all about Benjamin Franklin!"

"But I guess Jumbo celebrated, didn't he?"

"Yeah, we went to Hunterton. Have you ever been in Ohio? It's great over there. Do you think I could skip Mass tomorrow? I have homework for Monday."

Lady of the House

On Sunday morning, Jumbo took me out on the front porch. "Taddy, don't tell Vera anything about our trip to Hunterton."

"I won't," I said, "but is there any chance we might move there? Are you thinking about getting a job in the steel factory?"

"Where the hell did you get that idea?"

"You said hello to your friend. I hoped you were interested in moving us there. Seems like a nice town."

"Shut up about it. Shut up about the whole day."

"I liked singing in the truck with you."

"If you know what's good for you, you'll keep your mouth shut about Hunterton! You can talk about Belvedere but not about what happened after."

"I hope Ziggy gets along down there."

He turned his jaw to the side and glared at me. He often did that when his temper flared. I thought he was going to scold me for wetting my pants or something. What else? His brow reddened, and his eyes squinted.

"Not a word to Vera! And no, I'm not looking for a job in Ohio."

I had learned long before to be careful on mornings after Jumbo had been drunk. This obviously was not a moment to remind him about how close I felt to him in the truck the day before. Jumbo didn't want to hear anything about the day before. I had hoped the trip to Ohio might have brought us closer, but that was another wishful delusion.

He went back inside to have his breakfast. I waited outside in the morning chill, till I heard him talking to Vera and Lucy. Then I went back in to join them. I didn't speak about Hunterton or even Belvedere.

For several months after that, Jumbo was on his best behavior. I noticed he deferred to Vera's judgment on many domestic matters. Though only fifteen, Vera had matured early, in both physical and emotional ways. Once she sensed her new power over Jumbo, she did not hesitate to use it. Skillfully and willingly, she took over Mother's duties. She made some changes for the better, and I definitely benefited from them.

She insisted, for example, that we sell the cows right away. Now that Ziggy was living at Belvedere and I was attending Rehoboth Elementary every day, who would take care of the cows? Milking and feeding them twice a day and taking them out to pasture had become onerous. We could sell the cows and make enough to buy what we needed from the milkman for a year or two. Why were we keeping these animals? Besides, once the cows were out of the shed, Jumbo could expand his workshop.

Jumbo sold Rose and Mary.

Vera also insisted that we put new curtains on the parlor windows and that the front and back doors receive a fresh coat of paint, inside and out. Jumbo agreed, and he took everything a step further by sanding down the kitchen table and giving it a fresh coat of blue paint. Then he painted the kitchen cabinets blue.

By the time spring came, Vera was in control. Jumbo raved about her cooking, her attention to all the details of housekeeping, and how carefully she was looking after Kazzy and Blizzard. At one time, I heard him actually say in a casual way that if Mother could see the job Vera was doing, she would probably be jealous.

Looking back at that first winter after Mother's death, I think now that Jumbo's behavior was a veil. I did not suspect it then, but he was courting Vera's affection. I was too involved in the changes in my own life to pay much attention to Jumbo's seduction of his daughter.

I did not realize it, just as I had not understood till later that his visit in Hunterton was to a whorehouse.

That winter, I had no Ziggy and no cows. I felt liberated. Max, who was becoming more and more independent, often spent nights at a house next door to the Texaco. So, I now was alone in the bunkhouse.

I was overjoyed now to have homework in the evenings, and without distractions. I often did special assignments for Miss Beck. When I showed her my book from Belvedere, she suggested I give a report about Ben Franklin to the whole class. I did, and it was a hit.

The ironic thing for me personally was that Ben stayed in school till he was ten, then he had to stop his formal studies and go home to help with his father's candle making business. Not me. I was almost ten when I started school, and I planned to stay in as long as I could.

I returned home with As on my report cards, and Jumbo and Vera were very pleased. When I told Jumbo I wanted to model my life after Ben Franklin, he looked confused. Vera and Lucy explained to him that Franklin was a famous scientist and patriot, one of the nation's Founding Fathers. Aside from his career in printing and publishing and compiling a dictionary and founding a lending library in Philadelphia, he served during the Revolutionary War as an ambassador in France. He helped to craft the Constitution, and he was an inventor who discovered that lightning is electricity released from the clouds. He proved it by flying a kite during a thunderstorm. This was all news to Jumbo.

Vera suggested I recite my report right there in the kitchen. Jumbo said he would rather borrow my book sometime and read about Franklin. He never did. From his evasive glances, I saw he had no interest in learning about my hero. My father had grown up in Poland under the bitter reign of the Russian czar. His curiosity for American historical figures was negligible. He had come to America for a better life, not for the history.

What may also have happened was that after ten years of his struggles to sustain his family in America, and after suddenly losing his beautiful and obedient wife, Jumbo's desire for embracing a robust future had weakened. There was no longer any talk of starting another restaurant or even of revving up the secret alcohol trade again. My pipe dream of his applying for a new job at the Hunterton steel factory, starting a new life there, seemed absurd to him.

He continued to work at the mine. On his few days off, he puttered in his shed. I remember how happy I was when he was out there, leaving me inside to study. His presence inside the house was oppressive, and whatever he did out in the shed was his business. All of us felt that way.

Whereas Ben Franklin's father insisted every night on having engaging conversations with his wife and children, grooming their interest in moral issues and the affairs of the day, my father served us best by staying out of sight, preferably out of the house. He was a burden and a distraction. Ben Franklin would have felt sorry for all of us

When Mother was alive, she served as a buffer between Jumbo and us. Now, we had no protection. His rare moments of charm were temporary distractions, illusions from the reality that our father was an ogre.

Now that Ziggy was out of the house and no longer my constant charge, I had a wider vision of my family and of myself. But Jumbo now seemed a more threatening presence. He had little interest in parenting us. He expected us to serve him, and if we were not trying our best to please him, we had best stay away from him.

That meant I would have to take cues about morality and certainly about my education from people I admired outside of the family, perhaps in books like my hero Ben Franklin.

Mother had been able to encourage Jumbo's better traits and sometimes moderate his self-destructive impulses. Now without her, he floundered. He seemed to latch on to Vera for support, but despite her gorgeous looks and quickly maturing woman's body, Vera was still a girl.

We all were sinking. It was a plunge. We did not speak about it. The Black Madonna gazed out at us from the parlor wall. Her severe glance seemed almost threatening. "What do we say?"

Worse things were coming, She and baby Jesus seemed to warn. And indeed, they did, particularly to me.

BLOOD PUDDING

We were not surprised when one Saturday afternoon in March, Jumbo drove back from Curly the Greek's junkyard with an old metal tank and some copper tubing and what looked like the basic components of another still. He hauled all of it into the shed and disappeared. Soon he was unloading bushels of grapes and driving over to Rulandville to the Italian restaurant for empty wine bottles. By May, he regularly smelled of red wine at the breakfast table.

I knew Vera would say nothing about it, though she was the new lady of the house. By June he was teasing her and giving her sips. Sometimes she even smiled at him and said it tasted good.

Make a Wish!

Jasper Slattery and I began to study together a lot. We competed with each other for the highest marks on tests. Despite my bad leg, he encouraged me to participate in sports after school. Sometimes we tossed baseballs and footballs back and forth in the schoolyard. He took me to the sandlot baseball field out the road by the junkyard and pitched balls for me to hit. Jasper was kind and accepting to me about my handicap. I was grateful that he defended me when other boys made fun of me.

Before the bell rang each morning, I would usually be standing outside on the school steps, waiting to see Jasper's bushy red hair and freckled face. We were about the same height and build, and as he walked toward me up the sidewalk, I envied his perfect posture and jaunty stride. No matter how troubled I was about Jumbo back home, when Jasper waved and grinned at me, I knew I could forget about home for a while and enjoy my day in school.

I became loyal to Jasper, just as I had been loyal to Ziggy. It thrilled me to have a real buddy, who was bright and positive and almost as curious about Ben Franklin as I was. He thought my sister Vera was as beautiful as any movie star, and he thought Lucy was pretty, too, though maybe a little too serious. I told him Lucy sometimes pulled practical jokes on me, like short-sheeting my bed or hiding my toothbrush, and that deep down she had a pixie spirit. Jasper said he had never seen Lucy laugh, and he suspected her sense of humor was shallow. Jasper was an only child, so he did not know what to expect of siblings. I told him Lucy had her truly comic moments, but she rarely revealed them. "Lucy has a religious streak," I said.

"Maybe so, but she should try to have more fun. If she were my sister, I would insist on it."

Sometimes Jasper came over to Robert Street, and we goofed around with Kazzy and Bliz. They liked him, too, and I enjoyed sharing them with him. I asked him why his parents did not have more children, and he said they were Presbyterians. That did not make sense to me, but apparently, it did to Jasper.

It was new for me to have an independent party reporting to me about Max. I learned that my big brother had a reputation around Rehoboth as a motorcycle hotshot and a cigarette-smoking heartbreaker with the ladies. This confirmed my suspicions. I had seen Max in action, flirting with the daughters of customers at the Texaco. His usual come-on was to invite the girl to take a spin on his Harley, with or without the sidecar, depending on how brave she was. Despite the Prohibition laws against alcohol, Max was known to offer his date a nip prior to the motorcycle ride, to firm up her nerves. Max had perfected this formula, which also included splashing on cologne prior to picking up his date, the same way Jumbo did before going to the mine.

Max had Jumbo's personal magnetism. Some girls found him irresistible. Jasper said most Rehoboth families considered Max a rogue. Any girl seen zooming with Max on his Harley was considered fast and foolish.

This new information from Jasper troubled me. With Ziggy's infamous misbehavior at Rehoboth Elementary and with Max's escapades on his motorcycle with trashy girls and with Jumbo's drunkenness, I had a thick jungle of prejudice about my family to cut through. I was the opposite of my father and my older brothers, and I was grateful to Jasper and his parents for welcoming me.

Jasper admitted that he was afraid of Jumbo. I told him everybody was. But Jumbo was our father, so what could we do? That's when Jasper would stick his chin out and chew on his lip, as if he were thinking up a solution for me. He never came up with one. Nobody did, till I finally realized the only solution was escape. But it felt good to have somebody with a big heart to know all this about me.

After we had become true friends, Jasper said he had heard a rumor that my mother's death was not from natural causes and that Jumbo was perhaps to blame for it. I told Jasper that though Jumbo had been mean at times to Mother, I knew he was not responsible for her death. She had died from a bad pregnancy, and the autopsy proved it.

Even so, Jasper's parents balked at giving Jasper permission to spend the night at our house. I asked him why, and he said it was because of Jumbo.

Mr. Slattery was an officer at the bank. He and Mrs. Slattery seemed happy enough to let me sleep over at their house, and I was always thrilled to be their guest. Oddly, despite Max's fame as Rehoboth's bad boy, Mr. Slattery admired Max's mechanical skills. Once down at the Texaco, when they had discovered smoke coming out of the engine on the Slatterys' new Chevrolet, Max opened the hood, shot under the car, and in an instant spotted and fixed their clogged exhaust manifold.

"Surprisingly shrewd for a lad of seventeen," said Mr. Slattery. "I think your brother is a natural at the trade. He's got great instincts as a mechanic. Good skill to have these days with so many new cars on the road. He needs to put a damper on that wild stuff before he gets hurt. I suppose your father never says that to him?"

"No, sir," I answered. "With Max, it wouldn't do any good. He's just as stubborn as Jumbo."

Mrs. Slattery asked about Ziggy, and I explained that Ziggy was now down at a special school in West Virginia. I was looking forward to visiting him, as soon as Jumbo found a free weekend to drive down there again. It was a full day's excursion to Murphy's Forge, I explained, and circumstances had not allowed us to visit there yet.

"Your family has gone through a lot of changes lately," Mr. Slattery said one evening at the dinner table. "And is your father still able to hold down his job at the mine?"

Such questions confirmed what Jasper had already told me: that recently Jumbo had become a popular topic of town gossip. One day I mentioned this to Max at the Texaco, and he only raised his eyebrows. Joe Curtiss overheard me and said, "Hey, Max! Didn't you say you bumped into Jumbo on Water Street, last time you rode down to Hunterton?"

By that time, I had learned more about Hunterton's infamous Water Street, and I was not surprised to hear from Joe Curtiss that Max visited there too.

On my tenth birthday, Lucy baked a chocolate cake with coconut icing for me. Jasper came over to have a piece and sing "Happy Birthday." As a gift, he had built a sleek and sturdy kite with balsa wood sticks, twine, and brown wrapping paper. He had sketched a miniature portrait of Ben Franklin on it. The kite came with a huge spool of a thousand feet of string.

I told him the kite was so gorgeous, I didn't want to fly it. But Jasper said he didn't make it to decorate my room. We'd be flying it for sure on the first windy day. I grinned and looked him eye to eye. We shook hands. I knew he really was my buddy now. He accepted me, despite my crazy family, my bad leg, and my occasional gloomy moods.

Before I blew out the ten candles on the cake, I closed my eyes and wished for my right leg to grow back longer. While my eyes were closed, I also had an impulse to ask God for Jumbo's reputation to improve. But I figured that would be a wasted request. We all hoped and prayed he would hang on to his job, but that was really only up to Jumbo and his bosses. It also depended on the amount of wine he drank every night, before he pulled Vera into bed with him.

Vera said, "Make a wish, Taddy!"

She didn't know my wish was about her.

Cold Cokes

My feelings of independence grew. I knew I would always be grateful to Vera for stabilizing our home and for looking out for all of us, me in particular. She had originally taught me to read, then Lucy took over, and now Vera was signing my report cards and encouraging me in my studies and saying yes if I wanted to sleep over at Jasper's house.

Vera had thrown away her education to make our family at least partly functional. She said she did it out of loyalty to Mother. Maybe it was fulfilling for that reason. But I suspected that her only enjoyment in life now was when she left the house on Saturdays and worked over at the company store, helping out Daddy Mac. That's where she seemed relieved and happy.

When I said I should look for a part-time job like babysitting or a paper route to help out with the budget, she objected.

"Tad, we are getting by, and your job now is to be the best student you can be. Max gives me some money every week, and I am doing okay with the laundry business. Lucy helps a lot, but I know she would rather be doing some volunteer work for the church. Your job, my brother, is to read and study and earn the best grades you can. That's what Mother would want. You know that."

When summer came, I tried to finagle a job through Max, helping out at the Texaco. He refused to ask Joe Curtiss about it, because he did not want me around where he worked. He said I would be a nuisance. Then I applied for a job at the Bijoux movie theater as an usher. I would have worn a uniform and carried a flashlight and a broom and swept popcorn off the floor between features. The lady at the Bijoux liked me, but she said I was too young, and none of their uniforms would fit me. I was disappointed when they turned me down, because I would have been able to watch plenty of movies for free as part of the job. But it wasn't to be.

When Jasper and his family drove off for a two-week vacation at Atlantic City, I started missing Ziggy. None of us had been down to see him, but Jumbo told us the letters from Dr. Horvath were encouraging. Jumbo thought a visit from the family might ruin all the progress Ziggy had made over the winter and spring.

I finally told Vera that I was bored and asked if I could pitch in with the laundry work. She said okay. Early in July, Lucy was heading off to a religious retreat with the church youth group for a week, so I filled in for her. This gave me an opportunity to work side by side with Vera. I know she was grateful for my offer to help.

Working beside Vera, I could see that Jumbo had worn her down. She seemed to have adopted Mother's adage, "Nothing to do."

I was ten. I could not talk to her about this. What was I going to say to a sixteen-year-old? "Nothing to do" applied to me, too, I realized.

My understanding of the human sexual act was vague. When we lived at the farm, I had seen cats and rats mating. It all seemed disgusting to Ziggy and me. That Jumbo would have done it to Mother was terrible enough, but to imagine that he now was doing it to Vera, and we could hear it happening sometimes down in Jumbo's bedroom, made me sick. Then he would threaten her not to speak about it to anybody.

I wanted to take a baseball bat into the bathroom some morning while he was shaving at the mirror and bang his big bald skull to smithereens.

I knew Vera was ashamed. She tried to pretend nothing unusual was happening. She covered it up by saying, "Oh, Jumbo just wasn't feeling very well last night, and I had to look in on him. He seems fine this morning."

I tried to speak to Max about it.

"Do you know what is going on with Jumbo and Vera?"

"What about it?"

"Do you think we should help her?"

"How?"

"I don't know. That's why I'm asking you."

"If she keeps doing it, maybe she likes it. Girls like it. They say they don't, but they do."

"I don't think she likes it, Max. He makes her do it. Sometimes she cries out in the night. Last night I heard him say if she spoke to the priest, he'd make her regret it."

"He's right. What good would telling the priest do?"

"It's bad, Max."

"It's none of your business. Worry about yourself, why don't you?"

One sunny afternoon in August, I found Vera on the back porch, feeding sheets through the wringer, just as Mother had done countless thousands of times. She was shuddering, crying with her face twisted tightly in anguish. I saw some vertical worry lines on her forehead, like the ones Mother had shown the year before she died.

When Vera saw me, she put the sheets down. She raised her apron to her face and tried to dry her tears, but they came back and kept rolling down her cheeks. She was sobbing uncontrollably. Her chest jerked hard, like it would crack.

"Oh, Vera. Dear Vera!" I said.

I put my arms around her as tightly as I could to stop her body from shaking. At first when I held her, she jumped, like she was frightened by my touch. Then she held me close, and we both stood on the porch in each other's arms. It felt a lot like Mother's embrace, and that day she was wearing one of Mother's flowered dresses. I did not want to let go of her. I needed comforting too. We both were confused and desperate, probably more than anybody else in the family.

I believe she could feel my love, which I could not put into words. While we embraced, her chest quieted, and the sobbing stopped. We went back to work, cranking the sheets through the wringer.

"I hope someday I will have a boy just like you, Tad, once I go out on my own."

She smiled at me. With the sun to her back, she looked so much like Mother that I almost started to cry myself.

"She would be so proud of you, Mr. A Student!"

"Do you think?"

"Here's a quarter. Run over to the store and get us both a Coca-Cola? And keep the change."

"I love you, Vera. Thanks."

As I walked back with the open Coke bottles in my hands, I did feel proud of my report cards, and Vera was right. Mother would be proud too.

But I wondered how proud she would be of Vera. Mother was good at understanding almost everything, but Vera's predicament might stump her and would probably make her weep just as hard as Vera.

As I passed by the wooded lot where that fateful slippery elm stood, I paused and watched its green leaves rustling in the afternoon wind. The sight of it gave me a shiver. I thought how terribly Vera's life had changed because of the bark on that very innocent-looking tree. And who would ever know? Who would ever suspect? It looked like a normal tree. I went behind and ran my fingers along the scars on the bark. They reminded me of the slashes on the face of the Black Madonna.

I walked on further and pressed the cold Coke bottles against my cheeks. They felt good. They helped me hold back what my eyes wanted to do. Seeing the slippery elm sent that falling sensation back through me. That tight clutch of dread again squeezed my heart.

I wondered what punishment eventually would find me for what I had done to Mother and, now also, for what I had done to Vera.

Lady Liberty

In September, nearly a year after Mother died, the mine laid off Jumbo. It did not surprise us. He had been processing grapes and potatoes in the kitchen and distilling vodka and red wine under the shed. Since nobody came to the door to buy it, we concluded he was his only customer. We smelled it on his breath every evening. Often, when he left the house in the morning, he reeked. He stowed three or four shot-glass-size bottles of vodka into his lunch box to cover his hangovers during the day.

One afternoon, the mine foreman found him dozing in a coal cart and sent him home. He was told not to come back until he was fully sober and ready to work again. He came back the next morning smelling of vodka, and again he was banished and told not to return for a month.

He heard the zinc smelting plant was desperate for workers, and when he arrived there a week later sober and charming, he actually talked his way into a utility job shoveling slag, monitoring the conveyor belt that led to the roasting oven, and monitoring the outflow valves of the sulfuric acid pipes. Work at the zinc plant was hot and dangerous but paid more. He was told categorically that any on-the-job impairment from alcohol could impede his reaction times. Mistakes with that heavy equipment had caused amputations, burns, acid spills, and fatal falls into the boiling vats. He had to be careful, and he had to lay off the liquor.

Jumbo told us he relished this difference in his jobs, and we wondered if perhaps the monotonous grind in the coal mine had lulled him into thinking he could get away with drinking on the job. He knew that drinking alcohol at the zinc plant was out of the question, and for six weeks he abstained entirely.

On November 3, exactly one year after Eva Malinowski's death, he paid the priest to celebrate a brief early morning requiem Mass for Mother. After church, we all came home for a small reception, which Vera and Lucy had prepared. They served ham and Polish biscuits and a special lemon cake, which had been Mother's favorite recipe. The priest said a prayer before the Black Madonna, and a few neighbors and a couple of Jumbo's mine and zinc plant friends lingered for coffee.

When everyone had left, we started to clean up the house. Jumbo went into the shed and stayed there.

We checked on him at sundown and found him passed out by his vodka still. Vera put ice water to his face and managed to wake him up. She reminded him that he had to report to the zinc plant first thing in the morning, and that he should come into the house and go to bed.

He started to cry and said he was sure they would understand why he did not go into work. He was grieving. The foreman there was a lanky and sweet Polish fellow, Jake Milajeki, who had come to the Mass that morning and stopped by afterward. Jumbo had already told him he might not show up for work. He knew he wouldn't lose his job again, because they valued him and were even thinking of promoting him to assistant roaster controller.

Jumbo continued to drink for the next four days, and finally Jake Milajeki came to the house and told him he could not make excuses for him anymore. If Jumbo did not show up the next morning, he could forget the promotion to assistant roaster controller. He would lose his job entirely and forever.

That night, I heard Vera pleading with Jumbo to consider what he was doing to the family. She used some of the words Mother had used in her pleadings. Vera had heard those words, too, of course, but she emphasized the shaming component of the argument, so much so that Jumbo started weeping again and telling her how sorry he was that he had treated Mother so roughly. The result was that he did win back his zinc plant job and two months later was promoted to the assistant roaster controller position with a bump in pay. We were relieved and astounded.

At the work site, Jumbo displayed quickness and stamina that far surpassed men twenty years younger than him. But for the next year and a half, he continued to bounce back and forth between the zinc plant and the coal mine. He never tried the moly mill, though I think he kept it in the back of his mind as his "third strike," if he needed one.

He did binge drinking and then begged for work. I suspect the company took mercy on him and hired him back because of us, his children, who were living in one of the company houses. But when he became a risk to the mine itself or the zinc plant, they could no longer tolerate his habitual drunkenness.

A parade of priests came to talk to him. Miss Wilson made a house call. Jake Milajeki offered to let him stay in an extra room in his house so he could monitor his abstinence and keep Jumbo on the job and on the payroll. After talking with Vera and Jumbo, Jake went so far as to remove all the equipment from Jumbo's underground distillery. He personally hauled them to Curly the Greek's junkyard and made Curly promise he wouldn't sell them back to Jumbo.

However, after a few weeks more of doing impeccable work at the zinc plant, Jumbo went back out to the junkyard. Happy to make a sale, Curly caved. Jumbo bought the stills back. He installed them again in the pit in the shed, where he went about preparing more batches to be drunk at a later date. Jumbo was methodical and careful, as if it were his top priority in the world. He was sober when he did the preparations, which required attention to detail. He was a different man from the creature he would become, once fermentation and distillation had proceeded and he could imbibe.

After these cycles of futility, he was laid off permanently from both the coal mine and the zinc plant. The foremen at the moly plant refused to talk to him. Management allowed us to live in the company house, as long as we could find rent money.

By that time, Max had left the Texaco and had opened his own motorcycle shop, Malinowski Motors. Max had also begun to sell new and used Harley Davidson motorcycles. The shop started out slowly but became a success. Max made enough profit to pay the full rent for 7 Robert Street.

When Jumbo ran out of vodka or wine, he sobered up for a week or two and looked around town for any odd jobs available. He gardened. He cleaned out garages. He washed cars. He pumped gas at the Texaco. He even waited tables at the coffee shop in Rehoboth for several months, where he bragged to the customers that back in Poland he had once owned a first-class gourmet establishment. He said he had not ruled out the possibility that one day he would go back into the restaurant business once he found adequate financial backing.

All this while, in the cellar under his work shed, his vodka and wine were slowly fermenting in their vats. Then, when Jumbo determined they were ready, he would stop gardening or cleaning out garages or gutters or pumping gas or waiting on tables and retire to his private shed, where he would start drinking and not stop till he had drunk all the bottles empty.

Jumbo's addiction was colossal and terrifying. He would come into the house several times a day to use the toilet or to eat a sandwich, but those were the only times we would see him.

I recall one winter afternoon when I was done early with my homework, and I looked into the shed to be sure he was conscious. I found him sitting at his workbench, reading a Polish newspaper under the bare electric bulb. His hands were jittery, and the paper rattled in front of his eyes. I doubted he could read it. I thought at first he had the shakes due to the chilly air, but no, he was in withdrawal. He told me he could die if he did not have a drink at once.

He took three empty bottles from under the bench and handed them to me with three corks. He penciled an address on a small rectangle of pinewood. Then he drew a map for me to show me exactly where to go. I remembered the map Mother had drawn for Ziggy and me. That mission had turned out horribly, but again, I had no choice but to follow orders. I did not want Jumbo to die like this in withdrawal.

He reached into his pocket and produced a silver half-dollar coin and said, "Take the bottles and the money. Go in by the back door. Her name is Mildred. Can you remember that? Give Mildred the fifty cents and come back with the bottles full and corked. If you love me, Taddy, you'll do this for your father."

I put on my winter coat and followed his orders. I pocketed the corks and put the bottles in a brown paper bag, just as many of our customers had done when we had the family business. Following Jumbo's map, I headed about a mile and a half past Rehoboth Elementary and down an unpaved country road. I arrived at the address, which was a log hut stuck back from the road a hundred yards or so. Smoke was coming out of its chimney, so I knew somebody named Mildred was probably inside. I had never been on this road before, but obviously Jumbo knew it well. His rough map was exact.

I stopped in front of the hut, pulled the coin from my pocket, and inspected it. The image of Lady Liberty on the coin, her long skirt with plentiful folds, all flapping in the wind, triggered my imagination. She had a bunch of flowers in her left hand, and she strode forward with her right hand extended out, palm up, over a glorious rising sun. She looked as if she was showing everybody the way into the future. She had broad shoulders and a graceful tilt to her head. She looked inspiring, just as Mother might have looked from a distance. Mother could have been the perfect model for this Lady Liberty on the handsome silver coin.

Then I realized that I was only daydreaming. I was also shivering from the cold. My immediate future did not seem inspired in any way, despite Lady Liberty's sincere gesture.

I went around to the back of the shed and knocked. A voice called for me to come in.

A tired tall woman stood behind a wooden counter. On the counter lay a dead baby flat on her back in diapers, maybe six months old. The baby's skin was gray blue, and the eyes were open. There was a thick yellow film that clogged the nostrils and seemed to paste the gray lips together.

"Yes?" the woman said.

"Is your name Mildred?"

"Mildred."

"I'm Tad. I'm Jumbo's son," I said, pulling the empty bottles out of the paper bag.

"You're Jumbo's cripple," she said. "I heard his idiot got sent down West Virginia? That right?"

"Yes." I put the bottles down on the counter and set Lady Liberty down, right at the gray feet of the dead baby.

"You got corks?"

I took the three corks from my pocket and laid them on the counter.

The woman picked up the coin and the bottles and the corks. She disappeared into a back room, where I heard her open a tap and fill the bottles with moonshine. While she tamped the corks into the bottles with a wooden mallet, I stared at the baby and felt the urge to touch its hand to see if it felt the same as Mother's hand when she died.

But then Mildred came back with the three bottles filled with an amber liquid. "Don't touch her," she said. "Diphtheria."

We both gazed silently for a moment at the little corpse.

"Are you going to bury that baby?" I asked.

Mildred let out a cool chuckle. "What the hell else would we do with her?"

She watched me put the bottles into the bag and laughed again. "Tad, my boy, on top of being a cripple, you got a little bit of idiot in you too. Don't you?"

Crystal Set

At school, I put up with teasing and jeers.

"Where does he get it? Does he ever give you any?"

"I heard the cops took him home again last weekend?"

"I saw him yesterday. He was kicking a cucumber up Emery Street."

One night, Jumbo drove the truck down to Hunterton. He got lost on the way home and ran out of gas. A West Virginia state policeman found him by the side of the road. He had passed out in the truck cab. The trooper poured a couple gallons of gasoline into his tank and pointed him over the state line in the direction of Rehoboth. He made it home, apologized to us all, and stayed sober for two months.

"I heard your father is talking about opening his own restaurant. Did he really own one in Poland?"

I had nothing to say. I couldn't tell them how I hated him.

This period of my childhood was a minefield of insults, embarrassments, and humiliations. I tiptoed carefully and tried to steel myself from the mockery and from Jumbo's egregious treatment of all of us. I lived for school and for my studies and for whatever reading I could do. I asked for extra homework and special assignments to counteract having the town drunk as my father.

I followed Benjamin Franklin's example and started a notebook with a list of virtues to foster and tabulate in my daily life. I showed my notebook to Jasper, and he caught the bug too.

We both copied Franklin's technique and drew charts for each week, comparing our results on each of the thirteen virtues Franklin had listed: temperance, silence, order, resolution, frugality, industry, sincerity, justice, moderation, cleanliness, tranquility, chastity, and humility.

After several weeks, we showed our notebooks to Jasper's father.

"I'm impressed, boys. But it will be hard for you to live up to Franklin's example."

"Well, Mr. Slattery, that's what Jasper and I are trying to do. We're following Ben's instructions."

"Tad's right. And Ben says in his autobiography that many weeks he did not get a perfect score."

I added to Jasper's argument. "If Ben recorded a long streak of perfect weeks, there would be no reason for him to keep score. He was very careful about himself."

Jasper and I soon learned that a perfect week was impossible. But we kept trying. Every Friday, we would compare notebooks.

Once, Jasper asked if we should show them to Jumbo, just to see what he would say. I explained that Jumbo had little knowledge of Ben Franklin and would probably not be interested. Then I realized that Jasper was teasing.

"Oh, I get it," I said. I laughed, but Jasper's joke hurt.

Whenever I could, I slept over at the Slatterys' house. His parents enjoyed seeing the two of us acting like brothers. We both had good manners and eager attitudes. They said we were positive influences on each other. Jasper had those countless freckles on his cheeks, and when he was very tired from concentrating on his homework, his left eye drifted, making him slightly cross-eyed. Between my short right leg and his lazy left eye, Jasper reckoned we were even. I smiled with gratitude when he said that. He was trying to show compassion for my handicap and solidarity for our friendship.

At some point Jasper's father changed jobs. He left the bank and went to the mining administration, where he was chief accountant.

He also supervised, among other responsibilities, the payroll office and the employee housing department. That may have been why we were treated tolerantly those several times when we were negligent on our rent payments, but I cannot say that for sure. Looking back, it was strange that we were still permitted to live on Robert Street. I believe that Jasper's father was giving us a break.

The Slatterys' house was built of red bricks and was located up near the center of town, not far from the Texaco and two blocks down from Max's new motorcycle shop. Their house seemed gigantic with its high ceilings and a big dining room and a basement and a broad back porch. They also had a large backyard, where we tossed baseballs and footballs. For a family with only one child, it seemed extravagant, but I was happy to share in filling up its spaciousness. Honestly, there was simply no comparison between the Slatterys' house, which they owned, and ours, which nobody would want to own.

Jasper had a noisy beagle with black and brown spots named Bart, who loved to retrieve sticks when we threw them. He also liked chasing cars down the street. Bart's tail was white, and it had a kink an inch and a half from the end, the result of a skirmish with a panel truck wheel. When Bart wagged his tail, the tip flipped back and forth, opposite to the way the rest of the tail was going. This annoyed Bart. He would nip at it, as if he wanted to straighten it out with his teeth, and this always made us giggle. Apart from the constant howling and the curious tail defect, Bart was a perfect dog. When the three of us went out for a walk, we were proud and jolly, much different from how I felt when I was home.

Like our adopted mentor Ben Franklin, Jasper and I shared an interest in science. Jasper liked Tom Swift books, too, and we often imagined ourselves as budding inventors with brilliant ideas ready to hatch out in our futures. Therefore, when a representative from the Westinghouse Company on the other side of Pittsburgh stopped by our school with a dozen crystal radio kits to give away, Jasper and I ran to be the first two in line.

Radio was a new and spectacular phenomenon all over the country. But it was especially popular in Pittsburgh, where Westinghouse manufactured some of the country's first radio home models. Apparently, the Westinghouse marketing department wanted to promote sales of their new products by giving out free crystal sets to schoolchildren around Pittsburgh. Once children took these cheap and easily assembled contraptions home and started fiddling with them, their parents would listen in and perhaps consider buying an expensive console family radio with speakers, not headphones.

As the Westinghouse representative explained with blackboard diagrams, the crystal set used the radio wave itself as power. So, the apparatus did require earpieces but no electrical connection as a power source. I wished Mother and Ziggy would have been around to experience this new form of magic. They both would have been astonished

Jasper and I stayed late that day, reading the instructions pamphlet and winding our capacitor coils around old Quaker Oats cylinder-shaped boxes we got from the school cafeteria. We fixed the crystal in place and adjusted the skinny wire known as the cat's whisker exactly as the diagrams indicated. We hung two large wires out the schoolhouse windows for our separate antennas and grounded our contraptions to the giant iron radiators in the classroom.

Then we donned our headphones and moved the copper beads along the coil to tune in whatever the airwaves had to offer. We felt as though we were tuning in to the universe. We were. It was an incredible thrill. It was one thing to see the Westinghouse man do it then listen in through his earphones. But now we did it ourselves!

The first sounds were crackles and sputters. As I listened and adjusted my cat's whisker, I watched Jasper's lazy left eye deviate further inward. I could tell his mind, like mine, was caught in the spell, casting our imaginary lines to catch whatever form of broadcasting we could find.

My spine tingled when I actually heard "Carolina in the Morning" performed by Paul Whiteman's orchestra. The crooner's voice was clear as could be. Jasper said he had chills too.

"Ben Franklin would have loved this!" I exclaimed.

The next day after school, I trolled along the coil and heard a report about the recent discovery of King Tut's burial chamber.

"Jasper!" I shouted.

"I know, I know!" He beamed. "I'm hearing it too."

"This is magic," I said.

"It's not magic, it's science, Tad."

"But it's still magical!"

Neither of us wanted to leave the school building that afternoon, but the janitor kicked us out. Jasper said he couldn't wait to take his new crystal set home to show his parents. Maybe they would want to buy a radio for their house, and I could come over anytime and listen.

That made me think how wonderful it would have been for me to take my set home and play magic radio music to Mother. As for Jumbo, I never knew when I came home if he would be drunk or not, or if he might find something critical to say about this new miracle.

So, I waited. Unlike Mr. Slattery, Jumbo would never be able to afford a home radio, even if he wanted one. I sneaked the kit into my bedroom and every night waited till Kazzy and Bliz had fallen asleep in the room beside mine. Then I would dangle the aerial wire out the window, connect the other end to the radiator pipe near my bed, and explore the universe with my ears.

This went on for several weeks, until Vera spotted the aerial wire dangling down from the window and asked me what it was. I demonstrated the crystal set to her. She was stunned. If she had stayed in school, she would have known all about it, but she didn't. I had to demonstrate it for her.

Word got out, and Kazzy and Blizzard pestered me to try it. But they were much too young to operate a delicate device, I explained. I told them to keep their hands off my instrument.

And when Vera told Jumbo about it, he came up to my room and put the earphones up to his ear. He put them down quickly.

"It's a toy." He shrugged. "How much did it cost?"

"It was free from the Westinghouse Company. They handed them out at school."

"They give away toys at your school?"

There was no point in explaining the crystal set to Jumbo. If it did not seem obvious to him that a scientific invention of overwhelming power was in his hands, bringing information and entertainment from somewhere far away instantly into our house to penetrate his thick, shiny skull, then why run the risk of making him cross.

"Don't waste too much time with this thing, Tad," he said.

"I won't."

"You're smart, Tad. Maybe you can make money someday using your brain. Don't waste too much of your brain on this toy."

I held my tongue. What he said about the crystal set was dismissive and absurd, but I couldn't stop him from saying it. At least, this was a moment when Jumbo was trying to show some interest in me. He was trying to be my father.

And he had an important point about using my brain. If my legs never evened up, and there was no sign they would, it would not be wise for me to work in any capacity that involved intense physical labor. My body would not tolerate it. I was no Jumbo or Max. I thought maybe someday after graduation from high school, I could land a job in a radio station in Pittsburgh, maybe even at KDKA, the first broadcast station in the whole country.

I told Jasper about my idea of someday working for KDKA, and he was all for it. When I told him Jumbo said our crystal sets were toys, he shook his head in dismay. He even hugged me. I was deeply comforted that I had a buddy like Jasper, who could understand and sympathize with me. I had lost Mother and Ziggy. I had a brilliant fool for a father. But Jasper's hug told me I was not alone.

The crystal set was a big thrill, a connection to the world, a diversion of my imagination to events and cultures far beyond my dismal home. In retrospect, about the same time I was immersing myself in exploring the world outside with my new and amazing crystal set, I should perhaps have been more cautious about the intentions of people in my immediate vicinity.

Second Base

Nick Katsaros had a reputation for being a loner. People called him Curly. He was the Greek junk dealer. A bachelor probably in his late thirties, he owned and was the sole employee of Curly's Junk and Recovery, a seven-acre hodgepodge of over a hundred abandoned cars, jumbles of corroded farm equipment, dented oil drums and water barrels, old washing machines, bathtubs, sinks, gutters, and anything else sizable and made mostly of metal. The objects were strewn in clusters on a weedy knoll two and a half miles west of town.

A corrugated steel fence about six feet high snaked around the yard's winding perimeter. The face of the fence closest to town doubled as the outfield wall for our sandlot baseball field. Both the junkyard and the ball field were set back a dozen yards from a straight stretch of the road to West Virginia. Nick's rusty Ford tow truck had West Virginia plates, and people said he lived with his sick mother eight miles across the state line.

Nick had a saggy belly and a thick, flabby neck. He was fat and pigeon-toed, and he walked slowly with a slumped, side-to-side waddle. He was bald but wanted people to call him Curly because he said that's what Katsaros meant in Greek. Jumbo told us never to call him anything but Mr. Katsaros, and we did. Jumbo just called him Nick, but everybody else in town called him Curly, the name he preferred.

Like Jumbo, Curly had one gold tooth. It was on the upper left. His other teeth were dark and chipped or missing. To hide the gaps, instead of smiling, he sometimes pursed his lips hard, twisted his face, and blinked his bright blue eyes fast. This looked odd, and it didn't happen often, because Curly always seemed sad or maybe hungover. He had permanent stubble on his cheeks and neck, thick black hair on his arms and forearms, and black grease caked hard under the nails of his pudgy fingers.

He smelled of garlic and kerosene and sometimes alcohol, and his thick Greek accent made it difficult to understand him. If we asked him to repeat something a second or third time, he thought we were making fun of him and would frown and clam up. When Jumbo and Curly dickered over the price of a piece of junk, Jumbo's thick Polish accent versus Curly's dense Greek inflections made for confusion. Somehow the two men struck deals, like on a used fuel pump for our truck's engine or a wringer for Vera's washing tub or small stuff, like bobbins for Mother's worn-out Singer. Jumbo would usually pay Curly with vodka or wine, which made him a valued customer, especially after Prohibition started.

I describe Curly and his junkyard not because he was an eccentric Rehoboth town character, but because of what he did to me.

For a junk dealer, Curly seemed sensitive. For example, he refused to kill any of the skunks nesting in the darker nooks of his property. Instead, he discouraged them by firing BBs from an air pistol, which sent loud metallic pings around the yard when they ricocheted off bathtubs or fenders of the vehicles, sometimes three or four times a shot. We all thought this was fascinating sport but risky for the eyes. Once Curly had offered to let Ziggy fire the pistol, but as soon as it was in his hand, Ziggy panicked and handed it right back. I was glad.

The BB pistol kept the skunks off the front of the property, but we all had seen wandering tribes of them in the back acres near the start of the forest, where they burrowed under the fence to breed and raise their young in the trunk of an old Dodge or Studebaker.

Curly knew this. Maybe just laziness made him ignore the skunks. In any case, he said it would be cruel to kill the skunks with bullets or poison. Besides, he said, the skunks kept the rats away, and he'd rather have skunks. We all had seen rats, too, but why argue with Curly?

"Just make a lot of noise when you go back there!" he shouted to his customers in his high-pitched voice. "The skunks will clear out for you. No stinky stuff. Go on! Come get me when you find what you need."

Also odd for a junk dealer, Curly had no dog. A year before we moved to Rehoboth, Achilles, his pit bull, had been run over by a coal truck. Perhaps out of loyalty to Achilles, Curly never found a replacement, even though a dog would have settled the skunk and rat infestations. If somebody had offered Curly a dog, he might have accepted it, but nobody ever did. Unless they had business to do with Curly, everybody left him alone.

Curly could usually be found tinkering with tools and motors somewhere on the lot or smoking a cigarette and reading a Greek magazine on the tiny porch of the wooden shack near the front gate. In the winter months, he mostly stayed home with his mother over in West Virginia. In January and February, it was rare to see his truck in front of the gate or any smoke puffing out of the upright muffler shaft on the roof that served as the shack's chimney.

I recall that around the time when Mother was giving birth to Blizzard, that nasty storm dumped three feet of snow everywhere, including on Curly's junkyard. This left large ghostly lumps looming all over the irregular hills of his property. Ziggy and I had hiked out to see it. The snow-covered machinery appeared as giant loaves of powdered sugar, beautiful and eerie to behold from the road. Ziggy loved it, and he could not wait to get home and tell Mother about it.

That fairy world landscape lasted only a day. Shortly after the blizzard, the sun shone down and quickly melted the thick white canopy, which had acquired an orange film. The ugliness underneath reemerged, a confusion of disintegrating contraptions swamped in red mud.

Each year, by the time spring came on, Nick's truck and the skunks, who had hibernated in his vehicles and appliances, were back again and visible. The baseball field next door started to perk up too.

Nick was raised in Greece, and he did not understand baseball, but he always wore a Pittsburgh Pirates cap with the visor hiked up in front, probably to hide his bald pate.

He was cordial to the boys who played on the field. If a home run sailed over the fence and rolled into his yard, he never fussed when we asked to retrieve it. Eventually he cut a hinged door in the wall for us in center field, so we didn't have to go way around to his front gate and delay our game too long. There was no lock on the door, so we could slip in and fetch the ball without bothering Curly or losing much time. Later, he jigsawed a square window in the wall near the right-field foul line, so he could stand on his side of the wall, keep an eye on his front gate, and watch us play.

Sometimes he dropped off a watermelon or iced soda pops in buckets, which hit the spot on early July days, when our pickup games might last all afternoon. He had also once donated fifteen steel and wooden doors from an abandoned furniture warehouse along with a spool of baling wire and eighty yards of chicken wire. Max and the older boys used it all to construct a makeshift backstop behind home plate.

Occasionally we would see Curly peering through the square hole in the fence to watch our games, almost as if he had nothing else to do or any other friends in the world.

With my bad leg, I could not run fast to catch fly balls. I was usually assigned to right field, where the ball rarely was hit. If I glanced over and saw a gold tooth glinting from the peephole, I would wave to Curly, and he always waved back.

After Jumbo lost his work in the mine and the zinc plant for the last time, he often scavenged in Curly's lot. If the truck was up and running and had gas, we'd go to Curly's in it. At other times, we took Jumbo's wheelbarrow. Jasper considered these trips an adventure, and I was always happy to have my buddy along. We came back with items Jumbo could use. If he spotted an old pressure cooker or a copper vat, Jumbo was likely to bring it back to refine his distilling rig.

Jumbo also used Curly's lot as a source for fabrics. At a time when Jumbo was flat broke and sober, he surprised us by fashioning garments for us. I saw him take his razor knife into an abandoned Oldsmobile sedan and harvest the entire seat padding and black velvet upholstery and roof lining. He then brought it all home in the truck and laid out the material on the worktable in the shed. Using Mother's old Singer, he crafted winter coats for me, Kazzy, and Blizzard.

That same winter he also made primitive boots from old leather interiors. Treads from discarded tires served as soles. The children at school ridiculed me, though most of them wore frayed hand-me-downs too.

"Let me guess. Jumbo made that for you?"

"Yes. He's fairly clever with a sewing machine."

"I can see that. Very clever."

"It keeps me warm."

"I bet it does."

Lucy asked Jumbo why he didn't ask the priest if we could snoop into the rectory's used clothes inventory, the way we had done when Mother was working for Father Fernando. Jumbo said he had no interest in talking to the priest. She could get her clothes there, but he did not want to feel indebted to a priest who would nag him again about his alcohol habit.

Like Curly, Jumbo did not understand baseball. He never watched us play. But when Max found an old boat with a canvas sail in Curly's yard, he cajoled Jumbo into taking the sail home and cutting and stitching together three bases to use on the ball field. Jumbo stuffed the three bases with horsehair padding from the upholstery of a wrecked Buick. The bases served us well for several seasons, yet another example of Jumbo's diverse skills.

One day, while I watched Jumbo slice through the leather seats of a partially cannibalized Chevrolet convertible, Curly heard me say, "Any chance you could make me a baseball glove with some of that leather, Jumbo?"

"I sewed your bases a couple years ago. Now you want a glove?"

"I was just wondering."

"Keep wondering. What kind of player can you be? With that leg of yours? You're almost twelve now and you know it's shorter than the other. Your Mother's prediction was wrong."

"But I can throw, and I can bat."

I didn't need Jumbo to tell me I was a lousy baseball player. But a decent glove would at least give me a better chance of catching a ball. I was ashamed of the ancient flappy mitten Max had given me. There I was out in right field, the worst player, and with a pitiful glove to match my skills.

Then one afternoon, Jumbo came home and said Curly had found a new ball glove in the trunk of a car. All I had to do was go out and ask for it. Curly was offering it to me free, because he knew I wanted a glove.

"Now? Can I go now?"

"Be back for supper. She's making chili and rice tonight. If you're late, you'll go hungry."

It was early May, my birthday was approaching, and I knew I probably wouldn't be getting anything else for turning twelve. This glove might be exactly what I would have asked for!

There were puddles along the road from a sudden shower. On my way out to Curly's, I thought about Mother's chili recipe, how delicious it would taste, and then I started thinking about Mother, who had been dead three years now, and how much I still missed her.

My memories of Mother slowed my pace along the road, and I inhaled the fresh woodsy spring air. The rain had cleaned the usual zinc acid bite in the nostrils, and when I closed my eyes, I could almost imagine being again at the farm up on the hill at Ripple Brook Gardens. May was beautiful on the old Wells place with the robins and the larks chirping and wildflowers blooming everywhere.

Eventually I looked far ahead around a curve in the road and saw my destination. Worried that I would arrive too late, I quickened my pace but then saw Curly's truck parked by his gate. Due to the brisk rain, the ball field was empty. Nobody would want to play there that afternoon. Large round puddles of rainwater had formed around home plate and at the three bases Jumbo had made, each a little square island in its own separate circular pond.

I passed Curly's truck and walked in through the gate. He was locking his office door.

"Mr. Katsaros!" I shouted, "Jumbo said you found a baseball glove."

Curly turned. "It's nice. And it's brand-new. Want it?"

"My birthday is coming up, and I would love to see it."

He went inside the office and came out holding a brand-new Bill Doak fielder's mitt, the same one I had seen and coveted in the Sears catalog. The glove had a leather web stitched between the thumb and the pointer finger, and in the catalog, it cost nine dollars, more money than I had ever held in my hand at one time.

Curly's bright blue eyes started blinking fast, and he popped the brim of his Pirates hat back over his brow. "It's yours," he said with one of his rare smiles.

I slipped my fingers into the glove's fragrant leather. I buttoned my wrist in and brought the palm of the glove up to my nose. It smelled raw, luxurious, new. I thrilled at the thought of showing it off to the other boys. I couldn't wait to field a fly ball with it, knowing that my catching ability would be immensely improved.

"Where did you get this?" I whispered.

"See that Chrysler over there? Guy was in a big hurry. Said he was leaving Pittsburgh forever and had to catch a train to St. Louis and didn't have time to wait around and sell it. Said I could have the car for fifty dollars if I drove him into the train station. Yeah, the car's like new, and so is your ball glove."

I blinked, amazed. "I can't believe it, Mr. Katsaros. Nobody else has a glove this nice."

"You call me Curly now on?"

"Okay, Curly."

"I got a few other things you might like," he said. He put his hand on my shoulder.

"No, thanks. I have to run home to dinner."

"Bat and a brand-new ball. Came out of the trunk of that guy's Chrysler."

"I promised Jumbo I would run right back for dinner."

"Let me get the bat and ball. You can have them too. More stuff for your birthday."

"Thanks, Curly. But I have to go home." I started walking toward the gate.

As I headed out, he went back into the shack and came out, following me with the new ball in one hand and the new Louisville Slugger bat in the other.

"You can try it out," he insisted. "I'm happy for you. All this is yours. Happy birthday!"

"It's not my birthday yet. I have to go."

"Come on, the field's on your way home. It won't take you any time at all."

"It's all wet."

"Not so wet. You can still see all the bases. You got to try out the glove. I gave it to you. Now I want to see you use it. I'm your fan, know what I mean?"

As we passed his truck, the sun came out from behind the clouds in the west. Long beams of gold stretched across the May grass. It glowed green, and fingers of steam wiggled up from the four puddles in the infield. The glove felt delicious on my left hand, and the desire to field a grounder or a skipper became urgent.

His hand with the ball was on my shoulder again, steering me away from the road and over the wet grass toward the infield. Neither of us talked, and he started to whistle. I recognized the melody of "Take Me Out to the Ballgame." I was surprised Curly knew that song, and I almost laughed. My good luck had made me giddy.

He put the ball into the pocket of the glove. I squeezed it through the leather, anticipating my new catching abilities as a drastically improved right fielder. The ball was new and spotless. The red and black threaded seams traced their endless patterns round and round the bleached horsehide.

He stopped whistling. "Feel nice?" he asked, his blue eyes blinking again.

I nodded and smiled. "Feels wonderful."

"You happy?"

I nodded again.

"Don't you want to break it in? Let's have a toss."

"No, I really don't have time. I don't want to seem ungrateful, but I will be late for dinner. Thank you so much, Mr. Katsaros."

"I told you to call me Curly."

"Thank you, Curly."

When I started back toward the road, he grabbed the ball from the glove and said. "Let me give you a toss!" Before I could respond, he had lofted the ball high up into the air, and I ran to catch it, so the ball would not get wet on the damp grass. The ball dropped neatly into the webbing of the glove, and I grinned.

"See that! A good glove, and you know how to use it, don't you! I bet you can use this new bat too."

"Yes, I sure can."

I underhanded the ball back to him. He had the bat in his left hand and caught the ball with his right and tossed it up, even higher. I drifted under it and caught it.

"How's it feel?"

"Perfect!"

He jogged over and put his hand around my throwing arm and felt my muscle. "Man, you strong up here. I know you got a bad leg there. But your arm is strong. Nothing weak with that arm. I bet you're proud of that arm. I bet you can throw the ball a mile."

When I pulled my arm away, his hand slipped down onto my wrist and grasped it firmly. By this time, we were walking on the muddy infield. It did not feel like he would be willing to let me go. Then he was standing behind me, close enough that I felt his belly against my back. I could not see the road. We were in plain view, if cars passed by. But I realized that if a car moved fast on that straight stretch, it would be unlikely anybody would notice us. Due to the rain and the puddles, I doubted that Jasper Slattery or any of the usual sandlot gang would show up. I began to tremble.

He started to pant. I smelled the tobacco on his breath. He was sweating heavily, and his strong body odor was mixed with a nauseating stink of kerosene. I could feel his fat cheeks quivering in a scary way. I had buttoned the baseball glove tight around my left wrist, so I couldn't peel his strong fist away from my arm.

I heard my voice tremble. "What are you doing, Mr. Katsaros?"

"Curly. You call me Curly," he commanded. He squeezed me close to his body and swung the bat up hard into my belly. Holding the bat with both hands he pressed his huge body against me from behind. We still were walking very slowly, and I looked down at the Louisville Slugger label beside his fist on the bat. It felt like he was squeezing the breath out of me. We splashed through the puddle at second base, and when I started to scream in fright, he lunged against me.

He shoved me down onto the soggy canvas base. The padding inside was wet and hard, and when I landed, his full weight pounded down on me. I lay stunned, facedown, the muddy water everywhere around me. Nick's kerosene odor pulsed over me. He started kissing my neck. His panting was fast. He started to grunt into my ear.

"Let me go! That hurts!" I screamed.

I had no idea what I had done wrong to him or why he was treating me so violently and kissing me at the same time. In my stunned state, pinned to second base, I felt his hands working my belt buckle. He slid my pants down to my knees. His chest crushed against my shoulders. I smelled his hot foul breath. He snorted with a crushing vibration that ran all along my spine. I felt him and heard him spit thick snot into the palm of his hand.

His fingers with the slimy snot on them groped around my poop hole. He forced a thick finger into me and grunted in his high-pitched voice, "You like me? You like Curly?"

I did not answer, and he started kissing my ear. His tongue was all over my ear, like he would bite it off. I was in too much pain to speak or do anything but sob. Then I started to vomit.

"You like me? You like Curly? Don't you?"

I started to scream, and then all I could do was cry.

The grunts and snorts and kisses continued. After his fingers came out of my butthole, I shrieked. He shoved what felt like a hammer handle up into me, cutting me hard, then lurching back and forth, deep into me. He rammed into me over and over again. I felt like my belly would split. He was so deep. I knew I would surely die soon.

"You're killing me, Mr. Katsaros! Please stop!"

"You ain't gonna die. I love you."

As sure as I had watched my mother die, this cruel man on top of me was killing me from the inside out, and I had no idea why or how he was torturing me.

At one point, my nausea stopped. All I had was pain, thrust after thrust. He was pounding my guts to death inside me. Surely, if I did somehow live, I would feel this pain forever.

And suddenly he stopped, except for his heavy chest movements and his kisses.

I could not feel anything inside me anymore. I felt dead from my belly button down. I didn't know if my legs would move or not. I looked straight in front of me at the sun shining on third base. I started trembling again, and he rolled away from me into the puddle. We both lay there for probably a minute, me trembling horribly and him breathing slowly on his side.

Then I heard him splashing. He stood up, his feet sloshing behind me in the puddle. I didn't know what he was doing, but I heard him close the snaps on his fly.

Lying on second base on my belly, I stared around and saw squirts of my blood darkening the puddled rainwater. It was a deep maroon in the water. My butthole was bleeding. The pain was so bad, I wanted to die.

"Stand up," he commanded. "Stand up. Pull up your pants. I'm sorry."

I was able to roll over and bring my knees up to my chest, squatting on the base. The puddle around me had a mix of vomit and blood in it.

I saw him glance hastily toward the road. "Pull your pants up!" he yelled in his high voice.

I stood up and wobbled, my underpants tight on my knees. I took two steps in the water. It hurt to walk. I unbuttoned the wrist strap and flicked the glove off. Then I drew my bloody pants up over my thighs and buttoned the fly of my jeans.

He still had the bat in his hands. "Don't tell nobody."

"Don't kill me. Are you going to kill me now?"

"No. I won't. But you don't tell nobody! Hear me?"

"I thought you were going to kill me."

"Don't tell nobody!"

"No."

"Not your father?"

"No."

"Not the priest?"

"No."

He nodded.

"Do you want to kill me?"

"I'm sorry. No, I'm not gonna kill you. I'm sorry. I like you."

"Can I go home now?"

He pointed toward the edge of the puddle. "Don't forget your glove."

I picked it up from the water. The ball was floating beside it, the horsehide now all red and brown.

Too stunned to move, I watched him scuffle off silently toward his truck with the bloody bat in his hands. He locked the gate to the junkyard and climbed into his truck. I kneeled down and watched the truck drive off toward West Virginia.

The only thing I knew for sure was that I was not dead. I was in too much pain to be dead. And I did not know what had happened to me. Kneeling on the field, I watched the sun falling behind the trees. I cried from the pain and also from the thought that perhaps this was the punishment I had been expecting for three years. This injury, whatever Nick Katsaros had done to me, had been lurking in the dark shadows of my imagination ever since I helped Mother die.

This was the punishment I deserved. This was physical pain to match what my heart had been feeling. This was the falling sensation, this was the crash at the end of my fall.

I could feel more warm liquid spilling out of my butthole and leaking inside my jeans down my thigh. I touched the seat of my pants, and the pain was horrible. Yes, this was definitely the punishment I deserved. I wept fiercely.

After about twenty minutes, I stood up and breathed slowly in and out. Then I started to walk, taking small steps. I decided on a long detour back to town.

I dropped by the nearest strip mine pond. It was secluded behind its mounds, and I peeled off my clothes and soaked them in the orange water. I crept into the pond. My butthole stung horribly as soon as it hit the chilly water, but I could tell the bleeding had stopped. I put my fingers on it and looked at them. There was no more blood. Maybe the cool water helped to stop the bleeding.

At the edges of the pond I collected pebbles and jammed at least twenty of them into the fingers of the Bill Doak fielder's mitt. Then I threw it out into the middle of the pond and watched it splash and sink fast to the bottom. I heaved the brown and red baseball into the woods as far as I could throw it.

Then I remembered there might be traces of my blood on the canvas covering on second base, but I felt too weak to walk back and clean it off. I would leave that task to Nick, I decided. I was not going back there. Never would I go back there.

I limped home and sneaked into the house by the back door. Jumbo was drinking in the shed, so he did not notice me. I told Vera and Lucy I had taken a swim in the strip mine pond, and my pants and shirt had fallen in. I asked if they could wash up my clothes.

Vera looked surprised. "Jumbo said you went to the junkyard to get a new baseball glove."

"The junkyard was closed. So, I went for a swim instead."

"That was a long swim, Taddy."

"Yes, the water was nice."

They looked at each other. Why should they believe me? But my skinny dip in the strip mine pond would be easier to believe than what the truth was.

They saw from the way I walked that I was in pain. I asked if they had any aspirin anywhere, because I had fallen on my butt when I jumped into the strip mine pond. Vera asked if I wanted her to look at it, but I said no. She poured me a glass of cold water and produced an aspirin tablet. That was my dinner that night. I was grateful for it.

I lost my passion for baseball. I avoided going anywhere near the ball field or the junkyard. I knew Jasper Slattery would be disappointed, and I wondered if maybe I should tell him about what had happened. But I knew I would not. I had kept my secret about Mother, and I would have to keep this secret too.

That night, as I lay in bed, I wondered if Mother had been in that much pain when she died. And I wondered if somehow, wherever she was, that she might know what had happened to me.

After half an hour, the aspirin started to work, and eventually I conjured up some bunnies in the moonlight to fight off the horrible images of the junkyard and the ball field. I desperately wanted to go unconscious for a long while.

Somehow, I fell off to sleep and woke up the next day with horrible pains in my abdomen and butthole. I stayed home from school for two days. I could pee, but I could not poop. I did not want to poop ever again. I did not want to read about Ben Franklin or anything. Vera wanted to take me to the doctor, but I told her I was feeling better each day. On the third day, I went to school but had not done any homework.

It took two weeks to move my bowels, and when I finally did, it was horrible and I bled for a week afterward. In fact, it was impossible for me to take a normal shit from then on. Even into adulthood, my turds always came out skinny as pencils. There were times on the toilet when I wished Curly had killed me.

I should have warned the other boys about him. I don't know if he did that to anyone else. I was just afraid to say a word about it to anybody. And I didn't.

Several times, Jumbo asked me to go with him to get things from the junkyard, and I refused.

"Why?" he asked.

"Why do you think?" I looked in his eyes defiantly, and I could see he did not want to think very hard about me. "I have to do my homework."

"Did you ever get that ball glove from Nick?"

"It wasn't my size."

"Too bad."

"Yeah. It was a beautiful glove."

Shame

My grades in school slipped. When Vera looked at my report cards, she was puzzled.

"What's wrong, Tad? Are you trying?"

"Yes."

"Is there something wrong?"

"No. I just have to try harder."

"I wish you would. Mother would not be pleased with these marks, not at all. I see you in your room studying hard. But look at these grades! Is it because you still miss Mother?"

"Maybe that's it. Maybe I can't concentrate because I miss her."

"Come here. Let me give you a hug. Everything will be all right. You're still not blaming yourself, are you?"

"No. I don't think so."

"You're crying, Tad. Let me just hold you tight for a while. Things will be all right."

Jasper was concerned too. He saw I no longer shared his joy at solving the math homework problems or doing extra reading in our history or science lessons. I stopped keeping weekly tabulations in my virtue notebook, and when I told him I had lost track of it completely, he was angry.

I certainly could not tell Jasper what Nick Katsaros had done to me. I was too ashamed. If I told Jasper, he might tell his parents.

Then word would likely spread all over town, about what I had let Nick do to me.

For the longest time, I was not sure what he had done to me, except that I hurt a lot.

In the weeks and months that followed, I started to feel another kind of shame, that I had allowed him to do it. I was probably the only boy in our whole group who could not outrun Nick. He was fat and slow and clumsy. Maybe that's why he picked me out, set a trap for me, told me he was my fan.

Should I have fought harder? Should I have tried to hurt him? Should I have snatched the bat out of his hands and hit him with it?

I was ashamed for being a slow runner and for being too stupid to grab the bat to defend myself and then for letting him pull my pants and underpants down. So many things to be ashamed about!

I pondered the deficiencies in my body and my passive behavior on that terrible May afternoon. For the previous three years, I had obsessed about the slippery elm mission for Mother on that grim November morning. Was I now complicit in some way with Nick Katsaros, just as I was with Mother?

Every time I found gobs of blood on my underwear or on my sheets and had trouble washing them out in the bathroom with cold water, I realized the secret would be hard to keep.

My blurred thoughts prevented me from understanding bad things that happened to my family. The first was when Max informed Jumbo he was leasing a bigger building for his motorcycle shop. He said he could no longer help us pay the rent at Robert Street, at least not for the next six months.

Jumbo had not worked anywhere steady for most of that year, and his credit line at the company store had been used up. Daddy Mac had been kind, but he needed some payment on the interest, and Jumbo had nothing to pay. He would have to sell either the truck or the piano. Otherwise, the mining company would evict us, plain and simple, and we would all be sent to foster homes. Even Jasper Slattery's father would not be able to save us.

Jumbo spoke briefly about riding a bus down to Jacksonville, Florida, where he said he once had a high-paying job with the railroad down there. That sounded like a wonderful plan. He could send home money to support us.

Before that idea went very far, Vera talked to Daddy Mac at the company store and finagled a plan by which the store would buy back the Beckwith. Daddy Mac said he would do Vera a special favor and pay the mining company directly for the three months' rent that was in arrears and for three months in advance. She was able to put sixty dollars back into the credit line, and our eviction was temporarily averted.

Three months later, Max found a buyer for the truck, took a percentage of the deal for himself, but was able to hand Vera a clean thirty-five dollars toward the rent. Later that year, Jumbo sold the parlor armchair and the Black Madonna and some of the tools in his shed to a door-to-door peddler.

During this time, I slept over at the Slattery house whenever I could. I started to wish they would adopt me. We all saw our family situation as desperate, and it did not seem to have any chance of improving. As much as I enjoyed school, my homelife was terrible and lonely. Listening to my crystal set at night did not offer much consolation. Jumbo was crafting more garments and shoes for us, and Lucy sneaked us over to the rectory thrift shop, where we scavenged through their bins of clothes others had discarded.

One afternoon after school, Jasper said, "Do you want to stay over at our house tonight? Mother is making macaroni and cheese. Isn't that your favorite?"

"Sorry, not tonight."

"You haven't been over for a couple weeks. Are we still friends?"

"Vera says I should stay home for a while. She is worried I am wearing out my welcome at your house."

"Come on, Tad. You know that's not true."

I accepted Jasper's invitation. That was a mistake. The macaroni and cheese was delicious, but before I went to bed I had a very painful poop in their upstairs toilet. During the night, my butthole bled. When I woke up, my pajamas were stuck to the sheets. I checked the mattress, and fortunately, I hadn't stained it. Jasper was still asleep in his bed, unaware of the mess I had made.

I wasn't bleeding anymore, so quietly I washed off in the bathroom and rolled up some toilet paper to stick in my butt crack, in case there was any spillage. Then I put on my school clothes. After I neatly made the bed, it looked just as if nothing had happened. When Jasper woke up, he didn't notice anything. At breakfast, I pretended to Jasper and his parents that everything was normal with me, even though I was worried that I could spring a leak at any moment.

At school things went normally till after lunch. I had to poop again, and this time it felt like fire coming out. I sat in the bathroom stall crying from the pain. I knew what would happen next, so again I wadded up toilet paper and put it in place. As I was washing my hands at the sink, an older boy looked down at my pants as he was walking out and said, "Hey? What's that, chief? Looks like you're getting your period. Next time, use the girls' bathroom."

I went back into the toilet stall and sobbed some more and rolled up more toilet paper. I knew I should go to the nurse's office, but I remembered she was only there mornings.

I never mentioned the bloody sheets to Jasper, and he never said anything about them to me. I was not invited to spend the night at their house after that. One time when I was there for dinner, Mrs. Slattery took me aside and asked, "Tad, do you have any secrets you might want to share?"

I shook my head no and smiled.

Brother Gus

During the months I was trying to deal with what Curly Katsaros had done to me at second base, Vera and Lucy started pestering me about catechism class. I had yet to go to confession or take Holy Communion. My sisters were concerned that I had been acting quiet and strange and coming home with mediocre grades. Maybe confessing to a priest would help me lift my spirits and raise my report card marks. Certainly, participating in the sacraments would improve me in the sight of God, which was important. It was impossible for me to take part in confession or Holy Communion, unless I first attended catechism class and was officially confirmed in the church, they explained.

"Your soul may be in peril," Lucy warned.

"Max never went. Neither did Ziggy."

"Max did go," Vera said.

"Mother made him," Lucy added. "But he didn't finish the course."

Lucy scowled. "You are not Max or Ziggy." She pointed her finger at my heart. "There's something wrong in there."

I blinked at her. "Okay, I'll go."

Lucy did one of her affectionate tortures: she leaned her forehead hard against mine, so that all I could see was her one wide-open eye. Meanwhile, she pinched my tummy to make me laugh.

"Okay. I said I would go."

"Don't be scared, Taddy. I can coach you on all the questions. You'll do great. And you'll love Brother Gus. He's such a peach."

Brother Augustine was approachable, informal, and bighearted. If anybody could make catechism class bearable, it was burly Brother Gus. He insisted that everybody in his class call him not Brother Gus, just Gus. We all were nervous, so we did what he said. I did not know how many other children in the class had souls in peril, but we all were more than willing to do whatever we had to in order to get through the class.

And Lucy was correct when she said Brother Gus was a peach.

A stout man in his early thirties, Gus had a round head, wide pink cheeks, thick blond brows, and an easy smile that filled his face much of the time. His eyes were an intense crystal blue, and for a large man, his voice was surprisingly high-pitched, a full-throated tenor. His solo singing of Schubert's "Ave Maria" was the highlight of our most recent midnight Christmas Mass.

Though he had prematurely lost most of his hair, Gus had retained an isolated island of curly blond strands about the size of a thumbprint at the peak of his forehead and then rich yellow curls around his ears and up onto the back of his head. He was a friar, not a priest, which meant instead of wearing tight clerical collars and black garments like the other Rehoboth rectory residents, Brother Gus walked around in a loose wool robe that was light brown and tied at the waist with a rope.

On cold days, he wore a hooded black cloak on top of it. Unless there was snow on the ground, he wore sandals without socks, probably like what the people wore in the Holy Land during Jesus's time. This meant that when he started talking very seriously about a question in our catechism book, we could see his toes wiggling rapidly. In fact, his whole trunk would rock about on his chair. This extra body language sometimes distracted us from the point he was trying to put across in his explanation. Once we got used to it, we stopped staring at his feet and his wriggling torso and looked him in the eyes, which is what he wanted us to do when he spoke. Eye contact with Gus was key.

"If you aren't looking at me, you're not listening to me," he said several times on the first day.

"When you speak, I look at you. So please do the same for me, and you will learn a lot. We all will have a great time! At the end of the course, you'll go to your first confession, take your first Holy Communion, and then I'll treat you to ice cream. How does that sound?"

Gus told us about his background. His parents were farmers, originally from Sweden. They were strict Lutherans. He was born and grew up on a corn and cattle farm in Iowa.

Gus looked the part, every pound a proud farmer: jutting jaw, wide shoulders, brawny forearms, and a broad, ambling stride. His long wool robe also had a wholesome human body odor in its thick folds, consistent with farmwork. When I told him I first grew up on a farm, he chuckled, his eyes beaming brightly as he shook my hand hard.

"Did you talk to your animals, Tad?" he joked.

"Sometimes."

"Yes, they like it if you talk to them."

"We used to have a pair of cows here in Rehoboth. We milked them twice a day. My brother Ziggy and I sometimes talked to them all day. And they liked it when I played my harmonica for them. We called them Rose and Mary."

"Yes, Tad. People simply don't realize how much animals enjoy music. And I bet your music made their milk sweet?"

"I guess it did. I'm not really sure."

"Of course, it did."

Gus said his parents sent him to college in St. Louis to study agriculture, but then "one golden dawn" while fishing on the banks of a little river that flowed into the Mississippi, God called to him from the sky.

"Just like that. No turning back. No questions asked. No more agriculture studies. No more being a Lutheran," Gus said.

His life was changed by an irrevocable decision.

"Was it like when the risen Christ confronted Saint Peter on the road away from Rome?" I asked.

"How do you know about that?"

"*Quo Vadis*," I answered.

"Gosh, Tad, you must study your Bible hard."

"Not really. *Quo Vadis* is a famous book in Poland. My mother told me all about it."

"Well, yes. My decision was immediate, just like Peter's. I think you're going to do great in catechism class!"

To Gus's parents' shock and disappointment, he joined the Roman Catholic Church and entered a Franciscan order. He traveled around now as a catechism specialist, mostly in the mid-west, and with occasional postings in West Virginia and Pennsylvania. He had a reputation of being great with young people. The Pittsburgh Diocese had assigned him for a two-year stint in Rehoboth. Lucy's youth fellowship group felt lucky to have him as their leader.

Gus lived in the same rectory building near our first house in Rehoboth. He conducted the catechism class, attended by about a dozen children my age, every Tuesday afternoon after school in the rectory conference room. The course lasted three months. I wished that Jasper Slattery could come with me to the classes, because there were some pretty girls from outside Rehoboth in the group. And Jasper would have enjoyed meeting Brother Augustine too. But Jasper was Presbyterian, so that was out. I didn't bother to suggest it to him.

In the class, we all sat on folding chairs in a circle, which made eye contact with all of us easy. On that first meeting, he handed around pamphlets and explained that over the twelve-week course, we would consider the ninety-five questions listed in the pamphlet, taking up ten questions each week, and with a review at the end.

We were also expected to memorize the definitions of important words like magisterium and monstrance and chrism and the Assumption.

Lucy proved to be a great resource. She knew her catechism cold. She could spout out all the definitions without blinking, and she helped me memorize them before each written quiz. I could tell Brother Gus was pleased with my weekly performance, and I actually began to look forward to our sessions. When he asked me why I was so interested in the various topics presented and why I showed up first to class each week and scored high on the quizzes, I said I was keen to look after the welfare of my soul. He tilted his head and winked at me approvingly.

"That's unusual for a boy your age."

"Thanks," I said.

Some weeks in class, I would jump ahead to topics that were not scheduled for the day but that seemed crucial. The lockstep question-and-answer method of the catechism struck me as too rigid. No room for explanations. No gray areas, no give-and-take on why or why not. Questions 48 and 49, for example, looked bleak to me, which I mentioned to Gus on the second week.

> *48. Q: What is purgatory? How do people get there? How do they get out of there?*
>
> *A: Purgatory is a place of temporary punishment for souls that die in the state of grace but who must be purified of venial sin or of any temporary punishment still due to their sins before they can enter heaven.*
>
> *49. Q: Will people in hell ever get out?*
>
> *A: No, the punishment of hell is eternal.*

As gracious and welcoming as Gus was, he admitted there was no way he could sugarcoat the answers to questions 48 and 49. The catechism was the law. Hell is hell. Period.

Of particular concern to me, also, was number 53:

> *53. Q: What is sacrilege? What kind of sin is it? Give examples of it.*
>
> *A: A sacrilege is the irreverent treatment, or mistreatment, of sacred persons, places, or things; it is also the reception of any of the sacraments unwor-*

thily. It is a mortal sin. Examples of sacrilege are knowingly receiving Holy Communion in mortal sin; or knowingly not confessing all of one's mortal sins in confession.

As I pondered all these onerous issues and went over them in detail first at home with Lucy and then with Brother Gus, my heart pounded and ached. Brother Gus reassured me that at my early age, I surely would not have all that much to confess.

He said once I had made my first confession, I would feel a wonderful freedom, a sense of a burden being lifted from my shoulders and from my heart. Jesus would forgive me through the priest. All I would have to do was pray some Our Fathers and Hail Marys, do a "ring around the rosary," as he called it, and poof, onward to my everyday Christian life with a pure heart and a clean spirit.

In class when I looked into Brother Gus's twinkling eyes, confession seemed like it would be a cinch. The other children seemed eager to get on with it, ready to charge into the double-chambered booth and spill their darkest thoughts and deeds to the forgiving Lord through his agent on earth, the whispering man behind the lattice screen.

But on my way back to 7 Robert Street, I would recall that my soul was probably very much in greater peril than their souls, so maybe I should think it all through again before venturing into that booth.

In week nine or ten of the course, I became increasingly worried. I asked Brother Gus if perhaps I should enroll in his next catechism class, too, prior to making my first confession, just to be sure I understood fully what everything meant.

He frowned. Then he tried to reassure me by saying that it's all about mystery.

"Mystery is the most wonderful part of being a Christian, Tad. Not until we see our Maker himself will any of us actually have a real understanding of Jesus. Right now, while we are alive on earth, we should follow the rules of the Church and enjoy and praise its mystery."

When I did not seem convinced, he looked peeved.

"No. You do not need to take the course all over again. That would confuse you even more. You've already made 100 percent on all the quizzes, and you're one of the best catechism pupils I have ever had. That includes children from all nine of the states I've taught in."

His flattery did not comfort me. I did not want to be the best catechism student in the country. I wanted the problems with my soul to be fixed.

I pointed out to him part of the answer to question 84: *If we deliberately withhold a sin in confession, no sins we have confessed are forgiven; moreover, we commit another mortal sin of sacrilege.*

"That's right, Tad. When you go into the booth, you've got to tell the whole story. If you hold back anything from the priest, you might as well not even go into the booth in the first place."

"Holding back is bad?"

"Holding back is the same as lying to God. No matter how many Our Fathers or Hail Marys you say, Jesus will know you're holding back, and you weren't serious about the whole effort. He will feel personally betrayed."

"I would not want to do that!"

"Sometimes I think you're too serious about all this."

"But we're talking about the future of my soul, aren't we?"

"Yes, but back off a little bit. Remember what Paul wrote to the Corinthians: 'The letter kills, but the spirit gives life.'"

The next week I asked him about questions 87 and 88.

87. Q: How do we make up for the punishment due to our sins once they have been forgiven?

A: We can make up for the punishment due to our sins by performing the penance imposed after confession and by prayer, attending Mass, fasting, almsgiving, the works of mercy, the patient endurance of sufferings, and indulgences.

88. Q: What is an indulgence?

*A: An indulgence is the remission of all or some of
the temporal punishment due to our sins.*

"So, Gus, I read up about indulgences in the school encyclopedia, and I wonder if it is still possible to buy indulgences, if somebody could afford them?"

"The Church gave up that practice back in the sixteenth
century."

"Yes, I read about the Council of Trent. But if I give a lot of
money to the church, can I avoid hell?"

"No. But don't worry. I know you are not going to hell."

"How do you know?"

"Because Jesus always forgives our sins. Stop worrying so much
about it. Promise me you will. Enjoy the mystery of it all."

"That's what Jesus wants us to do?"

"Yes. Just by pondering that mystery, you will grow much closer
to Jesus. And that's what you want. That's what we all want."

48

Confession and Communion

The Tuesday before our first Holy Communion, Brother Gus awarded each of us a string of rosary beads: glass crystal for the girls, olive wood for the boys. We drilled on them in class, going all around the circle and saying the prayers out loud. After class, we stepped out of the rectory and into the church, where we sat in one of the pews and waited for the two priests, who sat in the two booths, to hear our first confessions. It was just a regular sunny spring day outside in Rehoboth, but it seemed to me like the end of my soul's future.

The course had proved to me that my soul was doomed. I also concluded I would worsen my already dire condition if I left the confession booth not telling the priest anything about Mother's death or my encounter at second base with Curly Katsaros.

"I played with my dinky four nights in a row last week, Father."

"That's all?"

"Maybe five nights. Twice in a row on two of those nights."

"No, I mean are those the only sins you wish to tell me about?"

Brother Gus saw me leave the booth, and he gave me a proud grin. He waved me over to where he was sitting at the end of the pew. Afraid to look into his eyes, I stared down at his feet. His toes were wiggling to beat the band.

"Hey, look at me. That wasn't so hard, was it?"

"No, not hard at all."

"And you weren't in there more than a minute. See! I knew you'd sail through it easily."

"It wasn't as hard as I thought. The priest was nice."

"See that? Jesus loves you, Tad. Isn't that a wonderful relief?"

"I haven't done my penance yet. I must run home and do that right away." I pulled my rosary beads from my pocket and squeezed them in my fist, so Gus would see I meant business.

Communion the following Sunday did not go as smoothly. I kneeled at the Communion altar and whispered the phrase from the catechism handbook, *"Lord, I am not worthy that you should enter my roof but only say the Word and my soul shall be healed."*

I bowed my head, straightened my spine, and stretched my palms out, left above right. The priest came down the line, paused, and murmured, "The body of Christ." Then he dropped the circular white wafer into my palm. Fortunately, I had my eyes open, because it was so light, I could barely feel it. If it weren't for my eyes open, I might have dropped it. Pure luck.

I raised my palms to my mouth and felt the little dry wafer stick to the roof of my mouth and suck up all my saliva. Almost immediately the priest brought the silver chalice with the wine and tilted it toward my mouth. My upper lip bumped the chalice, and a wave of wine, smelling exactly like Jumbo's home product, sprayed into my mouth and down my chin.

The odor and taste of the wine instantly brought up the vile scent of Jumbo's breath. I had smelled it countless times. I had barely closed my lips before my stomach heaved and pitched its bitter liquid contents into my mouth.

The priest saw me and jumped back to avoid vomit spraying on his white raiment. Fortunately, my lips were sealed tight, though part of my vomit, mixed with the wine, shot up the back of my mouth and out my nostrils.

I choked. I couldn't breathe. Lucy, who was kneeling beside me, instantly pulled her handkerchief from her pocket and covered my face and pounded my back. This helped me get my breath back.

We stood and turned to leave the altar with my face masked by the handkerchief. Lucy guided me down the steps, but not being able to see where I was going, I stumbled. Lucy caught me by the elbow, or it could have been worse.

I heard her quickly whisper the post-Communion prayer, which I had memorized from the catechism handbook, but could not recite at the moment.

"I thank you, O holy Lord, almighty Father, eternal God, who have deigned, not through any merits of mine, but out of the condescension of your goodness, to satisfy me a sinner, your unworthy servant, with the precious body and blood of your Son, our Lord Jesus Christ."

Outside the church after the Mass, Brother Gus called all of his pupils together for a photograph. I was embarrassed to be around anybody, because I knew I must have smelled of wine and vomit, and nobody seemed to want to stand near me. Due to my vomiting, I did not actually swallow any of the blood or the body of Jesus Christ. Almost all of it went out my nose. This may have been an unconscious impulse of my soul. Since I had not confessed my most important sins, I realized that I had unwittingly not compounded my sin by swallowing correctly. Vomiting was actually a good thing for the future of my soul, I reckoned secretly.

Brother Gus spread his long arms out beside the photographer and smiled broadly. "You did great, class! How does it feel now to be a real Christian, freed of sin, and to know how much Jesus loves you?"

After the photograph was taken, the other children cheered and thanked him for our excellent instruction. He then treated everybody to ice cream cones, as he had originally promised. I wasn't in the mood for ice cream. I was just glad the course and the ordeals were over, because I did not feel great to be a real Christian that day. I was hardly free. I was doomed, and I knew it. Let the children with clean souls enjoy their ice cream. They earned it.

As for Brother Gus, a few months after our class, he was transferred to a parish way down in Thurmond, West Virginia, another coal mining town, to continue his catechism teaching to yet another group of immigrant children. This disappointed many of us, since it meant we would not hear him sing Schubert's "Ave Maria" again at midnight Christmas Mass.

Years later, I concluded that Brother Gus, because of his upbeat and glowing personality, served the church brilliantly as an itinerant preceptor. He was the ideal vehicle to deliver the bitter fear of an inevitable hell into the pliant minds of children.

Taken seriously, the lessons of those ninety-five questions and answers in his pamphlet were terrifying. And yet his glowing disposition gave the illusion that there was almost nothing to worry about, as long as you followed the rules spelled out in the pamphlet.

Ben Franklin's weekly virtue checklist, which I had failed repeatedly, was a cake walk compared to the book of catechism.

How could Gus reassure me that I was not going to hell? How could he know?

Still nauseated from my first Communion that Sunday, I watched skeptically as Gus dipped the ice cream from the clay bowl in the cooler and spooned it into big waffle cones for the others in my class. His blue Swedish eyes flashed, and his large round head with the golden curls on the sides rolled around with a smile of jolly optimism for all of us. Everybody was supposed to feel wonderful around Brother Gus, and most did. I did not.

However, I am grateful to Brother Gus for a tip he gave me, quite by accident. This tip was incredibly useful to me, but it wasn't in the catechism pamphlet.

As I mentioned before, one of Brother Gus's odd bodily habits, while he was conducting class, along with wiggling his toes, was to shift around a lot on his folding chair. At first, we all thought it was because of his dynamism and his passion for what he was teaching. It seemed like he was so possessed by what he wanted us to learn that he literally squirmed in his seat while teaching us.

But he also sometimes leaned forward and reached his large right hand back behind the chair. He did this when we were praying, and all our eyes were supposed to be shut. He would scratch the back portion of his brown wool robe far below the knotted rope at his waist, sometimes even down near his butthole.

I was not the only one in the catechism class to observe this. Several of the boys made wisecracks about it later. Sometimes, never to his face, they called him Brother Ants in his Pants.

291

Several days after our first Communion, I went over to the rectory to pick up my confirmation certificate. Nobody was in the hall where we had our classes, but I found the certificates all laid out in alphabetical order on a table against the wall. I found my certificate and had it in hand, but then I realized I urgently had to poop.

I ran up to the second floor, where there was a large men's bathroom with white ceramic tiles on the walls and floors. There were four toilet stalls with curtains, half a dozen sinks, and a gang shower where the priests all washed up. I knew about the bathroom, because cleaning it had been one of Mother's jobs back when she first worked for Father Fernando. I sometimes watched her work there, often with Vera, scrubbing the sinks and the toilets. To tell the truth, whenever I had a chance and was in the area of the rectory, I liked to run in and use that bathroom. It reminded me of Mother.

That day the toilet stalls were empty, and I ran into the first one, near the shower. While I was sitting and waiting for it all to come out of me, I heard the water spraying out in the shower and a couple of voices talking loud enough that I could hear what they were saying. One was Brother Gus's high-pitched voice and the other was a priest I did not know, whose voice was deep and loud. They both had raised their voices to speak above the noisy spray of the shower water.

While I sat in the stall, I looked down at the floor near the shower curtain. I noticed on the white tiles leading into the shower a string of wet, round blood droplets that looked like a curving row of red pennies.

I knew that blood had not come out of me. I had done a beeline directly into the toilet stall and did not go near the shower threshold, where the blood drops lay.

"Yeah, it's my goddamn hemorrhoids," Brother Gus said in the shower. "Pretty embarrassing!"

"Do they bleed often like that?"

"No, only now and then. But it sure can be messy. And sometimes they itch like hell."

"How did you get them?"

"Hemorrhoids? A lot of people get them. That's what the doctors tell me."

"But aren't you kind of young to get hemorrhoids?"

"I was raised on a farm. Farmers do a lot of heavy lifting. On my dad's farm, I had to heave bales of hay, sometimes from dawn till sunset."

"So, you toiled in the fields?"

"Yes, everybody in Iowa knows that can give you hemorrhoids. I've been to several medical men about it, but all they do is give me cream to put on. Nothing stops the bleeding, especially after I take a big crap. And sometimes the itching drives me nuts. They said I could have an operation, but frankly I would be scared to have anybody put a knife near my asshole. Wouldn't you?"

When I was finished in the toilet, I wiped myself quickly, didn't see any blood on the tissue, and then washed my hands at the sink as fast as I could. As I ran out the bathroom door, I looked back and saw Brother Gus, a towel around his waist, swabbing the white bathroom tiles with a paper towel.

The next day during recess at school, I went to the encyclopedia in the school library and looked up hemorrhoids, a tough word to spell. I learned that hemorrhoids are swollen veins near the butthole, or anus. They can grow big and can itch and bleed like crazy. Women apparently acquire them during pregnancy, and men often can bring them on by becoming chronically constipated or by repeated heavy lifting, as Brother Gus had mentioned to the priest in the shower.

I knew I could use this tidbit of medical knowledge to avoid embarrassment. In the future, if anybody noticed blood on my underwear, for example in the school lavatory or in the locker room, I could say I had hemorrhoids. I got them from lifting heavy buckets of milk every morning and afternoon from our family cows, Rose and Mary. Nobody could dispute that fact. The excuse was a lie, but it seemed like a reasonable alibi. I used it successfully as I got older.

Years later I thought that, after all the catechism class discussions about hell and purgatory and rules of the church and my inevitable damnation from my sins, Brother Gus's revelation about bleeding hemorrhoids was probably the most useful tip of all, though he would never know he had taught me.

I want to add that I believe Brother Gus's story that lifting hay bales on the farm in Iowa had given him hemorrhoids. I hope it was not a false claim to cover up something bad, something like what happened to me.

Big Shot

Max motorcycled over one night after dinner and surprised us with a thick wad of cash to help with the rent. He had sold two Harleys that week, and he wanted to share the profits. He said he also wanted to tell Jumbo something important in private. Overjoyed with the money, Vera started counting the bills, and Max and Jumbo headed out toward the shed.

Now nineteen, Max stood an inch taller than Jumbo and broader in the shoulders. As they made their way out through the kitchen hallway, I watched that same swagger in their steps, which I would never be able to copy. But Max's strut seemed more exaggerated than usual that evening, and no doubt he had knocked back a whiskey or two prior to his arrival. From the keen glint in his eyes, I suspected Max's news was important. In the shed, Jumbo would likely make more alcohol available to lubricate their man-to-man chat.

After twenty minutes or so, I sneaked out on the back porch. In that short time, their voices, animated and fortified by vodka, had already risen in volume and intensity. I tapped on the shed door and poked my nose in. I told them if this was an important matter that they wanted to discuss in private, they should quiet down and not agitate Kazzy and Bliz or worry the girls.

They were standing by the worktable, squared off, their faces flushed and sweaty. A half-empty vodka bottle stood on the worktable, flanked by a pair of empty shot glasses. They both were fuming and clearly annoyed that I had bothered them. Max grabbed the knob and shoved me out. "Scram, Tadpole!" he shouted and slammed the door.

They did not lower their voices. I remained on the porch and listened. I hoped Vera and Lucy could not hear them.

"Damn it, Max! Don't you know better? Those Hunterton whores carry all kinds of bad stuff. Crabs for starters. Clap. Syphilis. You name it. Those girls will get your cock clogged up so bad, you'll be pissing out your ass!"

"Look who's talkin'. Didn't I see you down there again last Friday night? Right there on Water Street? What, did you hitch a ride all the way down there just to get laid?"

"Must have been somebody else looks like me."

"Nobody else looks like you. And I know you probably rode right back here and fucked Vera, didn't you?"

"No."

"Bullshit! You're preaching to me about crabs and clap. For all you know, you're bringin' all that disease back from Hunterton and giving it to Vera. And what happens if you make her pregnant?"

"You shut the fuck up about Vera. I'm careful with her."

"Listen, if you don't stop fucking my sister, I'll kill you. People around town talk about you and her, you know."

"Who the hell do you think you are, some kind of big shot? All grown-up suddenly, are you? And now you tell me you're getting married. What's her name?

I sneaked over to the window and saw the two of them, their faces flushed under the bare light bulb.

"Benny. Benny Papallardo."

Jumbo poured some vodka into his glass and gulped it down. "Papallardo? You're gonna marry a wop? Christ, is she pregnant?"

"Hell, no."

"Are you sure? How do you know?"

"She said she missed two periods, but that doesn't mean she's pregnant."

"Well, what else could it mean? Benny Papallardo? She's the daughter of that bar owner over in Rulandville? The guy who gave me the corks and the wine bottles?"

"Yeah. Pasquale Papallardo. It's not a bar. It's a restaurant. A nice restaurant."

"So, you mean I'm gonna have a dark-skinned guinea grand-child? Just what I always dreamed of! Coming to America, so my first son can have lots of little Sicilian wop rodents running around on the floor? Is that what you're telling me? And I hear Pasquale Papallardo is in with the mob. He has a numbers racket that covers every town from out Monroeville clear down to Wheeling. And you, my boy, are in for some serious crap now, you idiot. Knock up a wop girl like that? How old is she?"

"Sixteen."

From the window, I saw Jumbo sneer. "The girl is sixteen? Sixteen?"

"Yeah. So what? I thought she was a little older."

"In terms of fucking up your life, stupid, you make Ziggy look like a genius!"

Jumbo nodded at Max, taunting him with a sneer.

Before I could blink, Max's big right fist shot up and ramrodded Jumbo's exposed chin. He popped him right on the dimple. Jumbo's neck snapped back, and his head crashed onto his workbench and then down onto the floor. A loud sustained clattering followed as half a dozen tools fell loose from their workbench hooks and slammed down around Jumbo. One of the hammers and the sharp blade of a chisel just missed his forehead.

He lay there, unconscious at Max's feet, the electric light swing-ing wildly on its wire and casting shifting shadows through the shed.

Max stood red-faced, his chest heaving and his fists still clenched. With his broad brow knit tightly in rage, he fixed his glance on Jumbo's face. It was vacant, no inkling of consciousness in it.

For an instant, I feared Max would kick Jumbo's skull. But he seemed spent, satisfied with what he had done and that Jumbo was still breathing.

His nostrils flaring, Max grabbed the vodka bottle, drained it, and bolted through the door. He blew past me, strode quickly around to the front of the house, not bothering to go inside and say goodbye to my sisters. Out front he leaped onto his Harley and took off into the night.

Vera and Lucy burst out of the kitchen door. They ran through the shed door and kneeled by Jumbo. I stood paralyzed in the doorway. Vera slapped Jumbo's cheeks. Lucy listened to his chest for his heartbeat. I gazed at my sisters kneeling by their father and toiling to revive him amid the clutter of scattered screws, bolts, tools, and broken bottles.

I confess it: while they were doing their best to bring him to consciousness, I hoped Jumbo would die right there. This would be a chance for all of us to be free.

I imagined Brother Gus's clownish round face looking me in the eyes as he waved his finger to shame me. I could not recall any question in the catechism pamphlet that said what the penalty was for wanting your father to die. Such a sin was too evil even to mention for someone who wanted guidance on the journey of his soul.

But I savored that feeling. It was in me, as real as the hard and fast thuds of my heart. I had felt it before, but while I peered at my sisters trying to revive Jumbo, it had never seemed as realizable as now. And I doubted there was any way to atone for that feeling, not for someone like me, who couldn't even swallow Communion wine.

Blended with my hate for Jumbo was my gratitude for Max. At that moment, I loved Max for what he did. I loved him.

I even whispered it to myself, "I love you, Max."

It surprised me to feel that, but I did love him.

Piccolo Palermo

Max's wedding was assembled in a rush. Guests on the Malinowski side of the sanctuary would be sparse. Jumbo assumed nobody at the mine or the metals plants would want to attend, and he, therefore, invited exactly nobody. He said he was embarrassed that Max's bride, Bennedetta Papallardo, was sixteen and obviously pregnant. The fewer in attendance, the better, he said.

Vera invited two of her laundry clients plus Mrs. Lewis. They accepted, but when they found out the father of the bride was Pasquale Papallardo and that the reception was to be at *Piccolo Palermo*, Pasquale's ristorante, they all declined. *Piccolo Palermo* was known for late-night poker games and was said to hide a speakeasy in the basement, purely a rumor, according to Max.

Daddy Mac from the company store was the Malinowski family's only guest.

I invited Jasper. Without speaking with his parents, he said no. When I asked him why, he reminded me that the year before, Vera and Lucy had forbidden me to go with his family to their Presbyterian service. They both said it was against Roman Catholic rules to enter a church of heretics. So, Jasper assumed his parents would not approve of his going with me to St. Augustine's over in Rulandville.

"But it's a wedding. It's not like a real Mass or anything."

"Is it one of those services where the priest serves wine?"

"You don't have to drink the wine. I already asked about that."

"My parents are strict. Besides, my dad said Max is getting involved with a very shady family."

"What's that supposed to mean?"

"My father is an accountant. He has to protect his reputation."

I realized again my relationship with Jasper, once so important to us both, was weakening. His excuse about not going with me to Max's wedding was further evidence of that decline. I was hurt, but I tried to understand that religious prejudice can divide families from each other, even when the head of the family isn't much of a believer, which was certainly the case with Jumbo. But as Mother used to say, "Nothing to be done."

Gathering the widely dispersed Papallardo family for a hurry-up marriage was complicated. Max said he heard that weddings were important to people from Sicily, and not attending was considered a deep insult. Benny had two uncles in Chicago, for example. Neither could attend, which offended Benny's father. Their excuses seemed almost flippant: they had restaurants and other business matters to take care of.

Pasquale had similar responsibilities, but out of family loyalty, he had attended three weddings in Chicago. So now what was their problem? Another branch of the family up in Massachusetts also declined. This led me to believe that there were levels in the hierarchy of the Papallardo clan. Perhaps the Rulandville branch might rank lower than Pasquale would like. But I did not mention my theory to Max. He had enough concerns on his hands without worrying about marrying a bride with an inferior Sicilian pedigree.

On the plus side, two Papallardo families from New York and another from New Jersey said they would take the train out. This consoled Pasquale. And on a local basis, all the Papallardo uncles and aunts and cousins from Hunterton, Ohio, and Wheeling, West Virginia, planned to come, so there would be plenty of mouths to feed at the reception in *Piccolo Palermo*.

Pasquale booked six cabins in the charming new Twin Oaks Motor Court, just two miles out of Rulandville. He happened to be part owner of the motor court, and his out-of-town family would stay in comfort and for free.

Kazzy and Blizzard were old enough now to get excited about the event. After a stroll with Lucy up to the rectory, where we once again picked around in the boxes of used clothing, we were all able to look presentable at the ceremony.

On the day of the wedding, Benny's father sent a Cadillac limousine over to Robert Street to pick us up. Jumbo stood ramrod erect in his black suit and derby as we stepped out in the morning sunshine in front of St. Augustine's. He smiled proudly as he watched the chauffeur help Vera and Lucy step up onto the sidewalk, followed by Kazzy and Blizzard, hand in hand. A photographer took pictures.

Jumbo said little that whole day. Due to the injuries he sustained in the shed two weeks before, when the groom coldcocked him, all Jumbo could do was smile and whisper and bow at the waist. Max's swift uppercut had fractured Jumbo's jaw in three places, and when Jumbo's skull smashed on the floor, one of his neck vertebras shattered. When he regained consciousness, an hour after the fall, he had severe jaw and neck pains and darting electrical spasms in his hands and feet.

The next day, Dr. Zankowski came to our house, examined Jumbo, and immediately sent him in an ambulance to St. Agatha's Hospital in Pittsburgh, where Mother had died. The oral surgeons and neurosurgeons took X-rays. Steel wires were strung through Jumbo's teeth to clamp the jaw shut. They said all he could eat for the next two months was soup. Then they would see him again to take off the wires, if the bone fragments healed smoothly.

The spine specialist wrapped him in a thick padded brace to keep his head straight. This helped to limit the excruciating pain that ran right up into his skull and into both shoulders when he looked up or down or to either side. On the morning of the wedding, Jumbo had shed the brace, because it did not fit under the collar of his starched Sunday white shirt. Vera assisted him with shaving that morning, including his scalp and neck, and she helped him tie his bow tie so that he did not move his head. In fact, he looked convincingly intact, despite the wobbly skeletal components, which nobody could see.

Several times that day, when I watched him in the church, his eyes squinted and his lips pursed in agony. I presumed it was dangerous for him to be without his neck brace. The doctors at St. Agatha's insisted he should never take it off, except to wash his neck. He risked instant and permanent paralysis. To look sharp at his son's wedding, however, he disregarded medical advice.

Another medical factor at play in the church involved Jumbo's drinking history. In the two weeks leading up to the ceremony, Jumbo had continued to sip wine and vodka through a glass straw. This was Dr. Zankowski's recommendation.

Knowing Jumbo was an inveterate alcoholic, Dr. Zankowski said he thought it would be best to allow him to drink small amounts of alcohol every day leading up to and at the wedding to prevent his coming down with delirium tremens. The shakes, hallucinations, and convulsions of the d.t.'s could wrench his neck and sever his spinal cord forever, paralyzing him. Better to stave off the d.t.'s with maintenance alcohol, suggested Dr. Zankowski. Not surprisingly, Jumbo complied.

There was another consequence of Max's punch to Jumbo's chin, more cosmetic than medically serious. The day after the fall, the whites of Jumbo's eyes had bloodied up and the sockets had blackened grotesquely. He suffered no change in vision, and he could roll his eyes around without difficulty. Dr. Zankowski said the blood from the combined blows to his chin and the back of his head had resulted in the release and pooling of blood around his eyes, which in time would resolve without serious consequence.

Still, Jumbo looked hideous when he grimaced, which he did frequently due to the pain. Shining pate, gold tooth gleaming, and his red eyes glaring out from black caves, he was a gruesome creature. Jasper Slattery said Jumbo looked like the skull on the Jolly Roger flag.

Vera worried about how he would look at the wedding, but as the days passed, the red blotches faded from his eyeballs, and his black sockets lightened to yellow and then to their usual flesh color. We were all relieved, especially Jumbo, whose obsession with the appearance of the fellow he saw in his shaving mirror every morning was critical to his self-esteem.

At the church, I spent much of my time in the first row, glancing over at Jumbo on the far side of Vera. I wanted to be sure he was not moving his head around and becoming suddenly paralyzed. When the organist played "Here Comes the Bride," he stood with the rest of the congregation, then he cranked his whole body around toward the middle aisle and watched as Benny proceeded slowly to the altar. Max and the priest were waiting for her, along with the best man, Travis Arsenault, Max's newly hired assistant mechanic in the motorcycle shop. They wore rented tuxes and looked nervous but handsome. A week before the wedding, Max had finally gone to the dentist and had his fractured front tooth capped.

As she passed us, I had difficulty making out Benny's face, due to the puffy mounds of fine white lace shrouding her head and veiling her eyes and mouth and then flowing down over her shoulders and bosom. She carried an enormous bouquet of white roses over her tummy, apparently a Sicilian tradition honored by all brides, lickety-split wedding prep or not.

I was curious to see her face. Max boasted that Benny was a knockout beauty, but I wanted to catch a clear look for myself. I had never seen her up close till that moment in the church, but that glance was far from satisfactory. I would have to wait a little longer, I realized. Max had never brought her by Robert Street, and I rarely, if ever, had reason to pass through Rulandville. So, I hadn't seen her.

Max said she was only two and a half years older than me. She had dropped out of Rulandville Central Catholic, because her mother had developed rheumatoid arthritis. They needed Benny to waitress full-time in *Piccolo Palermo*.

Max first met her one evening when he parked his Harley outside the restaurant and went in alone for a dish of their famous Sicilian lasagna. Benny served. Max flirted. She gave him a free second plate of the lasagna and for dessert a pair of her mother's own specially prepared cannoli. He asked if she would like to take a moonlight spin on his motorcycle after her shift was done. Benny said yes to that and to Max's other overtures, which resulted in her finding out she was pregnant three months after his first mouthful of *Piccolo Palermo*'s pasta. Now, here we were in the church.

Apart from my preoccupation with Jumbo's medical condition, the ceremony was long and boring, much of it in Latin. When they offered Holy Communion, Jumbo and I stayed in the pew. Vera had instructed me to keep an eye on him. Lucy also pointed out that I had not been to confession in a long time, and it would be a sin for me to eat the body and drink the blood of Christ with an unclean heart. I agreed and gladly stayed put in the pew with Jumbo.

At the end of the ceremony, when Max lifted Benny's veil to kiss her, I finally saw her face. She had strong eyebrows and dark skin, like her father, Pasquale, and fat lips and a sunken chin, like her mother, Giuseppina. Her eyes were small and black, but she did have a beautiful almost electric smile with double dimples on both cheeks, which she showed off as she strode back down the aisle with Max.

Max said Benny's smile was like that of the famous *Mona Lisa* painting. When we arrived at the restaurant for the reception, I compared Benny to the *Mona Lisa* print behind the *Piccolo Palermo* cash register. Max was fooling himself with the silly comparison, but not me. Benny had buck teeth. The *Mona Lisa*, as far as I could perceive, did not.

We saw much more of Benny's smile at the reception, where the Papallardo family, many of them clad in traditional Sicilian folk costumes, danced and laughed and drank jugs of the *Piccolo Palermo*'s homemade Chianti. I saw some of the younger girl cousins, who were near my age and prettier than Benny and whose bodies had developed early, like most of the Italian girls in Rehoboth. I wanted to walk up to them and introduce myself, but I was not feeling brave.

Most of the time, I stood back and listened to the music and watched the crowd. I noticed Daddy Mac took a few spins on the dance floor with Vera, and they both seemed to enjoy it. He bowed and kissed her hand when he took her back to her chair, which charmed me.

Kazzy and Blizzard ran around with the little Papallardo brats, scampering everywhere like manic monkeys. They all were exploding with energy pent-up during the long wedding. My little brothers joined a game of tag, giggling and shrieking, and hiding under tables and darting in and out among the adults. Noisy chaos pulsed through the reception in waves, and the adults all looked game for it too.

The kitchen staff provided an abundant Sicilian buffet with printed labels on chafing dishes: *risotto al gambero rosso* (pasta with shrimp), *cozze grattugiate* (breaded mussels), and towers of *prosciutto* and *reggiano* cheese. The most popular item was *babbaluci a picchi-pacchi lumache*, or snails with garlic and parsley, which looked and smelled repulsive.

Up from Wheeling, five Italian musicians (two mandolins, a violin, an accordion, and a trumpet) played nonstop Sicilian folk tunes. There was much clapping and yelling and cavorting, but not among the Malinowski family. They could have held the party without us, and I wished they had.

Two of Benny's cute girl cousins, twins from Hunterton, Ohio, of all places, showed off in a fast group dance called the *tarantella*. Their footwork was dazzling. Vera told me the *tarantella* was first inspired by a Sicilian peasant child, who had been bitten by a poisonous spider. In her delirium from the tarantula's toxin, she spun about furiously and actually saved herself from death by sweating out the venom through her pores.

Lucy coaxed me onto the dance floor to try it, which was a mistake. She quickly caught on to the steps, imitating the girls from Hunterton. But I tripped and nearly fell. Lucy grabbed my arm and saved me. I left her to dance without a partner, which she did not mind.

Lucy rarely let herself go like that, and I wondered if she had possibly sneaked some wine. Later she denied it and reminded me that she hated the smell of red wine as much as I did, except for the kind the priests served at the altar.

Gripping his glass straw, Jumbo appeared calm and steady through it all, though obviously in pain. No sign of impending d.t.'s. He sipped the Chianti from an iced tea glass and sat stiffly beside Pasquale and Guiseppina, nicknamed Pina. Max had warned us ahead of time that Benny's father expected to be called Don Pasquale, not just by his restaurant staff, but by anybody he met, particularly new family members. I wondered if Pasquale, like Jumbo, might not harbor pretentions of royal descent.

It was eerie how at a distance the two fathers resembled each other, side by side at the honor table in black, wide-lapelled suits. Both were about the same age, and both were bald and had jutting chins, prominent cheekbones, and waxed mustaches. The Don's complexion was much darker, and he was narrower in the shoulders and more than a foot shorter than Jumbo. Also, his mustache was very thin, less grandiose than Jumbo's. But despite their variant ethnicities, they looked like brothers.

I suspect their conversations were limited. The music all through the event was engaging but loud and unrelenting. Also, Jumbo's fractured neck kept his gaze rigidly straight out at the dancers and the musicians. He could not look over at Don Pasquale, except at the risk of sudden pain and paralysis. Furthermore, Jumbo's teeth were wired together, and when he spoke, his Polish accent made whatever comments he might utter about Benny and Max nearly unintelligible to the Don. Still, they seemed immediately chummy with each other, and I wondered why.

In regards to the question of noble blood, I scanned all the Papallardo grandchildren galloping on the dance floor to see if any of them showed potential as being a royal idiot, similar to what Ziggy had once been reputed to be. I did not pick out any obvious candidates, but that meant nothing. There could be a slow-witted Papallardo child running around at a restaurant in Chicago or Massachusetts, just as Jumbo's was locked in a high-fenced institution down at Murphy's Forge.

Reluctantly I went over to meet Don Pasquale and Pina and shake their hands. The Don smiled as he glanced down at my leg. "Jumbo," he said, "you got yourself a fine-looking blond *invalido* here. When he's ready to work for a living, send him over to me. I'll put him to washing dishes. A boy with that bad leg wouldn't last long in the mine or the plants."

I thanked Don Pasquale and smiled at Pina, who spoke next to no English and had large knuckles, deformed by arthritis. But like Benny, Pina had a beguiling smile with an overbite, though she seemed sincere when she flashed it.

Having paid my respects, I stepped away from the table. I felt uncomfortable. Don Pasquale insulted me with the first words he said to me. I understood why so many of the people we had invited to the wedding had declined, including Jasper. Mr. Slattery's suspicions were correct. Don Pasquale really was a shady character, possibly a criminal. And some of his grandchildren seemed nasty. A pair of boy cousins from Wheeling apparently heard what Don Pasquale had said about me to Jumbo. Later, when I walked by their table, one of them pointed at my leg. "*Invalido! Invalido!*" they snickered. They giggled at me then scampered back onto the dance floor.

My first impressions of Don Pasquale were confirmed a few weeks later when Max came back from his honeymoon up at Geneva-on-the-Lake, Ohio, and I asked him how he liked his father-in-law.

"Hate his guts. He wants people to be afraid of him. I'll tell you honestly, Taddy. The day before we got married, he asked me to give him a spin on my Harley. He said he wanted to have a little talk with me."

"About your drinking?"

"No. That afternoon, I rode him over to Beaver Creek Park. We got off the Harley, and I lit him a cigarette. We walked around the entire lake. He kept his mouth shut for the whole forty-five minutes or more, till we had circled clear around the lake and were ready to get back on the bike. He's little, and he had trouble keeping up with me. I thought he was getting out of breath, so I slowed up a couple times to make it easier for him to speak. But no, he clammed up till just before we got back on the bike."

"Was he teasing you, trying to keep you in suspense?"

"Maybe. Finally, just before we got back on the bike, I asked him if he had something to say. He said yes. He asked me if I really love Benny. I said yes."

"That's all? Just wanted to know if you loved his daughter?"

"No, there's more. Then I feel his finger stab me in the chest. He looks up at me real close and says, 'Listen, boy, I'm not going to repeat this. Don't you ever let me hear about you fucking around on my daughter. Don't let my people in Hunterton come back to me and say they saw you whoring around down on Water Street. If I hear anything like that, I'm not going to ask you for an explanation. I'll have you dragged right off your Harley by the side of the road and have your nuts cut off. Faster than you can say ouch. Got it, Mr. Malinowski?'"

Back to Belvedere

Max said Benny would not shut up till she met Ziggy. At the wedding reception, she had been introduced to everybody but him, and why wasn't he invited? She had heard about the goofy and lovable Ziggy, and she simply had to meet her other brother-in-law, even if he was a royal idiot or whatever Jumbo said about him.

"I'm Sicilian," she said. "To us, family is important. Everybody in the family is important. And you mean it's been over three and a half years since you people drove down there to West Virginia and gave Ziggy a hug? What kind of family would treat their own flesh and blood that way? Even on Christmas and Easter?"

I agreed with Benny. Jumbo had effectively abandoned Ziggy at Belvedere in the hands of Dr. Horvath. Except for the typewritten letters postmarked Murphy's Forge, West Virginia, which none of us except Jumbo read, we had heard nothing about how Zig was doing. No, not even Christmas mail!

"Ziggy is fine," Jumbo reassured us. "Nothing to worry about. He loves it there. Gets along fine with everybody. Never gets homesick. Horvath says he's a popular guy."

I had asked several times if we could go down to visit him, but then Jumbo had to sell the truck, and a trip down to Wheeling was fairly impossible. Bus service was spotty and complicated by several transfers, and Max had always said he was too busy at the shop to motor down there with me. I wrote Zig a letter once, hoping some-one at Belvedere would read it to him.

When he saw the letter, Jumbo took it from me and tore it up. "The doctor tells me Ziggy is happy where he is. Don't stir up trouble. Besides, if somebody reads your letter to him, he'll want to come back here. Do you want that to happen? Aren't things messy enough around here without him? Leave Ziggy alone."

Benny, however, would have her way. As Max said, she would not shut up about Ziggy.

Benny had several cousins in Wheeling. We had met them at the wedding. So, a trip to visit her family members and then drive on to Murphy's Forge and make Ziggy's acquaintance seemed natural and necessary. What was the problem with us, she asked. Now that Max was her husband, he owed her a trip to meet Ziggy, didn't he? Don Pasquale would lend us his Cadillac convertible for the day. What were we waiting for?

"I know I will adore my new cousin Ziggy. He's a lovable teddy bear. Maybe we could take him for a ride through the West Virginia woods or at least take him out to dinner. Could we bring him some presents? What kind of food does he really like? Does he need a new sweater or a tie? What's his favorite color? Would he maybe like a new baseball glove? Or a bat? Or a football? What is his favorite sport? What kind of gift? I have to bring him something, don't I, Max? Maybe my cousins in Wheeling would like to meet him. I bet they would. They could come along with us to Belvedere, and then we could all go out together, maybe have a picnic in Wheeling Park. Maybe he would like a new bathing suit? Tad, what do you think? You probably know him best."

I agreed. The sooner Benny met Ziggy, the sooner she would hush up about him. And it was clear to me that Max's life was changing in ways he could not control. He was freshly returned from his honeymoon on Lake Erie, and already the girl with the electric smile and the baby in her belly was dictating his marching orders.

For now, at least, Max seemed tense but willing to go along with Benny's desires. But I knew enough about my oldest brother to realize that he was not likely to be content for long in this role. For all my years of fearing and resenting Max, the bully, I now felt some sympathy for him.

Max would never admit that he might want support from me. As I became more familiar with the bossy sixteen-year-old he had just made pregnant and married, I realized I would have to open my heart up to him. I was reluctant to do so, but brothers sometimes have to stick together.

That Saturday morning broke gray and drizzly and stayed that way. Just after ten, Max and Benny pulled up on 7 Robert Street in Don Pasquale's new red 1924 Cadillac Phaeton convertible. I had seen the fancy car outside the church on the day of the wedding. After the reception, the newlyweds had jumped into it and drove up to Lake Erie for their honeymoon. When I climbed into the Phaeton's back seat with Jumbo, white rice kernels from the honeymoon send-off still lay strewn on the floor and stuck between the leather upholstery seams.

The red Phaeton was far and away the most beautiful car I had ever seen. I wished the weather that day would have been better, so that we could have put the top down for the ride to Wheeling. The rain came in fierce and chilly gusts, but the Cadillac had a great heat system that kept us all warm and cozy, almost to the point of feeling stuffy.

I asked Max how Don Pasquale could afford so luxurious a car. Was *Piccolo Palermo* really that successful? He said Don Pasquale had several other enterprises besides *Piccolo Palermo*, and it would be best if I did not ask Benny about them that day or, at least, until I had a more trusting relationship with her.

Jumbo, in his neck brace, sat beside me in the back seat. Unless I asked a question, he said nothing, occasionally sipping from his vodka-laced iced tea.

Benny up in the front seat provided a nonstop narrative of their honeymoon adventures on Lake Erie, which mainly included trips to some of Cleveland's finest department stores. Then she gave us a rundown of the various employees of *Piccolo Palermo*, the ones she liked and did not like, and then she gave a lengthy description of the classy restaurants owned by her relatives out in Chicago.

During this lively, entertaining monologue, none of us needed to say a word. It was Benny and the windshield wipers pretty much the whole way, which was fine, because only twenty minutes out of Rehoboth and just over the West Virginia line, I noticed Jumbo's eyelids batting shut. The continuous drone of Benny's voice and the electric heat and the hypnotic wiper blade swipes on the windshield lulled him into deep slumber.

I was relieved to learn that we would not stop in and visit Benny's relatives on our way through Wheeling. We did have the option to do so, if we wanted to, after we visited Ziggy. But Ziggy was the real reason for our trip, and Benny did not want anything to stand in the way of her meeting him. She wanted to fill out the full mental picture of her new family.

For our trip, Benny's mother specially baked two dozen chocolate pistachio biscotti and put them in a painted tin for Ziggy.

"They are my favorites! He'll go crazy when he tastes these. Everybody does. And Ma made enough so he can share with his buddies. And I hope he likes the sweater I bought him at Higbee's in Cleveland. Wrapped it all up so beautiful, see? Like my bow? Max helped me. I used his pinkie to tie it, didn't I, Maxie? Max says Ziggy has probably grown some, so the clerk thought I should buy him a size larger. Does he like argyle? Is that another cigarette already, Max? That's three since we left your house. You gotta cut back. You're stinking up the Don's car. He don't like it all stunk up."

Max remained silent throughout Benny's monologue, clutching the wheel, his eyes not wavering from the road ahead. Finally, when we were approaching Wheeling, Benny grew quiet and watched out her window as we drove south along the Ohio River.

I wondered how Ziggy would respond to our unannounced visit. I worried that he would be cross with us, and he would have good reason to be.

Would he hug me or turn away from me? I felt guilty about our family's long silence. But when I thought back through the years of how much time I had spent looking after Ziggy, staying out of school for half a dozen semesters to mind him and the cows, sacrificing my early years of education, I could not heap too much blame on myself.

Ziggy had established a new life at Belvedere, I told myself. I hoped that we would see him now as content with his situation, that our absence would not be a betrayal. How long he might live there, Jumbo never said. But if Dr. Horvath reassured us that Zig was happy and adjusted, no matter what Benny might say about family obligations, we probably would let him stay as long as he wished. I would be starting high school in a year, and I simply would not agree to alter that goal. I would not drop out and be his keeper. No. I had put in my time.

I looked up at Max smoking incessantly beside Benny. He seemed to seethe, annoyed by Benny's unrestrained chatter and most likely angry with himself. He had found his way into this situation all by himself. He could not blame anybody else, except maybe the tasty lasagna, and he knew it.

Some of the changes for Max were positive. Don Pasquale had honored the Sicilian dowry tradition by paying off the lease on the motorcycle garage for the next three years. On top of that, Don Pasquale had prefinanced a contractor to redesign, enlarge, and fully redecorate the couple's new two-bedroom apartment above the garage. When the baby arrived, everything would be perfectly prepared. Little Pina or little Pasquale, for those were the only naming options Benny would consider, should be all set.

To my left was another soul whose life had changed rather abruptly. Max's punch had made a lasting impact. Along with Jumbo's voice, the sock to his jaw had stifled Jumbo's narcissistic personality, at least temporarily. And I realized, as I sat in the silent car and looked out at the wind rippling the gray surface of the river water, that I did not fear him anymore. I hoped that feeling would continue once his neck was out of the brace and his jaw was free again to bark out commands at any target within range. For now, Jumbo had been silenced and had to listen to what other people had to say, including his motormouth daughter-in-law.

I wondered if my life would change anytime soon. I had given up on my right leg's chances of catching up to my left, and the problem with my butthole seemed to have healed as much as it ever would. But in a way, as I rode along the river that morning, I knew I, too, had changed fundamentally. I had brought along the little book I had borrowed from the Belvedere lobby's library. I wanted to return it to Dr. Horvath's collection.

True, Ben Franklin's autobiography had been helpful and inspiring for a year or two. I had followed some of Ben's recommendations and tried to live up to his disciplined approach to life's challenges. In my imagination, I had eagerly drawn parallels between his life and mine.

But that stage of my life was over now. It was time to put Ben Franklin and his vows of virtue back on the shelf.

Such exercises now seemed like vanity. The fact is, if a fat junkman had ever raped Ben Franklin when he was a boy, had kissed his neck and cheeks while ramming his long, malicious penis into him again and again till he thought he would die, then Ben likely would have stopped recording weekly tabulations of his virtuous acts.

Yes, I would leave his book back on the shelf at Belvedere. It no longer applied to me or belonged in my possession.

52

Someone Else

When we arrived inside the gate at Belvedere, we saw three large buses parked in the courtyard. The guard at the front door welcomed us in and explained that lunch was served, after which all the residents would pile quickly into the buses and ride into Wheeling to watch a double feature: Buster Keaton in *The Navigator* and Charlie Chaplin in *The Pilgrim*. The guard said he was going along as a chaperone with the boys and was looking forward to it.

We told him we had come to see Ziggy Malinowski. The guard said that we would have to clear that with Dr. Horvath. He suggested we wait in the lobby while he went to find Dr. Horvath.

Nothing in the lobby had changed since our previous visit. The same heavy leather chairs and couches were arranged exactly where we had left them. Over the fireplace the late Archibald Murphy still stood stocky and proud in front of his riverside iron factory. It seemed that the hundreds of books on the shelves of the lobby had been dusted but not opened. I found the empty slot I left in the row of books when I removed the Ben Franklin autobiography. I slid Ben back into his proper place, as if he had never left the shelf, had never been to Rehoboth, had never been my mentor and companion and inspiration.

I looked over at Jumbo, quiet and in pain. He had found a stiff-backed wooden chair near the entrance and had sat down with his neck and head fully erect. He stared up at the large grandfather clock near the stairway. When its loud gong struck noon with twelve deep brassy notes, his gaze fixed on the decorative face and detailed metal hands of the clock. I had seen him that subdued at times when he was drunk, but now he was almost sober, waiting to see Ziggy, and he did not seem interested in looking at any of us.

Max with the biscotti tin and Benny with the gift wrapped argyle sweater paced around on the Persian carpets. Benny fidgeted and tapped her toe nervously. When the clock stopped chiming, Benny asked, "Do you think he knows we're here?"

"Everybody's having lunch," Max snarled. "Can't you hear them all?"

Indeed, channeling softly up through one of the carpeted corridors that led into the lobby we heard the voices and clattering utensils of two hundred residents having their noon meal. They were talking, laughing, sometimes shouting at one another. The aroma of a hearty beef stew, ideal for a cool rainy day, wafted in along with the noises of the dining hall. They all sounded quite animated, probably excited to venture off campus and go see the comical movies.

"But does he know we're here? We've come a long way, and we're his family. Where did the bellhop go? He said he was going to get the doctor."

At a quarter after twelve, by the chime of the clock, we heard slow and measured footsteps descending the central stairway. Looking up, I saw Dr. Horvath, tall and authoritative in his white clinical gown. The four of us met him at the foot of the stairway. Shaking our hands cordially, Dr. Horvath welcomed us back. He squinted and cupped his hand behind his ear to understand when Jumbo explained in whispers that he was recovering from a minor automobile accident, hence, the neck brace and marked speech impediment.

"Oh my, we must all be careful on the roads these days," Dr. Horvath said sympathetically. "I hope that beautiful red Cadillac outside wasn't damaged in the collision."

"Oh no, that's my father's car," Benny interjected. "That car's brand-new. We took it on our honeymoon two weeks ago. That's all. No, it's never been in an accident. When was your accident, Jumbo?"

Jumbo whispered, "You didn't tell her about my accident, Max?"

I watched Dr. Horvath's long nose dart between Benny and Jumbo and then over at Max. On the spot, Jumbo had conjured an imaginary motor vehicle accident to explain his current locked jaw diction and ramrod posture.

Max and I knew enough not to question the story. We were used to Jumbo fibbing to cover up for embarrassing misadventures.

But Benny wanted clarification. Fortunately, we were spared further discussion on the matter when a deep, resonant gong rang in the mess hall. Then we heard two hundred chairs screech loudly as they slid back from the tables. A cacophonous mix of two hundred male voices echoed at us down the corridor and grew louder as they approached.

"Ziggy should be along shortly," said Dr. Horvath above the din. "You will see that he has recovered and developed nicely during the year since the operation."

"Operation?" Max exclaimed.

"I'm sure your father told you."

"Ziggy had an operation?" I asked.

"Castration. But should the young lady in her condition be here for this discussion?"

"What are you talking about, Doctor?" Benny squealed. "You did an operation on my dear cousin Ziggy? What kind of operation?"

"I didn't do it, Mrs. Malinowski."

"Who did?"

"Our urologist, Dr. Finley, performed the bilateral orchiectomy. As I explained to Ziggy's father in my letter, we simply had to. Ziggy gave us no choice. And he sailed through it splendidly. He had a little pain for a week, but that was easily comforted with a few aspirin tablets. He had no signs of infection, and before anybody could believe it, there he was again, back in the fields, working right alongside all his friends on the farm. Good as new and without all the problems he had before the surgery."

Max glared at Jumbo. "You let them cut off Ziggy's nuts?"

"What?" Benny said. "They cut his nuts off? Why? I never heard of such a thing."

Dr. Horvath put his long fingers on Benny's shoulder and smiled. "Oh, young lady, I assure you, we saved Ziggy from some very big problems. Major legal problems."

"Like what?"

"The penitentiary."

"They would send him to jail?"

"If you don't mind my saying it bluntly, Ziggy was oversexed. He could not control himself. He had not been here more than a month when the other residents began to complain about him. Totally inappropriate, they said. Shocking, they said. Disgusting, others said."

"But all young boys jerk off, Doctor." Max said, still staring in disbelief.

"Let me go on, please. Before we knew it, the other boys started doing it too. And then we had a huge problem on our hands. Ziggy turned the dormitories into a disaster. We were afraid to give the lights-out order. We couldn't control them. Every night, sometimes multiple times. And they started doing it in the fields, too, right out in the open. Ziggy would egg them all on."

Max's face opened into a slight grin. "Our Ziggy?"

Dr. Horvath frowned. "It was not funny. We really had no choice but to proceed with the operation. I wrote to your father, and he gave his written consent. Then, once Ziggy was neutralized, so to speak, the problem ceased. He spent a week in the hospital and returned, and then, just like magic, the dormitories were peaceful again all night. Work in the fields proceeded without embarrassing interruptions. Now Ziggy gets along fine with everyone. A few months ago, he even apologized to me for his previous misbehavior. And at the annual banquet, we gave him the Most Improved Resident award! Wait. You'll see."

Our disturbing conversation was interrupted when the first wave of residents emerged from the corridor. Thirty or forty of them streamed past us and out the front lobby door to the buses. I watched them carefully, and they did not look odd or unintelligent to me. They were teenagers and young men dressed in neckties and jackets, looking like normal fellows, chattering away and anxious to go to Keaton and Chaplin. I wished I could join them for the afternoon.

318

It sounded like great fun, and I really did not want to think much about Ziggy's surgery.

Then I saw Zig emerge from the corridor into the lobby. He was walking with two others, and when he saw Dr. Horvath in his white coat near the stairway, his head jerked. Then he recognized us standing there, and he froze. His wrists started to bang together, and his eyes squinted and blinked behind his glasses.

I waved at him, and he stepped toward us slowly. He had not grown much since I had seen him, but I was stunned by how much weight he had put on. Zig had always looked pudgy, but now his cheeks blended with his neck and the fatty flesh beneath his chin lopped over his shirt collar. His shoulders were round mounds, and his fingers, cocked back while the wrists banged together, looked doughy and pale. He even had visible bulges under his nipples. Boy tits is what Max called them later.

As the other residents hustled past us and out into the buses, I approached him. Tears now were dripping from his eyes, and his clear snot dripped from his nostrils down to his lips. I did not know if he would allow me to hug him, so I offered my hand, but he closed both his arms around my chest and squeezed me tight.

"Taddy, where have you been? I missed you," he whispered. "You are taller than me now. Do you want to go to the movies?"

"I missed you, too, Zig. I don't think I can. We came to see you, not a movie."

"Do I seem like someone else to you, Taddy?"

"No, Zig. You're still my favorite brother, but you've grown up a lot."

Zig did not want to release me from his hug, and I wanted to keep holding him too. As he pressed his chest against mine and held me against him, I could feel the soft bulges on his chest. They felt like actual tits, almost like Mother's felt when she hugged me, but smaller.

I reached for my handkerchief to clean the tears from his face, but he released his grip and grabbed his own handkerchief from his jacket pocket. "You don't have to do that anymore, Taddy. I can take care of myself." Then he bumped his forehead into mine and gave me a close grin. "I grew up a lot, Taddy. I'm someone else. Who's the pretty girl with Max?"

"I have news for you, Zig. Max is married now, and he's going to have his own baby. You're going to be an uncle. Uncle Ziggy!"

Zig shook his head. Behind his glasses his eyes rolled around and settled on Benny's tummy. "A baby? Max got married?"

"Two weeks ago."

"They say I can never have babies now, Taddy. I can never have babies. Never. Even if I get married, I can't have babies. My dinky's dead. I can pee, but that's all."

"Come over and meet Benny. And give Max and Jumbo a hug. Be gentle with Jumbo. His neck is hurting him pretty bad. He had a fall."

"Can we all go to the movies? Buster Keaton. Double feature with Charlie Chaplin."

"Benny brought you some cookies and a present."

"Would she like to go to the movies with us?"

Dr. Horvath came over to us, followed by Jumbo and the newlyweds. "Ziggy, I told your family how well you have been doing since the operation. Isn't that true?"

"My dinky doesn't work anymore, Dr. Horvath," Zig repeated. "I try, but nothing happens. Not since the operation." Then he laughed, and shook his head. "Anybody want to go to the movies? The buses are leaving."

Meadowlark

The next day was Sunday, and I told Vera I did not feel well and would not attend Mass. I also refused to go over to *Piccolo Palermo* afterward, where Don Pasquale had invited us all for Sunday dinner. From the upstairs window, I watched my family walking up Robert Street in their church clothes, Vera holding Blizzard's hand and Lucy holding Kazzy's.

Jumbo strode stiffly alone behind them, his neck and jaw clamped in place. He did not stride with his habitual swagger. I noticed he clasped his hands behind his back, the same way all the priests who lived at the rectory did. Seeing him walk that way made me think that Max's punch had made Jumbo walk like an old man. It did not bother me to see that.

The morning was sunny and windless. Yesterday's rain puddles had evaporated through the night, and the grass of the little front yards up and down the street was drying out. It was unseasonably warm, an ideal day for what I had in mind to do.

As soon as they had all disappeared around the corner, I changed out of my pajamas and put on my shirt and jeans and my boots and jacket. I grabbed my harmonica, which I had not played for probably half a year. Before leaving the house, I picked out a sturdy paring knife from the kitchen drawer and folded a napkin around it before stowing it with the harmonica in my jacket pocket.

I turned left out the front door and swung down toward the opening in the woods, the same path Ziggy and I had followed with Rose and Mary on hundreds of mornings. I could have found my way along that path with my eyes closed, and Ziggy could have, too, if he were with me.

But today I was alone. I wanted to be strictly alone.

I crossed over the spring and paused briefly at the place near the birch tree, where I once buried what Mother had called her blood pudding. Nobody would ever notice that spot near the birch, and nobody else knew that the remains of an unborn sibling lay disintegrated two feet down, exactly where I had buried them, gradually mingling with the detritus of nature's many other cycles of flowering and death.

I recited an Our Father and a Hail Mary for Mother and her unborn child, and then I stepped on through the woods toward Ben Curry's meadow, where Ziggy and I had spent countless mornings and afternoons reading, snoozing, playing the harmonica, eating lunch, being chased by yellow jackets, and sometimes wandering under the summer sun down to skinny dip in the colored strip mine pools.

Those days were done for Zig and me, but as I strolled through the tall meadow grass, I pulled out my harmonica and played his favorite "Little Red Wing," just as though he were walking beside me. I played loud and soft, fast and slow, sometimes skipping as I played and imagining Ziggy humming along, as he so often loved to do. The meadow seemed incredibly empty without Rose and Mary grazing in it. Strange how only two cows can seem to fill up a huge, rolling pasture.

I had thought all along that Ziggy would never have to atone for the sin we committed together. In his own peculiar way, Zig had often expressed to me great guilt at helping with Mother's slippery elm suicide, but I never suspected that life would penalize him physically for the crime just as I had been punished.

Ziggy's intelligence was limited, and he, like I, was fully ignorant of what we did for Mother when she asked us to do it. Nevertheless, we were guilty. Brother Gus's catechism class had singed that moral fact deep into me. Over and above whatever torture purgatory would offer Ziggy and me in the afterlife, physical punishment had been meted out to both of us. I had been raped, and Ziggy had been castrated.

As I walked through Curry's meadow, I kept mulling over our conversation at Belvedere. After the three buses had driven off to the movie theater, Dr. Horvath had explained at length to us that Ziggy's behavior at the institution had been grotesque and unacceptable.

"You're saying he's a sex fiend?" Benny asked. "My new cousin Ziggy's a sex fiend?"

"No. That would be unfair."

"So, what was his problem? Did he hurt anybody?"

"The problem was his lack of discretion. We could not reason with him. He had no understanding of how his behavior affected others and the institution itself."

"So, you made him have the operation," Max added.

"Ziggy could not be controlled. When I went to the board of directors, they wanted to expel him at once, but I explained to them that sending Ziggy back to Rehoboth would only make matters worse for him and for his family. I explained all this in several letters to your father."

While Dr. Horvath continued with his account, Jumbo blinked and nodded from the waist. Max, who had recently been threatened with castration, was likewise mute and asked no further questions. Neither did I. We all listened and nodded.

Did we all agree that surgery was the best option for Ziggy? Years later, I concluded that it probably was.

And from the short chance I had to embrace him and look him in the eye in the Belvedere lobby, he seemed fully adjusted to his condition, chubbier but less tense, and he now had friends and a purposeful life working on the institutional farm, probably more satisfying to him than minding cows.

Dr. Horvath said that as long as Belvedere remained open, Ziggy could reside there for the foreseeable future. They did have an age limit of twenty-seven, so we would have to find a place for him after that. But that was almost ten years into the future, and hopefully all of our lives and circumstances would be significantly different.

I wondered how Mother would have reacted to Dr. Horvath's recommendations. If she had been alive, I suspect she would have agreed to the procedure. She usually supported Jumbo's decisions.

As a psychologist, Dr. Horvath had cautioned that such behavior problems often became much worse as young men grew into their twenties and began interacting with young women. When he mentioned that such individuals could become a danger to little girls, Benny shook her head and said she wanted to go home immediately.

We left the tin of biscotti and the argyle sweater there with Dr. Horvath. During the drive back from Belvedere, all of us, especially Benny, remained silent. She decided not to visit her relatives in Wheeling, and instead, we stopped at a diner north of Wheeling for a fast hamburger, tomato soup for Jumbo. After lunch, he climbed back into the car, sat back in his seat, and soon fell asleep. Max chain-smoked, and Benny did what I did: tried to adjust to what we had found out at Belvedere.

Eventually, in the luxurious comfort of the Cadillac with the windshield wipers lulling us, I saw she fell asleep too. I closed my eyes and invoked bunnies in the moonlight. Soon, we were back on Robert Street.

Walking through Ben Curry's meadow, I passed Ziggy's favorite apple tree and saw no apples or yellow jackets. I marched on, scaled the fence, and followed the trail down to the strip mine pools. I saw nobody around anywhere, and as the sun by this time was high and bright, the sky blue and vacant, I left my clothes on the bank and jumped into the water. Shivering with goose bumps at first, I lay on my back and felt the push of the heavy water, warmer than I expected, buoy me up. I wished Ziggy could be there with me, giggling and splashing the way we used to do.

As I noodled around in the wetness, I felt my ball sack shrinking tight. My dinky was getting firm and wanted me to be play with him. I was in the very pool, where Ziggy had first showed me how to do it, and I wondered if this was the real reason why I had stayed away from Mass and the *Piccolo Palermo*. As I flopped around on my back, I saw in the distance the soaring tip top of the moly stack with its effluent wafting out in a tiny white tuft against the blue sky. I paddled around, and as a silly experiment, tried to line up my straightening dinky with the tall brick column. There they were: two vertical sticks thrusting up to the heavens, the one in my hand warm and hard and begging for delicious attention.

It started as a game in the water, me doing what Ziggy had showed me to do, but very soon, I felt desperate to make it happen. I wanted it to come out of me, just like the tiny white stream high up in the blue sky. I did not imagine any pretty girl helping me. I did not need her. It was just me and my dinky and the smokestack.

It took only seven or eight strokes to make it happen. Perhaps if I had not used my thumb and fingers but just lay there perfectly still in the sunshine, with the water a smooth flat pillow boosting me up and the smokestack straight and tall over the mine mounds, it still would have happened.

Yes, I would have felt that white liquid squirt up above me, higher in the sky than the moly stack, and then drop down in thick drops into the orange water.

It had felt so powerful and necessary, and as my breath slowed down, I was unutterably content not to be at Mass, but to be alone where I was, doing what I was doing, and having this fierce power within me to prove with every thrust that I was alive. I had told the sky, this is me. I could not know how or why, but doing it made me feel who I am. That may sound peculiar, but it was true and it was me and it was wonderful.

Ziggy would have giggled. But then I realized he would have been jealous. Now my injured brother would not have a chance to share such pleasure with a girl and someday make a baby. That someday would never come for Ziggy.

With my triumphant dinky limp again and my heart beating slowly, I looked around and saw nobody else around. I paddled over and stepped up onto the bank. I took the napkin with the knife in it out of my jacket pocket and dried off my skin. The white cloth napkin turned orange from the pond water, but I didn't care. Then

I dressed and wrapped up the knife and walked back up into the meadow, tooting more songs on my harmonica as I went along.

My music soothed me on my way back across the field and put me into a lazy trance. The sun shone hot on my head and dried my hair. On the other side of the meadow, I went through the gate and reached the tall oak tree that had dropped acorns near Mother's buried blood pudding. I stopped and unsheathed the knife from the napkin.

I recalled how Ziggy had always loved it when I read to him about Zorro, the Fox of Capistrano, whose lightning-quick sword carved a Z at scenes of his vengeance. But Ziggy and I had never carved a Z anywhere on anything, because Mother never allowed us, except that one fatal occasion, to take any knives out of her kitchen.

Today would be different, and I went about cutting the thick oak bark with the paring knife, first with three quick slashes at eye level, as Zorro would have done, so that nobody would miss the message. Then I gouged down deeper on each slash, till I reached well into the bare white pulp of the oak. Nobody walking along would miss this Z for Ziggy. It was right in the center of the oak's trunk, five feet high and a foot tall and at least a full inch into the wood.

Someday Ziggy would come back to Rehoboth, and we would go for a walk together. I would show him his oak tree. But I would never tell him what I had buried just on the other side of the birch. Even if we dug down to find it now, probably nothing would be left, except my memory of our sin. I would never want to remind him of that.

Never. Ziggy had paid his debt, and I wished that I had paid mine, too, both of us changed, scarred, brothers in sin, and not looking forward at all to our march up the trails in purgatory. And that's if we were lucky, according to Brother Gus's catechism book.

54

Wheels

When I returned home to the house that afternoon, Max had driven the family back from dinner at *Piccolo Palermo*. He was leaving when I arrived. He said Don Pasquale had voiced annoyance that I had not joined them for the meal. Sicilian families always have Sunday dinner together, Max explained. Also, Don Pasquale had a surprise gift for me. Max wouldn't say what it was, but the Don would have it delivered.

The next afternoon when I came home from school, Vera met me at the door. She told me to stand right there and close my eyes, and she would be right back with a surprise for me. I waited on the front steps, and then I heard her and Lucy walking around the side of the house toward me. Before I opened my eyes, a very loud bicycle horn blasted at me twice.

When I opened my eyes, Vera and Lucy were grinning and holding a genuine new Iver Johnson cushion frame roadster bicycle with a blue truss bridge frame, black fenders, the loud horn, and pneumatic tires. I was shocked.

"It's for you. From Don Pasquale," Lucy said, blasting the horn again.

"I can't believe this. Jasper will be so jealous."

"Jumbo is too." Vera laughed. "Isn't it gorgeous?"

"Just as a gift? This bike probably costs almost fifty dollars!"

"Yes, a gift!" my sisters responded in unison, both nodding with huge smiles.

Though I had never owned a bicycle, ever since I had grown tall enough to fit on it, I had practiced plenty of times on Jumbo's old Sears and Roebuck rattletrap. This new blue creature was utterly deluxe! Immediately I dropped my books on the front steps and grabbed the handlebars. I swung my right leg up over the saddle and balanced carefully on my left foot.

"Go ahead," Vera urged. "See how you like it."

"Like it? Are you kidding?"

Tentatively I cruised down the sidewalk and then out onto Robert Street. The new bike had coaster brakes, which were tricky to use at first, but after a couple of trips around the block, I quickly acquired the knack. The seat had a pair of thick springs, so when I went over bumps, I hardly felt them. The frame was so light and graceful, and I could accelerate without becoming short of breath. I wanted to stay on the bicycle and ride it all over Rehoboth, but I had homework to do that evening. After half an hour of exploring the neighborhood and showing off to anybody I saw on the street, I rode back home and rolled my new prize behind the house and stowed it in an empty corner of the shed.

"Next Sunday, you don't want to miss dinner at *Piccolo Palermo*," Jumbo said that night. "The Don will expect you to thank him."

"For sure," I said, still a bit dizzy from receiving such a beautiful and useful gift. I had never dreamed of owning such a bike. And now it was mine. Just like that. Right out of thin air! I had not even wished for it or prayed for it or anything!

I could not wait to ride it to school the next morning. Only a dozen or so kids had bicycles at the school, and I was sure to be the envy of everyone. It had a sturdy metal basket in front of the handlebars that was big enough to carry all my schoolbooks. Luckily Don Pasquale had included in the gift a sturdy padlock with a large U bar to slip between the spokes of the back wheel.

All that week I locked my new Iver Johnson to the handrails on the school's front steps, and even though I knew it was secure where

I had left it, sometimes between classes I popped out front to be sure nobody had stolen it.

When some of my eighth-grade classmates caught sight of me riding my new bicycle, they did the down-up-down visual double take. But now I laughed at it. They were not noticing my limp. No, this was probably the finest bicycle they had ever seen.

It certainly was the best, most important gift I had ever received, even nicer than my Ben Franklin kite from Jasper. Though I had reservations about accepting it from Don Pasquale, I figured a bicycle is a bicycle, and there was no way, other than a gift outright, that I would ever own one as nice as this. And when people asked me how I happened to own it, I told them it was from a friend who wanted to remain anonymous.

The kids at school were used to seeing me occasionally in old clothes and apparel created by my father out of car upholstery. So, this new treasure raised eyebrows. But no matter where it came from, it was mine! As Vera had said, even Jumbo was jealous.

The next Sunday, we went to church in Rulandville, and after Mass, we walked to the restaurant for dinner. *Piccolo Palermo* had several rooms for family events, and a special one for the Don's family meals.

As soon as Don Pasquale was seated, I went over to thank him for my gift.

"How's my handsome blond *invalido*?" he asked. "So, you like your new bicycle?"

"Very much. Thank you, Don Pasquale."

"I figured it would even things out for you. Now you can go wherever you want as fast as you want. Maybe faster than anybody else!"

Though I was afraid of the Don, I laughed at his comment. "Yes. Thank you so much!"

"So maybe some weekends, you might want to come over here and help in the kitchen a little bit? We always need an extra set of hands around here. Hear what I'm saying?"

"I see."

"Yes, Jumbo tells me he used to own a big restaurant over in Poland. He and I thought maybe you want to follow in Jumbo's footsteps. You know, start here, get the lay of the land, see how a restaurant works. Get the big picture. Maybe wash a few dishes first, then move on to clearing tables, maybe become a waiter, maybe become a chef. Who knows? The sky's the limit, like we say."

"Yes, who knows? The sky's the limit!"

"And maybe when summer comes, you could work here full-time? You might even like working here more than going to school. You never know. You're still young. You got a lot to learn. But you like the bicycle?"

"So much! You're very kind, sir."

"Maybe we see you next weekend here at *Piccolo Palermo*?"

Apprentice

"Give it a try," Jumbo insisted, whispering through his teeth. "And what else are you going to do with yourself this summer? When I had my own bistro near Vilnius, people came from miles around to taste my dishes. I was famous, a little bit like what your mother and I had over in Ripple Brook Gardens, but much bigger. You may find you have natural ability, Tad. Give it a shot. You could do worse than *Piccolo Palermo*. Don Pasquale is offering you a chance. Take it. It's the least you can do, since he already gave you that bicycle. Hear what I'm saying? I'm just looking out for you. With that bad leg, you know, you'll need some kind of trade that doesn't involve heavy physical labor. No mine or zinc plant for you, Tadpole."

For the next several months on Saturdays, I rode my new bicycle the seven miles from Rehoboth to Rulandville and put on the white pants and shirt and apron, washed dishes, swept and mopped floors, took out garbage, and picked up litter in the parking lot. Then I rode the seven miles late at night in the dark back home. Although this routine exhausted me, on Sunday morning, I had to wake up, dress up, and ride back to Rulandville with the family in Don Pasquale's Cadillac. We were now going to church in Rulandville, Jumbo's new rule.

After Mass, I would sit through Sunday dinner with the Papallardo family, sometimes including their relatives from Wheeling and Hunterton. I only had Sunday night to do my homework for Monday mornings.

Once the doctors took the wires out of Jumbo's teeth and removed his neck brace, he became more animated and bossy. "Who cares about your marks in school?" he asked, which meant only that he did not care about those marks. "Believe me, if you go into the restaurant business, all you need to know is how to count your money. Well, you've got to learn to be a chef, but I can teach you whatever you want. Pina and the Don will teach you Italian style. Your mother would be so proud! Do you remember Jumbo's Tavern? Wasn't that fun?"

After three months, I asked Jumbo when Don Pasquale would pay me for the work I did.

"Pay you? Hell, he already gave you that beautiful bicycle and you want him to pay you too?"

"I thought the bicycle was a gift."

"It was a gift. And now you're giving him a gift back, like you should. We're all family now, Taddy. You don't want him to think you are an ungrateful brat, do you? He's giving you a big chance here. You're like an apprentice to him. And don't mess things up for me. Now that I have my teeth and tongue back to working again, and my neck is out of that damn brace, he says he may give me a job as a waiter. You have to be patient with a guy like Don Pasquale. Show him respect. Be patient. Wait your turn. I'm waiting my turn. You should wait yours. There's plenty at stake."

I detested everything about the job. The other people who worked in *Piccolo Palermo* were pleasant enough, but in the kitchen, everybody spoke Italian. I picked up a few words, just to get by, but if I dropped a plate or a glass or if Pina found a fleck of dried pasta on the back of a clean platter, she lit into me in a fierce Sicilian rant, as if I had murdered her baby.

They also made me memorize everything on the menu, first in Italian, then English. They said they wanted me really sharp, if I ever made it up to the grade of waiter. Every good waiter could recite the menu by heart. That was critical to any quality restaurant, did I understand?

But I never took orders from the customers. I spent most of my time back in the kitchen, so why did I need to memorize the menu?

There was another complication. From my long bicycle rides, sometimes in thick snow and over icy, bumpy roads, I developed an embarrassing problem. If I was late to work and waited too long to have a bowel movement while I was pedaling furiously toward Rulandville, when I finally got a chance to poop, my butthole started to leak blood. I hoped nobody would notice, and though I wadded up toilet paper and tucked it up there, sometimes telltale stains would show up on the seat of my white kitchen pants. When this happened, I tried to cover up my backside by picking out an extra-large apron and double-folding it behind. If I bled through the apron, when nobody was looking in the kitchen, I would spoon out some simmering Bolognese sauce from the stove, wait a few seconds, and then smear it with my fingers over the apron stains. I hoped this trick would mask my problem, but apparently people noticed.

During one Sunday dinner, Don Pasquale called me aside, sat me down, and said he wondered why I never took Communion at Mass. I told him that the smell of red wine made me puke, which I don't think he could believe.

"You have to get over that fast, boy. You can't get along in the restaurant business if you puke when you drink red wine. Got it?"

"I guess so."

Then he came very close to me and whispered in my ear, "Another question, Taddy boy. Some of the people in the kitchen are wondering if maybe you got hemorrhoids or something. They say maybe they thought you were bleeding or something. I never noticed it, but Pina said she saw it herself. Bloody stains around your ass."

I blushed hard and drew back from him, partly because up close, his breath smelled strongly of Chianti, and partly to adjust to the shivers his words had sent down my spine. I breathed in deeply and answered, "Yes, I do suffer from hemorrhoids."

He pulled me toward him again, and I was close enough to his eyes to see the little red veins under his lids. He blinked twice, and then he reached in his pocket and said, "I got just the cure for you. Hold out your hand."

I drew back again, and he handed me a garlic bulb that was slightly bigger than a golf ball.

"Put this in your pocket for now. But when you go home tonight, shove it up your ass. Try to leave it in overnight. Works great on hemorrhoids. Shrinks them down to nothing. It's what we do in Sicily. You're gonna thank me. Believe it or not, I once had the same problem. Now I don't. Take it from the Don, you're gonna love me for this. Lay on a little olive oil over it before you stick it in. That helps."

"Thank you, Don Pasquale."

He sat back in his chair and smiled, patting me on my shoulder. "Hey, don't worry. I won't say a peep to nobody." Then he winked at me and drew his fingertip along the lower border of his mustache, nodding his reassurance.

I was puzzled why Jumbo, a large and dominant personality, might fall under the spell of someone like Don Pasquale, a small egotistical man, who demanded obeisance from everyone he knew and certainly from everyone who might qualify as a relative. Although Max had married into the Papallardo family, it felt like we all were now subject to a strange new set of oppressive rules, most of which made me uncomfortable, sometimes miserable.

Yet Jumbo went along with everything the Don said and expected me to do the same.

Part of Don Pasquale's appeal was that he provided a steady source of free alcohol to Jumbo. I heard the details from Max. The Chicago branch of the Papallardo family was involved in the black market importing of alcohol across Lake Michigan. Delivery trucks bearing Illinois license plates arrived late at night to the back entrance of *Piccolo Palermo*, unloaded several dozen cases of their liquid cargo, and then drove on, presumably to Hunterton and Wheeling as their next stops. After the wedding, according to Max, Don Pasquale had promised Jumbo a weekly supply of bootleg wine and vodka with nothing expected in return, no questions asked, just a family gift, part of the dowry.

Somehow, that did not seem to me sufficient cause for Jumbo's fealty and for his insistence that I follow through on everything Don

Pasquale advised me to do. I also resented the trend that the two families should become more intimate. Mother would never have put up with them. Don Pasquale had two grown sons, Carmen and Luigi, both currently running wineries in Sicily, which meant to me that they might be training to become *cosa nostra* functionaries. Max thought so too.

However, not all of it was bad. For example, when Don Pasquale handed me the full bulb of garlic, I cringed. Most of the turds that came out of me, at their widest, were the caliber of blackboard chalk, and stuffing in an object the size of a golf ball through such a scarred and narrow opening was impossible. I did, however, find that splitting the full garlic bulb down to individual cloves, peeling them and then inserting them with some olive oil as a lubricant did soothe my condition. The technique also reduced the bleeding, so much so that I continued to use Don Pasquale's remedy for years, even though it was technically not for exactly the same diagnosis. It worked, and nothing else I knew did.

I apologize for dwelling on this unpleasant medical problem, and I realize that it may seem that my fixation on it goes beyond what is necessary to portray my suffering. If, however, anyone should ever read these words, who might be tempted, for some depraved and inscrutable reason, to molest a boy or a girl or a man or a woman with a sexual attack, please realize how selfish and evil your action would be and how terrible and long-lasting the emotional and physical pain can result from your brief moment of sick and selfish pleasure. Please, never do it! Stifle those impulses! It's one of the very worst things anybody can do to another human. In my opinion, it's right up there with murder. All the garlic in the world will never soothe that pain, and it isn't funny, either. You don't need a catechism pamphlet to figure that one out, so please do not do it!

I wish I had possessed the courage back then to deliver the same message to my own father. Jumbo surely twisted and scarred dear Vera's tender body as well as her soul. I will say that, as far as I can recall, Max's powerful punch that evening in the shed ended Jumbo's selfish incestuous behavior with her for once and for all. Thank you, Max. Bravo, brother!

For whatever reason, Jumbo's loyalty to Don Pasquale increased with each passing month, and Jumbo's improving health did make it possible for him to start busing tables twice a week at *Piccolo Palermo*. On Saturdays, I felt ridiculous riding on my Iver Johnson and with Jumbo sometimes trying to race me on his clunky Sears and Roebuck rig.

Eventually I realized that Jumbo was getting paid for his work, while I was not. I was the apprentice, Jumbo reminded me. Don Pasquale was giving me a wonderful chance. I should never forget that.

Whether Jumbo had in mind that he himself would assume a higher rank in Don Pasquale's restaurant, I never could say. I predicted to myself that Jumbo's alcoholism eventually would become evident, and Don Pasquale would fire him. But for the first several months, Jumbo was on his good behavior: affable, punctual, gregarious, charming. I had seen this before every time Jumbo started a new job, but I kept mum about it, though I resented that he was being paid and I was not.

All that winter, I thought ahead to the summer with dread, when school would be out, and Don Pasquale would expect me to work full-time for him. I could not imagine riding the bicycle every day to and from Rulandville and then returning Sunday for Mass and Sunday dinner, now required of the whole family. This was what I would do, no discussion, no reconsideration, no option. These were Jumbo's and Don Pasquale's orders.

As the weeks went by, I began to feel desperate, perhaps terrified. I was turning fourteen, starting high school in the fall, and feeling that my life was a prison and that I would never find a way out. It was at this time that I recalled that young Ben Franklin, the tireless and intrepid pursuer of virtue, had at one point fled from his printing apprenticeship. Ben up and left Boston and traveled to Philadelphia to start a new life on his own, because he was fed up with a situation that made him miserable.

If Franklin could jump his apprenticeship, why couldn't I? If a person is in a bad situation and doesn't try to get out of it, perhaps that person deserves to be in that situation. Despite all the constrictive webs weaving around me through Jumbo and Don Pasquale and Pina and her entire restaurant staff, that person would be me, and I knew I did not deserve it.

I pondered pulling a Franklin, running away from Rehoboth, maybe hopping on a train and finding my way to another city.

I don't know why, but I liked the idea of moving to someplace in Ohio, someplace like Cleveland or Geneva-on-the-Lake, somewhere fairly far from where I was now. I had no idea what kind of job I could find or how I would secure lodging in a strange place or how I could continue with my education, which seemed like the most important thing in the world now. In the back of my mind, I did fear moving to someplace new and running into some predator like Nick Katsaros again.

Every time Jumbo or Don Pasquale reminded me that I would never be able to work in the mines or in a zinc smelting plant or probably even in an automobile or motorcycle garage, due to my bad leg, my mind started to spin through other ways I could make a living. But I could not figure out what I would want to do. Clearly, spouting off menu items and standing near hot stoves all day and night and pretending to smile at everyone because I loved to cook and serve and clean up meals would only guarantee me a career of personal frustration and misery. I would hate myself and everybody else.

I figured if I did cross Don Pasquale and quit my job, I would have to leave Rehoboth immediately. I even wondered if the Don might lean on Max to rough me up a bit to teach me a lesson, perhaps convince me to come back to the restaurant, bite the bullet a bit longer till it tasted sweet.

I doubted that Max would treat me that way. I knew he hated Don Pasquale and might follow his orders on many accounts, but he would not likely threaten to do me any physical harm. My relationship with Max had actually become fraternal, not to brag.

Plus, as Benny's pregnancy went along and the baby grew inside her tummy, she seemed to become bossier, more hysterical, sometimes uncontrollable, and demanding. Max's motorcycle shop, in the garage right below their new apartment, was busier than Max could keep up with, and having to run upstairs to check on Benny several times a day was playing on his nerves. He smoked continuously, and three different times in February, I heard him arguing with Jumbo when he came over to cadge a bottle of vodka from Jumbo's free stash. Jumbo didn't want him to take it, but Max said he would take it anyway, and he did.

I realized I was probably the only person Max could talk with, and I was flattered that he opened up to me about the pressures of being an expectant father. Several times, he said he wished he had never stopped by at *Piccolo Palermo* for that serving of lasagna. That's when all his problems began. That's when he started to feel his freedom being snipped away.

One evening, we even went for a walk together up Robert Street and then all through the neighborhood. He was not surprised when I told him my own frustrations about how Jumbo had bought into the Papallardo family to the hilt, and how now I was somehow expected to fulfill a delusional calculus that Jumbo and Don Pasquale dreamed up together about my future in the restaurant business.

At the conclusion of our walk, Max tossed his cigarette in the gutter, and before he climbed onto his Harley, he held out his arms to me and hugged me hard. "You're a good brother, Taddy. I should have been nicer to you a few times. How about you and I ride out to Mom's cemetery. I ordered a gravestone for her, and maybe we could take a look at it and plant some flowers for her. Would you like that? I bought myself a nice little Kodak, and we can take a picture of the stone to show Jumbo."

I was stunned. As his Harley sped up Robert Street, my heart went out to him. And he was good to his word. Later that spring, on a sunny day, Max drove me out to Mom's grave, and we planted pansies and snapped a photograph.

And not long after that trip to Mother's grave, Max's Harley would take me on a terrible ride that would change both of our lives in major ways and allow me to jump my apprenticeship at *Piccolo Palermo* and escape from my prison in Rehoboth. Yes, and forever.

Bliz and Kaz

I have not mentioned much about my two little brothers. There are reasons for this.

Once I started school and became a serious student, working conscientiously to complete my homework assignments, Blizzard and Kazzy became for me both a distraction and a nuisance. As they grew older and wanted to play sports with me, occasionally I would toss a football or baseball with them, but only if my homework was done and they could not find other playmates in the neighborhood. Vera and Lucy did the feeding and washing and mothering as best they could, and as a father, Jumbo was as good as absent, often an inebriated presence not fit even for babysitting.

I know the boys resented me to some degree, because I was distant and sometimes solemn, especially after I began my odious job in the restaurant. Though I never treated them cruelly, as Max had done to Ziggy and me, I know I was not a pleasure to be around. I did not show much love for them.

I felt sorry for them. They had never really known Mother as I had, and though Vera gave of herself completely, she was only a teenager, hardly the woman in her prime that I knew as my mother. So, both of my younger brothers were deprived of that critical blessing. Our poverty and the baffling randomness and occasional violence in our household surely affected their development, enough so that early on, I noticed their behavior showing selfish and unpleasant tendencies.

Sometimes Kaz bullied Bliz severely, much like Max had done to me, and Bliz often sassed back at Vera or Lucy, shouting, "You're not my mother, you know!"

When Blizzard and Kazzy paired up in defiance, they were a tough team. My sisters could do little to discipline them, and occasionally the unruly little imps would flare up in simultaneous tantrums that involved throwing crayons or forks and spoons or Lincoln Logs at my sisters. Jumbo, whose razor strop had served as the ever-threatening sword of Damocles in my early childhood, had become passive and uninterested in his youngest two sons. With no firm hand to guide them, they grew up brash and routinely rude. Good behavior happened in church but nowhere else.

I was not surprised that when Kazzy started to school, he often had to stay late for detention. I had no doubt that Blizzard would follow a similar course at Rehoboth Elementary.

Finally, I preferred to ignore them both as best I could. Eventually, they grew hostile to me. Bliz and Kaz, my constantly antagonistic little brothers, were yet another reason for me to fantasize about running away and living in another place. They resented my presence in the house, and I had trouble finding shelter from them. I certainly did not have the will or the ability to discipline them, and it pained me to think how ashamed Mother would be of them. She could have made a huge difference in shaping their sense of right and wrong. Or so I would wish. Vera was not up to the task.

One sunny Saturday morning before I set off for work at the restaurant, I looked out the front window and saw the two of them clowning around on Robert Street.

"No, like this," Kazzy chuckled.

"No, watch! More like this," Bliz shouted.

"Yeah, and he always swings his arm like this."

"Oh, yeah! You've got it. You look just like him. Benny calls him the *invalido*!"

"What's that mean?"

"*Invalido* is Italian for cripple."

I felt my cheeks burn. They were taking turns mimicking me, having a grand old time limping up and down Robert Street.

"That's Taddy all right. You're funny, Bliz. Let me try it. I'm the *invalido.*"

"You're overdoing it!"

"Yeah, but this way is funnier!"

Riding to Rulandville on my bicycle that morning, I thought how impossible my life had become in Rehoboth. I knew, as time went on, that Kazzy and Blizzard would become worse. I was now a sport for them, a convenient target of ridicule. As far as I could tell, they had not detected any of my blood leaking on the bathroom floor near the toilet, but that discovery would certainly be a cause for cruel hilarity from them.

And Jumbo and Don Pasquale were conspiring to force me into a summer job I did not want. Their plans for my future seemed even more dire and unacceptable.

I found solitude and sanctuary with my harmonica in Ben Curry's meadow and the surrounding forest. And at night in my bedroom, I fastened my headphones to my crystal set and listened to jazz or classical music that transported me momentarily. But, as I mentioned, the Black Madonna had disappeared from our parlor, so even now at night, that meditative option was out. I could not light a candle and pray before the holy image of her and her baby.

And yet, despite my recurrent feelings of falling and spinning and losing all control and hope, I believed that my mother's love would possibly sustain me. Her love would always endure in me, and I was sure of it.

Even now, however, I find it astounding that her love proved an active force in helping me escape, which it truly was. Perhaps this sounds mysterious and far-fetched, but I can find no other valid reason in this world, other than pure chance, to explain my deliverance from Rehoboth and from the sticky and paralytic blood pudding, which my family had become for me.

I have learned that the ancient Greek tragedians in Athens used a plot device called *deus ex machina*, when a god in a chariot would be lowered onto the stage by a crane to resolve the dramatic conflict.

In my more contemporary personal drama, that *machina* was a rehabilitated veteran of the Great War and had been manufactured by the
Harley Davidson Company in Milwaukee, Wisconsin.

57

Slag Heap

I trembled uncontrollably. Max flew his beast down the road at seventy or eighty miles an hour. He blew by cars and trucks on very narrow roads and around curves and over humps and ridges, as if nobody else should dare to occupy the pavement. In ten minutes, we were in West Virginia, and then he turned at the Paris Community Cemetery and shot back along the same stretch going even faster, right past the junkyard and the ball field, barely a blur in the corner of my eye. I did not think of Nick the Greek or of baseball. All I thought about was hanging on to Max's leather jacket as tight and hard as I could.

Did he want to crash and kill us both? I was too terrified to shout those questions to him, but they certainly reverberated in my brain. The Harley rumbled and vibrated so violently that as I shook, I felt in my gut the terrible conviction that my big brother and I were hurtling to a violent and painful doom. As a last resort, I closed my eyes and whispered a quick prayer to Mother's favorite, 57 angel. She did not seem to want to manifest, at least not immediately and not at seventy-five miles an hour, according to the speedometer on Max's handlebars.

I was not reassured when he slowed down briefly and pulled onto a dirt road and stopped. With the engine still idling under us impatiently, he reached into his jacket pocket, pulled out a stainless steel flask and took a long swig.

"Just want to let off a little steam, Taddy. Don't worry. Hang on."

Off we flew. Again, I gripped the thick brown leather of his jacket for all I was worth, which did not feel like much at that moment.

Why did I get on this motorcycle, I asked myself, now in tears. I have often asked myself that question, for that madcap trip with Max changed my life forever. And again, I will always wonder if perhaps Mother herself had willed this journey.

Max's reputation as Washington County's top motorcycle mechanic and wildest daredevil was widespread, but I thought that this trip was putting everything in his notorious past far in the distance. The speedometer needle ticked passed ninety.

We whipped down Main Street in Rehoboth, past the blurs I knew as the school, the library, the police station, and the Presbyterian church, past the Texaco, beyond the Slattery house, went airborne over the rails of the train crossing track just as the bells were ringing and the warning gates were coming down, and then scooted further along past the company store and toward the mine and the zinc and moly plants.

Max had bragged often about shooting his Harley up and down the giant slag heaps that occupied the back seven or eight acres of the zinc plant's grounds. The waste material from the giant roasters came out of the plant daily, steaming in railroad hopper cars. It was hot and smelly, spewing sulfurous orange smoke into the air all along the tracks that led to the dumping area. People said the plant had plans to recycle all the slag at some point, but in the four and a half years we had lived in Rehoboth, the mounds accumulated ever larger and farther out. Now they resembled steep orange and gray sand dunes like in the Sahara Desert or maybe on the red planet Mars.

Ziggy and I had climbed on the mounds out of boredom from time to time, pretending that we were French Foreign Legionnaires or interplanetary explorers. But those idle games never lasted long. Footing on the slag was unpredictable. On stormy days, the rainwater sometimes pooled in pockets in the gritty silicon-rich substance, and then after the pockets dried out, they could be treacherous, easy to fall into. In addition, the slag pellets could vary in size from sand granules up to pieces as large as loaves of bread or even fire hydrants.

None of these literal pitfalls bothered the thrill-seeking Max, whose stated intent that day was to let off steam on his trusted war veteran Harley.

The trick of conquering the slag heaps, he often bragged, was to fire up to maximum speed and keep it up as long as possible. It was dangerous to slow your machine down, he said, because the bottom could fall out from under your wheels. High speed alone kept that from happening, and the faster, the safer.

We blew past the mine administration building and the parking lot attendant's shack and tore down the bumpy road past the zinc plant with its four belching smokestacks and the giant moly stack looming several miles further on. A quarter mile along, we spotted our goal, the irregular field of giant slag heaps.

The slanting rays of the late afternoon sun cast peculiar undulating shadows, one against the other, for as far as we could see. The distant recently deposited mounds were still letting off stinky orange vapors at the end of the lot, and I had a brief and baleful vision that surely hell's landscape could not be too different from what we were looking at.

Forget the Sahara or Mars! Hell seemed much more accessible and relevant at this horrible moment.

I also deduced that Max was no longer aware I was holding on to him, let alone that I was trembling and weeping with fear. He did not stop to explain what he had in mind. It would become obvious. He was letting off steam. I screamed for him to stop, but he did not. Now he was uniting, becoming one, with the Harley and his slag mounds, perhaps becoming one with hell.

He cruised rapidly along the edge of the field and scouted for the most challenging heap. When he saw what he wanted, he went for it. I saw it charging quickly toward us.

He jerked his wrist on the handlebar throttle, and we accelerated. My neck snapped as the Harley reared back and jumped forward. Like it or not, I was locked into a ride far more terrifying than any Kennywood roller coaster.

Suddenly we were ascending the gritty sulfurous edge of a freshly deposited mountain of slag, its orange surface still hot and spewing fumes. Then, in less than a second, we were on top of it and shooting down the other side, only to rise again and jerk forward and up to another soggy sulfurous peak. Dust and smoke and orange steam were all over us. I vomited into my mouth then swallowed it and vomited it again. I pressed my chin and the side of my head against his leather jacket and the tense muscles of his rigid back.

My eyes stung from the sulfurous steam. I tried closing them, but that made the dizziness worse. I wondered if I should open them, at least to see my death.

With whatever wits I had left, I wondered how long Max wanted to pursue this death ride. Was he really this fearful of becoming a father? Had Benny driven him to the point of vehicular suicide? I cursed the day he married her, as I am sure he had done many times in the past months. She would give him as much lasagna as he wanted, and she would never run out. And today, Max was not going to run out of slag heaps, because there were easily a hundred or more, of random heights and girths, products of Rehoboth's industrial bounty.

We zipped up and down over a fast dozen and were heading back in the direction of the zinc plant when Max attacked a fresh and very tall heap at the edge of the field. We shot up to the summit and immediately plunged down toward the railroad tracks, but he could not brake us in time. Two-thirds of the way down, his front tire jammed into a boulder-size lump of slag, hard as concrete, and the cycle flipped up into the air with both of us on it. With no traction, the wheels spun furiously, shedding pinwheels of red sand.

I lost my grip and fell onto the soft warm slag, but Max kept clutching the handlebars and landed sideways under the bike. The full weight of the engine crushed his left knee against the sharp slag rock. Blessedly there were no flames, but we both lay still, looking up at the sky.

We were stunned and still for a moment. The engine continued to idle while we tried to assess the damage done, but then Max killed the ignition switch.

I heard him shout, "Motherfucker! My knee is fucked."

I was able to stand up and walk down the side of the mound. I didn't really hurt anywhere, and I was amazed that the motorcycle engine now was silent.

I was alive, breathing, and walking gingerly on the slag.

I looked up the mound at Max, who was trying to stand. He could not. His face had a large gash that looked like somebody had carved a machete blade into his forehead. Blood rippled down his face. His rearview mirror had split off the handlebars and splintered. Either the mirror glass itself or the broken support rod had slashed a four-inch gouge down to his skull bone.

"Help me, damn it!" he screamed. "My knee, Taddy! My knee!"

I climbed back up the mound and hoisted the Harley a few inches, high enough for Max to grip his leg with both his hands and pull it out from under the engine. When his leg cleared the frame, we saw bone chips from his shattered kneecap scattered in a yawning red wound that had granular dark orange slag dust crammed all through it.

From the knee down, his left leg angled out toward the zinc plant, while his other leg pointed back toward our neighborhood. There was plenty of bleeding, but nothing squirted.

He slid down the slag pile head first on his right side. At the bottom of the heap he tried to sit up, but his face turned gray and sweat poured onto his brow on either side of the bloody gouge.

There was nobody around. I looked up at the giant smokestack, and only a wisp of smoke drifted up above it. No activity anywhere else.

"I better run get some help," I said.

"Damn, this is bad!"

"I'll shoot back to the plant and talk to somebody."

"Do it fast! I could lose my leg. Fuck, does it hurt!"

"It looks terrible, Max. Are you in a lot of pain?"

"Hell! What do you think?"

He was able to reach inside his jacket for his whiskey flask. He swigged what was left of it then tossed it out into the slag.

"Looks like the Harley will survive."

"How do you know? Shit!"

"I'll come right back. I promise."

"Hurry, Taddy boy."

The parking attendant sat cross-legged on a folding chair in front of his shack. He was smoking a cigarette and reading a Zane Grey paperback, *The Rainbow Trail.* He did not look like he wanted to be disturbed.

"I really need some help, mister."

"I saw you two stupid hell-raisers fly by here fifteen minutes ago. Heard your engine cutting up over by the heaps."

"Yes, that was us."

"Well, what am I supposed to do?"

"We really need help. We crashed. My brother could lose his leg."

"Dr. Zankowski went home at noon today."

"He needs to go to a hospital. He will need surgery, I know."

"How do you know?"

"Please, do you have a truck or something to go get him? My father works in this mine."

"Who's your dad?"

"Jumbo Malinowski."

"I haven't seen Jumbo here for well over a year or two."

"Please! My brother needs help fast. Do you want him to lose his leg?"

"You got a limp yourself. Do you need a doctor too?"

"Please, can you help my brother? If he bleeds a lot, he could die, like my mother."

The attendant went into his shack and, mouthing his cigarette and still holding his novel, picked up a telephone. In a few minutes, the mine ambulance arrived. The driver was more sympathetic than the parking attendant. He and his colleague, who wore white medical smocks and white police hats, told me to jump in the back.

I directed them to the pile where Max lay, and in minutes, they had rolled Max onto their stretcher, and we were lifting him into the ambulance.

Through his groans, Max asked if they could stop at his shop. He wanted to tell Benny what had happened. They refused. They said every minute they wasted getting to a Pittsburgh surgeon increased the chances of his losing his leg. They straightened his leg in a splint, covered his open wounds with gauze, and shot his shoulder with a syringe full of morphine. They gave me a large wad of cotton gauze to press into his forehead gash to staunch the bleeding.

Then we were speeding full throttle with a siren screeching to make everyone get out of our way. Max winced when we hit the Rehoboth railroad crossing, and he actually let me hold his hand for a few miles. I could see he was scared.

Slowly the morphine took hold of him. His fist loosened around my hand. His eyes snapped shut, and then he dozed off.

"Where are we going?" I asked the driver.

"St. Agatha's. They're charity. You're charity, aren't you?"

"My mother died there."

"You want to go somewhere else?"

"No, St. Agatha's. They fixed up my father pretty good. We are definitely charity."

"You're Malinowski, right?"

"Yes."

"Didn't your father work at the mine? Big guy? Bald? Mustache?"

"Yeah. Jumbo."

"I heard a rumor couple years ago that he ran a little bootlegging business. Made his self some money. Is that why he left the mine?"

"No. I think he just got tired of digging all day."

"And your brother Max here has a reputation. He's a wizard with motorcycles, right?"

"You saw what the wizard did at the slag heaps."

"Hate to say it, but he's a fucking crazy Polack is what he is."

"Our family is a little crazy."

"I'm a crazy Polack too. Kruszewski's my name. Call me Chris. Join the club. Now keep that cotton pad tight on his forehead. He'll likely have an ugly scar."

Sister Joseph

Chris Kruszewski offered me a Lucky Strike. I declined. He and his buddy smoked and chatted, while I kneeled beside Max's stretcher and applied pressure to his forehead for the rest of the trip.

Max slept, courtesy of the morphine. The siren blared the whole way. At sundown we zipped through the Liberty tunnels and emerged on the highway along the Monongahela with all the lights of downtown Pittsburgh gleaming across the river. As we crossed the bridge, I glanced upriver to see if I could make out the Kennywood Ferris wheels, but I couldn't. The sky had darkened, and since it was only April, Kennywood hadn't opened yet and the twin wheels would not be lit up.

Sirens wailing, we barreled on toward St. Agatha's, which stood about three blocks in from the river in a crowded neighborhood not far from the downtown business district.

I recalled St. Agatha's from the night we brought Mother there. The building was a redbrick behemoth, four stories tall, and spread out over an entire city block. The facade had high twin spires, also of red brick, that made the huge structure resemble an ancient fortified abbey or even an armory, solid and sturdy enough probably to withstand an earthquake.

I found out later that St. Agatha's was the first Catholic hospital in Pittsburgh, and now they had professors and house staff doctors from Pitt Medical College. Like Mother and Jumbo and now Max, almost all the patients at St. Agatha's were charity. Though Jumbo hated priests, even he might admit that some of the money dropped into the collection baskets at Sunday masses found its way to worthy causes like St. Agatha's, which had tried to save his wife's life and helped set the bones in his jaw and neck. Now St. Agatha's surgeons would try to salvage the leg of his eldest motorcycle-maimed son.

Max woke up as they rolled him on a hospital stretcher into an examining room. A pair of nuns with clipboards, both of them short ladies but with bulky black habits and towering white hats that looked like beekeepers' hoods, took information from Chris Kruszewski and me. One of the nuns looked familiar, and I noticed she had a scar above her mouth, like a harelip that had been repaired. The two nuns kept asking me questions, and out of courtesy, I tried not to look at the harelip one's mouth.

In the accident, Max's wallet had fallen out of his pants and was likely buried somewhere in the slag heap. He was delirious from the morphine and wasn't able to answer coherently, so the nuns relied on me to tell them his identity and home address and report what happened. I quickly added that Max had a pregnant wife at home, and she might not know about the accident. I gave them the phone numbers of Max's shop and of *Piccolo Palermo* and told them the hospital might get in touch with Benny that way.

I was still in my school clothes and had slag dust jammed up my sleeves and under my collar and in my hair, but I tried to present myself politely and responsibly. After I washed Max's blood off my hands, the nuns asked if I had been injured.

"No. I'm okay," I added with a smile.

I could hear Max groaning behind the examining room door when they started his intravenous line. The surgeon came in and manipulated him to test for the viability of his injured limb. Then the orderly rolled him to the X-ray chamber. I went along and helped hoist Max up onto the hard flat table. He moaned every time they moved his knee even slightly. While they took pictures, I waited outside in the hall.

In a few minutes, the surgeon walked toward me, holding the X-rays. He raised them up to the light. He showed me three different bones badly shattered in his knee, and one fragment had cut an artery that fed down to his foot.

"We have to take your brother right away. Otherwise, he could lose that leg. The operation might take three or four hours, minimum. We will have to give him ether, clean out that joint, sew up his artery, and screw his bones together. And we'll sew up that forehead gash. We took an X-ray of his skull. It's okay."

"Where should I wait?"

"Sister Joseph will take care of you."

Then the surgeon and an orderly hauled Max off to the operating room. I walked back to the entrance hall and found a chair.

The two little nuns came out and smiled at me. Under their hoods, their habits had white round collars with silver crucifixes dangling in front of their bosoms. They asked if I would like something to eat.

As I nodded to the shorter of the two nuns, she gave me a familiar wink.

"Sister Joseph?" I asked.

"Yes?"

"You took care of Mother the night she died. That was over four years ago. Eva Malinowski."

Sister Joseph's gray eyes blinked quickly. She grabbed her silver crucifix and thumbed it up and down, as if to jog her memory.

"Remember?" I said. "Eva Malinowski. The doctors couldn't stop her from bleeding. And she had a bad infection. My father is the big bald guy with the mustache. And Max was there that night too."

"Oh, that beautiful woman from Rehoboth? The one who lost her baby?"

"Yes. Mother was beautiful. You remember her?"

"And your father. I remember that mustache."

"He still has it."

"Coal miner, right?"

"Part-time. My name is Tad."

"I remember you. You have grown a foot since then. When was that?"

"Like I said, over four years ago. Now I'm thirteen."

"Oh my! To lose a mother so young."

"And with seven children."

"Seven? Did your father get help in the house?"

"He gets by."

"Do you help him?"

"When I can."

"You look very hungry, Tad. Why don't you come back with me to the kitchen? I'll make you a nice ham sandwich with all the trimmings."

"I would love that. Is there a place I can wash my hands again and my face and use the bathroom?"

"Yes. And we called Benny. Her father will drive her in to the hospital tonight, so you can ride home with them later, once Max gets out of surgery."

"Will Max have to stay overnight?"

"Several days, at least. It all depends on what Dr. Hershel decides. Max's leg is bad. You saw the X-rays?"

"And his forehead?"

"Oh, that cut won't kill him. It will leave him a scar, but he's not handsome like you, so he probably won't mind. Do you know you take after your mother?"

"You really do remember her?"

In the staff kitchen, Sister Joseph fixed a feast, including strawberry ice cream and three chocolate cookies for dessert. Then she said, "Make yourself at home," and she left me alone at the kitchen table. After several minutes, I put my dishes and silverware in the sink and then went back and folded my arms on the clean tabletop and lay my head down.

Alone in the kitchen, I closed my eyes and relaxed for the first time all day. I liked the feeling of St. Agatha's. I liked the clean smells of iodine and rubbing alcohol and disinfectants. All the uniforms impressed me: the nuns and the orderlies and the doctors, all in pressed white pants and white socks and shoes.

Also, a sense of high purpose seemed to be at work in the huge building, emphasized with statues of saints in the halls and with walls adorned with large relief medallions of pilgrims and angels and oil portraits of great doctors. I had not spotted any Black Madonna icons, but perhaps there was one somewhere upstairs. The building felt like she was around somewhere, and maybe she was watching me. Or was it 57 angel? Some force of grace had saved me from injury that day.

And the place seemed so physically and spiritually solid, despite all the busy activities occurring around every corner.

"Make yourself at home," Sister Joseph had said.

And I did feel at home. Did that have anything to do with the fact that Mother had breathed her last in that building, that her heart had stopped beating not very far away from where I now was laying down my head?

I dreaded those last visions of Mother as she died, but it was right here in this building where I had last touched her as a living creature. Being so close to where she had breathed her last made it easy for me to imagine her arms around me, comforting me, consoling me, telling me that Max's leg would be all right, promising me that she still loved me more than I could ever know.

I fell asleep with my head on the table. When I woke up, Sister Joseph said, "Max is done with surgery, and Dr. Hershel says the leg has a good chance. All the blood vessels are intact, all the way down to his toes. And he can wiggle them!"

I blinked my eyes several times to find my bearings. I still could feel Mother's arms gently holding me, and I was reluctant to wake up and lose her presence. "Thanks, Sister Joseph. That's wonderful news."

"And Benny and her father are here. They will give you a ride home after you say good night to Max."

"Oh, Sister, you've been so kind to me. Thank you."

"That's what we do here, Tad. I wish we could have done more for your mother. It is so unfortunate what happened to her. I'm hoping that God forgave her."

When Sister Joseph said those words, I immediately broke into tears. I had been certain for so long that God had forgiven Mother, and now this kind nun had brought the issue into question all over again.

With my lips quivering, I stood up from the table. I saw Sister Joseph's eyes look at me with alarm. She pulled me to her and hugged me. Though I did not like what she said, I did feel comforted by her arms about me. My tears stopped, and I dried them with the cloth table napkin she had given me with my dinner.

Sister Joseph's hands held my shoulders, and she looked up at my face tenderly. I saw her eyes dwell briefly on the little scar under my left nostril, a flaw that only slightly resembled hers. Still, it was a scar like hers, and she noticed it.

"Tad, you seem like a fine boy. When do you turn fourteen?"

"I'll be fourteen in May. Why?"

The dreamy feeling of Mother's presence was still with me. It was as if Mother's embrace had fused into Sister Joseph's.

When I smiled very gratefully to her, she said, "Wait. Sit down again."

And this is when I became utterly convinced that Mother's spirit was there in that hospital kitchen and engaged in helping me.

Sister Joseph took a seat across the table from me. She palmed her crucifix again and squinted a few times as she looked at me, as if she was collecting her thoughts.

I stared straight at her gray-blue eyes and noticed that when she smiled, her eyes twinkled brilliantly. She seemed quite old to me, much older than Mother had ever been, probably at least fifty. She had thick knuckles that whitened when she gripped the crucifix, but her eyes glittered with a girlish playfulness, as if she had a silly joke she might want to spring on me.

But what she said was no joke. Rather, it was Mother's will.

"So, do you finish eighth grade in a couple months?"

"Yes. I start high school in the fall."

"We might have a job for you here this summer. But you would have to leave home and come to live at the hospital. Once your school lets out, would you like to come and work as an orderly on our accident ward and live right here in our building? The pay is not good, but you'll have uniforms and three meals a day in the hospital cafeteria, and you can sleep in one of the little rooms on the top floor of the nuns' residence building. We will look after you. Why are you crying again?"

She smiled broadly, which nearly erased the scar above her lip, and her eyes beamed at me, dazzling me with the wonder of her proposal.

I blinked at her in amazement.

How could Sister Joseph possibly have suspected that her gracious smile was, at that very moment, unchaining me from my dismal existence in Rehoboth and offering me shelter, nourishment, and a simple path straight through the barriers in my life.

"If you like it here, we can probably give you an evening job in the fall, and then you can enroll in the high school down the street. It's called Fifth Avenue High, one of the very best in the city of Pittsburgh."

"Do they teach Latin?"

"You want to learn Latin?"

"Benjamin Franklin studied Latin. I want to be like him."

"My, Tad. You seem ambitious. Perhaps you are the very fellow we've been looking for."

My heart was racing almost as fast as when I had been on Max's motorcycle. Sister Joseph could have told me almost anything about the job, and I would have welcomed it without question. I kept exploring all the features of her face, her white cheeks pinched by the edges of her beekeeper's wimple, her pale finely wrinkled brow, her soft-sloping chin, the asymmetrical and shiny silvery scar that led from the lower part of her left nostril down to the middle of her upper lip, wondering if she really was serious or only telling me a fairy tale.

With her thick knuckles clutching her crucifix and her wonderful eyes blazing at me, I thrilled as her lilting voice declared in a quiet tone that something incredible was happening to me.

No more Rehoboth. No more pedaling to Rulandville. No more Sunday dinners at *Piccolo Palermo*. No more Don Pasquale. No more bratty little brothers or constant fear of encountering my inebriated father.

None of that anymore.

If what Sister Joseph said was true, all of that would be over. I shook my head with gratitude and dried my eyes again on the napkin. "When can I start?"

"Your father will have to sign a statement of permission."

"Before I go home tonight, could I ask you to show me the room where I will be sleeping? Would you have time to do that? I don't know when I'll be able to come back here to have a look."

"Yes, of course. You see, we need a high-minded and mannerly boy like you to serve as an orderly on our emergency ward and to operate the elevators sometimes in the hospital and also in the staff dormitory. You would be a big help to us. Please consider this."

"Okay, stop right there. I'll do anything. When do I start? But please, show me the room?"

"Don't you want to see Max?"

"Yes. But first show me my room. Will they let me play my harmonica? Does the room have a window, so I can use my crystal set?"

"Follow me, Tad. Let me show you everything. I'll tell Benny and Mr. Papallardo to wait. My, but she is pregnant!"

"But for now, my job will be a secret, okay? Please?"

59

Spring Fever

At seven pounds and fourteen ounces, Pasquale Ignaz Malinowski arrived a week before predicted and was baptized on the first Sunday in May at St. Augustine's in Rulandville.

Again, branches of the Papallardo family assembled in the church, mostly the Hunterton and Wheeling relatives. The Chicago and Massachusetts clan members could not attend, again citing business commitments, but they sent lavish bouquets to welcome baby Patsy. The New York Papallardo branch declined, but they sent flowers too. With the May sun beaming down through the stained glass windows on all the hyacinths, primrose, camellias, and tulips, the sanctuary looked and smelled exquisite.

The Malinowski family sat at the front of the church, in the same places where we had witnessed the wedding a few months before. Max's smashed-up leg was sheathed in a heavy full-length plaster cast. He hobbled down the aisle, supported by a single crutch. Still, he was able to hold chubby little Patsy in his free arm. He carefully suspended him over the baptismal font while the old priest mumbled Latin phrases and tipped Patsy's head backward, dousing holy water on his scalp.

Max looked awkward and tense. As the old priest's knobby fingers flicked the water, the fidgeting baby looked so small and cherubic. Max loomed above him, huge and injured and with a deep vermillion scar running at an angle across his forehead. Benny stood beside him and dabbed Patsy's head with a lace-bordered towel. Several times she flashed her smile at Don Pasquale in the front row.

Though I did not take Holy Communion at Mass and refrained from dancing at the restaurant, I enjoyed the entire event. I grinned at almost everybody, and when Don Pasquale toasted to Benny's new baby, I sneaked a couple of experimental sips of the house Chianti. Later, I was surprised to see Jumbo sitting beside the baptizing priest, both of them chuckling like longtime cronies. I recalled Jumbo's contempt for priests, but there was no evidence of that. Good for Jumbo. Bless his heart, I thought.

Nor did I fret or feel annoyed about anything that was happening around me that day. None of it threatened or disgusted me, not even the occasional unavoidable eye contact with Don Pasquale.

In my mind, I had already made my escape. I had moved into Pittsburgh, specifically to a single room of my own on the top floor of St. Agatha's staff dormitory building. The simple chamber had a firm comfortable bed, a work desk, a cozy wingback chair, a reading lamp, a bookshelf, a closet, an iron radiator, and a south-facing window. From that window, I could look out over the Monongahela River to where it met the Allegheny and formed the wide Ohio. I could watch the rising and falling of the Mount Washington funicular railroad, the incline train, which scooted slowly up and down the four-hundred-foot slope.

I fantasized that my new room, though Spartan in appointments, was probably not unlike chambers in the local preparatory schools, like Kiski or Shadyside, where wealthy Pittsburgh families sent their sons to be groomed for college. From that window, or surely from the roof of the building, I also could spy upriver and make out the twin Ferris wheels of Kennywood Park and enjoy excellent reception on my crystal set. Who could ask for more?

True, the Pittsburgh air was thick with fumes from the many steel factory smokestacks belching along the river. But I had sniffed carefully that night outside St. Agatha's, and I noticed the Pittsburgh atmosphere lacked that sharp bite of Rehoboth's zinc plant effluent. The Pittsburgh air was polluted, but it was les acrid than what I had been breathing routinely for most of my boyhood.

Sister Joseph had been extremely cordial at St. Agatha's and afterward true to her promise. She sent me a letter to be signed by my father. The letter said I would start my job as an orderly and elevator operator at St. Agatha's for the summer, beginning in June. For compensation, I would be given three meals a day, a tidy room where I could study and sleep, uniforms to wear on the job, fresh towels and sheets every week, and fifteen dollars to be paid in three separate monthly installments of five dollars.

When Sister Joseph's letter came, I showed it to Vera. She read it with a smile and advised me not to show it to Jumbo. She was overjoyed at my good luck in meeting Sister Joseph again and in now having an opportunity to escape Rehoboth. I was not to give Jumbo the chance to say no. What? And mess up such a splendid opportunity?

Better, she said, to fake Jumbo's signature. She was pleased to do it herself, stick it in an envelope, and let me run off to the post office with it right away.

"Taddy, we won't tell him you're leaving, not till a couple days before."

"What should I say to Don Pasquale?"

"Nothing. No, do not say a word to him or to anybody at the restaurant."

"Would that be fair to them?"

Vera rolled her eyes. "Have those people been fair to you?"

"You're right. But can I tell Jasper?"

"Do not tell anybody, Taddy. Keep it secret. This is a golden chance. Don't let your father ruin it, because he probably would. Don't let anybody know till you are out the door!"

I wondered if Max, who had to stay a full week at St. Agatha's after his surgery, might have heard anything about Sister Joseph's plans for me. Apparently not. They released him with his whole leg in the cast and a bottle of morphine pills for when the pain was bad, but nobody had mentioned my future employment.

I could tell Max was aggravated by the comments the Papallardo people gave him about how, now that he was a father, he would be expected to behave less recklessly. Let this be a lesson learned.

They also wondered how I could have been in the same accident and escaped without a blemish. I loved it when they said the word "escaped." It reminded me of what I would be doing very soon.

I was so grateful to Vera for her forgery and her advice to keep silent, but it was hard for me not to brag. That last month in school, my classmates several times mentioned that I seemed unusually content and agreeable and even silly.

"You're crazy as a magpie, Tad!" one of my classmates said.

"Spring fever," I said with a giddy smile that probably looked idiotic.

Sometimes, Jasper peered at me suspiciously. I think he guessed that I was holding something back from him. I saw he felt I was not being fair. I wasn't. But I didn't want anything to ruin my chances for what seemed a once-in-a-lifetime breakthrough.

Though I gave my solemn word of honor to Vera that I would keep my mouth shut, what truly preserved my silence for the final few weeks was a more sacred conviction: that Sister Joseph had been with Mother and me in our last grim moments together, and that four years later she now could feel Mother's will calling to her to shelter and protect me. Mother knew I needed help, specifically someone to shepherd me out of Rehoboth and set me straight on a higher road, where my imagination could take wing, and where I could find my own path to an education and to personal freedom.

I concentrated so hard on keeping my secret that I was unaware of other changes happening at home. One June evening after dinner, I was caught off guard when Lucy asked me if I would like to take a walk with her. She wanted to speak privately to me. At first, I feared she had heard of my plans from Vera, and that she wanted to take a stroll to convince me not to leave Robert Street.

Several blocks down the street, Lucy grabbed my arm and said, "Taddy, Vera told me that you are planning to leave us and go to work at a hospital in Pittsburgh for the summer. Vera said that if you do good work, they may ask you to stay on at the hospital and that there's a fine high school nearby."

"Yes, Lucy," I said, "but Vera told me not to tell anyone. She's worried Jumbo will find out and try to stop me. Please don't say a word."

Lucy nodded. "Oh, I'm sure he would."

"That's why I haven't told anybody, not even you. I'm sorry."

Lucy smiled and shook her head. "Oh, don't apologize. I'm excited for you."

She embraced me hard, and I could tell the tears in her eyes were joyful. We walked a few blocks further, and then again, she stopped and held my hand.

"Look at me, Tad. I have my own secret, and I'm hoping you can keep it too. Do you remember Father Fernando?"

"Father Fernando? How could I forget him? He's one of the nicest people I ever met."

"Yes, he is. A couple months ago, I wrote him and told him I want to become a nun. I explained about how terrible our lives have been since Mother died. He wrote back and said that he knew of a wonderful convent for me in Detroit. The Sisters of Mercy."

"You want to be a nun?"

Lucy's eyes instantly grew large and bright. "Father Fernando will come here in July and take me to Detroit to join the Sisters of Mercy."

"Are you sure? There are other ways to leave here, besides becoming a nun."

"Oh, I think I know what you're saying, Tad. But, Jesus has called me. His voice is clear and loud and loving. I will marry Jesus, and I trust Father Fernando. I have read all about the order. They do work in America and in Argentina. Isn't it exciting? Maybe they will send me to Argentina!"

Feeling a conspiratorial thrill, we embraced again. Then, right there on Robert Street, we both burst out laughing. I could tell Lucy felt very much the way I had been feeling. She was escaping too. And even though Jasper had once said that Lucy did not have a sense of humor, her explosion of laughter that night reassured me that Jasper could not have been more wrong.

The night before I left Rehoboth, I went into the shed and told Jumbo I would be leaving in the morning. He was enjoying some of his Papallardo dowry vodka and did not seem to understand clearly what I was saying. I told him he could use my Iver Johnson bicycle for the summer. That pleased him. The next morning, I did not wake him up to say goodbye. And I did not mention anything to Blizzard or Kazzy. They would, no doubt, bid good riddance to the *invalido*, but I preferred not to see the glee in their eyes when I went out the door.

I had packed my socks and shirts and underwear and pajamas and what other clothes I would need, along with my crystal set, into a small suitcase, the same one Mother had carried from Poland and hauled over with us from Ripple Brook Gardens. I also took the Ben Franklin kite Jasper had made me out of the closet, rolled it up, and put it into the suitcase. I planned to put the kite up on the wall in my new dormitory room. Then I hugged Vera and Lucy on the front porch.

The sun was bright on Robert Street as I walked toward the bus stop on Main Street, Rehoboth. I had written a farewell letter to Jasper, and I dropped it in his mailbox on the way past his house. Then I stopped at Max's shop to tell him I was leaving and asked him to say goodbye for me to Benny and Patsy.

Max was out of his cast but still using a crutch to hobble around the shop. His forehead gash was filling in, but it still was a deep vermillion gully on his brow. He would wear it till he died. But it could have been worse, we all knew.

"This is great news, Taddy, you lucky shit! But you'll only be gone for the summer?"

"Probably."

"Are they paying you?"

"Not much."

"Did you tell Don Pasquale?"

"I asked Jumbo to tell him later today. I gave Jumbo my bicycle."

"Hope he doesn't wreck it."

"That's funny, coming from you, Max. You know, I want to thank you for socking Jumbo that night. I never said anything to you before about it, but he really had it coming."

"Maybe I should have hit him harder."

"Harder and sooner."

Max grinned. He reached into his pocket and pulled out five silver dollars. Offering them on his large square palm, he said, "You might need these in the big city."

I hesitated before I took them, half expecting him to close his fist and put them back in his pocket.

"Take them, Tadpole," he insisted. Then he gave me a viselike bear hug and spread his lips into his broadest Genghis Khan grin and said, "Now get out of here! See you in the fall. Let me know if I can sell you a motorcycle. I'll give you a sweet price."

When the Pittsburgh bus pulled up at the stop, I climbed aboard. The bus was almost empty. I bought a one-way ticket from the driver and sat at a window near the back.

We bumped over the railroad tracks in the middle of town and then took a left and headed toward the main highway. As I looked out at the Rehoboth buildings vanishing behind me, I knew I was only taking a trip into Pittsburgh, something lots of people did every day.

Was I really escaping? Was I only fooling myself?

It might seem like an ordinary commute for someone else, somebody who lived in Rehoboth but worked in the city. But not for me. No, I truly was fleeing.

As I reached down and ran my fingers along the tattered brown leather of Mother's suitcase, I wished that I could have helped her escape too. I wished that I could look into her eyes on the bus and ask, "*Quo vadis?*"

Then she would smile and shake her head. "I'm wondering the same about you, Tad," she would say with a kiss. "*Quo vadis*, my son?"

"And, Mother! I'm going to start learning Latin too!"

"You don't want to turn around?"

"What? Go back and let them crucify me upside down or worse in Rehoboth? Not on your life, Mother! Not on your life!"

Nutshells

The bus ride I took into Pittsburgh at the age of fourteen signaled a radical change in my life. Not only did I dodge a miserable future in Rehoboth, but also, in time I found a chance at St. Agatha's Hospital to pursue a path toward my eventual career as a medical doctor.

I was blessed. From my first day at the hospital, Sister Joseph watched over me carefully. She arranged for me to work as an orderly in St. Agatha's emergency ward, and she set up other jobs, primarily as an off-hours operator in several of St. Agatha's elevators. She saw to it that I was outfitted continuously in quality secondhand clothes from the hospital thrift shop, and she arranged for me to enter and finish Fifth Avenue High School, which happened to be the first chapter in all of America of the National Honor Society, a proud inductee of which I became. I went through Pitt in two years and then the medical school in four years, all while living at St. Agatha's. Finally, I served my medical internship at St. Agatha's, too, living for a total of ten years in that grand, noble, and indestructible master-piece of a Romanesque building.

I have always believed Sister Joseph was an active agent of my mother's spirit. If it were not for Sister Joseph's patient and unblink-ing attention to my welfare, I would never have bootstrapped out of my grim and peculiar childhood to enter medicine, a profession that has allowed me to aid human suffering and make enough of a living to support my family. Eventually I settled in Hunterton, Ohio, the smoky steel town on the banks of the Ohio, where, oddly, I had once waited patiently in the car for most of an afternoon, while my father Jumbo had his fun, letting off steam in a house of prostitution. Despite the town's dismal reputation, I have always loved Hunterton, Ohio, for its honest, hardworking citizenry, several thousand of whom I am proud to have cared for as my patients and delivered many hundreds of their babies.

One early benefit from my working at St. Agatha's was that the diagnostic enigma of my foreshortened right leg was resolved in the first year. A kind pediatrician named Dr. Wilson Fogarty pulled me aside on the ward one afternoon and asked about my limp. I said I had no explanation for it and that I had limped since I first learned to walk. He ordered some X-rays and later informed me that as a baby, perhaps in Poland, I had most likely contracted infantile paralysis. The shortened leg and the muscle atrophy in my right calf and foot were obvious residuals of polio. He arranged for me to be measured for orthotic devices for my shoes. My limp remained as I grew to adulthood but became much less noticeable than it had been during my boyhood.

I did not find help for my other nagging medical problem until much later. It was not until age forty that I mustered the courage to go to a colleague, Dr. Miles Black, a rectal surgeon. I confided in Dr. Black about my rape on second base that terrible afternoon in Rehoboth. Dr. Black examined me and told me I had a correctable rectal stricture. The next day, he took me to the operating room, snipped the stricture, and I was healed.

It is difficult for me to describe how grateful I am to both of these doctors, Dr. Fogarty and Dr. Black, for what they did to improve my life. I wish I had sought help on my rectal stricture sooner. I suffered miserably for almost three decades with the problem, and the relief following Dr. Black's operation was astonishing. Of course, my being fixed doesn't make what Curly did to me less wrong.

What happened to me after I left Rehoboth is not within the intended scope of this narrative. I plan to continue my story, as well as that of my siblings and my father, in a subsequent account. However, I feel compelled now to thank the reader for following the

Malinowski family this far, and rather than leave our stories up in the air, I conclude here with nutshell descriptions of what took place subsequently to each.

Lucy first. Accompanied by Father Fernando, she left Rehoboth a month after I did. On the morning they caught the train from Pittsburgh to Detroit, Lucy and my very favorite priest stopped by St. Agatha's to say goodbye. Sister Joseph was ecstatic to meet Lucy on her way to becoming a novitiate, and Father Fernando promised me he would look after her in Detroit. Lucy's letters to me from the nunnery were always tender and loving and happy, and she relished her order's mission aiding the needs of Detroit's poor. The order eventually sent her to Argentina, where she has remained for several decades. She sends me a letter every Christmas from there, and I send her pictures of my wife, Ruth, and our three children. Father Fernando, Lucy informed me several years ago, had become a bishop out in Seattle, Washington.

Max quickly sold his Harley Davidson franchise and moved up from motorcycles to owning a Dodge dealership in Rulandville. His charisma and bravado have made him a very effective car salesman, and it was rare for a customer to walk out of his showroom without the keys to a new car.

Max's marriage with Benny lasted four years. They had a daughter Pina two years after Patsy. When Don Pasquale died of lung cancer, Max quickly took up with a beautician from Wheeling named Dolores and left Benny to deal with the kids. I was worried that Benny's brothers, who had returned from Sicily, might try to settle scores with Max for abandoning Benny. But they never showed up for Benny's wedding or the christening, so why expect them to drive down and honor their deceased father's threat by removing Max's manhood by the side of the road? That never happened.

Max never stopped drinking. He also gambled and cheated frequently on Dolores, with whom he had two more children. When I had moved to Hunterton and started a medical practice and saved up enough money to buy a car, Max gave me a deal on a new black Dodge coupe with a rumble seat. Later I discovered my brand new

Dodge had used spark plugs, a secondhand battery, a reconditioned carburetor, and retreaded tires. What else did I expect from Max?

By the way, though Max sold Dodges, he always drove Cadillacs. And for all the taunts he stung me with as a child about my being a cripple, his limp through the rest of his life was more obvious than mine. In his showroom, he often told new customers he had been injured in the war in Europe and would prefer not to describe the details of the explosion. He figured that patriotic fable would soften them up when it came time to dicker the deal on their new Dodge.

As for Jasper Slattery, after graduating valedictorian at Rehoboth High School, he went off to Penn State and then on to law school in Philadelphia. He settled there, started a family, and eventually entered state politics. Occasionally, I saw his name in the Pittsburgh newspapers when election time came around. I assume he felt hurt that I never went by to wish him farewell in person when I left Rehoboth. He never sent an answer to the letter I dropped in his mailbox, so I figured he just wanted to forget about me. Of course, I sometimes think about him on nights when I cannot fall asleep and have to visualize some bunnies in the moonlight to help me doze off. I'm sure Jasper never realized what a help that has been for my sleep hygiene throughout my life. So, Jasper, if you ever read this, many thanks! And I kept your Ben Franklin kite on my dormitory wall for ten years. It's still somewhere in our attic in Hunterton. And I think it's wonderful that you've had such a successful career in Ben's own city. You literally followed in his footsteps!

Two years after I left Rehoboth, Vera married Mr. MacAdoo, who had grown quite fond of her. Daddy Mac had also become quite wealthy, and he built a huge brick house out the road from town. It was large enough for Blizzard and Kazzy to have rooms of their own, and the yard was immense. Daddy Mac also put the old Beckwith in the new parlor, so Jumbo could come over and play it.

Vera had a pair of sons with Daddy Mac, so their house was always busy. In fact, a number of years later, Ziggy came back and lived with Vera and Daddy Mac. Zig also helped out doing grunt work at the company store, and Daddy Mac said he was always jolly and agreeable, even popular, with the customers. Once I drove Zig over to Robert Street and showed him the big *Z* I had carved in the oak tree by Curry's Meadow. He ran his fingers over the bark. Then he blinked and hugged me. He didn't say a word, but I could tell by his nodding grin that he felt honored.

Behind Max's Dodge dealership in Rulandville was a small shed, where Jumbo finally resided. Dolores fixed him sandwiches for lunch and a hot dish for dinner, and Max provided enough alcohol to keep the old man happy. Jumbo occasionally would push a broom or clean tools back in the working area of the garage, but Max forbade him to enter the showroom or mingle with the staff or clientele. Jumbo eventually had given up on his habitual preening in front of the mirror, and his beard grew, long and white and ratty looking. When he grinned, the gold tooth played peekaboo from the middle of it.

I used to drive out to Rulandville a few times a year and visit Jumbo in that little shed. I once noticed a woman's form under the covers in his bed.

"Go ahead, Taddy, pull back the covers if you want to see her," he suggested.

I lifted the blanket and the sheet. I saw a shapely, full-bodied and big-breasted dummy with painted-in red lips and green eyes on the face. A blonde theater wig was glued to her head. Jumbo had sewn this female form himself from silk fabric and stuffed her with cotton batting. He kept her beside him every night to keep him company. She wore one of Mother's old white silk nightgowns.

"I get lonely, Tad. I hope you understand. Doesn't do anybody any harm."

"Does she have a name, Dad?"

"What do you guess, son? Yes, Eva."

T H E   E N D

Acknowledgments

Sincere thanks for inspiration and support to Jib Ellis, Peter Halperin, Barbara and Andy Senchak, Rose Styron, Nancy Aronie, Gesa and Klaus Vogt, and Karlee Dies.

Note: The characters and events of Blood Pudding are fictional. Any resemblance to real people, living or dead, is coincidental.

About the Author

Ivan Cox lives with his wife, Martha, on Martha's Vineyard, where he practices medicine. His first novel, *Cruise Ship Doctor*, is considered a classic of comic nautical literature. Ivan Cox also acts and writes plays and screenplays. His occasional essays and reviews appear in the *Vineyard Gazette* and the *Martha's Vineyard Times*.

THE MARITIME HOTEL

M · NEW YORK CITY ·

SKYLINE PARK PERIMETER LOOP
→ COUNTERCLOCKWISE

SKYLINE WILDERNESS PARK

STEVENS MEMORIAL TRAIL
HIKE TO TOP OF MT. ST. HELENA

OENTORI - ITALIAN
TORC
CELADON

CPSIA information can be obtained
at www.ICGtesting.com
Printed in the USA
BVHW070835240323
661078BV00001B/26